Dance
of Seduction

SABRINA JEFFRIES

Dance of Seduction

An Avon Romantic Treasure

AVON BOOKS
An Imprint of HarperCollinsPublishers

This is a work of fiction. Names, characters, places, and incidents are products of the author's imagination or are used fictitiously and are not to be construed as real. Any resemblance to actual events, locales, organizations, or persons, living or dead, is entirely coincidental.

AVON BOOKS
An Imprint of HarperCollins*Publishers*
10 East 53rd Street
New York, New York 10022-5299

First Avon Books paperback printing: April 2003

Avon Trademark Reg. U.S. Pat. Off. and in Other Countries, Marca Registrada, Hecho en U.S.A.
HarperCollins® is a registered trademark of HarperCollins Publishers Inc.

Printed in the U.S.A.

To my parents, my brothers, and my sister,
who have all, in your own ways,
dedicated your lives to making
the world a better place.
Clara and I salute you.

Chapter 1

London
May 1819

> In Books or Work, or healthful Play
> Let my first Years be past,
> That I may give for every Day
> Some good Account at last.
> *"Against Idleness and Mischief," Isaac Watts,*
> Divine Songs attempted in Easy Language
> for the Use of Children

Lady Clara Stanbourne was descended from a long line of reformers and rogues. Her late father's side had produced Quakers and Whigs whose passion to effect change was surpassed only by their respectable station. Her late mother's side, the Doggetts, boasted a broad assortment of feckless scoundrels who'd gloried in gambling, delighted in debauchery, and wallowed in wild living. The Doggetts possessed no respectability at all except through their tenuous connection to the Stanbournes through marriage.

Fortunately for England, the Doggetts had virtually died out. Only Clara's uncle Cecil, the card cheat, carried on the family tradition of wreaking havoc upon the unsuspecting and the virtuous. But he did it in America now, having fled England eight years earlier, when his cheating had landed him on the wrong end of a very large pistol.

Thus Lady Clara was surprised when she came downstairs on a bright spring Monday to learn that her uncle's American solicitor, a Mr. Gaither, had just arrived at Stanbourne Hall from Virginia. She didn't even know her uncle possessed something so lofty as a solicitor. Yet Samuel, her new footman, insisted that such a creature awaited her in the front parlor.

With a sigh, she glanced at the clock. "They're expecting me at the Home any minute. After my being away in the country for two weeks, they'll worry if I'm late. I suppose you'll have to send a boy round with a note."

"Yes, m'lady," Samuel said nervously, looking very smart in his new footman's uniform. Samuel was her most recent success from the Stanbourne Home for the Reformation of Pickpockets. Though he was a bit short for a proper footman, he performed his duties well enough, which was all that mattered.

An eruption of barking from the front parlor warned that her aunt, Verity Stanbourne, had reached the parlor first. Clara hastened to the doorway, groaning to find her aunt's three beribboned miniature poodles dancing around the American. Poor Mr. Gaither teetered on rickety legs atop a footstool, crying, "Shoo! Go on, you beasts! Get away!"

Aunt Verity flapped her hands fruitlessly at the capering, yapping dogs. "Now, Fiddle, you mustn't— Oh, come away, Faddle! And Foodle, if you don't stop this—" She cast Mr. Gaither a helpless look. "See how you've upset my lassies?

They're all much annoyed, I tell you." A sharp woof preceded the entrance of an old spaniel bitch. "Lord have mercy, here comes Empress—stay put, Mr. Gaither! If she doesn't approve of you, she's liable to bite you!"

Clara crossed the room and threw herself into the midst of the dogs. "Down, all of you, this minute! No one's biting anyone." She glared at the poodles until the barking turned to whimpers and three curly heads drooped in shameless obeisance.

When Empress kept woofing at poor Mr. Gaither's feet, Clara added sharply, "That's enough, Empress," and the aging spaniel retreated to Aunt Verity's side.

Unfortunately, Clara could do nothing about the low growl the dog continued to emit. Empress had taken a distinct dislike to their guest, which boded ill for Mr. Gaither. The dog had an uncanny ability to judge people accurately. Whomever she growled or barked at was eventually shown to possess serious character flaws. Empress was so adept that Aunt Verity used her to sift out good applicants from bad when interviewing new servants. As a result, Stanbourne Hall's staff was the envy of all Aunt Verity's friends.

Judging from Mr. Gaither's scowl, his character flaw was a hatred of dogs.

Clara held out her hand to help him down from the stool. "I'm so sorry, sir. I'm Lady Clara Stanbourne, and I see you've already met my aunt. Please forgive us for our chaotic ways. I fear we aren't much used to visitors."

"I can see why," he grumbled as he climbed down. Bestowing glares all round, he brushed at his frock coat to eliminate any remaining essence of canine.

"It's your own fault, sir." Aunt Verity sat down on the settee and arranged her skirts as carefully as any coquette. "You wouldn't let them sniff you, and they don't like that." One of the poodles jumped into her lap, and she clutched him close.

"You tried to kick Faddle, and she's very sensitive about these things."

"Sensitive! She's a blasted dog! And furthermore, I don't think—"

"Won't you sit down, Mr. Gaither?" Clara put in. "Perhaps you'd like some tea?"

That brought him up short. He glowered at her. "No, madam. I'd just as soon attend to business and be done with this." Fixing his gaze on the still growling Empress, who'd plopped down on Aunt Verity's feet, the solicitor took a seat as far away from the dogs as possible. "Letting beasts run wild . . . setting them on strangers . . . I swear, the whole country is mad."

Ignoring his complaints, Aunt Verity patted the settee, and Fiddle and Foodle leaped to cram their little bodies into the coveted space next to her. With a sigh, Clara sat on her aunt's other side. Good Lord, what a day. And it wasn't even noon yet.

Still keeping a wary eye on the dogs, Mr. Gaither opened his satchel to rummage through some papers. "I'm here to inform you, my lady, that Cecil Doggett is deceased."

He made his statement so baldly that Clara was sure she'd misheard. "What? Uncle Cecil? Are you sure?"

"Do you think I'd come all this way and endure these . . . these creatures if I weren't?" He drew out an official-looking document and handed it to her. "Here is the death certificate."

"Oh." She took it from him, her heart sinking as she scanned the paper. The facts were stated clearly enough.

A lump lodged in her throat. Uncle Cecil might have been a scoundrel, but she'd always harbored a certain fondness for him. He'd humored her hobby of collecting books for children. He'd never called her interest "frivolous" as Papa had been wont to do, or "nonsense" as Mama had. He'd simply given her what she'd craved—sweet little chapbooks of fairy tales and fables and stories of derring-do.

She read the certificate through tear-filled eyes. "It . . . it says here that he died of heart failure."

Having regained his composure, Mr. Gaither nodded with grave solemnity.

"I don't believe it." Aunt Verity took the paper from her and looked it over. "How very uncharacteristic of Cecil." She glanced up at the solicitor. "Are you quite sure it wasn't poison? Or something equally sinister?"

Oh dear, as usual Aunt Verity was living up to her name.

When Mr. Gaither looked taken aback, Clara figured she ought to explain. "The Doggett men are . . . *were* . . . adventurous sorts, you see, and all died badly. My eldest uncle was shot in a duel, and the youngest was hanged in Madrid for forgery."

"So death by heart failure isn't what one expects of a Doggett," Aunt Verity added.

"I assure you that if I hadn't been certain of the circumstances of his death, I wouldn't have left America to come here," the solicitor said loftily. "And I certainly wouldn't be passing on his bequest to her ladyship."

Clara regarded him blankly, but Aunt Verity pounced on his comment. "What bequest? The man never had more than two shillings to rub together."

"When Mr. Doggett died, he possessed fifteen thousand pounds. He left ten thousand of that fortune to Lady Clara. If she agrees to accept it."

Clara's mouth fell open. "Ten thousand pounds!" She tried to assimilate the astonishing news. This was straight out of a fairy tale by Charles Perrault. And like all fairy tales, it seemed much too good to be true. "Did my uncle happen to say how he came by such a fortune? When he left London, he was nearly penniless."

"I was told he won a plantation in a card game. The owner's brother, a wealthy man, offered him money in lieu of the property, and Mr. Doggett accepted. Said he wouldn't much like the life of a planter. But alas, he didn't live long enough to enjoy his newfound fortune."

A weight settled onto her chest at the thought of Uncle Cecil dying all alone in a strange country.

"And . . . umm . . . Cecil won the game honestly?" her aunt asked.

Clara groaned. She hadn't even thought of that.

"Of course!" the solicitor exclaimed. "I assure you I would never take part in any illegal endeavor."

Clara flashed him a weak smile. If Uncle Cecil's companions hadn't caught him cheating at the time, there was no point to explaining his proclivities now. And for all she knew, he hadn't cheated.

And pigs flew, too.

"This is quite sudden," Clara remarked. "Are you sure Uncle Cecil meant for the money to be left to *me*? I'm merely his niece. Perhaps you've confused me with one of his . . . er . . . mistresses or by-blows. I've heard tell he had several of both."

"Clara!" Aunt Verity clapped her hands over Empress's floppy ears. "You shouldn't speak of such matters before Empress. She's chaste!"

The dog squirmed to escape Aunt Verity's hands, clearly eager to drink up every scandalous word.

Clara shrugged. "Uncle Cecil was always perfectly forthright about his vices, so I don't see why *I* should pretend they don't exist."

"Good lack-a-daisy, niece, you'll shock all of my lassies with such talk. They're very sensitive about the proprieties." When the stony-faced solicitor snorted, Aunt Verity glared at him. "Well, they *are*. They have to be, living in the Stanbourne household as they do. My brother, Clara's father, was a clergyman, you know. A very fine man."

"I beg your pardon," Mr. Gaither retorted, "but I was given to understand that he was the marquess of Pemberton."

Clara gave him a pained look. "He was. Later in life, when he unexpectedly inherited the title. Until then, he was a clergyman. Now, about my uncle's estate . . ."

"Yes, of course. To answer your question, the other five thousand of his fortune is going to his 'mistresses and by-blows.' So the ten thousand is most assuredly for you. Unless you wish to refuse it? Mr. Doggett did mention that if you refused it, I was to accept that without murmur."

"I suppose you really ought to refuse," Aunt Verity put in. "Your father was always adamant that your mother not accept any proceeds from your uncles' ill-gotten—"

"She means *ill-conceived*," Clara broke in. "My uncles' *ill-conceived* schemes."

"No, dear, that's not what I meant—" her aunt began.

"Yes, it was," Clara said firmly. Perhaps Uncle Cecil had cheated. She would never know for sure and could do nothing about it.

But she could put ten thousand "ill-gotten" pounds to very good use. Not for herself, of course. Papa had left her a nice annual allowance of a thousand pounds. Between that and Aunt Verity's portion, there was plenty for them both to live comfortably in Stanbourne Hall all their days. But with ten thousand pounds, only think of the improvements they could make to the Home!

"So you do want the money, Lady Clara?" the solicitor asked impatiently.

Ideas already rushed through Clara's brain. "I do indeed."

"Very good, madam." Mr. Gaither began to explain the process of transferring the funds to her.

"If you're taking the money anyway, Clara," her aunt broke in, "you could put it to good use."

"Exactly what I was thinking, Aunt Verity," she said patiently.

"You could finally get married!"

Clara glanced at her, bemused. "What has money got to do with *that*?"

"Why, everything, my dear. With eight thousand pounds added to your present dowry, you'd have your pick of the respectable eligible gentlemen. Especially after we use the other two thousand to fix you up." She paused to pat Clara's knee. "Not that you aren't nicely fixed up already, you understand. For myself, I prefer your way of dress. But I've noticed that even respectable men like women with . . . umm . . ."

"Expensive clothing?" Clara said archly.

"No, dear. Elegance. Your wool gowns are all very well for reform, but you need elegance to attract a man. Once you've got a husband with your elegance and your fine dowry, then you can go back to dressing as you please. But you have to catch him first. Isn't that so, Faddle?"

Faddle barked enthusiastically. Clara rolled her eyes.

"I hear that the newly widowed Lord Winthrop is looking for a wife," her aunt went on slyly.

"Good Lord, not Winthrop again," Clara said.

That had certainly been a tempest in a teapot—the stodgy earl had paid some attention to her during her coming out but had retreated when his mother had protested Clara's "sordid" connections. Clara had hoped she was done with him forever when he'd married another woman eight years ago, dashing Aunt Verity's hopes.

Then the earl's poor wife had gone and died on him, leaving him with five children. So clearly Aunt Verity was back to planning the match. "Once we've got you properly done up," her aunt said, "and he hears of your newfound wealth, he's sure to look your way again."

"I don't want him looking my way again. He was a pompous twit back then, and he's a pompous twit now."

"Respectable, God-fearing men sometimes are, dear. But with your responsibilities, that's the sort of husband you need, don't you think?"

Clara scowled, though her aunt was probably right. When Clara married, it should be to a solid citizen who'd approve of her reform activities. The trouble was, Clara couldn't seem to warm to such men. Perhaps it was her unfortunate Doggett blood, but she found them so . . . tedious. One day, she'd have to take her medicine and align herself with such a husband, but she couldn't bring herself to do it just yet.

Aunt Verity bent down to croon in Empress's ear. "What do you think, girl? Wouldn't Clara look lovely in an elegant French gown, with pearls in her hair? Even a high stickler like Winthrop would overlook her mother's scandalous connections, and—"

"I shan't use the money for a dowry," Clara interrupted with an embarrassed glance at Mr. Gaither before her aunt started going on about reticules and pink bonnets and what all. "I intend to use it for the Home."

Her aunt straightened abruptly. "The Home?"

"With ten thousand pounds, I can expand it enormously." Excitement built in Clara's chest. "The children can have a real schoolroom, and we can provide financial incentive for tradesmen to take them on as apprentices. We might even start some little business of our own that the older children could run."

"But Clara, must you use it all on the Home? You could give half to the Home and leave half to enhance your dowry." Her pale brows knit in a frown. "But then there'd be nothing for fixing you up. Hmm, perhaps if we settled for an English modiste—"

"I'm not using one penny for my dowry," Clara snapped, her patience at an end. "Lord knows it's ample enough already."

Her aunt's hands fluttered against her pigeon breasts. "Dear girl, think what you're saying. You're getting on in years, you know."

"Thank you for pointing that out," Clara said, mortified to be having this conversation in front of a stranger. "I'm only twenty-eight, hardly old enough to be reduced to buying myself a husband. There's still plenty of time for marriage."

"Good lack-a-daisy, Clara—"

"Enough! I've made my decision."

Aunt Verity appealed to Mr. Gaither, who'd been listening to the conversation with smug interest. "Do tell her she can't use all the legacy on reform."

For the first time that morning, a smile lit Mr. Gaither's thin, bookish features. "Mr. Doggett made no stipulation whatsoever on how the money was to be used, madam. He left it entirely up to his niece."

"Clever man, my uncle," Clara muttered under her breath.

Mr. Gaither went on, almost maliciously, "If she wants to use it to make gold cages for your little beasts, she's perfectly free to do so."

Horror filled her aunt's face. "Cages! Clara, you would never—"

"Of course not, Aunt. I wouldn't think of it." Clara added teasingly, "Unless you persist in this notion of using it for my dowry—"

"I'm only trying to help," Aunt Verity grumbled. She was no fool—she knew when to retreat, though that didn't mean she'd given up. "If you insist on ignoring the possibilities, I don't suppose we can do much about it, eh, lassies?"

The poodles' yapping wiped the smile right off Mr.

Gaither's face. He leaped to his feet. "I'd best be going. I must pass on those other bequests, you know."

Clara smiled at the American as she rose, too. "Yes, to Uncle Cecil's by-blows and mistresses. I don't suppose you could tell me who—"

"Don't even think it, Clara Stanbourne," her aunt protested. "Reforming pickpockets is one thing, but if you begin associating with *those* sorts of women—"

"Actually, madam," the solicitor broke in, "Mr. Doggett thought that his niece might ask such a thing, and he instructed me to keep everyone's identities secret. I think he was afraid that if his . . . er . . . consorts knew of his exalted connections, they might take advantage of the association."

Tears sprang to Clara's eyes again. It was so like Uncle Cecil to try to protect her. "Thank you, Mr. Gaither, for carrying out his wishes so faithfully."

To her surprise, he winked. "I'll inform you when all the papers are drawn up, my lady, and you can collect the funds. Now, if you'll excuse me—"

"Yes, of course, I'll just see you out." Clara shot her aunt an indulgent smile. "Aunt Verity, I'm going to the Home, but I'll be back for dinner."

"Do be careful, Clara," her aunt called after her. "Take one of the footmen!"

"I always do," Clara said irritably as she ushered Mr. Gaither into the foyer.

Samuel jumped to his feet and hastened to bring Mr. Gaither's overcoat. But as the young man helped the solicitor into it, she saw his right hand flash.

With a groan, she stepped forward to manacle Samuel's wrist before Mr. Gaither turned around. "Oh, dear, Mr. Gaither," she said smoothly, "I believe you've dropped your purse. Samuel seems to have found it."

Samuel colored, but held the purse out with such lightning speed that nobody but Clara would have known it had resided in his pocket for a full five seconds. "It was on the floor, sir. Is it yours?"

With a look of complete bewilderment, Mr. Gaither patted his pocket, then said, "Bless my eyes, it is indeed."

"It must've fell out when you put on your coat," Samuel said helpfully.

"I suppose." Mr. Gaither eyed Samuel with suspicion as he accepted the purse. Then turning to Clara, he made a sketchy bow. "Good day, madam. I'll send a note round when everything is done. Perhaps it would be better if we meet elsewhere next time."

"Certainly," she agreed quickly. "Good day, Mr. Gaither."

The door had scarcely closed behind him before she whirled on Samuel. "I cannot believe that you—"

"It ain't what you think, m'lady," Samuel hastened to say. "I would have returned the purse before the carriage drove off, truly I would. I was just practicing."

"For what? You're out of that life now."

"I got to keep my skills up, because you never know . . ." He trailed off as if to keep from saying too much.

But he'd already said enough. She knew what he was thinking. *Because you never know when you'll lose a position. Because one day the dream will vanish as so many others have, and you'll have nothing to stand between you and starvation but your skills.*

She took one look at his anxious face and sighed. "From now on, please practice only on me and the servants, all right?"

He blinked at her. "You mean you're not dismissing me?"

The hopeful yearning in his face made her heart hurt. "No. Though if you ever do anything like that again—"

"Oh, yes, m'lady . . . I mean no, m'lady . . . I mean I'll never do it again, I swear!" Grabbing her hand, he kissed it with a slavishness bordering on desperation. "I won't disappoint you. I'll never pick a pocket again, and I'll be the best footman ever to work at Stanbourne Hall!"

"You'll certainly be the most nimble." When he looked downcast, she smiled reassuringly. "There, there, you're a good, hard worker, and I have every faith that you'll put your quick fingers to better use than you have in the past." Gently she extricated her hand. "Now go on with you, and summon my carriage."

With a quick nod, Samuel scurried off. She shook her head as she watched him go. Samuel was one of her successes, yet even he had his moments. How much hardship must it take to bludgeon such a promising young man into believing he had no hope of a future beyond stealing? That he must always expect life to hand him lemons?

She squared her shoulders. She was here to counteract all that bludgeoning, and with this new source of funds, she could do it on a grand scale.

The carriage rumbled up at once. As Samuel took his place on the back, she climbed inside and began to contemplate plans for her new inheritance. There were the practical improvements, of course, expansion of the children's dormitories and a new stove for the kitchen, not to mention at least two more teachers and a whole slew of books. Mama had always wanted better heating. Indeed if they'd had adequate heating during the cruelly bitter winter of 1812—

She sighed at the dark memory. Her mother had died of pneumonia during that winter. Clara herself had taken ill, for they'd spent many hours at the Home trying to keep the children warm. But her mother hadn't possessed the youthful constitution to survive frequent exposure to the dank, cold air.

Tears stung Clara's eyes, and she brushed them away impatiently. How silly to dwell on what couldn't be changed. The news of Uncle Cecil's death had made her morbid.

She smoothed out the skirts of her practical worsted gown, the sort she always wore to the Home, and straightened her spine. The best way to honor the dead was by making their passing useful to the living. Mama would be pleased to know she'd indirectly contributed to the Home's present windfall. Indeed, if not for Mama's steadfast insistence that Clara associate with the Doggetts as well as the Stanbournes, Uncle Cecil would never have known his niece well enough to warrant giving her such an inheritance.

Clara smiled. She hoped Mama was watching from heaven and smiling, too.

By now they'd entered the grimy, despair-ridden environs of Spitalfields. The passing of her carriage was scarcely noted—the bleary-eyed denizens of the streets were used to seeing the black-and-gold Stanbourne equipage trundle by nearly every morning. Clara had been coming this way alone for the seven years since Mama's death, and for three before it.

They lumbered onto Petticoat Lane, a street notorious for its receivers of stolen goods, who often worked out of pawnshops. She gathered up her leather reticule and striped wool shawl as they rode within sight of the Home.

Then something caught her eye in the alley very near her destination. Normally, she wouldn't give a second glance to two people squabbling, but a flash of red arrested her attention.

Johnny Perkins in his favorite scarlet coat. And the twelve-year-old, a resident of the Home, was having a spirited discussion with a tall, broad-shouldered stranger, who seemed to be restraining the boy from running off.

Reminded of this morning's incident with Samuel, she shouted, "Stop the coach!" As it shuddered to a halt, she opened the door and leaped out. Telling the coachman to go on and Samuel to wait at the top of the alley, she headed toward the imposing gentleman dressed in a ragged frock coat and battered beaver hat.

The alley stank of fried herring and cabbage and the quiet fear that pervaded Spitalfields. It wasn't fear, however, but alarm that spurred her toward the man gripping Johnny's shoulder with firm intent. Because morning sunlight glinted off the gold watch dangling from Johnny's hand, and that could mean only one thing.

Another one of her pickpockets was headed for trouble this morning.

Chapter 2

... converse not with any but those that are good,
sober and virtuous. Evil Communications
corrupt Good Manners.
A Little pretty pocket-book: intended for
the instruction and amusement of little
Master Tommy and pretty Miss Polly, *John Newbery*

Vainly trying to smother her distress, Clara vaulted the
rest of the way down the alley. She was just in time to
hear Johnny's squeaky voice say, "Now see here—"

"Johnny!" she said sharply.

The boy's head whipped around, and his ruddy cheeks
paled to the color of milk. "Bloody hell," he mumbled as she
approached.

She leveled on him her famous Stanbourne Stare, which
generally sent her children scurrying to behave. "Give the
gentleman back his watch this minute!"

Johnny hesitated, then handed the watch over. As soon as

the stranger had it, he lifted cool black eyes to her. Fear banished her irritation at Johnny. The only men in Spitalfields with that direct a stare were watchmen. Or worse, officers of the law.

Sick with worry, she stepped up to place a proprietary hand on the other shoulder of her hapless charge. "Please, sir, I'm sure Johnny didn't mean to take your watch—"

"What concern is it of yours whether he did or not, madame? Are you the lad's mother?" The man's hand still gripped Johnny's shoulder and seemed to tighten as they both stood there holding on to the boy.

Her panic increased. The stranger's faintly accented English wasn't a foreigner's exactly, but it wasn't an Englishman's either. Which didn't rule out his being an officer.

She forced a conciliatory smile to her lips. "I'm a guardian of sorts to him."

"Me mum is dead," Johnny interjected helpfully. "This here's Lady Clara."

"*Lady* Clara?" Instead of tipping his hat or begging her pardon, he muttered a French curse under his breath. Then he surveyed her hair, her gown, and even her boots with a brusque, impersonal scrutiny. "What's a lady of rank doing in Spitalfields?"

"I run the Stanbourne Home for the Reformation of Pickpockets. It's the brick building on the next corner. Johnny is one of my residents."

A thin, ironic smile touched the man's hard mouth. "I see that his reformation is progressing nicely."

She colored. "Lapses happen occasionally, sir, but they're unusual. I'm only sorry you had to witness this one. Now if you'd be so good as to release Johnny, perhaps we could better discuss the . . . er . . . situation."

Johnny remained silent, his gaze bouncing anxiously between her and the stranger.

The man stared at her long enough for her to glimpse a native intelligence in his fathomless eyes and wary expression. Then he shrugged and dropped his hand from Johnny's shoulder. Casting the watch a cursory glance, he shoved it into his coat pocket.

She breathed easier. "Thank you, Mr. . . . Mr. . . . ."

"Pryce." Then he added, almost as an afterthought, "Captain Morgan Pryce."

Oh, dear, a captain. But what kind? When he offered no more information, she examined him more carefully. He dressed shabbily—patched fustian coat and waistcoat, decidedly ragged stock, scuffed boots—and his black hair curled far down past his frayed shirt collar. But other details of his appearance revealed a man with gentlemanly habits. He'd tied his stock with considerable care, and his fingernails were clean and well groomed.

Still, that didn't make him an officer of the law. "Are you a captain serving with the River Police? Or the Lambeth Street Police Office?"

At Johnny's inexplicable snort, the gentleman cast the boy a quelling glance. "I'm a captain serving Her Majesty's Navy."

"In Spitalfields?" she blurted out.

A faint amusement crossed the surprisingly handsome face. "In case you hadn't heard, England isn't fighting any wars these days, so there's little call for naval captains. We're all on half-pay."

While his profession explained his educated speech and air of command, it didn't explain what a foreign-sounding gentleman who'd managed to obtain a captain's commission was doing in an alley in *her* part of town. "Half-pay or not, surely you can afford to board your family in better surroundings than Spitalfields."

"I have no family. And I live here because I own a business concern in the area." He jerked his head toward the tumbledown building on her right with a door that stood half ajar. "That's the side entrance to my new shop. I sell nautical goods to sailors."

"But why here, of all places?"

"Why not? Plenty of sailors live in this part of London. Should I have set up my business in the Strand among the milliners and the tailors? So I could tap the lucrative market for young ladies buying compasses?"

His sarcasm made her arch one brow. "Certainly not. But there are parts of town where you're less likely to risk having your shop robbed."

Oh, bother, thievery was the last thing she should have mentioned.

He shot Johnny a meaningful glance. "Excellent point."

She sucked in an anxious breath. Captain Pryce might not be a police officer, but some navy men could be rather surly about such things as being robbed in the street. And he definitely seemed the surly sort. "I hope you realize, sir, that little would be accomplished by taking Johnny before the magistrate."

Johnny flashed Captain Pryce a panicked look. "I ain't going to no magistrate, am I?"

"No," Captain Pryce said firmly. "Of course not."

Relief flooded her, but she couldn't risk the man changing his mind. "Where you're going is back to the Home this very minute." She squeezed Johnny's shoulder. "Go on then."

"But you gave me leave to visit Lucy this morning—"

"Which you used to ill effect, so your leave has been revoked." Lucy was Johnny's sister. If necessary, Clara would take him to visit Lucy herself later. "Now go tell Mrs. Carter I said to put your clever fingers to work in the kitchen. A long stint helping peel potatoes will give you time to contemplate how close you came to disaster this morning."

"I could connemplay it better dusting the parlor," Johnny offered hopefully.

"Contemplate," she said, enunciating the consonants. "It means 'think.' As in, 'think about your sins.' Perhaps you could do it best by cleaning out the chamber pots."

"Oh no, m'lady!" Johnny looked appalled. "Now that I consider it, peeling potatoes is just the thing for thinking. Aye, just the thing."

"Good choice." She shoved him none too gently toward the entrance to the alley. "Go on with you. I'll be there in a moment."

Casting Captain Pryce a last furtive look, Johnny scurried off. She held her breath until the boy slipped past Samuel and around the corner, then let it out in a long *whoosh*. Another disaster averted.

Well, not entirely. She still had to deal with the suspicious captain. But when she turned to face him, she read interest rather than suspicion in his eyes.

This time when his gaze swept her, it wasn't brusque or impersonal. It was slow, thorough, and intimate—the look of a man examining an attractive woman. To her annoyance, it set off an unfamiliar fluttering in her belly. And when his gaze rose to her mouth, as if drawn there by her quickened breath, the fluttering in her belly grew positively frenzied.

How absurd. He was a neighbor, nothing more. A decidedly attractive neighbor, true, and certainly more interesting than any other man she'd met in Spitalfields, but still merely a neighbor.

She fought to regain her composure. "Thank you for your indulgence with Johnny, sir," she said in a breathier voice than she would have liked. "I know he's given you the wrong impression of my children, but I assure you that most of them are not like him."

The gaze he lifted to hers was once more icy and remote. "You mean, they're not foolish enough to get caught."

This captain might be handsome, but his manner was worse than the gruff Beast's in her favorite tale by Madame Le Prince de Beaumont. "I mean, they try to avoid behavior that lands them in trouble." When he cocked an eyebrow skeptically, she stiffened. "They *are* only children, you know. They do err from time to time."

"As long as you keep them away from my shop, I don't really care what they do."

His bluntness brought her up short. "If you're worried they'll steal from you—"

"I'm worried they'll get underfoot."

"They won't." She forced a smile, determined to be congenial even if he was not. "I assure you that the residents of Spitalfields find us to be very good neighbors."

Scowling, he glanced to the top of the alley, where Samuel stood polishing the brass buttons of his yellow-and-black livery with a handkerchief. "Tell me, madame, do you spend a great deal of time in the neighborhood?"

"Every day."

"Your father or husband or whatever man is responsible for you doesn't object?"

That got her dander right up. "I beg your pardon, but I'm perfectly capable of taking care of myself—I need no man to be 'responsible' for me."

"Oh?" He nodded toward the head of the alley. "So why is that incompetent fool there standing guard?"

Thank heavens Samuel was too far off to hear this audacious captain's insults. "Samuel is my footman. He accompanies me everywhere as a matter of principle. And he's not an incompetent fool."

"He is if he thinks he can protect you while remaining several yards away."

"I *told* him to stand there. Quite frankly, I didn't think I'd be in any danger."

He stepped closer, his dark gaze drifting to her lips, then her breasts. It fixed there meaningfully before rising casually to meet hers. "Then you're as much a fool as he."

Color rose in her cheeks despite her attempts to squelch it. Though she was draped from neck to ankle in sturdy brown worsted, his look seemed to lay her bare. Or at the very least, imply that he'd *like* to lay her bare. A sudden image of the large, virile captain stripping her clothing from her one piece at a time affected her pulse most alarmingly.

She struggled to regain the upper hand. "Are you always this rude?"

"Are you always this careless of your safety?"

"I happen to consider some things more important than safety."

"Like what?"

"The well-being of my charges and my fellow creatures. The future of mankind."

"What lofty concerns for such a *petite jeune fille*," he said sarcastically. "And here the rest of us merely worry about surviving from one day to the next."

She lifted her chin. "That's why I believe being born to privilege means I must help those less fortunate. You might say I do my own part to keep the ship from sinking."

"By bailing it out with thimbles?" His voice held a taunt. "Take care, my lady, or you'll find yourself sinking faster than you can bail."

"If I had a shilling for every time some well-meaning person predicted disaster, I could buy your entire shop, lock, stock, and barrel. Yet despite the naysayers, I've managed to place sixty-three of my charges in positions as apprentices or servants throughout the city."

Surprise showed in his face. "You convinced that many

people to hire pickpockets? *Pickpockets,* for God's sake? *Bon Dieu,* how long have you worked here?"

"Ten years, though I've only been in charge for seven. And before you ask how 'whatever man is responsible for me' could allow it, I should tell you that my late father is the one who first brought me to work at the Stanbourne Home."

"And your husband approves?"

To her utter mortification, she blushed again. "I-I'm not married."

He rolled his eyes. "That explains everything."

"What do you mean?"

This time the sweep of his glance was insultingly insolent. "No man with any sense would allow his pretty young wife to saunter about this part of town unprotected."

"I *am* protected," she countered smoothly, refusing to be intimidated. "I have Samuel. And despite his appearance, he's quite effective. He used to be a pickpocket himself, so he knows the dangers of this area. And he carries a wicked-looking knife." She smiled sweetly. "Shall I have him brandish it for you?"

His gaze flicked past her to Samuel. "Don't bother. It would take him too long to fish it out of his boot. Which isn't where it should be, since it does him little good there." When she started, surprised that he'd know where Samuel kept his knife, the captain swung his gaze back to her. "Besides, a knife is useless against a man with a pistol. A villain could dispatch your foolish footman with one shot before you even gathered breath to scream, mademoiselle."

She would consider the blunt words a threat, except for one thing. Though he looked stern and his tone was rough, concern glinted deep in his eyes. Good Lord, the man was actually trying to caution her . . . in his own boorish, arrogant way.

"Why, Captain Pryce," she cooed, "I hardly know what to say. While I'm flattered by your concern for my well-being, it's entirely unnecessary. After all, I've been coming here for ten years with nary an incident."

"Until now," he said mulishly.

"So you plan to assault me in the alley in broad daylight, do you?"

"Confound it, that's not—" He looked thoroughly exasperated. "I only meant that women of your sort shouldn't be prancing about Spitalfields."

"I'll have you know that I do not 'prance' anywhere. And I had no idea I had a 'sort.' Precisely what is my 'sort'?"

"You know what I mean. A young, unmarried lady of rank with more time on her hands than sense."

"Such compliments! Aren't you the gallant gentleman? I begin to think you might truly be a naval captain after all."

Her sarcasm made him cock one eyebrow. "Did you think I was lying?"

She shrugged. "You sound like a Frenchman, and I doubt the navy commissions many French captains."

"I'm as English as you are."

"I don't see how. You mix French too easily and too well in your speech. The English are always mangling it, myself included."

"I grew up in Geneva, that's all. So I tend to use both my childhood languages." He crossed his arms casually over his chest. "And anyway, it's no business of yours where I'm from and what my profession is."

"Ah, but there you're wrong. You're my neighbor, and I must consider my children's welfare. With your shop so close, I'd like to know what sort of person we'll be dealing with in the future."

His heavy black brows lowered in a scowl. "Stay away from my shop, and you won't have to deal with me at all."

Abruptly, he turned on his heel and headed for the open door.

For a moment, she could only gape at him, the sheer enormity of his rudeness knocking the wind out of her. But as he reached the door, she recovered her composure. "You certainly set me straight, didn't you? God forbid that a person should try to be neighborly."

Cursing under his breath, he whirled toward her. "Let me make this clear, Lady Clara. I'd rather that you *not* be neighborly." Then he paused, a decidedly sinful expression spreading over his face. Resting his hand on the doorknob, he allowed his gaze to play over her suggestively. "No, I take that back. Be as neighborly as you like as long as you leave your brats at home. I always welcome female . . . companionship, especially when the female is so choice."

She'd have to be an idiot to mistake his meaning. "Is that your idea of a compliment? Because if it is, it's in very bad taste."

"That was my idea of an invitation. I beg your pardon if I wasn't clear enough."

"Oh, you were quite clear, sir. But you'll have to use the establishment down the street for that sort of companionship. I'm afraid my talents don't lie in that area."

"What a pity," he said coolly. "Because I have no other use for you as a neighbor, and no use at all for your charges. So keep them away from my shop. Understood?"

"Perfectly." She wouldn't let her children near his shop now even if he gave them his goods for free.

"*Adieu*, mademoiselle." He entered his shop and closed the door with a bang.

Good Lord, what a man! First to act as if he feared being robbed by every one of her charges and then to give her a most insulting invitation! She hoped she never had to deal with him again. Such rudeness went beyond the pale.

Still muttering to herself about their astonishing neighbor, she turned toward the top of the alley, where Samuel waited for her, scowling.

"What did that fellow want?" Samuel asked as she neared him.

Thank heavens Samuel hadn't heard what the beastly creature really wanted. "Johnny picked his pocket. I was trying to soothe things over."

Samuel eyed her oddly. "Are you sure that's what Johnny did?"

"I caught Johnny red-handed. And he wasn't only 'practicing,' I assure you. Fortunately, Captain Pryce was willing to overlook the matter." And lecture her and insult her in the bargain.

Samuel kept staring at the closed door to the shop. "*Captain* Pryce?"

"He claims to be a captain in Her Majesty's Navy."

"Looked too rough to be a naval officer, if you ask me."

Rough? Oh, yes. But if his behavior weren't so appalling, she would call him attractive—in a roguish sort of way. Those formidable thick brows . . . strong, aggressive features . . . intriguing eyes. A pity he had the manners of a troll.

A small smile touched her lips. He should fit in nicely around here.

No, that wasn't entirely true. For all his surliness and rude suggestions, he bore little resemblance to one-eyed Briggs with his coarse language and filthy habits. Or that brutal boxer Harry, who leaped out with his fists to avenge any offense, large or small.

Still, she could understand what Samuel meant by "rough." Captain Pryce had a certain hardness . . . an authoritarian air and rampantly masculine strength that sent delicious shivers along her spine. Any "female companion" would probably be well pleased to find herself at his disposal.

Good Lord, what was she thinking? The man was a beast. It was just as well that he'd warned her and her children away. Any woman of good sense would avoid dealing with him entirely.

Besides, she had far more important matters to attend to now that Uncle Cecil had bequeathed her a fortune. "Oh, Samuel, I haven't yet told you the news, have I?" As they left the alley, she explained about her new inheritance, thankful that her revelation took his mind—and hers—off the disturbing Captain Pryce.

When they reached the Home, she paused to survey the faded brick façade with an assessing eye. "What do you think should be done first with the money?"

"That's easy—you got to fix the roof. Leaks every time it rains. You got to put up new tiles."

"And something should be done about the listing shutters and the windows, too."

"Sturdier ones is what you need, tightly hung so as not to let in great drafts."

She nodded. "Poor miserable old matron." It had weathered a hundred years, first as a hospital for the insane until Bedlam had edged it out, and then as her own imperfect Home. "I'd dearly love to dress her up a bit—paint the trim a bright blue and replace the crumbling cornices with more magnificent ones—but then the old girl would look entirely out of place in Spitalfields."

"And that'd surely mean trouble, m'lady."

"Yes." It would mean the difference between being left alone or being continually robbed. "I suppose we'd best confine repairs to the practical." She smiled at Samuel. "I'd better go in. Mrs. Carter will want to hear the good news." Mrs. Carter managed the Home as lovingly as any hen with a brood of chicks, though she was getting on in years and often spoke of retiring. Clara didn't know what she'd do without her when she did.

"When shall me and the coachman return to fetch you? Five o'clock as usual?"

"That's fine. Oh, and Samuel?" She glanced back down the street to the alley. "Ask Aunt Verity to hunt up the navy lists and send them over at once. I know she has them. She used to follow her cousin's postings rather closely in the lists."

"Planning to check up on the cap'n's claims, are you?"

She shrugged. "It's always good to know who your neighbors are."

Samuel eyed her shrewdly. "You never checked up on old Mrs. Tildy, when she moved in down the street, or—"

"Just tell my aunt to send over her navy lists." Then she hurried up the stairs, not wanting to see her footman's curious expression.

It was simply a precaution. She wanted to make sure Captain Pryce was who he said he was. After all, with him so close by and her children so vulnerable, it only made sense. There was nothing more to it than that. Nothing at all.

She was so intent on her self-avowals that she didn't notice five-year-old Timothy Perkins until she'd crossed the foyer. He hadn't yet seen her. His eyes were fixed on the floor, and only when he suddenly smashed something with his foot did she realize he was absorbed by one of the many bugs that plagued the old building.

She started to ask why he was waiting outside the library, the one room her charges avoided. Then she thought better of it and glided toward him silently. But as she neared him, he looked up and froze. When he glanced to the library door in a panic, her eyes narrowed. She recognized a lookout when she saw one.

He opened his mouth to give the warning, but she shot him the Stanbourne Stare and held a finger to her lips. He slumped. Poor lad. His brother Johnny might defy her, but little Timothy was still young enough to be cowed.

Laying one hand on his shoulder for reassurance, she stepped up to the door and held her ear to the crack.

"So are you going back?" asked a voice she recognized as David Walsh's.

"Bloody right I am." That was Johnny's voice. "At least to get me money. The sly knave didn't give me a farthing for the watch. I know it's worth at least eight shillings."

"Well, you could hardly expect him to give you money with m'lady standing there," David said. "Then she'd know what you were both doing. And I've heard tell that the cap'n ain't stupid. He wouldn't let himself get caught in the act by her."

The captain? Giving Johnny money for a watch behind her back?

The truth hit her with brutal force, settling in her belly like a lead weight. Captain Pryce, curse his hide, was one of those awful men who provided the other half of the thievery equation: a receiver of stolen goods.

Of course! That explained so much. Why a naval captain— if he really was such a thing—had settled in Spitalfields. Why he and Johnny had been in the alley.

God rot that scoundrel! While she'd been away paying a long overdue visit to Papa's relations in the country, he'd been settling in here, coaxing her children back into crime. And she'd actually thanked him for letting Johnny go. How could she have been so stupid?

A shop for sailor's goods, indeed. She ought to know better. Fences often marketed their stolen wares under the guise of legitimate shops. Especially in Spitalfields, where legend said you could "lose" a snuffbox in one street and buy it back a few minutes later in another. No doubt that's why he'd set himself up here.

Devil take him! Until now she'd been fortunate to have no fences operating so close to her Home. This end of the street held mostly taverns and rag shops, neither of which tempted her children to stray. Having a fence half a block away would be disaster.

"Did the cap'n say how much he'd give you?" queried a feminine voice. Mary Butler, no doubt. She worshipped Johnny the way Johnny worshipped fat purses.

"No, we didn't get to it before m'lady came up."

"When you go back to the shop, tell us how much he offers," David said. "'Cause I heard it's more than any of the fences who work for the Specter. And the cap'n might be less rough to deal with than them."

The Specter? The hair rose on the back of her neck. Rumor had it that every fence in Spitalfields worked for the master criminal. His nickname came from his ability to run his business in utter anonymity. Wearing a hooded cloak that hid his face, he handled transactions in dimly lit rooms that changed with each encounter. Even his fences didn't know who he really was, which was why he'd eluded the authorities for years.

The pickpockets, being superstitious by nature, thought his uncanny ability to escape capture was supernatural. Rumors abounded that he could fly over the water, that he'd once floated from one building to another while being pursued.

Nonsense, all of it. But his reputation for ruthlessness was not. Anybody who crossed him eventually turned up in some forgotten alley with a slit throat.

"We don't know for sure he ain't in league with the Specter," Johnny said. "That cap'n looks as hard as any of the Specter's men. I heard he was once a pirate."

"I heard he was a smuggler," Mary said in a whisper. "I'll

wager he could slip a knife in a man's belly as easy as any of the Specter's men."

Was that just the typical exaggeration of children? Or was this captain really so dastardly? Clara strained closer, hoping to hear more.

"You should stay away from him, Johnny," Mary went on plaintively. "Let that cap'n keep the watch. Why would you want to return to the old life? There ain't naught but trouble in it."

Clara smiled. At least one of her children had good sense.

David snorted. "You only say that 'cause you're jealous, Mary. You couldn't lift a watch off a cully even if he was blind, deaf, and dumb."

"Could so!" little maligned Mary cried. "I once took a lace wiper off a gentry mort while she stared right at me!"

A "wiper" was a handkerchief. Stealing them had been Mary's specialty.

"It don't count when the lady offers it to you to blow your nose," David retorted.

"She didn't, you arse! I stole it fair and square!"

"And anyway, a wiper don't compare to a gold watch like Johnny told us about. You know how hard it is to filch a tick like that? And Johnny here lifted a ten-pound note from a wrestler once and got away without a scratch. You never done nothing like that."

Wonderful. Now they were competing for the title of Most Talented Pickpocket.

Johnny said offhandedly, "Leave her be, David."

"Why? Is she your flash-girl?"

"At least *I* do my own filching," Mary shot back. "I don't hide behind Johnny while he does all the work."

"Odsfish, I'll get you for that!" David cried.

At the sounds of scuffling, Clara decided she would hear nothing more of use and hastily pushed open the door. David and Mary were engaged in a hair tug-of-war that Johnny was trying to break up.

"That's enough!" She separated them swiftly, grabbing Mary with one hand and David with the other. "I don't want another word about who steals better! And no more about that cursed captain either, if you know what's good for you."

All three went pale when they realized how much she'd overheard. They glanced accusingly to little Tim, standing behind her.

"Bloody hell, you let her listen in?" Johnny snapped at his poor brother.

"I tried to warn you," Timothy cried, "but m'lady wouldn't let me!"

Johnny snorted in disgust. If Clara hadn't been so upset by the whole mess, she would have laughed. Johnny was a fool if he thought a five-year-old could stand firm against the Stanbourne Stare.

It certainly was keeping Mary and David frozen in place. David was her primary concern. Mary had pegged him correctly—he'd landed in the Home precisely because he was as light-fingered as a goat. He'd been caught on his first venture and released only when Clara had begged the judge to let him be put into her care. Unfortunately, his hero worship of Johnny put him at risk of trying to prove himself, and Mary wasn't helping.

Clara didn't know which was worse—an inept, insecure pickpocket like David or a competent, charismatic one like Johnny. "You all know better than to encourage this sort of activity. There's no future in thievery, no matter how skillful."

David and Mary hung their heads. "Yes'm."

Johnny pushed in front with a belligerent air. "They had naught to do with it, m'lady. It was all me. I'm the one you should punish."

His willingness to take responsibility for his actions surprised her. Perhaps there was hope for him after all.

But only if she stood firm now. "Don't worry, you're the one who *will* be punished. You know the rules, Johnny. Three chances, that's all. You engage in acts of thievery once, you receive a warning and a week's worth of chores. Do it twice, and you receive a lecture and a month's worth of chores. Do it three times . . ."

She didn't have to finish the sentence. They all knew it. Three times and you were kicked out of the Home. You couldn't return for a month, and then only if you'd shown that you'd truly changed your ways.

She despised that rule. Her father had established it, and though she often thought of dispensing with it, she knew she dared not. She had no choice: if she allowed children like Johnny to "lift" things while still living in the Home, she risked not only their corrupting all her other charges but also having the authorities shut down the entire institution. That would do no one any good. Nasty and overly strict it might be, but the third rule was a necessity.

She forced herself to continue, though Johnny had gone as still as the rest at the reminder. "This is your second offense, Johnny. You're dangerously close to eviction."

A small gasp beside her reminded her that little Tim was watching everything. Her heart twisted in her chest, and she quickly reassured him. "Not you, Timothy, just your brother. You will always have a place here, as long as you abide by the rules yourself."

The relief in his face showed that she'd guessed his concern correctly. Poor lad. Too young to be a hardened criminal, yet old enough to fear abandonment.

There was hope for Tim, but Johnny unfortunately teetered on the edge. He could tilt either way. And she greatly feared that she knew which way he was leaning. "Mary, David, and Timothy, join the others in the schoolroom."

With downcast eyes, the children headed off, but as Johnny started to slip past her, she grabbed his arm. "We're not done yet, my boy. I want to know whom you stole the watch from."

Johnny stared down at his feet. "Some gentry cove in Leadenhall Street."

She shook her head. "I don't understand why you feel compelled to steal. You've done so well. It's been four months since your last offense. Why ruin everything after coming so far?"

He shrugged.

"That's not an answer, Johnny."

"Ain't got an answer for you, m'lady."

His refusal to confide in her worried her. If Johnny had been caught stealing by that "gentry cove," he'd have been hauled to the magistrate straightaway.

The fact that he might risk it for some reason she couldn't fathom terrified her so much that she spoke without thinking. "Very well, don't talk to me, but if you go to the captain's shop to collect money for that watch, you know it'll be your third offense."

The minute his gaze shot to hers, anxious and scared, she regretted her words. But she dared not take them back. Leniency and kindness hadn't worked with Johnny—he was as incorrigible as ever. So perhaps sternness would.

She swallowed her apprehension. "I mean it. 'Acts of thievery' includes selling the goods to a fence. So stay away from Captain Pryce's shop if you want to remain here."

His solemn nod gave her hope that he would do so. Then he was gone.

Her knees buckled, and she had to lean against the wall for support. If only she could be sure she was handling Johnny properly. But it was so hard to know the right thing to do.

One thing was certain—the longer he stayed in the Home,

the better it was for him. Yet how could she keep him here now that she'd laid down that ultimatum? The moment her back was turned, Johnny was sure to run back to Captain Pryce's shop for his wretched money. Somehow she had to prevent it.

She could give Johnny money for the watch herself, but that would be rewarding his crime. No, she must make that cursed captain give her the watch, that's all. Once she told Johnny of it, he'd have no reason to ask Captain Pryce for the money, since the captain wouldn't pay him for something that had never brought a profit.

Of course, that meant she had to deal with the captain again. She scowled. That scoundrel—she could strangle him for dangling temptation before her children's faces. She'd had him all wrong. He wasn't the Beast at all. At least the Beast had turned into a prince once Beauty tamed him.

No, Captain Pryce was the Wolf from Perrault's "Little Red Riding Hood." And like the Wolf, he had only one purpose—to devour his prey. He pretended to want nothing to do with her children when in truth he planned to draw them in. No doubt he'd been trying to allay her suspicions when he'd warned her to keep her children away.

Well, if he thought she'd stand idly by while he corrupted her lambs beneath her very nose, he'd better think again. Her children might fall for his foolish promises of riches, but she was no Little Red Riding Hood, to be lured and then devoured. He could disguise himself however he wished. Because no matter what his disguise, the Wolf was about to meet the huntswoman.

Chapter 3

The ladies all thought him divine,
The nobles invited him home;
The castle he gave for their use,
And he for adventures did roam.
"The History of Jack the Giant-Killer," anonymous
Cornish legend, this version printed by J.G. Rusher

Captain Morgan Pryce, known in other circles as the Honorable Captain Morgan Blakely, stood at the window of his musty shop, examining the gold watch in the sunlight. The inscription on the inside of the cover read, "To my darling boy." He shook his head. It must have belonged to some sentimental fellow too young and green to know how to avoid pickpockets, though it looked awfully old and worn for that. Perhaps a family heirloom?

He snapped the cover shut, then idly shifted the watch from hand to hand, gauging the weight of the gold, watching the chain glitter in sunlight with the brilliance of gems—or Lady Clara's smile.

He scowled. Just what he didn't need, a complication like her. She was going to be trouble. He'd known it the moment he'd looked up to see her standing there in all her glory—seemingly descended from heaven into the alley, with the morning sun encasing her slender frame in an angel's halo.

L'ange d'allée. Yes, that's what she was—the angel of the alley. She came to the defense of children despite the cost to her own safety because "the future of mankind" mattered more. She glided about Spitalfields in worsted wings and berated a man for not being gallant. She responded to said man's randy insults with tart insults of her own.

And blushed prettily when that man looked her over.

The sudden perverse quickening of his blood made him curse. Damn that Ravenswood! What had possessed the man to set this up so close to an institution for pickpockets? And why couldn't the woman who ran it be a pinched-face spinster with a sour disposition? Instead of a teasing vixen who smelled of jasmine and almond oil. He could almost imagine her dipping one dainty finger into an apothecary's bottle, then smoothing it over the pulse that beat so enticingly in her fine, slender neck . . .

Bon Dieu, he must be mad. This was no time to be lusting after a woman, especially one like her. Lady Clara wasn't some French demi-rep with whom he could take his pleasure in passing or a bored Spanish wife who shared his need for a few hours' entertainment. Even if he hadn't already made her despise him, she wasn't a woman he could pursue.

She was a virginal Englishwoman, for God's sake. She had morals and scruples . . . and Expectations. His own scruples dictated that he avoid any woman with Expectations. He couldn't possibly rise to them, and dashing them was always damned messy.

Besides, letting *any* woman distract him just now was not only unwise but dangerous. Pray God she'd taken his warning to heart, for herself as well as her charges. Because he suspected she was capable of great perception. If she figured him out, he'd have a disaster on his hands.

A tiny scrape at the side door put him on his guard right before it swung open and a tall figure dressed in unassuming garb slipped inside. "Good morning, Blakely."

Morgan watched as his superior from the Home Office sidled around a scarred display case to enter the cramped front room of the shop. "Don't call me Blakely in Spitalfields. They know me as Pryce. And why are you here anyway? We shouldn't be seen together."

Spencer Law, the fifth Viscount Ravenswood, rested one hand on a counter made of salvaged ship oak. "We won't be. I made sure no one was around. But even if anyone was, they wouldn't recognize me in this getup."

"If you say so." Morgan had to admit that Ravenswood didn't look nearly as out of place in the grubby, low-ceilinged room as pretty Lady Clara had in the alley. Despite his distinguished looks, the man excelled at blending into the woodwork. Before taking his highly visible position in the Home Office, he'd been the most successful spymaster in England. But though he didn't have his hand in it much anymore, he knew how to play the game when he had to.

Like now.

"To what do I owe the pleasure of this visit?" Morgan asked with a trace of sarcasm.

Ravenswood pushed away from the counter. "I wanted to make sure that the building suits your purpose. And that I'd provided you with everything you need to establish your business. Both your businesses."

Morgan crossed to the windows at the front of the shop. He'd left them murky to make it harder for curious passersby to witness goings-on inside. But Ravenswood was right—no one lingered nearby anyway.

Hanging the "Closed" sign in the window, Morgan faced his employer. "The building will suffice, though I wonder why you set me up within a stone's throw of the Stanbourne Home for the Reformation of Pickpockets."

"The boys in the Home will spread the word about you faster than anyone else."

"And if, in the meantime, one or two of them are sucked back into that life," Morgan said dryly, "you're not terribly concerned, I suppose."

Ravenswood shrugged. "It's a calculated risk we must take for the greater good."

"I suspect Lady Clara Stanbourne wouldn't see it quite that way."

"You've met?"

"Lady Clara caught me in a transaction with one of her lads this morning." Morgan dangled the gold watch in the air. "He was offering me this for sale."

Ravenswood blinked and stepped closer. "What the devil—" He patted his pockets, a scowl spreading over his brow.

As the truth struck Morgan, he began to laugh. "Don't tell me it's yours. *You* are the 'darling boy'?"

"Give me that!" Ravenswood snatched it from his hand. When Morgan kept laughing, Ravenswood said glumly, "My mother gave it to me when I was ten."

That explained why it looked well-worn. Ravenswood was in his mid-thirties, so the watch must be at least twenty years old.

The man examined the watch, then shoved it into his scruffy coat. "Bloody pickpockets. That's what I get for walking here. Must have been when I was crossing Leadenhall, before I stopped in at Pickering's for breakfast. Some lad burst out from behind a carriage and ran into me."

"Ran into you? You fell for the oldest trick in a pickpocket's book!"

"I have a lot on my mind these days," Ravenswood muttered. "So Lady Clara caught you while the boy was trying to sell you the watch?"

Stifling a laugh, Morgan gave up on tormenting his superior further. "Yes. Fortunately, she misunderstood and thought he was picking my pocket. I let her think it."

"And when she discovers the truth?"

"I'm hoping she won't. But to be safe, I warned her to keep her lads away."

"Devil take it, why did you do that? You'll rouse suspicion."

"I dislike corrupting children on the verge of redemption. That's too calculated a risk for my taste."

"You know very well that any boy who approached you with goods is already halfway to being corrupted again."

True. And yet . . .

He remembered too well what it was like to hover in doorways to escape the cold, gnawing on day-old baguettes filched from the bakery. To sleep in a thieves' den, where temporary shelter paid for by a pilfered handkerchief was preferable to a night spent listening to his mother coupling with her latest paramour.

No matter how corrupt, no child deserved such a life. Turning his back on Ravenswood, he began to straighten the goods on a nearby counter. "Since I'm the one taking all the risks, I'll choose the ones I can stomach. Now tell me what I need to know about Lady Clara, in case she doesn't heed my warnings."

Ravenswood was silent, as if debating whether further argument was necessary. At last he sighed. "Lady Clara. Hmm. For one thing, she isn't your typical society female."

A fine understatement. A typical society female spent her Monday afternoons paying calls, not collaring impudent scamps. She avoided worsted unless she was poor, and even then she cheated the devil to gain the blunt for fine French muslin. She certainly didn't spar with lowly sea captains in alleys. "Is she as committed to her cause as she seems?"

"She'd fight the devil himself for those children."

Then the children were fortunate to have the likes of Lady Clara championing them. And judging from young Johnny's defection, the confounded scamps didn't even appreciate it. "Has she no family of her own to look after?"

"Only an aunt who lives with her, I believe. Lady Clara's parents died some time ago, and she never married. Since she hasn't attended a marriage mart in years and only goes to other social functions to persuade hapless ladies and gentlemen to contribute to her beloved Home, I expect she never will. Many gentlemen run the other way when they see her coming."

"There must be a great many idiots moving in her circle," Morgan muttered.

Ravenswood's low chuckle irritated him. "I'll admit that she's pretty. A bit too zealous for my tastes, though."

Morgan said nothing. Her zealousness fascinated him. To think that an English noblewoman would risk her own safety daily for children whom others ignored . . . it boggled the mind. "Is she successful in persuading others to help her?"

"More than one would expect. When Lady Clara turns that angelic smile on you, you find yourself offering your help whether you want to or not."

Morgan faced him, eyes narrowing. "I take it she's turned it on you?"

Ravenswood shot him a rueful glance. "She convinced me to hire one of her pickpockets as a groom. You wouldn't have thought it would work, but the stable-master actually raves about him." He paused. "Surely you're not worried about her interference in *this*. She talks a good game, but she's all bark and no bite. I can't imagine that a lady like her would take on the sort of hardened criminal you're supposed to be."

Morgan wasn't so sure. "I suppose not. And even if she does, I can handle her."

"If I'd thought you couldn't, I wouldn't have set you up so close to her Home. So how is the location otherwise? Any nibbles from the light-fingered sort, aside from Lady Clara's boy?" Just that quickly, he'd dismissed the young noblewoman.

Morgan prayed he could do the same. "Two river pirates, a peterman, and several plain thieves, not to mention the usual pickpockets. Since I offered all but the pickpockets too much for their goods, I wager I'll have even more 'business' as word gets around."

"Why 'all but the pickpockets'?"

"That isn't the business I want to encourage. The Specter won't feel the pinch of lost income if I'm merely drawing off the shilling trade."

"No sign of the Specter yet?"

He lifted one eyebrow. "After ten days? The Specter will only act when he considers me an important competitor. And that will require my sowing the soil with silver for a while."

"Not too long a while, I hope. I'm eager to have this re-solved."

"And you're tightfisted."

Ravenswood smiled thinly. "That, too. Especially since I'm funding this investigation with my own money."

Morgan scowled. "Are you sure you should have set this up without the knowledge and support of either the Home Office or the Navy Board?"

"After what happened to you with the smugglers, I'm not taking any chances. The less people who know, the better.

One man has already died in the course of this investigation. I won't risk another, and certainly not my best man." Strolling over to a stool, Ravenswood perched on the end of it. "I only hope your plan works."

"Give it time. If the Specter really has been trading in stolen bank notes, then my doing the same will present him with a serious problem."

Since bank note numbers were recorded, thieves could only receive hard currency for their stolen notes by sending them to accomplices in countries less concerned about a note's legitimacy. The accomplices used the notes on the Continent, and eventually the notes landed in unsuspecting foreign banks, which cashed them at the Bank of England. Since the Bank of England couldn't risk its notes not being accepted abroad, it honored them . . . and lost thousands of pounds every year in the process.

Morgan suspected that the Specter had his own connections on the Continent. "Once I cut into his profits, he'll have to deal with me. Either he'll offer to include me in his operation, or he'll try to get rid of me. Both will bring him out in the open."

"But in one of those scenarios, you end up dead. Like Jenkins."

Morgan shrugged. "Jenkins handled everything wrong. You shouldn't have sent a gentleman spy to deal with the likes of the Specter."

"Since you weren't in England at the time," Ravenswood pointed out, "Jenkins was all I had. And what's wrong with gentlemen spies? I used to be one myself."

"Yes, but you were ferreting out traitors in French society, not trying to catch a criminal in Spitalfields. You weren't running about asking questions of fences, pretending to be a thief when you couldn't tell a figger from a dive."

"What's a figger?" When Morgan arched an eyebrow,

Ravenswood added sourly, "All right, you've made your point. But you're as much a gentleman as Jenkins was."

"Ah, but Jenkins was raised one; I wasn't." He shifted his gaze to the window, and bitterness crept into his voice. "That's why you came to me, as you well know—because of my firsthand knowledge of petty thievery."

"Not to mention a certain cunning and an ability to blend in anywhere."

Especially here. Morgan glanced out into the somber street moldering with gray despair. Living among smugglers while doing his duty hadn't bothered him—they were naught but seamen like himself. But living in Spitalfields—

He'd suffered most of his first thirteen years in Geneva's streets before his father's family had found him. Such a childhood wasn't wiped away by a subsequent education and long service in the navy. Every day he spent on Petticoat Lane brought those thirteen years painfully back.

He swore under his breath. He couldn't wait to be done with this. "My point is, I'll be more convincing as a receiver of stolen goods than Jenkins was as a thief." Picking up a compass, Morgan breathed on the face, then polished it with his sleeve. "For one thing, Jenkins didn't already have a tarnished reputation to lend his role credence. Whereas Morgan Pryce—"

"So that's why you're using your old name instead of taking an alias."

Until Morgan's family had finally claimed him publicly last year, Morgan had gone by the name of Pryce, his mother's maiden name. It had been better for all concerned. "In practicing deception, it's always best to stick to the truth when possible. I'm known among thieves for consorting with pirates and smugglers. Fortunately, while Morgan Blakely was exonerated of all blame for those activities, Morgan Pryce still has the reputation for them. So why not use it?"

"Yes, but if you don't use an alias, people you care about—like your brother—might hear of your activities. Or have you already told him what you're doing?"

An image of his very respectable brother, Sebastian Blakely, the Baron Templemore, suddenly filled his mind, giving him a moment's regret. "I've told him nothing—ignorance is bliss and all that."

"Even though you're cheating on your wager? I thought his terms were that you were to stay in England and out of danger for one year."

"I'm in England, aren't I? And what could be dangerous about opening a small-business concern?"

Ravenswood rolled his eyes. "I suspect Templemore wouldn't agree with your interpretation."

"Then perhaps you should keep your mouth shut about it. I doubt he and Juliet will be coming to London anytime soon, so they'll never know. They're too busy up in Shropshire overseeing the wheat sowing or sheep shearing or some such nonsense."

Ravenswood shot him a speculative glance. "Have you never desired to join them? Surely Templemore would happily let you live on his estate."

"Don't even think it!" Morgan shuddered. "Much as I enjoy the company of my brother and his wife, I'd hate playing the country squire. The first three months of the wager period that I spent at Charnwood nearly drove me mad. My brother's estate is too peaceful." It afforded way too much time for remembering.

"I understand that, I suppose. I myself prefer London with all its entertainments."

"I prefer the sea. Activity. I've never been so bored in all my life as I was at the Templemore town house. If not for that damned wager, I'd have left England months ago, gone to India or Africa."

"Then I'll have to thank your brother for keeping you here when next I see him."

Morgan eyed him askance. "Thank my sister-in-law instead. It was actually *her* wager. Poor woman has some notion that I'll get into trouble without her interference."

A smile crossed Ravenswood's face. "Can't imagine where she got such an idea." He rose from the stool. "Well, I'd best be going."

"Don't forget what I want out of this—captaincy of a first-rater. Nothing less." This nightmare would be worth it if he could sail off on his own ship and leave this godforsaken city behind.

"Are you sure you wouldn't rather accept the position in the Home Office I offered you?"

"And stay in London? Not a chance. I want my ship, and if you can't give me that—"

"You'll get what you want."

"So you say. But I'm not entirely sure you can meet my terms, when the navy doesn't even know what we're up to."

"Don't worry, they'll honor my agreement with you once this is done. They always love a hero, and you'll certainly be a hero if you catch the Specter."

"And if I don't?"

He shrugged. "You'll be dead. Dead men don't captain ships."

Morgan frowned. "Stop talking as if I have one foot in the grave. I don't intend to die, and certainly not in this wretched place."

"I'll do what I can to make sure you don't. Speaking of that, the next time I need to reach you I'll send Bill with a message. You know him, I believe."

"Worried about having your pocket picked again?"

Ravenswood didn't rise to the taunt this time. "Bill will also come around once a week to fetch your written report. I want to hear about every suspicious fellow who approaches you, every rumor you get wind of—"

"I know how this works," Morgan said dryly. "I *have* done it before."

"True. You've survived disasters that would destroy a lesser man. But one day your luck will run out."

"If it were luck, I'd worry." Morgan grinned. "Since it's skill, I see no cause for concern."

Ravenswood gave a rare laugh. "I'll give you this—if sheer cockiness will keep a man alive, you'll live to be a hundred." He sobered. "Watch your back, my friend." He turned to leave.

"Ravenswood!" Morgan called out to stay him.

"Yes?"

"A figger is a boy put in at a window to gather up goods and pass them out to an accomplice. The accomplice, the real thief, is called a dive."

Surprise passed over Ravenswood's face. "How do you know all that?"

"I picked up some thieves' cant during those months I spied on smugglers and lived with pirates." He held the other man's gaze. "I also learned a few tricks about staying alive."

"You'll need them, I fear." And with that dire pronouncement, Ravenswood was gone.

Morgan shrugged off the warning. Ravenswood might have delved into the circumstances of Morgan's childhood, but there were whole sections of his life no one, not even his brother, knew about. Fighting for survival was second nature to Morgan.

It wasn't the danger of this endeavor that kept him awake at night. No, it was the damned memories. He'd kept them at bay for so long that he'd thought they would no longer trouble him.

Until he'd landed in Spitalfields. God, how he despised it. But he'd see his task through, as he always had. And once he had his ship and the wager was over, he'd sail as far from London as he could.

He flipped the "Open" sign back around, then spent the next few hours managing the thieves and customers who trickled in through the doors of his shop. Late in the afternoon, his stomach rumbled. He hadn't eaten since breakfast, but he couldn't close until six, when he would go to Tufton's Tavern for dinner.

Remembering the apples he'd stashed in the back room when he'd come in this morning, he scanned the street through the front window. No one seemed to be around, so he didn't bother to flip the sign back to "Closed," but merely hurried to the back. Fruit would have to satisfy him until closing time.

He'd retrieved an apple and was heading back to the front when he heard the bell at the door jingle. Preparing himself for the usual dismal encounter with a thief, he entered the shop, then stopped short.

A familiar female form bent over one of his lower display counters with her back to him. She still wore the dull brown gown from earlier, but her present stance hiked it up enough to display two well-turned ankles clad in fine silk stockings.

His mouth went dry. He'd give a year's pay to see what else those creamy stockings covered. If it was all as fetching as the slim-hipped, full-breasted form outlined by her solemn gown, it would be worth every penny.

When she began rummaging through his goods, however, he scowled. The little sneak! First, her nosy questions in the alley, and now this. So much for "all bark and no bite." Very well—this time he'd run her off for good, whatever it took.

But first he intended to play with her a bit.

Chapter 4

With luring tongues, and language wondrous sweet,
Follow young ladies as they walk the street . . .
Yet ah! these simpring Wolves, who does not see
Most dang'rous of all Wolves in fact to be?
"Little Red Riding Hood," Charles Perrault,
Tales of Times Past with Morals

Clara fumbled through the compasses, barometers, pipes, and assorted other sailor's goods atop the counter, but she found no watches. Bother it all. Where had the scoundrel put it? If she could find it, she would have accomplished half her mission here.

Then a deep male voice said behind her, "Looking for anything in particular, my lady?"

She nearly jumped out of her skin. Whirling around, she was startled to see Captain Pryce standing only a few feet away. "Good Lord, do you always sneak up on people like that?"

"Only when they're riffling my goods."

"I wasn't—"

"And I see you've brought your watchdog." He glanced beyond her to where Samuel stood just outside. "Though I'm not sure what good he'll do you out there."

"I wanted this conversation to be private." Some of what she had to say to him she wouldn't want *anyone* to hear, but especially not her pickpockets, even former ones.

"Private?" He slid behind the counter nearest her with an indolent smile. "I like the sound of that."

"Don't get any ideas," she snapped. "It's not what you think."

"You can't blame me for jumping to conclusions. I was fairly clear this morning about the only reason I'd want to see you in my shop. Yet here you are."

Yes. And here *he* was, all six feet of him. This morning, in the vast outdoors, he hadn't loomed quite so large or seemed quite so menacing. But in here the low ceiling barely cleared his head, and the gloomy, insufficient light tempted her imagination to supply bulkier shoulders and a broader chest than she'd noticed earlier.

Imagination, that's all it was. Now that she knew his true nature, she was attributing to him a more threatening appearance than he really possessed—deeper-set eyes . . . an unyielding male jaw with its ghost of whiskers . . . rougher-cut hair.

And when he lifted the apple he was holding and bit into it, it had to be her imagination that made his teeth seem unnaturally white and sharp. She felt less like the huntswoman and more like Red Riding Hood by the minute.

" 'What great teeth you have,' " she muttered under her breath.

"I beg your pardon?"

"Nothing." She steadied her nerves. "Anyway, I'm not here to provide you with companionship."

"What a disappointment. But then why *are* you here?" He chewed slowly, his insolent gaze never leaving her face.

"Actually, I was looking for a watch." Swallowing hard, she held out her hand. "The one that Johnny stole for you."

He cocked his head. "You mean the one that Johnny stole *from* me."

"You heard me correctly. You let me believe that the watch was yours, but you know perfectly well it isn't."

"Did Johnny tell you that?" He seemed utterly unperturbed by her accusation as he continued to munch on the apple.

"I overheard him and his friends discussing how he tried to sell it to you. Apparently you didn't think to mention that during our little talk in the alley."

His bland expression betrayed nothing. "I didn't want to land poor Johnny in more trouble. It's one thing for a boy to steal a watch—quite another to steal it and then attempt to sell it."

"And even another for you to buy it when you knew it was stolen," she retorted. "As I recall, being a fence is punishable by fourteen years' transportation."

"Ah, my lady, how dramatic you are!" He licked apple juice from his lips, making her think of secluded paths and whiffs of wolf in the woods. "The boy offered to sell me the watch, and I agreed. I thought it was a legitimate transaction. For all I knew, he was selling off his poor dead papa's lifetime treasure to buy his sainted mama a bit of bread. And I hate to stand in the way of virtue."

She snorted. His tales were even more glib than those her rogue uncles had tried to foist on her mother. "I swallowed your lies the first time because I was distracted by worry about what you'd do to Johnny. I'm not distracted now. If you'd truly thought it a legitimate transaction, you would have corrected me when I accused Johnny of stealing it from you in the first place."

He shrugged. "You caught me off guard, that's all."

"I'm sure I did. You weren't about to admit you're just another of the Specter's fences, here to wreak havoc and tempt my poor children to—"

"The Specter? Who is he?"

She sensed his sudden alertness, though no flick of a muscle or change in expression betrayed it. "You know perfectly well who he is, I'm sure."

"Tell me anyway."

"He's the king of the fences. They all work for him. He provides them with protection from the law, from what I understand."

"You seem to know a great deal about this Specter fellow," he said with a frown.

She glared at him for continuing the pretense. "My pickpockets are a fount of information. Until now, however, he's pretty much kept to his own part of Spitalfields, and I've kept to mine."

"Until now?"

"I assume you work for him like all the others. Before you came along, there were no fences on this end of the street. It made it easier to separate my boys from the life."

A strange, almost regretful expression passed over his face before he masked it. "I work for no one but myself."

"If that's true, it won't last for long. The Specter is very protective of his territory. He'll either insist you work for him, or he'll make sure you don't work at all. He's been known to dispatch competitors rather ruthlessly."

She didn't know what she expected, but it certainly wasn't his eruption of laughter. "Are you concerned for my safety, mademoiselle?" He clapped his hand to his breast in a mocking gesture. "I'm touched, truly touched that you care—"

"Don't be ridiculous, I don't care one pin what—" She

broke off with a curse. "I swear, you're the most annoying creature I've ever had to deal with in my life."

Leaning back against the wall behind the counter, he finished the apple, then tossed the core into a slop bucket. "Then you should have stayed away as I asked you to."

She ignored his threatening tone, forcing herself to breathe calmly, speak rationally. "I'm only here to retrieve the watch and demand that you stop your illegal activities, at least with regard to my charges."

"What 'illegal activities'? I'm but a humble shopkeeper—"

"Oh, stuff and nonsense." His smug confidence sparked her temper. "The one thing you are not, sir, is humble, and if you're a shopkeeper, I'm the queen. You refuse to accept that I'm not some naive girl foolish enough to believe all your ridiculous lies."

"That's one thing we both agree on." He pushed away from the wall, then leaned forward to plant his elbows on the counter, putting him at her eye level. His gaze slid slowly down her, devouring her. "You are hardly a girl."

"Stop that!"

"What?" he said in mock innocence.

"Looking at me as if you want to eat me up."

His crooked smile was the very essence of wolf. "That's exactly what I want."

She fought down a blush. "You'd find me quite indigestible."

"I doubt that seriously, *ma belle ange*."

"I'm not your pretty angel, sir. I'm not your *anything*."

"You could be," he said suggestively.

"Don't be absurd." But a secret thrill coursed through her at the thought, making her scowl. Only her cursed Doggett blood would make her even consider such an outrageous possibility.

She forced herself to ignore his speaking looks. "And don't try to distract me with such nonsense. I have proof that you're lying about the true nature of your activities. You've bought goods from enough thieves in the neighborhood to acquire a reputation."

He lifted one wolfish brow. "I see Johnny has been very talkative."

"That's what happens when you deal with children. They talk." She held out her hand once more. "Now give me that watch."

"What do *you* intend to do with it?"

"Return it to its rightful owner, of course."

"Who might that be?"

Flustered, she glanced away. "I don't know."

"That might hamper your efforts to return it, wouldn't you say?"

"I'll find out who it belongs to," she retorted. "Johnny would only say that it was a gentry cove in Leadenhall Street, but there are ways to learn these things."

"Oh? And what are these mysterious 'ways'?"

"I'll go to the police offices and see if anyone has reported a stolen watch."

If she'd hoped that mention of the police would frighten him, she was sorely disappointed. "Then they'll ask how you came by stolen goods, and your little Home will be put under immediate suspicion."

Curse him, he had a point. "All right, I'll tell them I found it."

He straightened from the counter with a mocking smile. "Then they'll take the watch, promise to find its owner, and keep it for themselves. One of them might even come sell it to me. Then you'd have gone to all that trouble for nothing."

She feared he might be right. Some of the police at the Lambeth Street Office must be corruptible, judging from the number of fences who thrived in Petticoat Lane. She might appeal to one of the magistrates who headed the office, but he'd simply send her back to his underlings for such a petty concern.

Still, it annoyed her to have this . . . this scoundrel pointing out the truth. "You are very cynical, sir."

"Why? Because I see all the disadvantages to your plans?" A sudden mischief leaped in his face. "Or perhaps you're not disclosing your *real* plan. Perhaps you don't intend to do anything with the watch at all." He lowered his voice to a conspiratorial murmur. "Except keep it for yourself."

"What! You dare to imply—" She broke off when he burst into laughter. "I see. You find this all so amusing. Very well. You won't think it's amusing when I bring one of the officers here to arrest you."

Though his laughter died, he didn't look terribly worried. "If it will satisfy your notions of morality, then by all means bring one." He edged around the counter until he stood on the same side as her.

Leaning one hand on it, he stood there, loose-limbed and nonchalant . . . and still taunting her with a smile, curse his hide. "But you have no proof of anything, as you well know. Besides, what police officer will take the word of a meddling lady reformer over that of a military man who served his country in our late glorious war? And yes, despite all your claims to the contrary, I was indeed a naval captain."

"I know," she muttered. "I found you in the navy lists." She'd spent half the afternoon scanning the huge volume for his name.

He looked surprised. "I'm flattered. I must have impressed you very much if our encounter sent you straightaway to learn all you could about me."

She ignored his sarcasm. "Five years ago, you captained a third-rater—the *Titan*. No mention of you appears after that, although rumor has it that you spent the time with smugglers and pirates. Not exactly the sort of thing to endear one to the police."

"You shouldn't listen to rumors. They're apt to be false."

"So you deny it?"

"I don't have to. The police won't take gossip as proof."

His smug self-assurance only drove home the futility of this debate. Threats wouldn't work with a hardened villain like him, especially if he had a police officer or two in his pocket.

But there was one incentive Captain Pryce and his kind always responded to.

"I'd hoped to avoid this, but you give me no choice." She drew herself up straight, trying to project a businesslike demeanor. "What if I make it worth your while for you to leave Spitalfields?"

"That sounds very interesting." He crossed his arms over his chest, fire leaping into his gaze as he lounged back against the counter with a sensual smile. "I can think of one way you could make it 'worth my while.'"

Oh, bother, she shouldn't have put it like that. She hastened to correct his impression. "I'll give you two hundred pounds if you'll close up here and reopen your shop elsewhere, preferably outside London, where you can't corrupt my charges."

At last she'd managed to wipe the mocking expression off his face. "What?"

"Consider it a fee for moving expenses if you wish. Two hundred pounds. But only if you leave by tomorrow."

"Have you lost your mind?"

"It's possible. But thanks to a generous uncle, I can now afford to indulge my mad whims, and this is my latest."

"To pay me off."

"Precisely."

He searched her face as if to gauge her sincerity. Then he

shook his head. "I like London. I like Spitalfields. I have no intention of leaving."

Somehow that didn't surprise her. She hadn't expected him to come cheap. "Three hundred pounds then."

"Ah, so that's why you stationed your footman outside. You wouldn't want him to hear you offering money to a scoundrel. Tell me, do you pay off *everybody* capable of corrupting your charges? If so, you must be very rich."

"Quite the bargainer, are you? Fine. Five hundred pounds. But that's the most you'll get out of me."

"*Sacrebleu*, I don't want—" He broke off, dragging his fingers through his hair with a look of frustration. "See here, I can make that sum in a matter of days. Your paltry offer is beneath my consideration."

"Aha! So you admit that you're receiving stolen goods."

"I admit nothing." He shoved away from the counter, his expression stormy. "Is this the purpose of your offer? To trap me into confessing to a crime?"

"No, truly it isn't," she said hastily. "It's an honest offer."

"I'm still not interested." His gaze flicked past her to the front of the store. "You'd better leave before your watchdog grows impatient. He's presently flirting with a milk-woman and has probably forgotten you're even in here. Good day, Lady Clara."

He turned on his heel and strode into the back room.

She hesitated. Though a quick glance at Samuel showed he was indeed preoccupied, she refused to simply give up. Throwing caution to the winds, she headed into the back room after her quarry. He was lighting a lantern, his head bent at the task.

"I'm not asking you to stop your activities, you know," she said.

He froze, his broad back to her.

She hastened on. "I merely wish you to do them else-where. It's a good opportunity for you to make easy money. It's funds you wouldn't have otherwise, and all you need do is pack up and move your shady enterprise."

"This isn't a shady—"

"Your accepting the money needn't even be an admission of guilt. In fact, if you're engaged in honest labor, you ought to leap at the chance to receive money for something so easy as moving your shop."

Slowly he faced her, eyes ominously black. "Perhaps I simply don't trust fine ladies when they offer me money for so little."

"It's not so little to me."

"All the same, you'll forgive me if I refuse to risk my life or livelihood on a dubious offer of funds."

"But—"

"Besides, I have a good berth here." He swept his hand to include the entirety of the small, windowless room.

She glanced around. This had once been a kitchen, judging from the small stove at the back, but for some reason he'd taken it for his bedchamber. Lord knows why, for with the stairway against the left wall, there wasn't much space. He had a rickety bed scarcely big enough for a man his size, a scarred dresser, a washstand, a basket of apples, and not much else.

Good Lord, for a wicked receiver, he certainly lived spartanly. "You call *this* a 'good berth'?" she said with disdain.

"It suits my purposes. More importantly, I pay no rent. In the long run, leaving here would actually cost me money, even with your attempt at compensation."

That roused her suspicions. "How do you manage to pay no rent?"

"Friends of mine own the building." His gaze hardened. "But that isn't any of your concern. Nor is my shop or my activities." All hint of his earlier smug amusement vanished, and only the menacing wolf remained as he stalked up to her. "So you'd best steer clear and mind your own business, Lady Clara, if you don't want trouble from me."

If she let him cow her now when the fight had just begun, she'd never defeat him. Tamping down her apprehension, she met his gaze evenly. "All right, if you won't listen to reason and leave London, just give me the watch and I'll be on my way."

"The watch?"

She glared at him. "The watch we've been discussing, for pity's sake. If you'll recall, you didn't pay Johnny for it, so by rights it's still his. Since I'm the one presently responsible for him, I demand that you give it back." At the very least, she must keep Johnny from coming here to get money for his thievery.

He glowered at her. "I can't give it to you. I don't have it anymore. I sold it to a man shortly after I acquired it."

"That's impossible. There hasn't been enough time, and your shop isn't that busy. Why, in the whole time I've been here, nobody has even ventured to come inside."

"Who can blame them with your watchdog standing guard? I tell you, I sold it."

"I don't believe you."

"I don't care." He paused. "But if it will ease your mind, I'll give you the payment I would have given Johnny."

"Certainly not! Then I'd be as guilty of a crime as the two of you."

"That's the best I can do. If you won't take it, you might as well leave."

"I'm not going anywhere without that watch." Sucking in a breath, she held out her hand. It occurred to her that Samuel couldn't see her now that she'd come into the back of the shop. Still, every ounce of her pride balked at letting the captain win. She forced herself to stare up into eyes chilly with threat. "Give it to me, and I promise I'll go."

"You'll go, all right." He stepped so close she could feel heat emanating from his body. "You'll go this minute. Because if you stay even though I've made it clear I don't have your confounded watch, I'll assume you have other reasons for waiting around."

He dropped his gaze deliberately to her mouth, and a trembling began somewhere in the vicinity of her belly. "L-Like what?"

"Like you've grown tired of your lonely existence corralling a lot of thankless scamps." He lifted his hand to run one finger down her cheek, sending a sensual shiver along her skin. "You'd like to experience something more . . . exciting." He bent close to whisper, "With me."

She jerked back. "Don't be absurd."

He dropped his hand and gestured to the doorway into the front room. "Fine. You know the way out. Good day, Lady Clara."

She stared at his self-assured expression. Clearly he expected her to abandon her quest for the watch and run screaming from his shop, clutching her virtue to her chest and vowing never to come back.

It was almost certainly a bluff, just the sort of tactic her roguish uncles would have tried on any hapless female who'd given them trouble. But did she dare to call him on it?

Why not? If he tried anything, all she had to do was scream and Samuel would be in here in seconds. But she'd wager good coin that he wouldn't try anything anyway.

She tilted her chin up. "I told you—I'm not leaving without the watch."

Disbelief, then anger, flashed over his face, and before she could even react, he advanced forward, forcing her to back up or be run down. She came up short against the wall, where he trapped her by planting his hands on either side of her shoulders.

She stared up into his determined expression and felt a moment's panic. "What in the dickens do you think you're doing?"

"Rousing your sense of self-preservation."

"I'm not afraid of you, you know," she said stoutly.

He flashed her a smile of pure wickedness. "You should be."

Then he kissed her. Hard. Thoroughly. As she'd never been kissed before.

His audacity so stunned her that she didn't react at first. Then she tried pushing him away, but it was like shoving a boulder. Nothing gave, nothing moved.

Nothing but his mouth . . . which explored every inch of her lips with merciless thoroughness. She smelled apples on his breath, mingling with the spicy aroma of bay rum that clung to his roughly shaven jaw.

A wanton heat flashed through her, mortifying her to her toes. Surely she wasn't actually responding to this. . . .

This incredible, alarming kiss that went on and on until she grew dizzy.

When he tore his lips free, she was so rattled that all she could do was stare at him. Her heart thundered in her ears as she fought frantically to rein in her wildly careening senses.

At least he looked nearly as rattled as she. His breath came in ragged, urgent gasps, and his face mirrored her own surprise.

Until he wiped it clean of all expression. "Now," he whispered, "I hope I've made it thoroughly clear why you'd best not come around here anymore."

She understood his words for the threat he meant them to be. "You mean, because you might kiss me senseless?" How dare he assume he could run her off so easily?

"Or worse." His eyes glittered wolflike in the dim light. "I might ravish you."

"R-Ravish me?" A bubble of hysterical laughter rose in her throat before she could prevent it. "Good Lord, that sounds like something out of a Gothic novel! Ravish me, indeed. Don't be ridiculous."

Judging from the flare of frustration in his face, her response wasn't what he'd hoped for. His mouth tightened into a grim line as he leaned into her, reminding her only too well that he had her trapped. "You think I wouldn't?"

"I think you're not that stupid."

That seemed to give him pause. "What do you mean?"

"You were right when you said going to the police to complain about your business affairs might gain me nothing. But if I complain about your attacking me . . . well, that's another matter entirely, isn't it? Englishmen are odd that way. They don't take a lady of rank seriously until she cries that she's been 'ravished,' as you so colorfully put it. Then I need only point the finger, and they'll hound you to the gallows."

Not that she for one moment believed he actually would "ravish" her. If he'd intended that, he wouldn't have stopped kissing her to deliver his dire threats in that bullying tone of his.

"Excellent point," he muttered.

"I thought so." She was finally winning a round. Buoyed by the possibility of success with this new tactic, she added smugly, "Indeed, if you don't move away and give me that watch, I might be tempted to complain of your behavior anyway. It would be my word against yours, and as I said, in such a case mine is more likely to be believed."

She'd expected to make him capitulate at last. Instead, humor glinted in his eyes. "Then I might as well be hanged for a sheep as a lamb, mightn't I?"

She had only a second to wonder what he meant before his mouth came down on hers again.

She didn't even attempt to fight him this time, angry that her tactic hadn't worked, annoyed that he would call her bluff, and . . . curious, too, God help her. How far would he take this absurdity?

She had her answer in seconds. Because his mouth was no longer the only thing touching her. He snaked one arm around her waist to pull her flush against him and caught her chin with his other hand to hold her still for his kiss. Then he melded himself to her, breast to thigh, while all she did was stand there, letting him.

She wasn't even sure why, except that his kiss was different this time, coaxing, more intimate than threatening. His lips played with hers, sipping at them, caressing them. Oh, bother, that made it so much more difficult to ignore.

The sudden intrusion of his tongue between her lips shocked her, but he gave her no time to fight it. With a deftness Lucifer himself would admire, he delved inside to explore her mouth.

The strange act intrigued her. No man had ever put his tongue in her mouth. She would never have expected it to feel so . . . pleasurable. And thrilling and decidedly wicked.

She swayed against him without even realizing she did so, and a noise half-growl, half-groan rose from his throat. He dragged her closer to give her one long, drugging kiss after another. With every plunge of his tongue, her pulse spiked higher and she grew more light-headed. Good Lord, but he certainly could kiss. She'd never dreamed men were capable of this much . . . passion.

No, that wasn't quite true. She *had* spied on her uncles kissing their tarts a time or two. Now she understood why the women had always been breathless and flushed and weak-kneed when they'd pulled away.

For the same reason she was growing breathless and flushed and weak-kneed beneath his hands.

His strong, masterful hands. The one at her throat stroked and caressed, treating her skin as if it were delicate and fine. The other splayed its fingers over her back to urge her against him until she feared that every button on his waistcoat would leave its imprint on her bodice. Yet despite the close embrace—and the magnificent swirl of feeling it incited—he still only kissed her. She knew there was more to ravishment than that.

Perhaps the wolf wasn't quite so dangerous as he pretended. Unfortunately, there was only one way to find out for sure—give him a little rope and see if he hung himself.

And pray that he didn't tie her up with it instead.

Chapter 5

The artful Angler baits his Hook,
And throws it gently in the Brook;
Which the Fish view with greedy eyes,
And soon are taken by Surprize.
A Little pretty pocket-book, *John Newbery*

Morgan wanted to stop, but he couldn't. *Bon Dieu,* she tasted like heaven. She felt like heaven, too, with her willowy body yielding in his arms. Which was precisely why he should let her go. Her eager response showed that his attempt to intimidate her wasn't working.

Yet he couldn't stop kissing her. Her warm, welcoming mouth inflamed his need, and her flowery scent teased his nostrils. He wanted to sink into her. From the moment she'd raced to Johnny's defense like an avenging angel, he'd itched to taste her, to touch her, to strip off her ugly gown and . . .

Ravish her. Yes, that sounded vastly appealing just now.

But he wouldn't. Not because of her silly threats, of

course. Ravenswood would handle any complaint to the police with swift efficiency. He wouldn't because he didn't take unwilling women, even when the force of desire made them temporarily willing.

So no matter how giving and lush her mouth, no matter how womanly the body pressed to him, and no matter how freshly scented her hair, he must put her aside before she got under his skin any further. He'd made his point. If she didn't flee his shop now, she didn't have the sense God had given her.

Releasing her, he stepped back and waited for the outrage to show in her face, waited for the inevitable slap. He needed it, wanted it. Then he'd be rid of her for good.

No slap came. Instead, she twined her arms about his neck and hung onto him. When she then stretched up to press her lips to his, he jerked back to growl, "What the hell are you doing?"

Her pretty eyebrows arched high on her forehead. "Kissing you, of course."

Her apparent eagerness confused him. But his body didn't think twice—every confounded muscle sprang to attention. "Why?"

Determination glinted in her eyes. "Without more proof, I can hardly complain to the officers that you were ravishing me. You have to be in the midst of something more incriminating than kissing me before I can scream for Samuel and have him march you off to the Lambeth Street Police. Of course, if you'd rather just give me that watch, Captain Pryce . . ."

The little fool thought to bluff him with her petty threats. She had no idea how close she was coming to breaking his control. Even knowing it was a bluff couldn't calm the havoc in his randy body. "If we're to be intimate," he taunted her, "don't you think you should call me Morgan?"

"Very well." Her voice dripped sweetness. "My dear Morgan, can we get on with this business of ravishment?"

"You still think I wouldn't dare, don't you?"

"I *know* you wouldn't," she challenged him.

He glared down at her, his hands tightening convulsively on her waist. "I ought to call your bluff. I ought to ravish you if only to make you see how foolish you are to risk your virtue so recklessly."

"I'm touched, truly touched that you care," she retorted, echoing his own mocking words.

"Oh, stubble it," he rasped and kissed her again, not bothering to hide one ounce of his need, determined to teach her a lesson.

But damn her if she didn't kiss him back. Her mouth accepted his reckless tongue as enthusiastically as any tart's, and if he hadn't known she didn't mean it, he would have laid her down right there and taken her. He wanted her that much. Too much.

Perhaps it was time he showed her how much. He slid his hand between them to cup one breast, kneading it through the worsted of her gown.

For one incredible moment, she actually responded, leaning into his hand and making his loins stir with keen excitement. Then she froze and jerked back, her eyes a brilliant, startled blue. "What are you doing?"

"Waiting for you to scream for your watchdog, my dear Clara." Holding her gaze, he lifted his other hand to caress her other breast. He tried not to imagine what color the nipple might be or how it would taste in his mouth, tried not to notice how well it fit his palm. "Go ahead—scream. This is *your* plan, after all. Or must I remove some clothing before you consider it sufficient evidence for the police?"

With a shocked little gasp, she slid out of his arms and away.

Thank God. Another minute, and he'd have abandoned any gentlemanly impulses entirely, reduced to a slavering beast with only one thing on his mind.

"All right, you win," she whispered. "You win." Her eyes were huge in her face, and her chin quivered.

He felt like a blackguard, but he pressed the point ruthlessly. "You must be more specific. What is it I win?"

She took a shuddering breath. "I won't go to the authorities."

"That's hardly a concession. I knew you wouldn't do it anyway—a woman of your position would never risk the scandal. So what other prize will you offer me?"

Though some of the fire returned to her face, she mumbled, "I won't insist that you give the watch back."

"Insist all you like, but I wasn't lying about it. I really don't have it anymore."

"If you say so." She whirled toward the doorway into the front of the shop.

"But I do want something from you," he called out.

She halted. "What?"

"Your word that you'll stay away from my shop."

Her sweet curve of a back stiffened rebelliously. "You are in no position to ask for anything, sir. You ought to be glad I'm giving up so easily."

She called this *easily*? "Fine, come back if you wish. And we'll play our little game again. Only next time leave your watchdog at home. That way I can take my time about ravishing you . . . I won't have to risk destroying your gown by ripping it off or—"

"Oh, stop that!" She whirled on him. "You would never—"

"Are you sure?" He took a step forward. "Care to try me, *ma belle ange*?"

The fire went out of her eyes. She shook her head mutely. "I have no desire to return, believe me, but if you insist upon corrupting my charges—"

"What if I promise not to buy goods from any of them?"

The instant the words left his mouth, he regretted them.

How could he manage that, short of questioning every pick-pocket who came through his door? Which he couldn't do without running off the very people he needed to lure the Specter.

The bright hope in her eyes only made it worse. "You'd do that for me?"

"If I can," he said evasively. "If I know they're from the Home."

"You won't buy anything from my children," she persisted, as if she didn't quite believe him.

He'd do whatever he must to keep her from coming back here with her nosy questions and pert demands and delicious glory of a mouth. "I'll do my best."

"That's all I ask," she said with a tremulous smile.

He shook his head. "Such a fierce defender, aren't you? And all for some ingrate rascals who'd as soon go back to their old ways as breathe."

"I'm the only defender they have, sir. If I abandon them, what's left for them but the workhouse or the noose?"

Envy of her charges stabbed through him so powerfully that he spoke without thinking. "Ah, Clara, what a pity there was no one like you around when I was a boy."

She dragged in a sharp breath of surprise. Then curiosity suffused her face, making him curse himself for his hasty words.

Fortunately, just at that moment the front door slammed open, sending the bell ringing madly as a voice called out, "M'lady, where are you? Are you all right?"

"I'm back here, Samuel!" she called out.

Seconds later, her footman loomed in the doorway, scowling blackly at Morgan. "What's going on? Why are you two standing back here in the dark?"

"A bit late for you to show concern, isn't it?" Morgan snapped.

Samuel paled to chalk. "If you so much as laid a hand upon m'lady—"

"Enough, Samuel!" Clara broke in. "Nothing happened."

"You have a strange definition of nothing," Morgan said, perversely angered by her nonchalant dismissal. "I don't call what we just did 'nothing.' "

"I'll gut you like a fish, I will!" Samuel darted forward, only to be restrained by Clara.

"You'll do no such thing." She turned her angry gaze on Morgan. "And you stop provoking my footman!"

"He needs to be provoked, damn it!" Morgan glowered at Samuel. "One of these days you could come to real harm while he's flirting and twiddling his thumbs!"

Her angry expression faded abruptly, replaced by a kind one that made his breath catch in his throat. "I'm sure he won't make that mistake again. Will you, Samuel?"

Samuel glared daggers at Morgan. "No, m'lady. Next time I'll stay glued to your side, I will."

"See that you do." Morgan knew he sounded like an idiot, warning her away from his shop with threats of "ravishment," then chastising her footman for not looking after her. But he couldn't help it. She roused some long-buried protective instinct in him. And he'd wager she knew it, too, from the way she was smiling at him now.

"Thank you for your concern, Morgan," she said softly. "And for your promise. Good-bye." Then, tugging a rigid Samuel off with her, she left his shop.

Only after she was gone could he breathe again. What was the wench doing to him? When she was around, he said what he oughtn't, did what he shouldn't, and burned where he mustn't.

He had to get it through his thick skull that Clara—*Lady* Clara—was not for him, not now, not ever. He wanted to be free of this cursed city, and if he took up with her, he'd never be. A Woman of Expectations would want him to stay put, to endure a life of domesticity too boring to drown out the bleak memories that plagued him. A life of squalling babes and society dinner parties and a dull position in the Home Office like Ravenswood's, guiding *other* men as they headed off into adventure and the blessed oblivion of life at sea.

Still, he had to admit he had trouble envisioning Clara as a domestic society matron sipping tea and paying calls. That would be too dull a life for her as well. But he had no trouble envisioning her heavy with some man's child, perhaps even . . .

Confound it all, now he was thinking about her ripe with his own babe! What madness was this?

Determined to purge such thoughts from his mind, he hurried into the front room and set about the task of closing up for the evening. What he needed was a good hot meal and a few mugs of ale, perhaps even an armful of willing wench, to set him to rights.

Night had fallen by the time he was done. He locked the front door, then let himself out the side door into the alley. He regretted coming that way almost instantly, for it made him think of *her*, and he was determined not to.

He was so engrossed in trying to drive the woman from his mind that his generally alert senses didn't warn him about impending danger until it was too late. The blow to his calves dropped him to his knees, but the knife that was then thrust against his throat made him struggle past the pain in his legs to focus on his attacker. He could think of only one person it could be—the Specter's weapon of choice had always been a knife.

"Now see here, Cap'n—" a faintly familiar voice began.

He wasted no time trying to figure out where he'd heard it, but drove his elbow into what he calculated would be the man's groin. He hit hard enough to make his assailant howl and release the blade.

Seconds later, Morgan was on his feet with his own knife drawn. Shoving the man against the wall, he pressed the blade to his assailant's throat. "If you don't want to die, tell me who you are and what you want with me."

"P-Please, Cap'n, don't kill me," the man whispered. "I-it's only me. Samuel."

"Lady Clara's Samuel?" Morgan asked incredulously.

For a second, only the sound of Samuel's quick gasps could be heard in the alley. "I-I wanted to . . . to give you a warning, that's all. Tell you to leave her ladyship alone."

Muttering a string of curses, Morgan shoved away from the wall and returned his knife to the sheath inside his coat. "That's a damned fool thing you did—coming up on me like that. I could have killed you."

"Aye, and I'm sore grateful that you didn't." There was just enough light for Morgan to see Samuel tug at his livery coat and straighten his stock. "It's only that m'lady has been good to me. I don't want to see her hurt."

"Neither do I."

"But after what you said just a while ago—"

"I was merely trying to provoke you, exactly as she claimed." Pray God she never told Samuel the truth of how she'd let Morgan touch her. Next time the foolish footman might shoot him. "But I swear that as long as you keep your mistress away from my shop, I'll steer clear of her. I want no trouble, either with you or with her."

Samuel slumped against the wall. "I do my best to watch out for her, y'know. But sometimes she makes it difficult. M'lady's a bit . . . well . . ."

"Headstrong? Independent? Determined to risk her life at every turn?"

"I see y've figured her out well enough," Samuel said morosely. "She thinks I can protect her against anybody, but I'm not that large and—"

"And just because you were a pickpocket doesn't mean you know a thing about guarding your mistress."

Moonlight shone just enough to illuminate Samuel's bowed head. "That's the God's honest truth."

He cast the young man a considering look. "You know, Samuel, it's possible to get the best of a man even if you're half his size. But you have to know how. I tell you what—if you'd like lessons in more efficient ways to use that blade of yours in attacking a man, I can give them to you."

"Why would you do that?"

Because the thought of your mistress running afoul of some villain due to your incompetence makes my blood run cold.

He could hardly say that. He had to remember what role he played. "Because I could use your help. Your mistress insists on meddling in my affairs. So you keep her out of my business, and I'll teach you how to keep her out of danger. All right?"

Samuel straightened. "Oh, yes, Cap'n! I'd be most grateful if you'd teach me."

"Then it's a bargain. I'll see you here tomorrow after you've accompanied Lady Clara to the Home. Though we should probably keep this between the two of us."

"Yes, sir, thank you, sir." Then Samuel added in a more subdued tone, "And thank you for not killing me. I don't much fancy being food for the worms."

"And I don't much fancy having to explain a dead footman in my alley to the authorities. So go on with you. Lady Clara is probably waiting for you at the Home."

"Oh, blast!" he cried. "I was supposed to meet her back there soon as it got dark."

As Samuel raced off, Morgan rolled his eyes. What had he gotten himself into? The man couldn't protect a gnat, for God's sake.

"Well done," rasped a voice from out of the darkness. "You handled him expertly, Captain Pryce."

Morgan's instinct to survive surged in him again. He whirled around, his hand already reaching for his blade, but he saw no one. The alley seemed empty, though it was too dark to be sure what lay in the shadows at the other end.

"Show yourself!" Morgan scanned the alley again. He thought he saw something move, but he couldn't be sure. An eerie chill ran down his spine. "I don't talk to anyone I can't see."

"That will make our conversation rather short, I should imagine. Because *I* don't talk to anyone who can see *me*."

The voice was as impenetrable as the night. The enclosed space and the distance of the speaker made the words bounce off the walls, giving the illusion that they came from everywhere at once. "Who are you? And what do you want?" Morgan had a good idea of the former, but not the latter.

"I could ask the same of you. You're the one encroaching on my territory."

"I don't know what you're talking about." With knife in hand, Morgan edged farther into the alley, staying alert with every step. "I run a shop, that's all."

A rumbling chuckle sounded all around him. "We both know what you do for a living, Captain. What I want to know is why you chose to do it in Spitalfields."

"What business is it of yours?"

"Everything that happens in Spitalfields is my business, as you will soon learn, if you haven't already."

A faint noise came from his right, and he whirled toward it. But it was only the scrabbling of a rat. Damn it all, he wished he'd brought a lantern into the alley.

"So tell me," the ghostly voice went on, "why have you settled in my part of town?"

"I figured it was as good a place as any."

"Then you figured wrong."

"I don't think so. I haven't lacked for business since the day I opened. And with Petticoat Lane's reputation for providing a diligent shopkeeper with . . . shall we say . . . incredibly cheap goods, I expect my profits to increase with every day I remain."

"I wouldn't count on that. Yes, the thieves will go where the pay is greatest, but to pay them well you have to keep your costs down. And I can be very good at making sure your costs increase with your profits."

"What do you mean?" Morgan fought to keep the excitement out of his voice. He was getting somewhere, and quicker than he'd expected, too.

"Fire is a constant hazard in this part of town. Nor is anybody likely to enter your shop if one or two of my brawnier friends lounge about outside. Or sneak up on you in the dark to put you out of business permanently."

"As you can see, I'm not that easy to sneak up on."

"I'll grant you that you can evade a footman with relative ease, but I assure you my men are better capable of causing damage. And you do have to sleep sometime."

"You'd be surprised. But by all means, send them on. As long as you don't mind losing your brawny friends, I'll be glad for the exercise." Morgan started to walk out of the alley. "Now if you'll excuse me, I'm too hungry to stand around being bored by your dire warnings. If you have any more to tell me, you can join me for a pint at Tufton's Tavern."

"But you haven't heard my offer yet, Captain Pryce," the voice called out, now tinged with irritation. "I'm willing to let you do as you please in Spitalfields as long as you meet certain conditions."

Morgan stopped. "What kind of conditions?"

"The main one is financial, of course. You'd share your profits with me."

"Not on your life," Morgan growled.

"It might be *your* life at stake if you do not."

With a disbelieving snort, Morgan faced the alley. "And what would I get for my generosity? Aside from my life, of course."

"Protection from the law, for one thing. My men and I keep our fingers on the pulse of every justice of the peace, every police officer, every magistrate in the surrounding boroughs. The moment the authorities set out to arrest anybody under my protection, that fortunate person is warned and aided in his escape."

Morgan sucked in a sharp breath. Was this merely the boast of a villain? Or could the Specter's tentacles actually stretch that far? Morgan had to find out. "I have my own connections, sir. Why do I need yours?"

He laughed. "If you mean the navy, we both know they lost sympathy for you when you showed up aboard a pirate ship."

"How do you know about that?" Morgan knew how, but he still wanted to hear what the Specter might claim.

"Word gets around. And I too have my connections in the navy."

It wouldn't require such connections—Morgan had personally made sure that the populace of Spitalfields learned of his time aboard the *Satyr.* Besides, even if the Specter had connections in the navy, they apparently weren't high enough for him to know that Morgan had been found blameless of any criminal activity related to his brief, somewhat unwilling stint with the Pirate Lord.

"All right," Morgan said, "I'll accept that you might afford me some protection from the law. What other advantages do you offer?"

"Higher profit. My fences adhere to a set rate for goods. I hear you've been paying more. You won't have to once you join with me."

"But I'd lose some of my profits to you, so it probably all evens out in the end."

"Not entirely. I can give you access to the truly productive thieves who pay you no notice now because they're loyal to me."

"They won't be for long if they hear I'm paying more for their goods, will they?"

"Ah, but you can't cash stolen bank notes for them. I can."

Aha, so Ravenswood had been right about the Specter's major source of income.

"As it happens, you're wrong. I have my own contacts for disposing of stolen notes. So you see, I don't need you that badly, do I?"

"Now you listen here, you little worm—" a voice snapped from just above him, then broke off abruptly.

Good, he'd riled the man enough so that the Specter had forgotten to practice whatever strange technique he'd used to make his voice hard to track. Morgan should have guessed that the criminal wasn't in the alley at all. He was speaking out of one of the windows in the adjoining building.

Morgan had to tamp down on his impulse to storm the building. Cornering the Specter would only tip Morgan's hand before he had the irrefutable evidence he required to build his case. Right now it would be the criminal's word against his. Morgan needed to link the devil to stolen goods, which required gaining the man's confidence.

Besides, storming the building would be fruitless. There were three exits at least—in front, on this side, and possibly a rear exit he couldn't reach from the dead-end alley.

"You're trying my patience, Captain Pryce," the Specter said, now firmly in control of himself once again. "Either accept my offer or you'll force my hand. And I become very nasty when my hand is forced."

The man certainly had a flare for the dramatic. "I'm trembling in my boots," Morgan said, sneering. He didn't want to rouse the Specter's suspicions by appearing too eager.

"So that's your answer? You refuse my offer?"

"I didn't say that. I have to think about it."

A long pause ensued. Then the man uttered a low curse. "Very well, I suppose that's understandable. At the end of a week, I'll ask you again. If you haven't made your choice by then, the offer will be withdrawn."

"Agreed. But if I decide to accept before then, how can I reach you?"

Silence met the question.

"Well? Mr. Phantom or whatever you call yourself, are you there?" When no answer came, he darted into the street. He got there just in time to see a tall, broad-shouldered figure on a black horse ride off at breakneck speed.

A sigh left his lips as he watched the cloaked man disappear into the twisting fog. Clearly, tracking the Specter wasn't going to be easy. But one thing was certain—the Specter was no supernatural entity. So eventually Morgan *would* have his man.

Chapter 6

And on the smooth Grass, by the side of a Wood,
Beneath a broad Oak that for Ages had stood,
Saw the Children of Earth, and the Tenants of Air,
For an Evening's Amusement together repair.
The Butterfly's Ball, and the
Grasshopper's Feast, *William Roscoe*

The children are as restless as I am, Clara thought as she sat with them in the library. And who could blame them? After her encounter with Morgan Pryce, the skies had opened, besieging the city with spring rains. Now, after three days of being cooped up inside with no visits to the market, no gambols in the park, no games of Thread the Needle in the back gardens, the children contained enough suppressed energy to fuel a mill for a week. Perhaps she should have skipped gathering the entire group of thirty-two residents for their usual story time before dinner.

"Which tale would you like to hear today?" The buzz of

answers made her dizzy. Packed into the library like bees in a hive, the swarming mass of limbs and bobbing heads only settled down when she cast them all the Stanbourne Stare. "One at a time now."

"Can we hear the story of Cinderella?" Mary piped up from where she sat on Clara's left with legs crossed.

"Aw, Mary," David called out, "you want to hear that one every bloody day."

"It's impolite to say 'bloody,' " Clara put in. Mary flashed David a taunting smile until Clara added softly, "But he's right, Mary, we did just read 'Cinderella' yesterday. Let's have someone else pick a story today."

When poor Mary's face fell, Clara felt a twinge of regret. Still, Mary's appetite for "Cinderella" knew no bounds. Though it was perfectly understandable, given the poor girl's hunger for a better life, the tale did grow tedious after the fifth telling in one month, especially for the boys.

Clara glanced back to where some of the older boys stood leaning against the bookshelves. "Perhaps one of you lads would want to choose. What about you, Johnny? Is there no story you'd like to hear?"

His sullen frown wasn't promising. "Don't like stories. They ain't true and they'll never be true, so what's the point?"

Clara sighed. Johnny had been a seething mass of rebellion and anger ever since his visit to his sister Lucy this morning. When Clara had sent him off accompanied by Samuel, she'd expected him to return in high spirits, but he'd dragged the rainstorms in with him and dumped them all over the rest of the children.

"You're wrong!" Mary protested. "Some of the stories is true. Girls do marry princes, don't they, Lady Clara?"

"Occasionally," she hedged.

"Come on, Mary, not even somebody as great as Lady

Clara marries a prince," Johnny shot back. "Why, she hasn't married nobody at all."

"That's because I choose not to marry just now," Clara said, a little defensively.

"Don't you want a husband, m'lady?" Mary asked.

"Some day, when I find the right gentleman. All the genuine princes seem to be otherwise engaged, but I might look for someone less . . . regal."

An image of Morgan Pryce flashed into her mind, and she cursed her foolishness. Never mind that he looked better than any prince of the realm. Or that his kisses were so imprinted on her senses that she woke each morning tasting him on her lips. Never mind that the scent of apples and bay rum and pure hot male pervaded her dreams at night.

Even if Morgan were the marrying sort—and she doubted that seriously—she could never marry a man who wore the unholy cloak of wickedness so easily upon his broad shoulders.

Though she must admit he'd shown brief glimpses of goodness. Like when he'd promised not to buy anything from her children. To her chagrin, a few of her charges *had* ventured his way despite all her rules to prevent it, or so she'd heard from her sources on the streets. But she'd also heard that Morgan had kept his promise. Every day he turned young pickpockets away, dealing only with grown thieves.

Then there was his chiding Samuel for not protecting her better. That made no sense whatsoever. One minute he threatened to ravish her, and the next he acted like her guardian? Every time she thought she'd figured him out, he turned around and did something like that.

That was the trouble—the contradictions in his character occupied her mind far too much. Sometimes she wished she'd never laid eyes on the perplexing Captain Pryce, with his unpredictable courtesies and his warm, delicious kisses.

Kisses he'd meant only to drive her off. She'd best remember that. She might have found him . . . interesting, but he considered her only an annoyance.

"I'm still waiting for somebody to suggest a story," she said.

"I thought of a story I want to hear." Johnny's eyes shone unnaturally bright. "How about 'Bluebeard'? Ain't that the one where the chap kills his wives and hangs their bodies in a closet? And then he gets his knife—"

"Enough, Johnny. There's a reason I never read that one. It's much too gruesome." She wasn't sure whether to be heartened that he'd apparently been reading stories on his own or disturbed that he chose the bloodiest tale in Perrault's book. "We don't want to give the small children nightmares."

"Why not? It'll prepare them for their future. What do any of us have to look forward to but a short life ended by the hangman?"

The bleak pronouncement fell on the children like a shroud, stunning Clara with its poisoning resentment. What in heaven's name had got into the boy?

A tug at her sleeve made her glance down to where Timothy Perkins cuddled close to her on her right. "I wanna hear about the grasshopper going to the ball."

She had to think a minute, but when she realized what he was talking about, relief swelled through her. "Ah, yes, 'The Butterfly's Ball.'" When Timothy bobbed his head enthusiastically, she added, "Excellent choice, my boy." A dose of William Roscoe's whimsical verse might be just the antidote for Johnny's gloomy predictions.

Twisting to scan the shelf behind her, she found the volume she wanted, then opened it and began to read:

*"Come take up your Hats, and away let us haste
To the* Butterfly's *Ball, and the* Grasshopper's *Feast.*

The Trumpeter, Gad-fly, *has summon'd the Crew,*
And the Revels are now only waiting for you."

She paused to glance at the still somber lads in the back.
Then an idea struck. "Since it's almost time for our own dinner, we should do this tale properly. David, you be the
grasshopper. Mary, you can be the butterfly. Johnny, we'll
need a blind beetle . . ."

The poem had seventeen bugs in all, and by the time she finished assigning roles—doubling them where necessary—even
the older boys reluctantly entered into the spirit of things. As
she lined them up to head into the hall, Robbie, the bee, buzzed
at her and the two moths flapped their wings, giggling. After
Tim begged him, even Johnny grudgingly agreed to heft his
brother on his back as the beetle in the poem did to the emmet.

Then they all marched through the Home. She read the
poem loudly, each child creeping or hopping his way through
his role when it was his or her chance to shine. By the time
they'd crawled and jumped and glided their way to the dining
room, the children had collapsed into laughter, and one storm
had passed.

As she watched Johnny swing his squealing brother into a
chair at the table, her heart twisted in her chest. The poor
boys—what was to become of them? When Johnny left
Tim's side, his momentary smile subsiding into the perpetual
frown he'd worn all day, Clara decided to find out what Lucy
had told him to make him so forlorn.

So she stopped him as he passed in front of her. "I haven't
had a chance to ask you how your sister is doing."

He glanced away, a muscle ticking beneath his beardless
jaw. "She's all right."

"Did she say if she'd be coming to visit Tim soon? He's
anxious to see her."

Johnny's angry gaze shot to her. "Lucy ain't coming here

no more. And she told me to leave her be, too. She said I wasn't to visit her at all. Nor Tim neither."

"What?" Clara shook her head, unable to believe it. "Are you sure you understood her correctly? She's always been so concerned about the two of you and—"

"She don't want us around, I tell you! Says she's got . . . important things to worry about." He struck a pose of nonchalance so false that even someone who wasn't familiar with him would have seen beneath it. "Looks like you're stuck with us for good, m'lady."

He threw the words out like a challenge, but she glimpsed the fear lurking behind them. "If you follow the rules, you're welcome to stay as long as you like."

That seemed to deflate all his bravado. "All right then," he mumbled, then stalked off, still frowning.

She glanced to where a giggling Tim scooped up gravy-soaked bread. Johnny had clearly not yet told the child about their sister's pronouncement. Poor Tim. He eagerly anticipated every visit from his beloved sister, and her abandonment would sorely wound him. Even having Clara there to comfort him couldn't possibly be the same as having his sister around.

Ah, Clara, what a pity there was no one like you around when I was a boy.

Morgan's wistful words of three days ago leaped into her memory from out of nowhere, striking her to the heart. They reminded her powerfully of Johnny and Tim. Had Morgan's family also abandoned him in his youth? That might explain why he'd returned to his criminal way of life even after he'd made something of himself in the navy.

The thought of a young Morgan scrabbling in the streets like her other children tugged at her sympathies. It was indeed a pity she hadn't been around when he was a boy. She might have provided him with enough encouragement to break him free of the world of crime that so often sucked her children in for life.

Well, Morgan might be past saving, but the Perkins boys were not. Clara refused to believe Lucy had meant to be so cruel to her brothers. But there was only one way to find out for sure. She must speak to the girl before Johnny got around to telling Tim what Lucy had said.

Turning on her heel, she strode out into the hall. Samuel was already waiting for her, since it was nearly time for her to head for home. "Ready to go, m'lady?"

"First, we must stop at Tufton's Tavern," she told him. Lucy worked as a taproom maid at the tavern nearly every night. "I must speak to Lucy about her brothers." Snatching up her pelisse, she headed for the door. "Has the rain stopped?"

"Yes, but—"

"Then we'll walk."

Samuel's eyes narrowed, but he knew better than to question his mistress's whims. He merely fell into step beside her as they left the Home's airy halls.

In the aftermath of the spring storms, mud clogged the streets, but the sky had cleared to a brilliant gold-and-red spectacle of sunset. Thanks to the heavy rains, the London air, generally thick with coal dust and fog, was clear and cool. Clara breathed it in eagerly as they strode toward the tavern, passing all the street sellers who'd come out to do business after the rain—the lavender girl with her crisp purple tufts and the orange-woman proffering citrus. With such scents of spring lingering in the air, it seemed almost a shame to descend into the cloying stupor of the tavern.

Tufton's Tavern was a long-standing institution in Petticoat Lane, part cookshop, part lodging house, and a large part alehouse. Having nursed many a thief and scoundrel at its gin-soaked teats, it was respected more for the quality of its ale than its cleanliness. After Clara pushed open the door and her hand came back with a greasy film, she had to resist the impulse to head straight for soap and water.

Wiping her hand on her apron, Clara paused just inside the door to scan the low-ceilinged room crowded with tables and settles. Candle and pipe smoke mingled with the smell of small beer and boiled beef to create a miasma that nearly choked Clara every time she came here, which thankfully wasn't often.

When her gaze landed on a familiar dark-haired man at a table in the corner, her heart tripped perversely. Morgan was here, in close conversation with two scruffy-looking men. She spotted the plate of mutton before him, and a smile touched her lips. What else would a wolf dine on but sheep?

He certainly looked every inch the wolf tonight, with his rakish clothing and his unruly hair tumbling thickly over his collar. When he reached to rip bread from a loaf with the casual violence of a man absorbed in his meal, her breath caught in her throat.

Next time leave your watchdog at home. That way I can take my time about ravishing you . . . I won't have to risk destroying your gown by ripping it off.

A delicious shiver skittered along her spine. Even knowing he'd spoken the words only to frighten her off, she couldn't help dwelling on the vivid image of him freeing her of her gown and sliding those sleek, knowing fingers over her belly, trailing kisses over her breasts and—

"If it's Lucy you want," Samuel broke in, "she's over there."

A blush staining her cheeks, Clara jerked her gaze from Morgan to Samuel, who watched her with clear suspicion. Grimly, the footman pointed across the room.

There stood the seventeen-year-old Lucy, serving pots of beer to a table of half-drunken men who eyed her with blatant admiration. No great surprise there. Taller than most girls, she always looked pretty, even in her thin, multi-patched gowns. Her hard life never seemed to dampen her determined good cheer, as evidenced by the jaunty pink feather stuck in her up-swept hair. She'd probably bought it in a pawnshop for tuppence, but she wore it like a crown while she chatted with the customers as if she hadn't a care in the world.

Which she didn't. Lucy had foisted her two cares off on Clara. And while Clara didn't mind receiving them, she did mind watching Lucy treat her brothers with such callous disregard.

Paying no heed to the whispers of curious patrons, Clara set off across the room. Samuel followed so close behind that he bumped into her when she stopped just short of the table where Lucy stood with her now empty tray.

"Good evening, Lucy," Clara said.

Lucy spun around, eyes wide. "Lady Clara!" Her gaze flicked to Samuel, and dark color suffused her cheeks before she jerked her gaze back to Clara. "And what brings you to the tavern this evening, m'lady? Fancy a bit of our fine mutton, do you?"

"Actually, I was hoping to talk to you about your brothers."

A decidedly guilty look crossed the girl's face as she shifted the tray to her other hand. "We're awful busy tonight. P'raps you could come by in a few days—"

"*Now*, Lucy. It's important."

Lucy sighed. "All right then. I s'pose Mr. Tufton won't mind if I sit for a bit with you. As long as you order something, that is."

Moments later, the three of them crowded with pewter tankards of India ale around a table graced by a single candle stuck in a grimy ginger beer bottle. With a decidedly false smile, Lucy leaned her elbows on the ale-stained table. "So what's this all about?"

Clara got right to it. "Johnny tells me you no longer want him and Tim to visit you."

"What?" Samuel growled before Lucy could even respond. He glared at Lucy. "Whyever not?"

Lucy glared right back. "Not that it's any of your business, Samuel Clark, but this ain't the sort of place I want my brothers hanging 'round."

"Never bothered you before," he retorted. "They used to live here themselves, until they got caught picking pockets off that gentleman and was sent to the Home."

Lucy tilted her nose up. "Yes, and I expect the boys would never have taken to thieving if they'd lived somewhere better than a tavern."

Samuel's skeptical snort echoed Clara's own opinion, but she merely flashed Lucy a patient smile. "Speaking of the boys, I've come because I'm concerned about what your refusal to see them will do to them. Johnny's very upset, and Tim will be devastated once he hears. They don't have to come *here*, you know. You could visit them at the Home when you have the time."

"No, I can't, I just can't." Bending her head, she busied herself with pleating her apron nervously. "It's better for them in the long run to stay off by themselves. I got prospects that take up all my time and—"

"Wait a minute," Samuel exclaimed, "I know what you're up to. It's that Rodney Fitch, ain't it? That bloody police officer from Lambeth Street has been courting you, I hear. That's your 'prospects,' I s'pose. You think he'll stop sniffing 'round if he knows about your two thieving brothers. Wouldn't do for a man in his position to associate with known criminals."

Lucy's head shot up. "For your information, he knows already. And it's got naught to do with him, Samuel. That's not what I meant by 'prospects' at all."

"You think he'll marry you, don't you? And set you up in

that nice house of his down in Grave Lane. But he'll never leg-shackle himself to *you*. Fitch might be a dim sort, but he ain't *that* stupid."

Clara kept quiet, eager to see where this surprising conversation was headed.

"He ain't no 'dim sort' neither," Lucy protested. Then the rest of Samuel's comment apparently registered, and she glowered at him. "And what do you mean, 'he ain't *that* stupid'? Why wouldn't Mr. Fitch marry me? I'm nice enough to look at, I am."

"I didn't mean—" Samuel broke off, clearly flustered. "It's got nothing to do with your looks. It's only that he's the sort to dally with a tavern maid, not marry one. Especially when her brothers is pickpockets. He's an officer of the law; he'll want a spotless wife."

Lucy drew herself up with a missish outrage. "Are you saying I'm not spotless?"

Samuel actually blushed. "Aw, Lucy, you know that ain't what I meant. I only meant—"

"I'm a good girl, and he knows it. And if I was wanting to marry Rodney, I could make him do it, too. Just see if I couldn't."

Samuel's face darkened to thunder. "Rodney? Is that how it is now?" He shook his head. "You're on the way to being a kept woman, and you don't even see it!"

"What?"

"First he'll have you calling him by his Christian name, then giving him a kiss or two, then it's 'Aw, ducky, won't you just let me—' "

"Now see here, you stop all that talk!" A brilliant blush bloomed on Lucy's cheeks. "I want nothing less than marriage. And Mr. Fitch respects that, he does. He's a gentleman, unlike *some* people I know."

All the fight seemed to go out of Samuel. He dropped his

gaze to his ale. "I remember a time when my manners was good enough to please you."

The naked vulnerability flitting over Lucy's face made Clara wonder what had gone on between the two before Clara had met Samuel. "That was a long time ago, Sam," Lucy mumbled. "Things has changed since then." Settling her shawl about her shoulders like a grande dame, she turned to Clara. "Now if that's all, m'lady—"

"No, it's not," Clara said. But clearly she wouldn't get far in this discussion if her lovesick footman continued to interfere. "Samuel, why don't you wait outside for me? I think Lucy and I should talk in private."

He scowled. "I don't want to leave you in here alone—"

"No one will bother me. Go on. I'll be there in a moment."

Casting Lucy one last mutinous look, Samuel rose and stormed out.

Lucy visibly relaxed once he was gone. "Thank you, m'lady. Sam don't understand that a woman's got to do what's best for her family."

"You mean, like marry a police officer to ensure her brothers' financial future?"

The girl's expression grew shuttered. "Don't you listen to Sam's nonsense. This ain't got nothing to do with Mr. Fitch. I just . . . don't want the boys around right now."

Lucy wasn't a very good liar, but Clara saw no reason to badger her on the subject. Samuel had already done enough of that. "I don't really care what your hopes are concerning Mr. Fitch, but the boys can't afford to wait until your 'prospects' come to fruition. They need your support and affection *now*."

"They're doing fine at the Home with you, m'lady."

"They're *not* doing fine. Did you know that I caught Johnny trying to sell a stolen watch to a fence only three days ago?"

Lucy dropped her eyes to the table. "Y-Yes, he told me.

Explained the whole thing. But I was very firm with him—told him that if he got kicked out of the Home because of such foolishness, he'd be on his own. I made it clear he can't come here to live, so he won't slip up again, I promise."

"You think not? Your brother is very stubborn. He isn't likely to forget that Captain Pryce still owes him money for the watch, and I've already told him that if he returns to the shop for it, I'll have to evict him from the Home. Those are the rules—none of my residents may engage in criminal acts. Since this is his third offense—"

"I understand, m'lady. But stubborn or no, Johnny won't break the rules a third time. Especially not after what I told him about that Captain Pryce."

That gave Clara pause. She glanced over to where Morgan was still huddled in close conversation with his companions. "What did you tell him?"

Lucy's gaze flitted to Morgan as well. She bent nearer, lowering her voice. "I warned Johnny not to get mixed up with one of the Specter's fences. It's too dangerous."

A chill ran through Clara. "But I thought Captain Pryce was independent of that awful villain."

"Not anymore, from what I hear." Lucy was whispering now. "They're saying that the Specter made an offer to the captain, and the captain took it."

Clara sucked in a tight breath. "They who?"

She shrugged. "Just people in the tavern."

"So it's only a rumor."

"Well . . . yes, but I daresay it's true. 'Round here, if a fence don't fall in with the Specter, he's done for."

Yes, and if Morgan *did* fall in with the villain, he'd no longer be able to keep his promise not to buy from her pickpockets. The Specter would never allow a lackey to make such a decision, and then Morgan would be back to tempting her boys again.

Her heart sank as she glanced over at Morgan and his companions. Were those the Specter's men with him even now? Had they come to confer with one of their brethren?

No, she mustn't jump to conclusions. False rumors did abound in Spitalfields, and until she knew for certain, she must keep an open mind.

She returned her gaze to Lucy. "I wish I could be as optimistic as you about the effect your warning will have on Johnny. But the boy has grown very willful of late, and I'm not at all sure he'll heed it."

"He will, I promise," Lucy asserted, her attention now caught by Mr. Tufton, who scowled at her from across the room. "My brother knows better than to get himself kicked out." She rose abruptly. "Now if you'll excuse me, I got to go back to work."

Before Clara could even protest, Lucy hurried off. Clara stared after the girl, a sinking helplessness settling in the pit of her stomach. She wanted to believe that Lucy was right about her brothers, but she couldn't. And what about this Mr. Fitch? If Lucy had set her sights on a police officer conscious of his reputation, what would happen to poor Tim and Johnny if he did not accept them?

In the meantime, how was Clara to keep Johnny from going back to that wretched shop of Morgan's? Frustrated and anxious, Clara rose and turned to leave the tavern. Then she caught sight of Morgan. He was sitting alone now, and he'd seen her.

Their gazes locked, hers fraught with anger, his full of curiosity. Then a dark, secretive interest spread over his face, making her blood run hot and her mouth go dry. He ran his gaze over her, as if trying to guess what pleasures lay beneath her layers of cloak and gown and chemise, as if waiting for her to let him find out . . .

Bother it all, why did she even think these things? Why

must he do this to her? The man might very well be one of the Specter's lackeys. *That* was what she should focus on—finding out the truth of his connections so she'd know what to do about them.

Her eyes narrowed. Perhaps she should just ask him. She couldn't pick better surroundings for it—a crowded public tavern, where he'd have to behave himself. There would be no "ravishing" here, to be sure.

Drawing herself up, she changed direction and headed purposely toward him.

Morgan smiled and rose as she approached, tipping his head in an abbreviated bow. "Good evening, Clara. Come to have a drink with me, have you?"

Given the intimacy of their last encounter, it seemed silly to protest his familiar tone or his easy use of her Christian name. "I wish to speak to you a moment, if I may."

With an extravagant wave of his hand, he indicated the settle across the table from his. She slid onto the seat, ignoring the curious looks of the other customers. When he took his seat again, his calf brushed hers under the table, and she caught her breath. Had he done it on purpose?

Then he rubbed one boot against hers, and she knew he had. Though a great deal of sturdy English leather separated their two feet, just that brief contact seemed so intimate that she jerked her foot back with a blush.

His low, husky laugh sent frissons along every nerve of her body. "I take it that you aren't here to renew our more . . . private acquaintance."

"No, indeed!" When he arched an eyebrow, she moderated her tone. "Actually, I've come to thank you."

He eyed her with suspicion. "For what?"

"Holding to your promise. Not buying goods from my children."

"It was no trouble. None of them attempted to sell anything to me anyway. They merely sniffed around. Apparently, you've trained your charges well." His gaze pierced her. "But that's not what you really want to talk to me about, is it?"

Good Lord, but the man could read minds. "No. I . . . um . . . wanted to ask you about a rumor I'd heard."

"Yes?" His tone was cautious.

"People are saying you've agreed to work for the Specter. And since you told me that you worked for yourself alone—"

"I never said the situation couldn't change."

"So you *are* working for him!"

Scowling, he crossed his arms over his chest. "Why do you care if I am or not?"

His evasion only alarmed her further. Yet he hadn't said for certain that he'd aligned himself with the Spitalfields Specter. "If you are, you can't keep your promise to me concerning my children. You'll have to take whatever goods are offered you, no matter who proffers them. Including those of my charges if they fall into their old ways."

He shrugged. "If one of your boys decides to return to the life, he won't care whether the fences reside nearby or five blocks away."

"You don't understand. When the fences reside five blocks away, the boys aren't forced to see old companions stroll past every day, crowing about their good fortune, flashing their illicit funds. Out of sight makes it so much easier for the children to put it out of mind until they're strong enough to risk temptation. But with you so near . . ."

The muscles of his jaw drew tight. "Do your job properly, and you won't have to worry about my influence over your charges, will you?"

His flagrant dismissal of her concerns sounded the death knell to all her hopes that the rumors might be false. Disappointment surged through her so powerfully that Clara had to stifle a cry of distress.

In that moment, she realized how foolish her image of him had become. His considerate behavior toward her pickpockets had led her to envision him as a gentleman down on his luck, a decent man who might need only encouragement to abandon his criminal pursuits.

Such wishful thinking had undoubtedly been born of her pesky attraction to the rogue. An attraction that now died a swift death.

"I take your meaning, sir," she managed to choke out. "I . . . I had foolishly begun to think that you . . ." She rose abruptly, eager to escape before she revealed just how much she'd believed his empty promises. "Never mind what I thought. I was wrong."

She turned from the table, but he stood to catch her arm before she could flee. "Now see here, Clara, don't run off. Let's finish our discussion like civilized people."

"Civilized people do not manhandle women." She glanced down to where his fingers gripped her, then lifted a cold gaze to him. "Kindly release me, sir."

To her surprise, he did so, though with a vile oath. When she started to move away, he said, "I haven't yet joined the Specter's men."

Stunned by his admission, she halted to stare at him.

He looked angry, defiant. "Is that what you wanted to hear?"

"Only if it's true."

His expression was stony. "It's true."

She swallowed. "But you're considering it?"

For a long moment he simply stood there, his eyes hot on her, though indecision clouded his features. Then he looked away. "Yes."

"I see. Then I shall know how to act."

His gaze shot back to her. "What the hell is that supposed to mean?"

She walked off without answering and threaded her way swiftly through the tables to keep him from seeing the tears welling in her eyes.

With a curse, he hurried after her, pushing his way through patrons until he'd caught up. "Confound it all, Clara, tell me what you intend to do."

She didn't answer because she couldn't. She didn't know what she'd do. But she couldn't allow him to continue running his business so close to the Home. She rushed outside, relieved to find Samuel waiting for her on a bench.

The faithful footman jumped to his feet. "M'lady, what—"

Morgan burst through the door behind her. "I'm not finished talking to you!"

Brows lowering, Samuel stepped forward between them. "Good evening, Cap'n Pryce. I hope you're not bothering my mistress."

That brought Morgan up short. He glared at Clara, then Samuel. Even in the poor light of dusk, she could see the fury roiling beneath the surface of his rigid expression. "Your mistress began a discussion she didn't finish. So if you'll excuse us, Samuel—"

"As far as I'm concerned, it *is* finished," Clara retorted.

"Begging your pardon, Cap'n," Samuel interjected in an oddly obsequious tone, "but I didn't know m'lady was planning to speak to you—"

"Don't you dare beg his pardon, Samuel," Clara snapped. "I have the right to speak to him whenever I please. And the right *not* to speak to him. And furthermore—"

"Very well, Samuel." Morgan shot the footman a weary look. "Take her home. I'm sure you did your best to hold to your end of the bargain."

At the word "bargain," Samuel groaned, then quickly offered Clara his arm. "Come on, m'lady."

Clara scowled at him. "What bargain is he talking about?" When Samuel hung his head, she turned her scowl on Morgan. "What do you mean, sir?"

The glance Morgan leveled on her was cool. "Our discussion is finished, remember? You don't answer my questions; I don't answer yours. Good night, mademoiselle." Then he strolled back into the tavern with the self-satisfaction of a man who knew he'd had the last word.

As soon as the door shut behind him, she exploded. "Oh, that man can be the most annoying, most . . . most outrageous—" Ignoring Samuel's proffered arm, she whirled to stalk off toward where the coach was parked near the Home. "He's always so smug and sure of himself. And now he's even got *you* involved in his secretive schemes."

"No, m'lady." Samuel hastened after her. "It's not like that, I swear."

She stopped short. "Then what is it like, pray tell?"

Samuel halted too, staring down at his feet guiltily. "He's been teaching me to fight is all. So I'd know how to protect you." When she gaped at him, he added, "I-I been meeting him for lessons in the mornings after I leave you."

That was not what she'd expected. Morgan was helping Samuel to protect her? "I don't believe it. Why?"

Samuel shrugged. "'Cause I asked him to. That one evening after we left the shop, I went back to give him a piece of my mind, and he held his own. Then he said he'd teach me how to look after you if I wanted."

"Just like that?" She tried not to be warmed by the revelation, but how could she not be pleased that Morgan had gone to such lengths on her behalf?

Then something occurred to her. "But he said a 'bargain.' What were you to do in return?"

Samuel sighed, shoving his hands into his coat pockets. "I'm to keep you from meddling in his affairs."

"Oh, of course." Her little bubble of satisfaction burst. She should have known Morgan did nothing without a purpose. In this case, the wretch figured that bribing her footman to keep her away would leave him free to conduct his illegal affairs without interference.

"Truly, m'lady, I don't think he's the devil you take him to be," Samuel said. "He's very concerned about your safety, and that means something, don't it?"

"Yes." It meant he'd found a way into Samuel's loyalties.

She would feel betrayed by Samuel's defection except that she knew how seriously the footman regarded his duty to protect her. And how adept Morgan was at manipulating well-meaning people.

Very well, at least now she knew she couldn't rely on Samuel in her fight against Morgan. She'd have to manage any interference with Morgan's enterprise alone. But one way or the other, she *would* interfere. Because she refused to stand by and watch that . . . that deceitful wretch tempt all of her charges into his camp. No, indeed.

The trouble was, what could she do? She would turn the wretch in to the police if she thought they'd act. But past experience had taught her that they required hard proof, which she didn't have. And even if they would investigate Morgan on her say-so, not all of the officers could be trusted. If she linked up with a dishonest one, he would merely take whatever bribe Morgan offered on the sly, and that would be the end of it.

Clara sighed. That was the trouble with Spitalfields. Everything was done on the sly, under cover of darkness or in secret transactions in closed rooms. If the activities of some of those scoundrels were ever dragged out into a public arena, they'd . . .

Yes, that was it! That's precisely what was needed! And she knew just the person to help her shine a light upon the dark doings.

She smiled as a plan formed in her mind. Morgan might have gained Samuel's loyalties and tempted Johnny into his old ways, but he hadn't won the war yet. Tomorrow she would set about scuttling the captain's battleship.

Chapter 7

I am inclined to believe that there have been but few
ages, if any, since the creation of the world, in which
vices did not reign as much as in the present.
"Introduction," Juvenile Trials for Robbing Orchards,
Telling Fibs, and Other Heinous Offences
By Master Tommy Littleton,
Secretary to the Court, *R. Johnson*

The tap-tapping of the hammer in Morgan's dream crescendoed to thunder, jolting him awake. Grumbling threats, Morgan rolled over to sit on the edge of his bed, head throbbing wildly. The knocking came from the side door.

Who the hell was that? He glanced at the clock and couldn't believe his eyes. Eleven o'clock, long past time for his lessons with Samuel. He was in no mood to deal with the footman this morning, especially after Samuel had failed to keep Clara at bay last night. He started to lie back and thrust a pillow over his aching head, then thought better of it. Samuel might know what Clara had meant by all her threats to "act."

That brought Morgan lurching to his feet. He stumbled forward, nearly tripping over his own boots, and had just enough presence of mind to realize he was naked. He reached for his rumpled drawers just as the knocking began again, setting off a series of explosions in his head.

"I'm coming, devil take you!" he cried as he dragged his drawers and trousers on. Pulling on a shirt, he headed for the side door, then swung it open so violently that it slammed against the wall, punctuating his headache with an additional stab of pain.

But it wasn't Samuel standing there.

"Quick, let me in!" Johnny Perkins begged, his gaze flitting along the alley as if he expected to be caught any second.

"What the hell are you doing here?" Morgan asked, scrubbing a hand over his whiskered face.

Johnny blinked at his harsh tone. "I've come for my money. For the watch."

Morgan glanced down the alley. "What about Lady Clara?"

"She ain't at the Home today. She sent word that she's going for a drive with her aunt in the park."

That would explain why Samuel hadn't come this morning. Morgan hesitated, debating. If Clara ever found out about this, she'd have both their heads.

On the other hand, perhaps he should give the boy his money and be done with it. As long as her ladyship never heard of it and Johnny stayed away, she'd no longer have a reason to fret that he was corrupting her children. "All right," he growled and let the boy pass inside.

Then Johnny slammed the door behind him.

"*Sacrebleu*, keep the noise down, for God's sake," he grumbled.

Johnny looked him over with narrowing eyes. "What happened to you? You look like you been hit by lightning."

"Blue lightning. Had enough last night to set a house afire. Not that it's any of your concern."

And who'd have thought a little gin could do so much damage? He didn't even like gin. He'd planned to spend his money buying drinks for *other* people, to loosen their tongues about the Specter.

But his plan had gone awry after his encounter with Lady Clara. Her looks of horror and her promises to "act," whatever that meant, had plagued him until he'd started downing one dram after another. Soon the rounds of drinks he'd bought for possible informants had become rounds of drinks for companions in crime, and he'd abandoned all control. He was paying for it this morning, damn her eyes.

He turned toward the back room, where he kept the safe. "Does Lady Clara often go for drives with her aunt?"

"Not since I been staying at the Home. But I reckon her aunt gets a mite lonely with m'lady away so much. She probably twisted Lady Clara's arm."

Or Lady Clara twisted her aunt's. What was the wench up to now? It was hard to guess. He'd never met a woman so unpredictable, so heedless of her own safety, so . . . generous to wayward children.

He swallowed. It was her caring toward *them* that stymied him. He'd never seen the like in his life. And how could Johnny not realize how lucky he was? "Won't anybody notice you're gone?"

"Not yet. I'm supposed to be scrubbing pots in the kitchen with Peg, but I promised her a shilling for letting me go. So I figure I'm safe enough until lunch."

Morgan relaxed. With any luck he wouldn't be getting the lad into trouble. Again. "I'll fetch your money." Morgan stopped Johnny from following him into the back room and gestured to the front of the store. "You wait over there."

When a gleam appeared in Johnny's eye, Morgan added, "If I find anything missing when I return, you'll pay for it later, and I don't mean in shillings. Understood?"

That banished Johnny's avarice. The boy bobbed his head, wide-eyed and fearful.

Morgan squelched a smile. It was amazing what an idle threat and a dire look could do to even the most incorrigible pickpocket. As he headed for the safe, he called out, "So how much are you figuring I owe you?"

"Two guineas," Johnny called back.

Morgan rolled his eyes at the lad's blatant attempt to fleece him. No self-respecting fence would give the boy more than ten shillings.

Keeping a wary eye on the doorway into the front room, Morgan released the hidden panel in the wall, opened the safe, and counted out a handful of coins. Then he closed up and returned to the front room, where Johnny now fidgeted as he stood at the window, scanning the street.

"Relax, boy," Morgan said. "Nobody's about in Spital-fields at this hour." Late nights guzzling gin meant late mornings for most residents. His thundering headache signaled that he'd been one of them in truth last night.

And for what? He'd learned nothing useful, no matter how many drinks he'd bought and how many stupid jokes he'd laughed at. His drinking companions had whined about hard times and schemes gone wrong, about troubles with the magistrate and friends in Newgate, but nobody had been willing to discuss Spitalfields' most notorious criminal.

All he'd ended up with was a serious case of morning-after regrets, centered mostly in his churning belly and pulsating noggin. He'd been so sure he was past the nightmare days of his childhood, but all it had taken was a little gin to make him cozy with companions he would despise when he was sober.

He scowled. One more sin to hold to Ravenswood's account.

Striding behind the counter, he plunked down Johnny's money. "Six shillings. That's all the watch was worth." No point in giving the boy enough to tempt him to return.

Johnny scowled. "I s'pose I got no choice when it comes to you bloody close-fisted fences."

He reached for the coins, but Morgan kept his hand on them. "Before I give you this, you must promise me you'll never return to my shop."

Johnny jerked his head up with a look of shock. "Whyever not?"

Morgan raised an eyebrow. "Because there's nothing here for you. I was under the distinct impression that you boys in the Home had abandoned the thieving way of life."

"I can't! Not yet."

"Why not? If Lady Clara gives you food, clothing, and shelter, you shouldn't bite the hand that feeds you."

"I got to get myself twenty pounds!" Johnny burst out. "I just got to!"

"Now what's a lad like you, with a place to stay and plenty to eat, need with twenty pounds?"

The typical defiance of all boys up to no good showed in Johnny's scowl. "What do you care, long as you get your own piece of it?"

Morgan gritted his teeth. Sometimes playing the fence could be frustrating. He switched tactics. "What if Lady Clara catches you stealing?"

"She won't."

"But if she does?" Morgan persisted.

Shoving his hands in his pockets, Johnny shrugged in apparent unconcern. "I'll have to leave the Home for a while is all."

Johnny's feigned nonchalance affected Morgan like a blow to the gut. When Morgan was Johnny's age, he too had hidden his fear behind a mask of bravado. He'd been damned good at pretending not to care that his and his mother's survival depended on her waning ability to hold a man's attentions. At hiding from her the truth of how he'd come by the few coins he daily added to their meager store. At living with the terror that one day he'd be thrown in jail for good, and she'd be left to struggle alone.

"Do you mean to tell me that if you steal again, Lady Clara would make you leave?" he prodded.

"The rules of the Home say if you pick pockets or sell stolen goods three times—and I already been caught twice—you're kicked out. You can't come back 'til you've changed your ways for a month."

Morgan remembered hearing of such "rules" from boys in the streets of Geneva who were in and out of charitable institutions like Lady Clara's Home. In truth, her rules were lenient. Other facilities sent violators to the workhouse or even to jail. If they even deigned to take in criminals in the first place.

But when it came to actually throwing Johnny out, would Lady Clara have the heart for it?

Awareness suddenly dawned. She was afraid she wouldn't. That was why she'd tried to retrieve the watch Johnny had stolen, why she was so frantic to send Morgan packing. She didn't want to have to evict the lad—or any of her other boys who might stray. And Morgan wasn't about to be responsible for holding her to her convictions.

"Will you give me my money or no?" Johnny asked with a boyish petulance.

"Will you promise to stay away from here? And tell the other lads they're not welcome either?"

Johnny shrugged. "Oh, all right." When Morgan handed over the coins, Johnny scooped them up, counted them greedily, then dropped them into the pocket of his ragged red coat. Then he tipped up his chin proudly. "I'll just go to another fence is all."

"Fine. Be a fool if you wish. Just don't be one in my shop."

A sudden clatter and wild barking outside made them both whirl toward the window. Morgan had barely assimilated the strange sight of an overly dressed matron with an armload of yapping dog descending from a carriage across the street when Johnny dropped to the floor. "Bloody hell, it's *her*!"

"Her?" Morgan asked, trying to see better around his window display.

"Lady Clara!"

Morgan strolled from behind the counter and up to the glass door. A footman was now helping a second woman out of the carriage. Morgan recognized her winsome form only too well. Confound the meddling wench, it *was* her. This was the last thing he needed on the day a menagerie of stamping beasts took up residence inside his head.

Then Clara straightened, and Morgan's headache was forgotten. God help him, but she was a treat for even his bleary eyes. Where was her sober brown gown, her no-nonsense bonnet? Today a perfectly tailored, snowy spencer nipped in around her bodice to accentuate her breasts and well-formed shoulders, while yards of pale blue fabric cascaded from beneath it to her ankles. When she moved, the faint breeze blew the gauzy stuff around her slender legs, hinting at a curve of calf here, an arch of dainty knee there.

The blood rushed to his head as he imagined sliding his

hands up beneath the gown to skim her silk-stockinged calves. Then higher past the garters to touch the warm, scented flesh that trembled beneath his fingers as he edged up to stroke––

"How does she look?" Johnny croaked from down at Morgan's feet. "Does she look angry? Is she headed this way?"

She's headed for my bed if I have anything to say about it.

Cursing under his breath, Morgan fought to rein in his lascivious imagination. "She's not headed anywhere right now. And she looks . . . fine." She looked elegant and poised, exactly as a marquess's daughter should look when out for a drive with her aunt.

And that must be her aunt—the beribboned older female with the curly-haired dog. Make that *dogs*. Four of them. One lolled in the aunt's arms while the other three capered or stamped about Lady Clara's dainty kid boots. Ignoring them, she strolled to the back of the carriage and issued instructions to her footman.

"She mustn't catch me here," Johnny whispered. Not that anybody could hear the boy over the racket those damned dogs were making. "She told me if I came back for the money, she'd kick me out for sure."

"She won't catch you," Morgan reassured him. But why the devil was she here? She couldn't possibly know Johnny was in the shop, because if she did she'd already have hauled the boy out by his ears.

The longer Morgan watched, the more bewildered he became. Clara directed her servant to erect a table and chairs on the opposite side of the street in front of a lodging house. The landlady, Mrs. Tildy, came out, conducted a seemingly congenial conversation with Clara, then went back in.

Casting Morgan's shopfront a quick glance, Clara took a seat beside her aunt at the table and began to set out inkwells and quills and a large glass jar.

"Are they gone yet?" Johnny whispered.

"No. From the looks of it, they're settling in for a long stay."

"Bloody hell."

Exactly. "Their vantage point gives them a full view of the alley and the front of the shop. There's no back exit, so you'll have to hide in here until they're gone."

"I can't do that!" Johnny wailed. "Mrs. Carter will start looking for me come lunchtime, and when she don't find me, she'll sound the alarm."

"Be quiet and let me think." Damn it, he was in no mood for dealing with Clara and her troublesome charge. "I suppose I'll have to get rid of her somehow."

"What if you can't?" Johnny's young voice cracked. "When m'lady sets her mind to something, it ain't that easy to change it."

"I've noticed. I tell you what—go into the alley and watch from where she can't see you. I'll try to convince her and her aunt to leave. If I can't, then wait until I've distracted her and make a run for it." He glanced down to where Johnny lay huddled against one of the counters. "Can you manage that?"

Johnny's face bore a painfully hopeful smile. "I can manage anything so long as you keep her from seeing me."

"I'll do my best. But first, I need your help." He eyed the two women, now bent in close conversation over the table. "What do you know about Lady Clara's aunt?"

"Miss Stanbourne? Not much. She don't come to the Home at all." He mused a moment. "But wait, there is one thing I heard from Samuel. Miss Stanbourne surely loves her dogs."

Chapter 8

His cap for much knowledge and skill,
He used in encounters most rare.
His sword all the giants did kill,
For speed none his shoes could compare.
"The History of Jack the Giant-Killer,"
edition by J. G. Rusher, Anonymous

Aunt Verity's dogs were performing precisely as Clara wished. Fiddle tussled with Foodle, Faddle barked ceaselessly at the sign swaying over Morgan's dirty shopfront, and Empress paced beneath the table, stopping occasionally to sniff Clara's boots.

Clara was as nervous as they were. She felt distinctly like Jack lying in wait for the Giant. Not that Morgan was physically as large as all that, but his imposing presence did remind her of something legendary, overwhelming, fearsome. In all her battles with him, he'd gained the upper hand with unsettling ease.

She wished she could don the Giant-Killer's cap of knowledge and arm herself with his phenomenal sword. Surely only mythical weapons would work on a man who could make a woman forget every principle, every intelligent thought, when he backed her up against a wall and kissed her.

Not that such a thing would happen today, thank heavens. Even Morgan wouldn't dare try anything naughty with Aunt Verity and the dogs about.

"Oh, stop that, lassie," Aunt Verity called to Faddle. "It isn't the least bit ladylike to bark with such persistence."

"Let her do as she pleases. She's not bothering anyone." Clara *wanted* the dogs to bark. That was why they were here, though Aunt Verity didn't know it.

Her aunt faced her with a sniff. "You tricked me, you know."

Alarm coursed through Clara. "What? How?"

"You told me that you would dress nicely and go for a drive on Rotten Row if I agreed to bring the dogs here afterward."

Clara relaxed. "I *did* dress nicely and go for a drive."

Aunt Verity snorted. "That wasn't a drive, dear girl, it was a dash. It was hardly long enough even to see anyone, much less be seen by gentlemen of consequence."

Clara bit back a smile. "I didn't specify how long a drive I'd go for."

"And when we finally met up with Lord Winthrop, you cut him off before he scarcely said two words."

"I only wish I had. He got in a whole slew of words, every one more tedious than the last. And he wouldn't even tell me about that incident with the pirates last year."

"What pirates?"

"Don't you remember? A year or so ago, he was aboard a ship that was attacked by the Pirate Lord. He made an enormous outcry against that man named Blakely, remember? The baron's brother? The one Lord Winthrop's crewman recognized among the pirates? The tale was hushed up when this Blakely fellow returned to England a few months later, but I wanted to know the real story. And Lord Winthrop refused to tell me."

"Good lack-a-daisy, niece, what do you expect? It was idle gossip—and probably every word of it false."

"That's not what *I* heard. Though I must admit I've never met this Blakely man in society . . . or his brother, for that matter. Still, parts of the tale must be true or Lord Winthrop would've denied it entirely." She sighed. "What a tedious man. He's had one interesting thing happen to him in his whole life, and he won't even discuss it."

"Oh, who cares if he's tedious? He's got wealth, respectability, and good connections. Surely that's ample compensation for any dullness of wit. And since he's now willing to overlook your own dubious connections—"

"Don't you find that curious? Nothing has changed from before. His mother undoubtedly still disapproves of me. So why the dickens is he sniffing about me again?"

Aunt Verity shrugged. "You're a fine woman, and he now recognizes it. More importantly, he's a fine man." She shot Clara a sly glance. "Your father would have approved of him enormously."

Clara laughed. "That's not exactly a recommendation. Though I dearly loved Papa, he was the most boring man I ever knew. Lord Winthrop is a veritable Charles Perrault by comparison."

"Why, Clara Stanbourne, I can't believe my ears! My brother might not have turned a clever phrase or danced like flashy folks, and his sermons might have been a trifle meandering, but he was as lively and interesting a man as you'll ever meet."

Clara raised her eyebrows, remembering only stern lectures about goodness and long evenings of readings. Her father had been born a clergyman's second son and had become a churchman as a matter of course. A series of unfortunate deaths and tangled family connections had brought him a distant cousin's title and estate when Clara was still a child, but Papa had never lost his early bent toward pontificating.

"Give me one example of Papa's liveliness, Aunt Verity, and I'll take back my assertion."

Aunt Verity clearly hadn't expected to be challenged, for she floundered a bit. "Well . . . he sometimes—No, I suppose that was rather tedious, but he did occasionally . . . that is . . ." She brightened. "He married your mother, didn't he? It was rather daring for a clergyman to marry a squire's daughter whose family gloried in scandal."

"I suspect he married her *because* of that family. The man needed something to liven up his dull existence, didn't he?"

Aunt Verity eyed her askance. "You're very severe upon your father, but your mother didn't seem to mind his dullness. I daresay she found it soothing after a childhood in the Doggett family."

Sighing, Clara stared off across the street. Aunt Verity had a point. Her parents had been happy together, and that congenial union had produced a great deal of good in the world. Clara had spent her life hoping to find someone with whom she could feel such closeness, even love, but it hadn't happened yet.

She doubted that it ever would. After all, she couldn't just marry anybody she fancied. She had important responsibilities, people who depended on her. She really ought to marry a man like Papa—dependable, respectable, *good*. A man whose passion for reform equaled hers, who wouldn't curtail the activities on which she thrived.

But after years of moving in society she'd come to one conclusion: men of that sort were decidedly dull. Or at least she found them to be so. Mama had adored her own dull husband, so clearly not everyone found dullness a deficit. Yet Clara yearned for something more. A man who intrigued and excited her. It was that wretched Doggett blood of hers, making her want what she couldn't have if she was to continue her work.

Every year, her frustration grew more acute. Faced with several gentlemen who would suit her stringent requirements, she nonetheless balked at the few who'd ventured to offer marriage. She simply couldn't raise an ounce of enthusiasm for any of them.

If even one of them had been like Morgan . . .

She frowned. What blessed idiocy was that? He was the most inappropriate scoundrel she'd ever found interesting. He didn't even *like* her, for pity's sake! He only flirted with her to distract her from his illegal activities.

All right, so he might be intriguing and exciting and he might be attractive in a roguish sort of way, but he failed in every other respect. Lord knows she could never find love with *him*. He would make use of her while she served his purposes, and be gone with the next hint of easy fortune.

Even living a spinsterish life like Aunt Verity or marrying a dull husband would be preferable to any alliance with a man like that.

Feeling a sudden surge of tenderness for her aunt, who at least recognized the practical aspects of Clara's dilemma, she reached over to pat Aunt Verity's hand. "I'm sorry if you think I tricked you into this, but I am grateful for your help. It would be very tedious sitting here without you. If you want me to use my inheritance for something other than the Home, then I must solicit donations."

Her aunt sniffed, clearly still put off by Clara's comments about Oswald Stanbourne. "I don't like coming into this part of town generally, you know."

"That makes me appreciate your sacrifice all the more."

"Well," Aunt Verity remarked, slightly mollified. "As long as you realize it."

Aunt Verity was as active a reformer as any of her relations, but she avoided the nasty parts of reform work. She knitted bandages for a leper's colony in Africa, collected clothing from her friends for the Home, and arranged tea parties to solicit donations—anything she could do from afar.

The idea of actually toiling in Spitalfields had always frightened her, so Clara rarely convinced her to venture into its environs. That was why she hadn't told her aunt their real purpose in being here. The possibility of confronting a genuine criminal would be a bit too much grim reality for poor Aunt Verity.

"I'm a mite worried about how Foodle will respond to being out here," her aunt continued. "She's so sensitive to strange surroundings." Foodle apparently excelled at hiding her sensitivities, for she was chasing her tail with great enthusiasm. "I don't see why you wanted the dogs here anyway."

"I told you—to scare off any dangerous-looking individuals." And call attention to any criminal sorts who might venture to enter a certain captain's shop. *That* should seriously curtail such activities.

"Well, I suppose that's a good enough reason. They are all excellent watchdogs. Particularly Faddle. Why, that dog's little nose—" She broke off as the shop door opened and a figure emerged. "Look, my dear, a potential donor."

Clara caught her breath as Morgan strolled out of the shop with the leisurely grace of a refined gentleman. He paused to glance up and down the street as if he scarcely noticed they were there, then looked straight at her.

When he smiled with wolfish delight, it was all she could do not to toss her donation jar at his head. "I doubt that this particular man will want to help our cause, Aunt Verity. He's something of a shady character."

"*That* fellow? Are you sure? He looks a bit . . . well . . ."

"Fearsome? Devilish? Wicked?"

"Handsome," Aunt Verity whispered. "Despite his scandalous attire, he's quite good-looking, don't you think?"

"I hadn't really noticed." What a lie. Morgan was devastating enough when fully dressed, but in only shirtsleeves, tight-fitting trousers, and boots, he gave new meaning to the word *sinful*. That a man should walk around with his hair rakishly tousled and his chest muscles rippling beneath thin fabric . . . no wonder she felt restless and hot after every encounter with the wretched beast.

"Not that a handsome man can't be a devil, you understand," her aunt continued. "Your uncles were all quite attractive, and they were as bad a lot as ever lived." She grabbed Clara's arm suddenly. "Good lack-a-daisy, he's coming this way!"

Morgan crossed the street, but he'd scarcely reached their side when Empress barreled out from under the table, headed straight for him.

"Aha! Let's see what Empress thinks of him," her aunt whispered, confident in the spaniel's ability to assess character.

So was Clara. Smiling in anticipation, she waited for Empress to bark and leap upon Morgan, looking for a prime bit of flesh to bite, or, at the very least, gnaw a little. If ever a man possessed character defects serious enough to gain Empress's dislike, it was Morgan Pryce.

Empress leaped upon him, all right . . . but her tail wagged and her tongue lapped his hand and her little paws scrambled to vault her right up into his arms.

What? Empress turned traitor? It was impossible!

When Morgan bent toward the dog, Clara jumped up, ready to fly to Empress's defense if he should hurt her.

Instead, he scooped the wriggling creature up with a laugh. "And who might you be?" He held the dog gently aloft, with her head a few inches from his face. Empress licked his chin, and he grinned. "Whoever you are, you're friendly."

So much for Empress's ability to assess character.

"Clara, did you see?" her aunt hissed, a little too loudly. "Are you sure that he's a shady sort?"

Morgan glanced at them, amusement dancing in his eyes. "*Who*'s a shady sort?"

"You know quite well who," Clara retorted. "Now put the dog down, Captain Pryce. You're frightening her."

"Yes, I can see her quaking in her . . . er . . . paws," Morgan retorted smugly, but he did set her down to approach the table. When he stopped directly in front of it, Clara could hardly resist gaping at the wedge of black hair showing in the vee of his half-buttoned shirt.

Eyes shining with mischief, he bowed as courteously as any of the lords they'd met on their drive. "Good morning, Lady Clara. And who is your lovely companion this morning?"

It would be highly inappropriate to introduce her aunt to a fence. But with Aunt Verity treading none too subtly on her foot, she had no choice. Sighing, Clara performed the introductions.

"Miss Stanbourne, is it?" Morgan cast her aunt a brilliant smile. "I can see the family resemblance between you and your niece. You have the same beautiful blue eyes."

To Clara's chagrin, her aunt blushed. Good Lord, it didn't take much to turn Aunt Verity up sweet, did it?

"As for you, Lady Clara," he said, turning an equally devastating smile on her, "you look . . . ravishing this morning." When he coupled his compliment with a pointed glance at her mouth, she glared at him. The scoundrel never could resist alluding to their intimate kisses in the shop.

"And you look rather ill," she replied.

"Clara!" her aunt said. "What has happened to your manners?"

"I speak as I find." Clara sniffed. It was true. He did look ill, and ill-groomed besides. Close up, she could see the beard stubble shadowing his jaw and the lines of weariness creasing his forehead. Not to mention his bleary eyes.

"It's all right," Morgan told her aunt without rancor. "I had a difficult night, and I imagine it shows."

Clara searched his face. Did he mean "difficult"? Or "wild"? When she'd left him at the tavern, he hadn't been drunk. But he certainly looked dissipated this morning—she recognized the signs from when one of her visiting uncles had stumbled down to the breakfast table after a night of debauchery.

A tight knot formed in her chest. Had Morgan left the tavern for a local brothel? An image of those large hands gliding sensually over some naked woman's body rose to plague her.

"Considering your 'difficult night,'" she said archly, "you're certainly very cheerful today."

"How could I not be? Two lovely females have set up a table outside my shop in plain view of all my customers." Sarcasm crept into his voice. "That's guaranteed to improve my temper. Though I'm curious about why you grace *my* shop with your presence."

"We hadn't even realized we were close to your shop," Clara said sweetly. "We set up here because Mrs. Tildy is always so supportive of the Home and wouldn't mind us being here."

He raised an eyebrow in abject skepticism. "I see. And exactly what is it you're setting up?"

"Our table for soliciting donations, of course. My aunt and I do that from time to time—speak to passersby on a heavily trafficked street about contributing to the Home."

"I suspect you'd garner more 'donations' if you set up your table on a street that caters to a richer clientele."

"Oh, I like to be close to the Home in case I'm needed. And I'm sure the residents of Petticoat Lane will be as generous as they can be."

His gaze flicked over to where the carriage rested, the

coachman and footman already dozing on the perch. "Where's Samuel?"

"I gave him something else to do today." She'd sent him to hunt up Mr. Gaither in Lincoln Inn's Fields. What a pity the solicitor was staying in a hotel in Cheapside.

Morgan cast her a considering glance. "So you and your aunt plan to sit outside my shop for what . . . an hour? Two?"

"Oh, much longer than that," Aunt Verity said cheerily. "Clara says we'll need to stay here from dawn to dusk a few days at least."

To Clara's delight, irritation flared in his face. "I see. And I suppose it won't bother you if my customers find your presence here . . . unsettling, shall we say?"

Clara couldn't repress her smug smile. "I can't imagine why a legitimate customer would stay away simply because two innocuous ladies are sitting all the way over here."

His eyes gleamed with what she'd swear was admiration. "No, you wouldn't, would you?"

She started to retort, but a movement in the alley made her glance that way.

"I do have to wonder," Morgan added quickly, drawing her attention back to him, "what has brought on your zeal for raising money for the Home, Lady Clara. From our conversation in my shop a few days ago, I assumed that you had all the funds you needed. Or have you already spent that five hundred pounds elsewhere?"

Clara tensed when Aunt Verity turned a bewildered look on her. "What five hundred pounds is he talking about, dear?"

Why, that wretched tattler! She glared at him.

He smiled at her aunt. "Apparently your niece neglected to tell you about my conversation with her." He shifted his knowing gaze to Clara, letting it settle on her mouth again, reminding her of the kisses she remembered only too well.

Heat stung her cheeks. "I don't bore my aunt with every

petty conversation I engage in during the day, sir."

"I wouldn't consider your offering me five hundred pounds 'petty,' Lady Clara," he retorted with clear relish. "As for the rest of our conversation—"

"What does he mean?" Aunt Verity demanded. "What's all this about five hundred pounds?"

Cursing him for a devil and a rogue, Clara decided she'd better admit some of what had passed between them before the man went any further. "I offered the captain a sum of money to remove his shop from this area. He turned me down."

Her aunt eyed Morgan curiously. "Why would my niece want you to remove your shop?"

Morgan graced Aunt Verity with a perfectly charming, perfectly devious smile. "Lady Clara has heard some rather inaccurate gossip about me, I'm afraid. And she won't believe me when I tell her that she's misinformed."

"Pay no attention to him, Aunt Verity. The captain knows perfectly well that my sources concerning his activities are reliable."

Just then Empress decided to enter the discussion. Apparently tired of circling her new beloved, she leaped up on Morgan's trousers again, streaking dirt all over them. Laughing, he picked the dog up, heedless of the mud caking her paws, now rapidly caking his shirt. Empress lolled about in his arms as shamelessly as a dockside tart.

"It's quite extraordinary, don't you think?" Aunt Verity told Clara. "You might wish to check your sources about the captain, given Empress's reaction to him."

"What do you mean?" Morgan scratched the aging spaniel behind her floppy ears.

"Empress only likes people of sterling character," Aunt Verity said.

Morgan cast Clara a gleeful grin. "They say dogs have good instincts."

Clara rolled her eyes. "Empress is a female, from a largely female household. I daresay she's merely relieved to have the attention of a male for a change."

"That's not true," her aunt put in. "She was quite horrid to that Mr. Gaither."

"Mr. Gaither didn't pander to her love of being scratched," Clara persisted.

"Empress loves being scratched because she suffers from a plague of fleas," Morgan remarked. "But I have a solution for that."

Her aunt pricked up her ears. "Really?"

He stroked Empress's silky fur, apparently completely at ease with the dog. "It's something we used at sea to rid ourselves of the fleas in the hold, a concoction of herbs. I'll write the recipe for you if you like."

"Oh, Captain, I'd be most grateful," her aunt gushed. "The poor lassies suffer so with them, and they're a torment to the household as well."

Just that easily, he'd won Aunt Verity entirely over. Clara could scarcely contain her irritation. "Don't you have work to do in your shop, Captain Pryce? My aunt and I don't mean to keep you from your business."

"I suspect business will be slow today, don't you?" he said dryly.

She'd hoped so earlier, but now she feared her hope was futile. He had a way of turning every situation to his advantage.

As if to acknowledge his control, he strolled over to her carriage and lifted himself onto the footman's perch, clearly settling in for a good long visit. "Besides," he went on, "I don't mind keeping you and your aunt company. This part of town can be dangerous."

"You know perfectly well you don't care about that. And don't pretend you merely want to make polite conversation either."

"Good lack-a-daisy, Clara!" her aunt reproached her. "The man might dress improperly, but he's behaving like a perfect gentleman otherwise. And being wonderfully kind to the lassies, too. Why do you insist on being rude to him?"

"Yes, mademoiselle," Morgan teased, "do explain yourself." Settling back against the carriage, he crossed his brawny arms over his chest. The muscles strained against the flimsy cambric shirt, making her mouth go dry. Why must a scoundrel fit only for hell possess a body fit for heaven?

He had the audacity to wink at her. "Is it because of that day in the shop when you let me—"

"Enough, Captain Pryce!" She rounded the table toward him so quickly that she startled Faddle into a paroxysm of barking. "If I could have a word with you in private?"

A slow burn of a smile tipped up the corners of that full, sensual mouth. "Whatever you wish. You know how I enjoy our private conversations."

He indicated the seat next to him on the perch, but she turned on her heel and walked down the street, away from the carriage and the table.

He let out a curse behind her. Hastening after her, he caught up just as she stopped even with the entrance to the alley across the street. "Where are you going?" he asked.

"Away from my aunt and the servants. You've already said quite enough about our previous conversations to ruin me, thank you. I won't give them further fuel for speculation upon our association."

He glanced across the street. But when she would have followed the direction of his gaze, he sauntered over to lean against the nearby building, forcing her to put her back to the street to look at him.

He gestured to the table. "I suppose you think this silly 'donations' maneuver will run me off."

"If you have no customers, you can't operate for long."

Cocking his head, he eyed her thoughtfully. "I wonder how enthusiastic your aunt would be about your project if I told her what we did in my shop the other day." His gaze drifted to her lips. "What if I mention that I know exactly how soft your mouth is . . . how rich and warm it feels on the inside . . . how perfectly shaped your breast—"

"You wouldn't dare!"

"Try me."

She eyed the determined set to his jaw and realized he would indeed dare. "Go ahead and tell her. Because if you do, it will destroy all her foolish illusions that you're an amiable gentleman, and then she'll be determined to help me."

"She's not determined to help you now?" His eyes narrowed. "Ah, I see. You haven't told her the real reason she's here, have you?"

"I-I don't know what you mean."

"Yes you do." Shoving away from the building, he ambled close. His gaze scanned the street behind her briefly, probably making sure no one heard them, before he continued. "You haven't told her that I'm a fence. Or that you're trying to put me out of business or any of that. Have you?"

She glanced away, but the truth was too obvious to deny. "So what if I haven't? I didn't wish to alarm her. But it makes no difference. She would support me all the same."

"You think so? Miss Stanbourne doesn't strike me as the adventurous sort. Perhaps we should find out what she'd do. I'll just tell her the truth—"

"Don't you dare!"

"I take it that you're not entirely sure of how she'd react."

Balling her hands into fists, she scowled. "You're the most infuriating, rude—"

"If you dislike me so much," he said with a smirk, "why do you keep coming around?"

"To make sure that you stop corrupting my children!"

Grinning broadly, he stepped closer and lowered his voice to a husky murmur that aroused her senses. "I don't think that's why at all. I think you come here because you like me, because you enjoy our little . . . encounters."

"I do not!"

Smoldering with heat, his wolfish gaze swept slowly down her, then up, so blatantly that she couldn't help but blush. He chuckled softly. "Liar."

The man was too smug for words. "Your adventures in the stews have gone to your head. Just because some soiled doves fawned over you last night—"

"Why do you assume I spent the night with 'soiled doves'?" he cut in.

"What else does a man do at night around here?"

"According to you, a great deal. Apparently I'm busy negotiating with criminals and corrupting pickpockets. When do I have time to cavort with tarts?"

"I'm sure I wouldn't know," she said stiffly.

He stared at her, then burst into laughter. "I'll be damned—the proper Lady Clara is jealous."

"Certainly not!"

"Then why do you care how I spend my nights?"

"I don't! I was merely saying—"

"Admit it, Clara." He leaned in, a self-satisfied smile on his face. "You're as fascinated with me as I am with you."

"Y-You're fascinated with me?" she blurted out, then could have cursed her quick tongue when hunger leaped in his face.

"Oh, yes. You're the first angel I've ever met." His gaze dropped meaningfully to her mouth. "Or kissed. The experience was distinctly fascinating."

His rakish smile rocked her to her toes. He had the most extraordinary effect on her . . . and he knew it, too.

Somehow she managed a laugh. "Does such glib flattery often work on women?"

"I don't know. I've never called anybody an angel before."

She ignored the silly increase in her pulse. "Of course not. Since you spend your time consorting with the fallen kind, you have no chance to try your insincere compliments on respectable women."

"*Ma belle ange*, I assure you my only companions last night were a bottle of gin and a motley assortment of thieves, fences, and publicans. I preferred your company to theirs, and if you hadn't run off when you did . . ." He lifted his hand as if to cup her cheek, then caught himself and dropped it again. Casting a furtive glance toward the table, where Aunt Verity watched them with avid interest, he murmured irritably, "Wouldn't you prefer to continue this conversation inside my shop?"

She seized on his annoyance with relief. "Not on your life. I don't intend to give you any more opportunities to assault me."

He arched one brow. "I wouldn't call it an assault when you throw your arms about my neck and beg me to ravish you."

"I did not beg—" She stopped short, realizing what he was up to. "Your sly flirtations won't distract me from my purpose this time. I shan't allow you to remain in Spitalfields and tempt my children back into crime."

Wild barking suddenly erupted from the table, and the dogs went racing off across the street. "What the dickens—" she began as she whirled around.

Only to see Johnny vainly trying to shoo the dancing Fiddle, Faddle, and Foodle away. Her heart sank. "Johnny! What are you doing here?"

But she feared she knew exactly what he was doing here.

Chapter 9

Reflect To-day upon the Last.
And freely own thy Errors past.
A Little pretty pocket-book, *John Newbery*

Morgan cursed under his breath as Clara hurried across the street. He should have known his plan to extricate Johnny would never work. Not even a serious flirtation could distract Clara enough to keep her from looking out for her charges.

And now poor Johnny Perkins wouldn't be the only one to suffer her displeasure. With a sigh, Morgan headed after her. While her aunt bustled over to herd the dogs back to the table, Clara caught the hapless Johnny by the arm before he could flee.

The boy gazed up at her, eyes wide with panic. "I was just going to the costermonger's stall for some potatoes for Peg—"

"Peg knows better than to send you off alone," Clara retorted. "Show me your pockets."

Johnny reacted much as Morgan would have at his age—he thrust out his chest in a gesture of defiance. "I don't got to show you, you know."

With a swiftness undoubtedly born of experience, she searched the lad's pockets herself. A low moan escaped her lips when she found something. Then she whirled toward Morgan and held up a knot of coins wrapped in a handkerchief. "You promised to leave my pickpockets alone. So where did he get this money, pray tell?"

Morgan strove to ignore her look of betrayal. No true fence would care about her wounded feelings, so he mustn't either, no matter how much they cut him.

He came toward her, affecting nonchalance. "Did you really think the boy would let that watch go without demanding payment? He's young, but he's not stupid."

"Please don't kick me out of the Home, Lady Clara," Johnny whispered from beside her, his courage vanquished. "I swear I won't steal again! Nor come near the cap'n's shop."

Guilt flooded Morgan with all the force of a tidal wave. He'd put her in an untenable position. If she followed her rules, she had to evict the lad from the Home. And for the sake of her other charges, she had to follow her rules.

She seemed to realize it, too, for her face was as white as her spencer. She stared down at Johnny, anger and worry mingling in her features. "You swore you wouldn't come here. You promised."

The boy hung his head. "I know, but . . . I . . . I . . ."

"I warned you of the possible consequences," she persisted, as if pleading with him would somehow change the circumstances. "How could you do so foolish a thing?"

Her despairing voice clutched at Morgan, made him speak without thinking. "I have a solution to propose."

Her head shot up, fury flashing in her eyes. "Haven't you done enough already?"

"I didn't ask him to come here. He came on his own."

"But you gave him the money."

Wearily, he rubbed his still throbbing temples. "Yes. A mistake. But I'm willing to make amends for it."

"How?" she said sarcastically. "By taking the money back?"

"By giving young Johnny gainful employment."

He must be insane. How could he take on the responsibility of anybody, especially a child, when he most needed to remain unencumbered?

Yet he couldn't stand idly by and watch the boy's situation tear Clara in half either. If she took Johnny back into the Home, it would erode her authority there and might eventually destroy the institution. If she evicted Johnny, the boy would surely fall back into old habits and end up dead or in the gaol by the age of fifteen.

Morgan refused to be responsible for either scenario. He was the one who'd wedged her between a rock and a hard place, and he would be the one to tug her free. Ravenswood might squawk, but the man should never have planted Morgan so close to the Home in the first place.

Since she said nothing, merely gaping at Morgan as if he'd gone mad, he repeated his offer. "I'll hire Johnny myself. And he can live in the storeroom upstairs."

That jogged her from her daze. "Do you really think I'd allow you to engage him as one of your own personal pick-pockets—"

"No, you misunderstand." He should have realized she'd take it that way. "I need an assistant in the shop. Johnny will sweep floors, polish silver, run errands, that sort of thing. No picking pockets, or I'll kick him out myself."

She stared at him, her trembling lower lip showing her confusion and uncertainty. He couldn't blame her for not trusting him. Fences often maintained scores of pickpockets who stole goods for them.

"It's impossible—" she began.

"Hear me out, Clara. You and I both know you can't let him stay with you after he's broken the rules." He nodded down the street to the Home.

She followed his gaze, her shoulders slumping as she spotted the anxious children's faces pressed to the windows and Mrs. Carter standing on the front steps with arms crossed.

"If you let him stay," Morgan went on in a low voice, "it won't be long before the others break the rules. Not to mention that it will get back to the magistrate. As you say, there are no secrets in Spitalfields. It's one thing if you can show the authorities that it's part of your policy to take him back, but if you can't, if you make an exception, they'll be suspicious of you from now on."

She closed her eyes, as if to shut all of it out. "I-I'll just have to prevail upon Lucy to take him in, that's all."

"I don't *want* to live with my sister!" Johnny cried. "Let her keep her 'prospects,' whatever they are. She don't want me there—she said so. And I don't want her neither."

Brave words from a boy who was clearly terrified about what might happen to him. Morgan went on relentlessly. "If you put him into my care, he won't be in the streets. If his sister won't let him stay with her, where else can he go?" He used the one thing he knew would sway her. "Unless you send him to the workhouse, of course."

Clara's eyes shot open. "The workhouse! No, he can't go there."

She glanced away, but not before he glimpsed her tears.

God, how he wanted to reach out and brush them away. But that would be foolish and probably unappreciated.

She turned her frustration on the boy. "A pox on you, Johnny! Why couldn't you just do as you were told?"

"Because he's too foolish to know a good thing when he has it," Morgan said.

"Hey!" Johnny cried. "P'raps I don't want to stay with you neither, Cap'n. Nobody's asked me what *I* want."

"And nobody's going to," Morgan said sharply. "If you know what's good for you, you'll listen to your betters for once."

Johnny blinked but wisely said nothing. Clara shot Morgan a considering glance, then sighed. "I don't know what to do. I don't see how I can trust you not to use him for your own purposes."

Wondering why he bothered to argue for something that did him no good, he turned to Johnny. "Tell Lady Clara about our conversation when I gave you the money. Tell her what conditions I put on it."

Johnny's gaze drifted warily between the two of them, but he answered. "The cap'n said he'd only give me the money if I promised not to return. And he said I was to tell the other boys they weren't welcome in his shop."

"There, you see?" Morgan turned back to Clara. "And if you'll recall, I asked you to keep your charges away from my shop the day I met you."

"Yes, because you were trying to lull me into trusting you."

"Because I have no use for children. They don't bring in enough money, and they can be trouble if they're caught."

Her gaze was steady on him now. "So you admit that you fence goods."

His soggy head reeled from the effort of keeping up with her arguments. Damn, but the woman never let an idle comment pass. "I admit nothing. I'm merely saying I have no reason to buy from pickpockets. Which is why Johnny would be safe in my care."

She hesitated, then shook her head. "I'm sorry, but I simply cannot allow—"

"I want to stay with him." Johnny glanced at Morgan, then squared his bony little shoulders. "I'd rather live with the cap'n than at the Home if it means I got a chance to earn a living."

"Oh, Johnny, you mustn't," Clara protested. "If you stay with him, you can never return to us. And what about Timothy?"

Who the devil was Timothy?

Johnny's face darkened. Then he stuck his lower lip out in a pout, as stubborn as ever. "Timothy don't need me around. He'll be fine with you. He likes it there."

And I don't. Johnny might as well have spoken the words aloud, for Clara's face showed betrayal once more. Morgan wanted to strangle the boy. Had the silly lad no idea of how lucky he'd been to have an angel of mercy like Clara looking out for him, willing to risk so much to make him a better life?

No, Johnny was too young to see it—he didn't realize that people sometimes got only one chance to turn their lives around. The idiot was throwing his away with both hands.

Well, Morgan would give him another, no matter how unwise it might be. He owed it to Clara.

Clara cast a mute appeal to her aunt across the street, but Miss Stanbourne ignored her. The older woman seemed none too eager to involve herself. Murmuring reassurances to the agitated dogs, she sat with the table as a guard between her and the rest of them.

"I can do what I want," Johnny went on. "And I want to work for the cap'n."

"Then that settles it," Morgan said smoothly before the

boy could say anything else to alarm Clara. "Johnny, go fetch your things from the Home. I need to speak to Lady Clara alone."

With an eager nod, Johnny raced off down the street. Clara watched him go, her expression so painfully tormented that Morgan's gut clenched into a knot. He'd never meant to hurt her, never meant to stand in the way of her kind heart. When this was done, he'd do all in his power to make it up to her—convince his brother to donate funds, make Ravenswood hire her boys, whatever would banish that look of desperation from her face.

She turned to him with her shoulders stubbornly set. "Must you draw him into our battle? He's just a boy—"

"—on the threshold of becoming a man," Morgan finished. "This is best for him, and you know it."

She shook her head. "Having him serve as an apprentice thief is not best for him."

"I won't let him steal, I swear it." He stepped closer to lay his hand on her arm. "I won't let any harm come to him while he's working for me."

Snatching her arm away, she whirled to face him. "If you think I'll simply stand by and watch while you corrupt him—"

"Let him go, Clara. He's old enough to make his own choices." He hated having her despise him so much. Even if initially he'd tried to make her do so. "You may come to the shop whenever you wish to check on him. And me."

"Don't worry." She drew herself up straight. "I intend to plant myself outside your establishment for as many days as it takes to run you off."

Gritting his teeth, he glanced over to Miss Stanbourne and their pitiful table. He didn't need this kind of trouble. "You don't have the time to sit out here monitoring my movements, and you know it. You have the Home to run. And annoying me will do you no good, in any case. You can't stay here day and night, and I'll simply do my business whenever you're gone."

"Then my aunt and I—"

"From the looks of her, your aunt can't wait to be away from here. And do you really think you and she and the dogs could stay long enough to make a difference?"

Her chin trembled, making him ache to step forward and kiss her hurts away. Stubbornness was bred in the woman's bones. Yet impossible as it was, he sometimes wondered what it would be like to have her lavish all that determined caring on him instead of against him.

"Come now, Clara," he went on, softening his tone, "at least have the good sense to acknowledge when you've lost a battle."

"I won't let this rest. I'll find a way to save Johnny from you *and* from himself."

His temper flared. Her and her damned principles . . . couldn't she see when she should keep her nose out of something? "You do what you have to, *ma belle ange.* Just remember that even angels know where to avoid treading. And when to accept defeat."

Then without waiting for her response, he returned to his shop. He had half a mind to turn right around and tell her the truth about his activities. Wouldn't she feel foolish for her outrage then?

He sighed. No, he couldn't do that. Clara was an open book, as honest as a nun at confession. Though she'd try to keep quiet about his true purpose, she might give him away without meaning to. And once she knew, she'd probably meddle. Too much was at stake to risk that.

As soon as he entered his shop and saw the meager appointments, it hit him what he'd done. He'd agreed to take on

Johnny. To care for and protect and shelter a *child*. When he should be concentrating on protecting himself.

Never mind that Johnny was the same age as most of the cabin boys that had been under Morgan's care when he was a captain. Never mind that boys his age went into danger on a regular basis at sea. Never mind that the "child" was a denizen of the streets used to fending for himself. It was still a big responsibility.

A commotion in the street drew him to the open door. Clara was arguing with her aunt. It didn't last long. The older woman soon had the footman loading up the carriage again, leaving Clara to stand helplessly gazing about her at the street.

Her aunt opened the door to the carriage and looked back at her niece. "Are you coming, dear?"

Clara straightened wearily, cast his shop a defeated glance, then looked at her aunt. "No. I'm going to the Home. You go on."

Frustration ripped through him as he saw her turn away from the carriage and wander slowly in the direction of the Home. Though he ought to be relieved, he felt horrible. He didn't want to be responsible for taking away her hope.

He stiffened. What the hell was he thinking? The woman would destroy him in a heartbeat if she thought she could. She was meddling with an important investigation, causing trouble where he could ill afford it.

Looking after children nobody wanted but her.

With a curse, he left the window. He couldn't consider any of that now. It would blunt his focus. Bad enough that he'd let his feelings for her lead him into doing something as stupid as taking Johnny. He wouldn't allow them any more sway than that. It was several days since the Specter had last spoken to him, and he must stay alert for the next confrontation.

The side door swung open to admit Johnny. "I brought all my stuff," he said brightly.

All his "stuff" consisted of a fancy cloak-bag, probably stolen, full of what Morgan hoped was clothing. He tried not to think of how pitiful it was that any boy should possess only enough belongings to fit into a cloak-bag.

"Where d'you want me to put it?" Johnny asked.

"Upstairs," Morgan said. "I'll show you."

As Morgan led the way up the dusty stairs to the storerooms, he said, "I imagine you passed Lady Clara on your way here."

When Johnny was silent, Morgan glanced back to see the boy scowling.

"Did she speak to you?" Morgan asked.

"She tried. I told her to bugger off."

Morgan managed to contain his anger until they'd both left the stairwell. Then he turned to fix the boy with a stern glance. "I truly hope you're not that stupid."

Johnny stuck out his lower lip. "What do you mean?"

"Do you know how rare it is to have a woman like that looking out for your well-being? You ought to be grateful she cares so much about what happens to you."

"You mean, because she's a lady and I'm just a pickpocket?" Johnny said, almost sneering. "You think she's better'n you and me?"

"I do, actually. Not because she's a woman of rank, but because she cares about people. She realizes that her actions have consequences and affect others around her. She takes her responsibilities seriously, no thanks to you and your heedless tongue."

Johnny stared down at his toes. "She's got too many rules."

"And you, my boy, don't have enough of them. But that's going to change." When Johnny's head shot up, Morgan went on firmly, "Rule one: no stealing of any kind. No picking pockets, no snatching cloaks off people's backs as they pass by alleys, no breaking into any houses."

"But I thought you wanted me—"

"I know what you thought. You were wrong. My ability to evade the law depends on my appearing to be legitimate, and I won't have you jeopardize that for a few wipers and a tick or two."

That seemed to mollify Johnny somewhat. "So you're not just keeping me from stealing 'cause *she* said to."

"Who, Lady Clara?"

Johnny nodded.

"No." But of course that was why. And it roused Morgan's temper sorely that her feelings mattered so much to him. He shouldn't care. It was dangerous to care. "Rule two: you rise in the morning when I tell you to rise, you go to bed when I tell you to go to bed, and you don't leave this shop without my express permission. Is that understood?"

"Might as well put me in a bloody gaol," Johnny mumbled under his breath.

"Which is where you're headed if you don't curb your impulses before you're an old and unrepentant scoundrel like me."

That got Johnny's attention. "You ever been in a gaol?"

"Several times. Before I was even as old as you. It was not a pleasant experience. I'd like to avoid repeating it. Which brings me to rule three: you are not to speak to anybody about what goes on in this shop. Not your sister, not your pickpocket cronies, and not this Timothy fellow."

"Timothy's my brother," Johnny put in. "He's only five. I don't tell him nothing."

Morgan caught his breath. "There's *two* of you Perkins boys? And a sister? *Bon Dieu*, I know you said your mother is dead, but have you no other relations? A father?"

Johnny hung his head. "He got seven years' transportation for forgery. He was passing forged bank notes when he was caught. We ain't got no family that'll claim us after what he did, so Lucy is all we got."

"And apparently even Lucy has despaired of you two and washed her hands of her responsibilities."

"That's not it." Johnny stuck out his lower lip. "Lucy's been spending time with a police officer." He lifted a hot gaze to Morgan. "But he don't like us, so she don't want us around. I reckon she wants to marry him 'cause he's respectable and he's got money. And if she does marry him, well . . . I expect Tim and I will be on our own."

Awareness dawned. "Is that why you've been stealing? To get enough money so you can coax her not to marry him?"

He shrugged. "I'm good at picking pockets, that's all."

That wasn't all, and they both knew it. Morgan swallowed past the lump in his throat, remembering his own hopes that he could steal enough to keep his mother in comfort. Perhaps then she wouldn't need to rely on lovers for her and her son's survival.

Despite all his attempts, however, he'd failed her in the end. He'd never been able to make her see what a snake her last lover was, not until that horrible night . . .

He cursed as the images rose in his head, a waking nightmare. They were only this vivid and powerful in Spitalfields. God, he had to finish this soon so he could leave this cursed place.

In the meantime, he had Johnny to deal with. "You may be good at picking pockets," he told the boy, "but I think you can do better things."

For the first time since they'd come upstairs, the sullen look left Johnny's face. "You do?"

"Yes. I can teach you—"

"About being a receiver?" Johnny's eyes lit up. "That

would be bloody good, because it's the receivers that make the real money."

"No," Morgan bit out, "not about being a receiver. About the sea. About the navy."

"You mean, being a sailor? That's as hard a life as stealing or worse."

"But it won't get you hanged," Morgan pointed out. "It's good honest work. Exciting, too. I might even get you a berth as a midshipman someday."

Johnny looked skeptical. "They don't take the likes of me as midshipmen. Even I know that. That's for gentry and gentlemen and people what have connections, and now that the war is over . . ."

"You let me worry about that. You concentrate on paying attention and working hard for me, and I'll see that you end up with a post you can stomach, one that doesn't require your looking over your shoulder for police officers every second." He paused. "But I can't help you unless you're willing to follow my rules. Can you do that?"

Johnny hesitated, glancing around him. Morgan could guess his thoughts. The place was warm and dry, heated by the stovepipe from the stove downstairs. With the room only half full of goods stacked on shelves, there was plenty of room. No doubt Johnny was weighing the possibility of hard work against the appeal of having a comfortable room to himself for probably the first time in his life. And the hope of a future.

Then he straightened to look Morgan squarely in the eye. "Yes, sir, I can."

Morgan smiled. "Good." Now he had himself an assistant, errand boy, and general lackey. The question was, what the hell was he to do with him?

Chapter 10

It is too often the case, I fear, that others, for certain considerations, wink at those crimes which at last terminate in very disagreeable consequences.
Juvenile Trials for Robbing Orchards, *R. Johnson*

Clara had come to the busy Lambeth Street Office before, but never on such important business. After two days of futilely hoping that Johnny would come to his senses or that Morgan would tire of having the boy about, she'd resolved upon this last resort: reporting Morgan to the magistrate.

As she sat in the office waiting to be shown in, she tried not to think of Morgan before the court, Morgan dragged off in chains, Morgan hating her. She tried not to remember all the bits and pieces Samuel had related to her about how Morgan was working with Johnny.

So what if Morgan had taught Johnny some practical skills? It was probably only to make the boy more useful to him as a pickpocket. And did it matter if Johnny claimed that

Morgan had forbade him to steal? Of course not. What else would he tell Samuel, knowing that the footman would tell her? No, any kindness Morgan showed Johnny was merely meant to soften her objections to his business practices.

What she must remember was Lucy's face, ravaged with her own guilt. Apparently, when the poor girl had found out where her brother was, she'd gone to the shop and begged him to go live with her at the tavern. Johnny had thrown the offer back in her face. He liked living at Morgan's, he'd told his sister. He didn't want to leave.

Full of remorse, Lucy had appealed next to Clara, but what could Clara do when Johnny refused to listen to reason?

No, there was only one alternative, and now she was determined to pursue it to the fullest extent. No matter what it did to Morgan.

After all, Morgan had never denied that he was a fence. He knew the consequences of his illegal actions. She'd given him plenty of chances to change his ways, and he'd scoffed at her every time. So now she would bring him down.

If the magistrate would take her complaints seriously. Which was by no means certain.

"His Worship will see you now," a clerk said and led her down a tiny passage to a cramped office.

His "Worship," Elijah Hornbuckle, sat behind a desk buried in papers. His broad, flaccid cheeks, protruding lips, and spotty complexion gave him the look of a bespectacled and bewigged frog. Fortunately, his fashionable attire added a certain gentlemanly air to his appearance, which somewhat compensated for his odd face.

But the tall man who stood with him, while being somewhat handsome, apparently lacked the inclination to dress well. His stock was crookedly tied, his shirt cuffs soiled, and his coat woefully ill-fitting. She would guess his age as forty-odd years, judging from his lined features and his bald spot, which shone like a polished apple where it peeped through the straggled hair combed over it. Mr. Hornbuckle introduced him as Rodney Fitch, police officer.

This fellow was Lucy's Mr. Fitch? Good Lord, the girl must be half-blind to choose him over Samuel, no matter how respectable or financially comfortable the police officer might be.

"Mr. Fitch will be investigating your complaint," Mr. Hornbuckle said, waving her to a chair.

The officer bowed more deeply than was proper. "At your service, miss . . . I mean, Your Grace . . . I-I mean, m'lady. It is 'm'lady,' ain't it?"

"Yes," she muttered, stifling a groan. Matters had just gone from bad to worse.

Under the best of circumstances, she would question the slovenly Mr. Fitch's competence, but his relationship to Lucy roused even greater concerns. If Lucy had any influence over the officer, the girl would make sure he found no fault with Morgan, since Morgan presently sheltered her brother. And Morgan would slip free again.

Yet Clara could hardly tell the magistrate her objections to Mr. Fitch without involving Johnny, which she was determined not to do. Wondering if this was a futile visit after all, she took a seat in the wooden chair before the desk.

The magistrate leaned back and folded his hands over his belly, which only made his chin double over his cravat, giving him an even more froglike appearance. "The clerk tells me you've come to report a Suspicious Character."

"Yes." Quickly she explained about Morgan and his shop.

Mr. Hornbuckle effected a most magisterial air, but other than that he showed little interest in her complaint. Fitch, however, whipped out a notebook and scribbled in it with a stubby pencil.

When she finished, Mr. Hornbuckle mused a moment. "Evidence?"

"I-I beg your pardon?"

"Do you have evidence?" He snapped his fingers impatiently. "Come on, come on, what is it? Give me your evidence."

"I already told you. A known pickpocket sold Captain Pryce a watch that I overheard the boy saying he stole."

"And the name of this pickpocket? We'll bring him in for questioning."

Mr. Fitch regarded her with great interest. She swallowed. "I-I can't say."

"You mean you don't know it?"

Unwilling to lie, she shrugged and hoped Mr. Hornbuckle would leave it at that.

"All right then, you have a suspected pickpocket—"

"A *known* pickpocket," she corrected.

He scowled at her over the top of his spectacles. "He cannot be *known* if we do not know his name, can he? Now then, what else?"

She blinked at him. "What do you mean?"

"Come, come," he said, snapping those cursed fingers of his again, "what other evidence have you? What other stolen goods have you witnessed being bought? Or sold?"

She stuck out her chin. "It's not as if I stood in his shop and watched what went on. That's what your police officer is supposed to do during his investigation, isn't he?"

Mr. Fitch's tiny shake of his head warned her that she'd strayed into a sticky area, but by then it was too late.

Mr. Hornbuckle puffed himself up like a frog preparing to belch. "Lady Clara, with all due respect, a great many individuals enter this office bearing evidence—*hard* evidence, mind you—of intrigues and thievery and general skullduggery. We scarcely have the time or officers to investigate all of those. We certainly can't run after every rumor that blows this way and that. When you have hard evidence, come back and we'll speak again." He rose officiously and gestured to the door. "Good day, my lady."

She rose, too, outraged by the curt dismissal. "But . . . but . . . this man works for the Specter!"

Mr. Fitch blinked. Mr. Hornbuckle scowled. Then they both exchanged glances. Apparently, she didn't need to clarify who the Specter was.

"Are you sure?" the magistrate snapped. "How do you know?"

"Well, he said—" She broke off, realizing that to explain herself she'd have to explain her own connection to Morgan, which would hardly help Johnny. "I-I heard it from several individuals. They said Captain Pryce worked for the Specter. Or at least was thinking of doing so."

"That's two separate things entirely," Mr. Hornbuckle said. "And rumor is hardly proof of anything."

"All the same, guv'nor," Mr. Fitch put in, "I don't mind looking into it. Might be sumpthing to it, y'know." When Mr. Hornbuckle frowned at him, Fitch added, "If he's with the Specter, sir, shouldn't we investigate?"

"I'll be the one to say what we investigate, Fitch, and I'm not about to waste a police officer on rumor and speculation."

"You mean, you refuse to do anything?" she said incredulously.

"I didn't say that, madam," the magistrate retorted. "In light of your information—such as it is—I'll consult with my superior and perhaps, if he agrees, we will—"

"Who is your superior, sir?" she demanded, not ready to leave the matter with a man so unwilling to give it weight.

He pursed his lips in a decidedly toadlike manner. "I am under the auspices of the Home Office."

"And to whom do you report?"

He looked as if he might not answer, but even Mr. Hornbuckle wasn't so brazen as to refuse to answer a lady of rank. "Lord Ravenswood, madam."

"Thank you. Then I shall speak to Lord Ravenswood myself." Turning on her heel, she started out of the room.

"He will only tell you the same thing!" Mr. Hornbuckle called after her. "You must have evidence, my lady, evidence!"

"I should like to hear it from him myself," she called back, not even bothering to take her leave as she stalked through the outer offices. All she wanted was an investigation, for heaven's sake. And the magistrate acted as if it were a great imposition, instead of his civic duty as an officer of the law.

Very well, she would go to his superior. She knew Lord Ravenswood from social occasions, and he seemed an honorable sort. Surely he would make the magistrate listen and send out an officer to investigate. She'd even take Lucy's Mr. Fitch if that was all she could get.

She was half a block away from the Lambeth Street Office when a voice called out, "Wait, m'lady!"

Halting, she turned around to find the spindly-legged Mr. Fitch galloping after her. He pulled up short, breathing much harder than ought to be necessary for a man of his age. "I want . . . to speak . . . to you," he gasped out.

"About what?"

He breathed heavily a moment longer, then straightened, tugging at his cravat nervously. "I'm wondering if . . . that is . . . I suspect that the pickpocket your ladyship spoke of is related to a certain female acquaintance of mine."

"Perhaps," she hedged, curious to see how much he would reveal.

"I hear that this particular pickpocket is in residence at the alleged fence's shop."

Her lips tightened. Word certainly got around fast. "If

we're speaking of the same individual, then yes, I believe that is the case."

"Well, then, m'lady . . ." He paused, hunching his shoulders. "I was wondering if your ladyship might know why the boy has associated himself with Cap'n Pryce."

She arched an eyebrow. "And I'm wondering why you're so interested in your acquaintance's relative, sir."

Mr. Fitch shrugged. "I'm speaking of his sister, as I s'pose you know. I look out for her from time to time. But I can't have nobody, especially Mr. Hornbuckle, thinking that I associate with criminals. Especially if you're right about this Pryce fellow."

Oh, dear, what should she tell him? She didn't want to ruin Lucy's chances for a better life, but Mr. Fitch certainly didn't seem the right sort of man for Lucy. "It's my understanding that the pickpocket resides there as a legitimate employee of Captain Pryce. And not to . . . er . . . steal for him." Or so Morgan said. She still didn't know whether to believe him.

A spark of speculation flickered in the man's gaze, but it was gone so fast that she might have imagined it. "Well, then, if you're right, that's not so bad, is it?"

"No, not so bad at all."

He bobbed his head. "Thank you, m'lady." Then he turned and trundled back to the police office.

She watched him go. How on earth had that fellow ever become a police officer? Except for a moment there, he hadn't struck her as being particularly bright and certainly not very brave. He'd barely questioned the magistrate's decision. He'd been more concerned about protecting his reputation than his "female acquaintance's" brother.

"You could do much better, Lucy," she said to the air.

But that wasn't her problem, she told herself as she headed up the street. Right now, her main concern was how to stop Morgan. Which meant she'd be paying a visit to the Home Office this afternoon.

The next morning, Morgan was in the alley showing Samuel how to hide his knife so no one would find it when Johnny came out through the open side door, towing an older boy. "This fellow says he's got to talk to you, Cap'n."

Morgan recognized Ravenswood's lackey at once. "Thanks, Johnny." When the lad stood there as if waiting to hear all the particulars, Morgan scowled at him and said pointedly, "Didn't I teach you better than to leave the shop unattended?"

With a mumbled oath, Johnny returned to the shop, dragging his feet every step. Morgan waited until he was sure the curious boy was out of hearing, then excused himself to Samuel and pulled his visitor around the corner.

"Sorry, Bill, but you'll have to come back. It's barely been a week, and I forgot all about the report."

"I ain't here for that, sir. Our mutual friend says he must speak to you. Tonight, at Lord Merrington's ball. Our friend is attending, and he wants you there, too."

A ball? "Can't he meet me anywhere more private?"

"He don't have time. He said to remind you that nobody at the ball would know you from this sphere."

Except Lady Clara. No, that wasn't probable. Ravenswood had already said she rarely attended social events, except to solicit funds. Merrington's ball wouldn't be the best place for that—it was a known marriage mart. Plus which, Ravenswood said she avoided those anyway, so he ought to be safe.

"Shall I tell his lordship that you'll be there?" Bill asked.

Morgan still hesitated. Tonight it would be a week since his encounter with the Specter. The man would want his answer. Then again, it might be better *not* to be here when the Specter showed up. The bastard might get angry enough to make a mistake. And it wouldn't do for Morgan to look too eager.

"Yes, I'll be there. I'll give him my report then, too." When Bill started to leave, Morgan stayed him. "Did he say what this is about?"

"Only that complications had arisen requiring your attention."

That was intriguing. "Thanks, Bill."

After the lad left, Morgan returned to the alley, deep in thought. He'd need to dress at his brother's town house, his only real home in London. He kept no clothing appropriate for a ball here. And there was Johnny to consider. He dared not leave the boy alone when the Specter might show up.

He smiled. Funny how automatic it had become to consider Johnny in every situation. In only three days, the boy's education had become as important to his life as Samuel's morning lessons and the business of being a fence. In truth, Morgan had come to realize why Clara was so concerned for the lad. Johnny had potential. He had a sharp mind, a sturdy and quick body, and, when he wasn't posturing and pretending not to care about anything, an eager disposition. With the right influences, Johnny might actually succeed in the navy.

If he could curb his tendency to flout authority.

Samuel looked up as he came down the alley. "Everything all right, Cap'n?"

"Yes." Morgan studied Samuel a moment. "I need a favor from you."

"I'll do my best, sir. But if it concerns m'lady—"

"No. It concerns Johnny. I have to be out this evening, and I want him looked after in the interim. Is there anywhere you could bring him to stay just for tonight?"

Samuel screwed up his face in thought. "I s'pose he could sleep in the Stanbourne servant quarters. I could keep him with me until late, then sneak him in after all the servants is asleep. S'long as it's just for one night—"

"That's all—one night. You can bring him back here early tomorrow morning."

"If you're worried he might steal from you while you're gone, I don't think—"

"It's not that. I merely don't want him here alone."

"Why not?" came a peevish voice behind him.

Morgan turned, then groaned to find Johnny in the doorway, looking raw and vulnerable. "You're supposed to be minding the shop," Morgan said.

"I been doing good, ain't I?" Johnny said plaintively. "I been careful and working hard and—"

"It's got naught to do with you, my boy. You've been a very loyal and trustworthy assistant, I assure you."

Samuel cleared his throat. "I could stay here with him if you want."

"No!" Morgan said sharply. The last thing he needed was Samuel and Johnny both tangling with the Specter. "I don't want either of you here tonight. Understood?"

When they hung their heads, he rolled his eyes. This was what came of being responsible for civilians. They didn't follow orders, and they got their feelings hurt when you didn't explain anything. It was damned annoying.

"You'll have to trust me on this. I have my reasons." He softened his tone. "I need you both to do this for me. It's important." Taking out a guinea, he flipped it to Johnny, whose eyes went round as he caught it in the air. "The two of you go out and enjoy yourselves. See a cockfight or a prizefight or something. Have a good meal and some ale. Just stay away from here until tomorrow morning, all right?"

With a nod, they both brightened, and he hid a smile. Amazing what a guinea would do to smooth over a pickpocket's objections.

The rest of the day couldn't pass quickly enough for Morgan, who'd grown tense wondering what "complications" had worried Ravenswood so much. When he sent Samuel and Johnny off together in the early evening and closed up shop, he wasted no time heading for his brother's town house.

He realized something was wrong, however, the moment he entered the town house and the butler called him "my lord," blinked, and then corrected himself. The only time Sebastian's servants confused the two twins was when both were in town.

Confound it all to hell.

"Morgan, is that you?" his sister-in-law cried as she hurried out of the drawing room. Juliet broke into a smile when she spotted him. "It *is* you! Oh, but it's good to see you. Sebastian was terribly disappointed when we arrived yesterday to find that you weren't in residence."

She greeted him with a hug, then belatedly noticed his scruffy attire. Holding him at arm's length, she surveyed him carefully. "Why are you dressed like that? For goodness' sake, you look like a vagrant."

"I . . . um . . . well . . ."

Her eyes narrowed. "You haven't been getting into trouble again, have you? The terms of our wager—"

"I remember the terms of our wager, never fear." He just hadn't been adhering to them, that's all. He cast her a fond smile. "My grubby clothing has naught to do with our wager." Not as far as he was concerned, anyway.

"Apparently, Morgan's been doing charitable work at the Home for the Reformation of Pickpockets," explained another voice as familiar to Morgan as his own. Sebastian strode into the foyer, eyeing his brother with a mixture of affection and suspicion. "Or so Ravenswood claims."

"You spoke to Ravenswood?" Morgan asked. Was this the complication that alarmed Ravenswood? It didn't seem likely. Ravenswood didn't care one whit if Sebastian knew what Morgan was up to.

"I saw your friend this morning," Sebastian remarked. "When you didn't come home last night and the servants admitted you hadn't been sleeping here, I thought he might know why."

Morgan tried to determine from Sebastian's expression whether Ravenswood had revealed Morgan's current undertaking, but he couldn't tell. He truly hated lying to his brother, but the alternative would put him on the outs with both Sebastian and his sweet wife, which Morgan didn't relish.

So he merely kept evading. "Actually, I've been sleeping in Spitalfields. Lady Clara, who runs the Home, has been having trouble with the local populace, and I was willing to offer my presence for her protection." Every word of it was true, even if they wouldn't take it the way he meant it.

"Oh, Morgan, that's wonderfully kind of you!" Juliet said so effusively that he felt guilty. "To sleep at the Home when you could have a nice bed here—"

"Yes, very kind," Sebastian put in, his eyebrows arching high. "And so noble, too."

Juliet babbled on. "I suppose you mean Lady Clara Stanbourne, do you? I met her during my coming out, but she doesn't go much into society, does she?"

"No."

"I don't believe I've met her," Sebastian put in.

"Judging from the fact that she didn't confuse me with you when we first met," Morgan said dryly, "I'd say that you haven't."

"Of course you haven't, dearest," Juliet chimed in. "You

go into society as rarely as she. How on earth would the two of you meet?" She shot Morgan a sly glance. "Tell me, is Lady Clara still . . . unmarried?"

He knew that look. "Don't get any ideas, Lady Matchmaker. I'm helping her, that's all. So stop envisioning chapels and wedding gowns right this minute."

"I was merely asking—"

"I know what you were asking, *ma petite*, but it's not going to happen."

Without warning, an image flashed into his mind, of Clara gliding up an aisle, sheathed in white and crowned with a halo of apple blossoms. On her wedding night, she'd be swathed in the filmiest of muslins to tease her husband with the curves he'd soon be free to fondle to his heart's content—

As his pulse began to pound furiously, he shook off the thought. Damn Juliet and her notions. Time to change the subject. "Is there any food in this place? I've not eaten since breakfast, and I'm starved."

Half an hour later, they sat in the kitchen, Sebastian and Juliet watching him as he devoured a plate of cold roast beef and pickles and washed it down with small beer.

"So what is it you do at the Home?" Sebastian asked.

Sacrebleu. He couldn't answer that without lying. Morgan concentrated on his food. "I teach the boys a few sailor's skills—how to tie knots, read a compass . . . that sort of thing." He taught *one* boy those things, after all.

"And Lady Clara doesn't mind your sleeping on the premises?"

"She doesn't stay there at night, you know. The housekeeper does."

"Oh." Juliet looked disappointed. "Do you have to go back tonight?"

"Actually, no. I'm going to Merrington's ball."

"Wonderful!" Juliet exclaimed. "So are we! Sebastian

didn't want to attend—you know how he hates such affairs—but I'm dying to dance, so I'm making him take me."

Morgan stifled a groan. They would all be there together then. Just what he needed—Juliet wondering why he was going off to speak in private with Ravenswood. Come to think of it, the arse had probably set up the meeting for tonight purposely after talking to Sebastian yesterday. No doubt Sebastian had mentioned the ball.

He glanced to his brother, whose gaze looked thoughtful.

"You know," Sebastian said, "you could accompany Juliet, and then I wouldn't have to. If you're going there anyway—"

"Oh, no, Mr. I'd-Rather-Be-Home," Juliet interrupted. "When I said I wanted to dance, I meant with *you*." She cast Morgan an apologetic smile. "No offense, you understand."

He grinned. "None taken." It was times like these when he actually envied his brother. Not that he had any desire to live Sebastian's sort of life. But once in a while he did wonder how it felt to have a woman care so much, to have her desire his welfare above all else, crave his company, warm more than just his bed.

Wondering was probably all he'd ever do. Women as fine as Juliet and Clara gave themselves to men who were willing to settle down. Morgan wasn't.

"So why are you going to Merrington's ball anyway?" Sebastian asked. "You do know it's notorious for being a marriage mart."

Juliet answered for him. "That's why he's going. To dance with eligible women."

Morgan started to protest, then realized it might be better to let her think it. That way he wouldn't have to come up with another explanation. "You read my mind, my dear sister-in-law," he said smoothly.

Her eyes sparkled. "And if Lady Clara just happens to be there dressed in her finest and eager for a dance with an eligible gentleman, well, he wouldn't complain. Would you, Morgan?"

That was so far from the truth that Morgan burst into laughter. "You're determined to see me married, aren't you?"

"I'm determined to see you alive and here for a while, so our children will have an uncle. If it takes your finding a wife to accomplish that, then yes, I want to see you married."

He sobered, remembering why he wasn't in the market for any wife, but especially not Lady Clara. "Then I fear you're destined for disappointment. The last person on earth who'd ever marry me is Lady Clara Stanbourne."

The moment he said it, he realized his error. He hadn't meant to say that Clara wouldn't marry *him*, but that *he* wouldn't marry *her*. And judging from the sympathy in Juliet's eyes, she'd taken his slip of the tongue very seriously.

He started to correct himself, then gave up. Without even seeing him and Clara together Juliet had decided that he felt something for Clara other than rampant lust. Very well, let Juliet spin her dreams. It would make it easier for him to come and go to Spitalfields while she and Sebastian were in town.

Juliet reached out and took his hand. "Don't you worry, Morgan. She'll come round."

He feigned a woeful smile. "I do hope you're right."

Then, to his chagrin, he realized he might actually mean it.

Chapter 11

There is no inclination, the gratification of which so
much degrades its possessors, or places them in such
humiliating situations, as that of CURIOSITY.
The Danger of Listening at Doors;
or the Curious Girl Cured, *Anonymous*

This might very well be a mistake, Clara decided as she
and her aunt navigated the throngs at the Merrington
mansion. The perfectly pitched orchestra made Clara's feet
itch to dance, and the smell of champagne, blended with
scents of the spring roses and lilacs spread throughout the
house, went right to Clara's head. If little Mary were here,
she'd think she'd stumbled onto Cinderella's ball.

Oh, yes, almost certainly a mistake. Clara wasn't here to
dance. She was here to corner Lord Ravenswood and make
him talk to her.

And why on earth was she reacting this way to a silly ball?
Aunt Verity generally had to drag her to such affairs, and then

Clara spent the whole time trying to convince wealthy people to donate money to the Home.

Aha! *That* was what was wrong with her. This was the first time she'd attended a ball without thinking about donations, the first time she felt free to enjoy herself. It was the only explanation for her urge to dance and have fun. Either that or—

No, she told herself sternly, it had nothing to do with Morgan and the restlessness he provoked in her of late. It had nothing to do with how he looked at her, how those smoldering eyes of his made strange cravings for excitement bubble up inside her belly until she just wanted to whirl and leap and . . .

Dance.

She sighed. All right, so perhaps it had a teeny bit to do with him. But that wouldn't stop her from accomplishing her mission here.

"Look, it's Lord Winthrop, way over there!" Aunt Verity exclaimed as she swayed giddily on her toes in a vain attempt to see above the crush. "We simply must get closer!"

Clara groaned. Yes, definitely a mistake to come here. Aside from the pernicious influence the music had on both her and her aunt, finding Lord Ravenswood in this crowd would take an act of God.

She should have forced the man's officious clerk to admit her into his lordship's presence yesterday morning when she'd first arrived there to speak to him. And yesterday afternoon when she'd returned. And this morning when she'd waited for three hours, only to be told he'd gone off heaven knows where and wouldn't return for the rest of the day.

Of course, nothing short of facing down Lord Ravenswood's clerk with a pistol would have kept that wretch from doing his civic duty. Which apparently included keeping Clara away from Lord Ravenswood.

Fine. Let the little squirrel bar her from seeing Ravenswood in his office. At least the clerk had no power *here*. Tonight, nothing short of an earthquake would prevent her from accosting the evasive Lord Ravenswood. She only hoped she'd heard the clerk right when he'd told someone else that Lord Ravenswood was attending the Merringtons' ball.

"Come on," Aunt Verity said, tugging hard at Clara's arm. "We must go speak to Lord Winthrop. It would be rude not to."

Clara rolled her eyes but followed along anyway. She wouldn't find Lord Ravenswood by standing on the edge of the crowd. "You know, Aunt, I'm beginning to think you should marry Lord Winthrop yourself. How many children does he have? Five? Only think of it—the dogs would thrill to the prospect of having a whole family to enslave. Empress could assess all the boys' friends for character flaws and run off all the girl's suitors who weren't up to snuff."

"Don't be silly." Her aunt threaded her way through the crowd with surprising agility. "His lordship is fifteen years my junior. Why would he want an old woman like me?"

"He's ten years my senior. Why would *I* want an old man like *him*?"

"That's hardly old. Besides, it's not the same, dear, if a *man* is older. Men are supposed to be older."

"And older men are supposed to be wiser, but I've seen little evidence of that in Lord Winthrop."

"Shhh," her aunt hissed. "He'll hear you."

"What?" They'd gotten so close that he might actually hear her? Good Lord, she should have jumped ship while she'd had the chance. Stealthily she unhooked herself from her aunt in order to head in another direction.

But it was too late.

"Good evening, Lady Clara," droned the earl, far too near for comfort. "I'm delighted to see you and your aunt in attendance at this fine affair."

One slight turn and Clara found herself practically nose to nose with Lord Boring. "Why, Lord Winthrop, what a surprise. Given your dislike of frivolous entertainments, I didn't expect you to be here."

Lord Winthrop forced a smile, which gave his generally somber face an unfortunate puppetlike appearance. "I do find the occasional party or ball refreshing. Indeed, I was about to ask you if you should like to stand up with me for this next dance."

It was amazing how being asked by the wrong man completely banished her desire to dance. Yet her search for Lord Ravenswood among the guests had been futile until now. Perhaps swirling about the ballroom would give her a broader view. And give her the chance to discourage Lord Winthrop once and for all.

So she accepted his invitation, and as her aunt looked on beaming, let herself be led onto the floor.

Unsurprisingly, Lord Winthrop's dancing skills left much to be desired, and more than once he headed the wrong direction in the turns. He was known for his sober temper, penny-pinching, and humorless railings against the lower classes, not for his dancing. Or card playing. Or wild escapades in the stews. In short, he would make the perfect husband for some fresh-faced girl eager to take on a house full of children.

Just not her.

After a few moments dancing, he asked, "How are things at your little Home?"

"Fine." Busy scanning the room for Ravenswood, she paid Lord Winthrop little heed.

"It is noble of you to try to save children, even if it is a futile enterprise. That sort is beyond redemption, I fear."

She gritted her teeth. However could Aunt Verity think this man suitable to marry?

He went on, apparently certain of her concurrence. "But it is sound preparation for your having children of your own. I assume that is your eventual intention."

She swung her startled gaze to him as another turn briefly separated them. His comment was as close as he'd come to hinting that he might be courting her. Then it dawned on her why he was courting her. She worked with children. He had five. He would undoubtedly consider marriage to her a tidy arrangement. For *him*.

When they were together again, she said, "Yes, I would like children of my own some day." *My own* being the operative words. "But at present I'm content to work with children who need me so much." A mischievous impulse made her add, "And speaking of my charges, we can always use the help of worthy gentlemen at the Home. If you ever have time on your hands and you'd like to visit, we'd be delighted to put you to work."

His appalled expression made her chuckle as the dance separated them again. Then while she encircled the adjoining dancer, she spotted her quarry across the room. Lord Ravenswood was headed out of the ballroom into a passageway that led only to the library and the conservatory.

Aha! At last she had him trapped. And the dance was ending, too. Perfect.

As Lord Winthrop came up to lead her off the floor, she wondered if she'd need to plead a headache to extricate herself from him. But her mention of his volunteering at the Home had thankfully been quite enough. Mumbling something about looking for his mother, he left her at her aunt's side and disappeared.

"Whatever did you say to that poor man to send him fleeing?" Aunt Verity asked.

"I can't imagine," Clara said sweetly. "We had a perfectly congenial conversation about the Home." When her aunt scowled and looked as if she were about to launch into a lecture, Clara added hastily, "And speaking of the Home, I see someone I must speak to about making a donation. I'll be back in a moment, Aunt."

Then she maneuvered her way through the crowd toward the passageway where Lord Ravenswood had disappeared.

Once she'd escaped the crush in the ballroom, she tried the conservatory, but there she found only a young couple, who sprang apart guiltily as soon as she peeked in. Mumbling apologies, she backed out.

That left the library. Lord Merrington generally kept it locked during parties, since he was very protective of his extensive book collection. Still, she headed there on the off chance that the library door might be unlocked.

To her surprise, when she tried the door handle, it turned. This time she was careful not to barge right in. Easing the door open, she peered inside.

She couldn't see Lord Ravenswood, but she was sure he was in there. She could hear a murmur of voices coming from the large bow window, which was the size of a small room itself. Unfortunately, the two pillars flanking it prevented her from seeing the interior from where she stood.

If that was indeed his lordship in there, to whom did he talk so secretively? Could it be a woman? She should probably return when he was alone, but she didn't want to miss this chance to speak to him. Deciding to get closer, she slipped inside the library.

Morgan leaned gingerly back in the dainty gilded chair to stare out the bow window at Merrington's fashionably appointed gardens. Some fellow beneath a tree pressed his attentions on a coy young woman with a fan. Watching them flirt roused Morgan's envy. They belonged here in a way that he didn't, despite the well-tailored evening clothes that Sebastian's valet had sweated blood bringing to perfection.

This whole affair made him nervous, and not just because of all the lordlings and their ladies who reminded him he wasn't really one of them. Even the house annoyed him. Velvet drapes, windows he could actually see through, immaculate carpets . . . it all seemed so clean and orderly after Spitalfields. It made him feel exactly like the fence he pretended to be—ill at ease, awkward, a real denizen of Petticoat Lane. It was all he could do not to tug at his uncomfortably tight cravat.

"Do you think it's wise to let the Specter twist in the wind by not being at the shop tonight?" Ravenswood asked.

Morgan dragged his thoughts back to the report he'd just finished giving. Ravenswood hadn't yet revealed why he'd been so eager for this meeting.

Morgan shrugged. "Bowing to the Specter's dictates won't force him out into the open. Defying them will."

"Or it will get you killed."

"I don't think I've irritated him enough for that yet." Morgan folded his arms over his chest, only belatedly realizing how that ruined the line of his tailcoat. "Anyway, that's all the information I have for you tonight. Now it's your turn. Tell me why you dragged me to this cursed ball."

Ravenswood sighed. "We have something of a . . . er . . . sticky problem concerning Lady Clara. She's been to the Lambeth Street police to demand that they commence an investigation of you and your shop."

Morgan just stared at him a moment, not knowing whether to laugh or scream. So the little meddler had finally reported him to the authorities? She must have been really angry over Johnny's defection. "You're sure?"

"Of course I'm sure—I'm in charge of those offices, you know." Ravenswood leaned forward and lowered his voice. "Hornbuckle said he urged her to abandon her demands. He refused to have you investigated without speaking to me first, but he discouraged her from following the matter further on her own. Apparently that didn't dampen her determination."

"No, it wouldn't. What has she done now?"

Ravenswood glanced away. "She . . . um . . . showed up at my office shortly after she finished with the police. My clerk put her off yesterday and again today, but I suspect she won't give up that easily."

"Oh, no, not the Lady Clara *I* know. Who is apparently vastly different from the one you know."

"All right, all right," Ravenswood grumbled. "I admit I was wrong about the 'all bark and no bite.' Bloody persistent wench. Who the devil would ever guess she'd carry it so far?" He eyed Morgan curiously. "But you don't seem very upset to hear it."

"It's possible that her opposition will work in my favor. The Specter hinted that he had connections in some of the police offices. When next I encounter him, I can gauge how much of that claim is true by whether he mentions Lady Clara. And if he does have lackeys among the police, then her persecution of me will only reinforce his belief that I'm a criminal. To be honest, I ought to thank her."

"So what shall I tell the magistrate about investigating you?"

The chair creaked as Morgan shifted to face Ravenswood. "Does Hornbuckle know I really work for you?"

"No one knows but me."

"Then why did he refuse to have me investigated when Lady Clara asked?"

"I gather it was because she offered insufficient evidence. And he said that she seemed to be hiding something."

Knowing Clara, she was hiding Johnny's involvement. "So why did he even bother to mention her concerns to you in the first placc?"

"Because she made a fuss. Because even though it peeves him to have a member of the nobility ordering him about, he didn't want to overlook her suspicions. And because you're a navy man and he found it odd that you might be a criminal."

"Good reasons, all of them. Very well, tell Mr. Hornbuckle to follow his inclinations regarding an investigation. It won't affect my work if he puts a man on me—the Specter will know how to get around that to reach me. How the investigation is handled might help us determine where your magistrate's loyalties lie. Not to mention those of his men."

"All right, but I give you fair warning that Fitch—the man he intends to use—could be trouble. Though he acts like that stupid Constable Dogberry in Shakespeare's *Much Ado*, he's really very competent. He's amassed himself quite a fortune in rewards for his successful investigations."

Police officers were told to investigate all crimes regardless of rewards offered, but in practice, the more the victim offered as a reward, the more strenuously a case was investigated. The good officers often made a very decent living from legitimate rewards. "That speaks well of your magistrate if he's willing to put a competent officer on the case. I can get around it—don't worry."

"And Lady Clara? What shall I do about her?"

Morgan grinned. "You're on your own with her, Ravenswood. I wouldn't tell her the truth, since we don't know how well she can keep it secret. But other than that, put her off however you like. I warn you, though—she's not only suspicious, but clever. She'll easily see through half your explanations."

Ravenswood glared at him. "I suppose you think I deserve this after placing you so near her Home."

"You're damned right I do. Have fun."

With a snort, Ravenswood stood abruptly, and at that moment Morgan heard a faint sound from beyond one of the pillars that bracketed the bow window. He couldn't be sure, but he'd swear it was a gasp.

Apparently Ravenswood hadn't heard it, for he turned toward the door to the library and asked, "Are you coming, Morgan?"

"No. I think I'll sit here a moment. But you go on. Oh, and ask Juliet to dance, will you? It'll flatter her but annoy my brother enormously. Then perhaps they won't ask me so many nosy questions about what I've been doing."

Ravenswood laughed. "All right."

Morgan watched as Ravenswood strode from the room without apparently noticing any intruder. If someone *was* lurking in the library, he was hiding.

Or perhaps Morgan had simply imagined the sound. He forced himself to stare out the window as if he'd noticed nothing, but he kept his ears attuned to every noise. When after a moment he heard the faintest swish of footfalls toward the door, he was out of the chair and after the man in seconds.

But it wasn't a man. A feminine cry sounded as a woman darted off at full speed. He caught her before she could even reach the door. Grabbing her by the arm, he whirled her around to face him.

Confound it all, it was *Clara*.

Looking pretty as a princess, she flashed Morgan a weak smile. "G-Good evening." Apparently sensing his anger, she backed away as if preparing to run, but he grabbed her arms to stay her.

"How much did you hear?" He dug his fingers into the bare skin showing above her long gloves and shook her. "Tell me what you heard, damn you!"

"Nothing, I swear! You were both speaking so low, and I couldn't get near because of those cursed pillars."

Should he believe her? He glanced over to the pillars. They weren't exactly close to the chairs. And he and Ravenswood had been discreet. He returned his gaze to her. "You heard nothing?"

She shook her head furiously. "Nothing. I promise you. And believe me, I tried."

"I've no doubt of that."

Now that he was almost certain she told the truth, he re-laxed his grip. But he couldn't bring himself to release her until he looked her over. He'd never seen her in evening dress. He'd never seen her lovely neck graced by pearls or her silky hair haloed by ribbons ... or her soft breasts swelling above the bodice of a rich, low-cut gown.

Without even realizing it, he skimmed his hands down the short stretch of bare arm to her kid gloves, then back up to the borders of the net puffing out over her blue satin sleeves. And all the while he drank her in, marveling at the change a little satin and some pearls could make in a woman. But when he reached to touch the pearls, she jerked and stepped back, breaking free of his grasp.

"That was Lord Ravenswood you were talking to, wasn't it?" she whispered, rubbing her arms as if to banish his touch.

That broke the pleasant spell she'd wound around him. "Didn't anyone ever tell you it's rude to spy on people?"

"Didn't anyone ever tell *you* it's wrong to fence stolen goods? And bribe government officials? And—"

"Bribe government officials?" he broke in before she could finish detailing all his imaginary crimes. "What are you talking about?"

"Don't play the innocent with me. Why else would you hold secret meetings with Lord Ravenswood if not to bribe him to ignore your crimes?"

He managed a laugh. "It wasn't much of a secret meeting if *you* stumbled upon us. You'd think we'd be more discreet."

"Don't laugh at me!"

"Then don't spy on me."

"I-I wasn't spying," she protested. When he stepped nearer, into a wash of light from a nearby sconce, she seemed to notice his apparel for the first time. "And why are you dressed like that?"

"Like what?"

She swept her hand down to indicate his cravat tied in the fashionable Oriental knot, his tailcoat finely cut, and his silk breeches drawn taut enough to bounce a shilling off of. "Like *that*. Like a gentleman."

"I *am* a gentleman."

She snorted. "You're a devilish, deceiving rogue, that's what you are. Dressing like a gentleman so you can sneak into the ball to bribe Lord Ravenswood—"

"I don't know where you get these notions," he snapped. "I was not bribing Lord Ravenswood. I merely encountered him in here and exchanged a few pleasantries. To bribe him, I'd have to tell him about my . . . er . . . activities, and why would I?"

She considered that with a thoughtful expression. How long would it be before she figured out the connection between him and Ravenswood and put the rest of it together? He'd best distract her before she got that far.

She tipped up her chin. "If you weren't here to meet with his lordship, why are you here? Tell me that."

A sudden mischief seized him. "Why do you think?" He waved one hand to encompass the library. "Lord Merrington owns a vast number of lovely and expensive items. He has excellent taste in china and some of the finest silver I've ever seen. His Rembrandt alone must be worth—"

"You wouldn't dare!" she exclaimed in clear horror. "You're a fence, not a thief!"

"That's true." He grinned, thoroughly enjoying himself. She was so delightfully easy to provoke. "The trouble with being a fence, however, is that I have to take what the thieves bring me. And since they generally don't have the education to recognize the choicest bits to steal, I've come ahead of time to pick out what I want. Then all I need do is send the professionals over here with their lock picks and their—"

"I won't let you steal from the Merringtons, you . . . you scoundrel!" Taking him by surprise, she whirled and took off for the door.

Erupting into laughter, he ran after her. She'd actually managed to open it before he caught her and slammed it shut. Still laughing, he twisted her around to face him, then planted his hands against the door on either side of her to trap her.

Judging from her expression, she didn't share his amusement. "Get away from me!" She thrust hard against his chest. "I won't let you do this!"

"Clara, stop it. Can't you tell when I'm teasing you? I'm not here to steal. For God's sake, calm down!"

It took a second for his words to sink in and another for her to stop pushing at him. But her pretty eyes still flashed, and her hands curled into fists against his chest.

"I'm not here to steal, *ma belle ange,*" he repeated. "I swear it."

Anger faded to uncertainty in her face. "And you're not here to . . . to determine what your cronies should steal?"

Choking back more laughter, he shook his head. "Come now, do you really think I'd reveal my plans if they were so wicked as all that?"

"I suppose not." Still stubbornly suspicious, she surveyed his clothing once more. "But if you're not here to steal and you're not here to bribe Lord Ravenswood, then why are you here?"

"The same reason most people are here, *cherie*. To attend the ball."

"Surely you were not invited—"

"I'm still a naval officer, you know. I do have friends from the old days."

Her eyes narrowed. "Lord Ravenswood? Is he one of your 'friends'?"

"Perhaps." Before she could pursue her interrogation, he turned it on her. "Now tell me why you're spying on him." As if he didn't know.

"I'm not spying on him. I was merely hoping for a word with him in private when I came upon the two of you."

"And why would you wish to speak to Ravenswood in private?" If she was telling the truth about not having heard his conversation with Ravenswood, then she'd want to hide what she was attempting to do.

That must have just occurred to her, too, for she blinked, caught in her own snare.

He tormented her gleefully. "Wait, I think I can guess."

Sheer panic filled her face. "Y-You can?"

"This is a marriage mart. You and Ravenswood are both unmarried. It doesn't take much to deduce the rest." He leaned in close to tease her. "Are you looking for a husband, Clara? I hear that Ravenswood is a most eligible bachelor. Have you set your sights on him?"

Her panic turned to annoyance. "Good Lord, no!"

"All it would take is your tempting him into a compromising position. Then, noble character that he is, he'd marry you. Is that why you wanted to speak to him privately, so you could entice him into a hasty marriage?"

"Don't be ridiculous."

"No?" He let his gaze trail over her to examine every aspect of her inviting attire. "Then why are you dressed in this pretty gown, if not to tempt a man?"

"I-I always dress well for these affairs."

He dropped one hand from the door to finger the blue

rosettes adorning her puffy sleeves. "Satin, isn't it? And very expensive, I'll wager."

"It's no more expensive than . . ."

She trailed off as he dragged one finger along the thin shoulder of her gown, then traced a line down her bodice. When her breath quickened and her eyes softened, he felt a fierce surge of satisfaction. Ever since that day in his shop, he'd wondered if he'd imagined her eager response to his touch. It pleased him enormously that he hadn't.

As she stared up at him with wide eyes, her lips parting in an unconscious invitation, he ran his finger along the trim of her low-cut bodice. It was all he could do not to touch the tempting swells of her breasts that peeked above the edge. What began as a way to distract her from his and Ravenswood's meeting was rapidly flaring into desire.

"Ah, yes, satin," he heard himself say hoarsely. "And trimmed with lace, too. Very costly." He lowered his voice. "Very provocative. An excellent choice for tempting a man to throw caution to the winds."

She swallowed, her pale throat trembling with the motion. "I wasn't trying to . . . I mean, this is the way I always—"

"I'll wager every man here has been watching you tonight, wanting to put his hands on you. Wanting to do this." He nuzzled her cheek, drowning in the jasmine scent of her. "And this." He kissed her impudent little nose. "And this . . ." He covered her soft mouth with his.

Every muscle in his body came alive. Her lips were even tastier than he remembered, honey-sweet and warm as summer. He could spend hours kissing her, touching her. He'd never met a woman so open and yet so innocent. She was sometimes an angel, sometimes a wanton, but always irresistible.

Like now. He ought to take advantage of her dazed response to escape, but he was doing this instead.

Nor had he any intention of stopping, not when he'd waited forever to kiss her again. The Specter be damned, Ravenswood be damned. As long as Clara continued to let him kiss her, they could all go to the devil.

Because he would enjoy this taste of her while he had the chance.

Chapter 12

Avoid sinful and unlawful Recreations, and all such
as prejudice the Welfare of Body or Mind.
A Little pretty pocket-book, *John Newbery*

The longer Morgan kissed her, the more Clara yielded.
How could she help it? She'd dreamed of this, dwelt on
it night after night. And it was every bit as delicious as before. The man knew a thing or two about kissing. His mouth
caressed hers so expertly that by the time he deepened it,
she'd given up any thought of resisting.

She rose to his kiss, opening her mouth to receive every
silken thrust of his tongue. Her hands crept beneath his coat
of their own volition, plastered themselves against his warm,
taut waist. With a groan, he leaned into her and kissed her
more deeply, making her heart pound so furiously she
thought surely he'd hear it.

Or feel it. Because the same finger that had traced her

bodice trim was drawing a line again. Except that this time he'd removed his gloves . . . and this time his bare finger stroked bare flesh. Boldly, seductively, he trailed it over skin that leaped to fire with his every touch.

Until at last he stopped at the inward curve between her breasts to dip his finger inside her bodice.

She tore her lips free, breathing hard. "Wh-What are you doing?"

His hungry gaze locked with hers. "Wondering about the temptations you were planning to offer Ravenswood."

"Oh, for pity's sake, I was not planning to offer—"

His mouth closed over hers again, so hard and plundering and needy that she scarcely registered when he slid his finger along the inside of her gown and chemise. But she definitely noticed when his fingertip grazed her nipple beneath the chemise—her bare nipple, for pity's sake. How incredibly erotic to have him touch her *there.*

And wicked in the extreme. Wrenching her mouth from his, she stared down at his deft finger, hardly daring to believe what he was doing. He stroked back and forth along the inside of her chemise, brazenly caressing her breast.

Her pulse thundered, and she could scarcely breathe. She should protest, but speech was impossible.

Resisting his attentions had been easier when his dress served as a constant reminder of his roguish character. It was so much harder when he dressed like any gentleman of her acquaintance. It made him seem almost . . . respectable.

Except that no respectable gentleman would do *this.*

"Perhaps we . . . we should return to the ball," she said weakly. But her hands remained fixed on his waist, putting the lie to her words.

His gaze pinned her in place, black, secretive, promising pleasures. "It's cozier here." His hand left her bodice, but only to reach behind her and lock the door to the library. "And private."

A shiver of fear and yes, anticipation, ran down her spine. "I don't think I should be private with you."

"Why not?" He shot her a smile of pure mischief. "You were planning on trying out your wiles in private with Ravenswood."

"I was not! Why won't you believe me?"

He planted an exquisite kiss on her neck. "Because you haven't offered any other explanation."

She dragged in a breath. No, she hadn't. And at the moment, she couldn't think of a single plausible one but the truth. Which she certainly couldn't tell him.

When she remained silent, he bestowed another kiss farther down, on her collarbone. "You see?" he rasped as she shivered with undeniable pleasure. "I'll stick to my explanation. Though I must say it was very cruel of you to plan such a thing. I hear Ravenswood has no interest in marriage, but the poor man wouldn't have stood a chance against your delights. God knows I'm completely helpless against them."

"You've never been helpless a day in your—" She broke off when he closed his hand over her breast, kneading it through the bodice so skillfully that she moaned. "Oh, my word, what do you think you're doing?"

"Touching you the way I've wanted to for so long," he murmured, "the way you've wanted me to." As if to prove it, he lifted his other hand to caress her other breast.

Good lack-a-daisy, as Aunt Verity would say. She would surely dissolve into a puddle right here, on the Merringtons' carpet. "Morgan, you really shouldn't—"

His mouth covered hers again in the most exhilarating kiss imaginable. Or was it exhilarating because his hands fondled her breasts at the same time, rubbing them in such a tantalizing fashion that she prayed he'd never stop?

What was wrong with her? She'd always figured that wantonness must have its pleasures for women, or some of them wouldn't be so willing to throw up their skirts for men. But she'd never expected it to affect *her* this way. Why, she didn't even *like* Morgan!

No, that wasn't true. She liked him too well. But not what he represented. Just as he didn't really like what she represented.

The thought gave her pause. Why was he using all his devilish powers of seduction against her? It couldn't be because he felt anything for her. No, it must be because of something else . . . like that day in the shop when he'd kissed her to distract her . . .

As the painful truth dawned, she jerked her hands from inside his coat to shove him away.

He staggered back, his heavy-lidded eyes glittering with a feral hunger. "What is it, *cherie*?"

"I know why you're doing this! Touching me and . . . and making me want you to— Anyway, I know why."

His hands closed into fists, as if he fought to keep from touching her. "Because I desire you?"

"Because you 'desire' to distract me." She fought to hide her hurt. "A man like you never gives in to urges unless they serve a purpose. And your purpose is to keep me from asking about what's going on between you and Ravenswood."

A palpable coldness spread over his features. "So you've figured me out, have you?"

She nodded, unable to speak the words for the sick tumult roiling in her stomach.

"I couldn't possibly just want to taste you," he said acidly, "or hold you in my arms or for one damned moment feel a connection with another fellow creature. No, not a man like me. Not a heartless criminal."

The force of his bitterness struck her with guilt. "I didn't mean—"

"I know what you meant." He glanced away, a muscle ticking in his jaw.

After a moment of wintry silence, she reached for the door lock, but he caught her hand. He braced himself against the door with his other hand as his gaze swept slowly down her body.

The need that leaped in his face was unmistakable. "All right, *ma belle ange.* I suppose you want answers to your questions. Well, contrary to what your suspicious little mind believes, I want to share a few moments of pleasure with you. So here's my offer—you ask your questions, and I answer them truthfully."

She started to speak, but he held his finger to her lips. "I'm not finished. For every question I answer, you give me something I want." He traced her lips with his finger. "A chance to taste you." He ran his finger past her chin to stroke the length of her neck all the way to her chest, and she shivered with anticipation. "To caress you." Tucking his finger inside her bodice, he inched it toward her nipple. "To fondle your bare flesh."

By the time he reached his destination, she ached to have him touch her there. And he knew it, too, for his face held a grim satisfaction as he stroked back and forth over her nipple, teasing her, arousing her. But when some prudent part of her rebelled and she reached up to stay his hand, he said huskily, "Those are my terms. For every answer I give you, you give me a caress or a kiss or . . . whatever I ask for."

Whatever he asked for. She was in dire trouble now. Because the very idea made her mouth water.

And confused her, too. Did he truly desire her as much as he claimed? So much that he'd answer her questions? Or was this only another ploy?

"You think I won't do it," she whispered. "You think because you ran me off last time with your . . . outrageous advances, that I'll let you do it again."

He merely arched an eyebrow.

"We're not in your shop now, you know. I'm not at your mercy. I can walk right out of here and . . . and ask his lordship all my questions."

Amusement glinted in his eyes. "You're welcome to try. He won't answer—I promise you that. But I will." He bent to press a shameless, open-mouthed kiss to the exposed curve of the breast he'd just touched. Then he lifted his head and cast her a wolfish smile. "If you give me what I want."

For some reason, her mouth had grown inordinately dry. "You want to ruin me."

"It needn't go as far as all that. You can stop me whenever you like. Whenever you're ready to stop asking questions."

She hesitated. This "offer" of his sounded risky and downright dangerous, like throwing rocks at a wolf from across a chasm. You never knew when the wolf might surprise you and leap the chasm, pouncing before you could even escape.

Then again, it wasn't as if they were entirely alone. A mass of society's most lofty personages swarmed only a few feet away. Aunt Verity would probably come looking for her soon. And Clara could scream for help if things went too far. Someone was bound to hear.

Besides, how else could she make him admit what was going on? Something odd was definitely going on. Morgan dressing as a gentleman and on easy terms with a very powerful viscount? Perhaps this matter of his shop wasn't quite what she'd thought. She had to have answers.

That was the only reason she'd do this. It had nothing to do with the pounding anticipation in her chest, the hot need pooling in her belly. Nothing to do with all the nights she'd spent wondering about him and wishing she weren't alone in her bed.

Steadying herself before she could change her mind, she said, "All right." The triumph that flared in his gaze made her wonder if she'd been outmaneuvered. She added hastily, "But you have to tell the truth. Because I'll know if you're lying."

He gave a wry chuckle. "I've no doubt of that." Then taking her by surprise, he scooped her up in his arms and carried her to the nearby chaise longue.

She felt a moment's panic. "Morgan, what are you doing?"

"I'd prefer to be comfortable for this interrogation, wouldn't you?"

"I-I suppose."

But instead of setting her on the chaise longue, he sat down and settled her on his lap. She started to scramble off, but he stayed her by throwing his arm around her waist. "Oh no, my pretty angel, you're not going anywhere. I want you near enough so I can make sure my part of the bargain is satisfied."

She cast him an outraged look. "Do you think I'd cheat?"

"Absolutely. Now give me your first question." He pulled her so close she could see the fine line of his lip, smell his wine-scented breath. And feel the hard bulge swelling beneath her bottom. "As you can tell, I'm more than ready to make my first demand, *cherie.*"

His clear arousal made her heart stammer and her blood run feverishly hot. He truly hadn't lied about desiring her. This wasn't only his way of distracting her.

Perversely, while that pleased her, it also furthered her agitation. Now all she could think of was how he might touch her next. So she asked the first, most obvious question that came into her mind. "What were you and Ravenswood talking about?"

"You." He reached for the edge of her bodice.

"Wait a minute!" she protested, grabbing his hand. "What kind of answer is that?"

His eyes gleamed down at her. "It's a truthful answer, so it meets all your requirements. And now I get my turn."

"But . . . but . . ."

He didn't wait for her to finish protesting that such a short, uninformative response raised more questions than it answered. He simply pulled her bodice and chemise down to expose one breast.

She blushed violently, her heart hammering so hard she thought she'd faint. Especially once he touched her. It was much more intense than when he'd fondled her through her gown or even when he'd stroked her bare skin. Just being this exposed to him lent a thrill to his caresses that made her breathless and trembly.

A greedy smile curved his lips as he watched her face, embarrassing her with his eagerness to see her reaction. And when she swallowed her gasps, not wanting him to know how he affected her, he took his time about plumping her flesh, then thumbing her nipple with ardent, silken caresses.

When finally she sighed and gave in to her enjoyment of the sweet sensations, he whispered, "You like that, do you?"

"I don't recall that your game required *me* to answer questions," she grumbled.

"Is it so awful to admit that you enjoy my touch?"

Her startled gaze shot to him. He looked uncertain of her, not what she'd expected. "No," she whispered. "It's just that no one's ever touched me . . . like that before."

"It's even better like this," he murmured, lowering his head toward her breast as if he meant to kiss it.

She should have known a rascal like him would cheat. But she was too quick for him. "Oh no, you don't." She stayed

him with her hand. "I only promised one thing at a time, and
you've had a caress. You don't get a kiss until you answer another question."

He lifted his head, his black eyes glittering with both need
and frustration. "I can see we'll be here all night at this rate."

"*You're* the one who gave me the barest minimum of an
answer. If you want more than the barest minimum of a caress for it, you'll have to be more forthcoming."

Irritation flickered in his face. "Has anybody ever told you
that you have the soul of a merchant? You bargain more
fiercely than a costermonger."

She smiled. "You were the one who set up this game, you
know. I'm merely following the rules."

"You're right. And I clearly didn't lay them out properly.
So here's what we'll do—you can decide when I've answered your next question to your complete satisfaction. But
once you have your answer, you must let me kiss or caress
you for the full length of the next song the orchestra plays.
Does that sound fair?"

The thought of him kissing her breast for three or four
minutes struck the breath from her lungs. Yet his request
seemed reasonable. They could hear the music in here easily,
and at least this gave him a finite restriction on his touching
and tasting. She'd simply have to steel herself for the on-
slaught of feelings he brought whenever he put his hands and
his mouth on her. It would be worth it to get the answers she
sought.

"I suppose it's fair enough. But give me a minute to think
of my question."

"Want to get the most for your . . . kiss, do you?" he said
smugly.

"Oh yes." And she could be as clever in framing her questions as he was in avoiding answering. "You said that you

were discussing me with Lord Ravenswood. What did he tell you about me tonight that you didn't already know?"

He opened his mouth to answer, then shut it with a scowl.

"Not so cocky when the questions are hard, are you?" she taunted.

His eyes narrowed. "I'll make you pay for this eventually, *cherie.*"

"Just answer the question."

A long moment passed. Then he sighed. "All right. Ravenswood told me that you'd reported me and my activities to the magistrate."

"He did?" she cried. "Why would he do such an awful—"

"Ah, ah, ah, not so fast." He held his finger to her lips. "That's another question. And I believe you owe me something before I answer any more."

She swallowed. She had to admit that he'd told her a very vital piece of information. To claim that it wasn't good enough to win him his kiss would be grossly unfair. "All right."

With a grin, he lowered his head. But apparently, it wasn't a kiss to her breast that he sought. Not exactly. Instead, he took her breast in his mouth and sucked it. Hard. Flicking his tongue against the nipple over and over in the most shocking fashion.

Oh, good Lord. Now he was nipping it, then soothing it with tempting strokes of his tongue that made a slow ache uncurl in her belly and spread throughout her trembling body. She closed her hands in his hair to hold him there, and he obliged her with a rampant eagerness, kissing her breast, laving it, making her feel as if she would come out of her skin if he did much more.

This could get dangerous very quickly, she realized, and she forced herself to listen for the end of the song, not sure how many songs had passed. When seconds later the orchestra grew silent, she could have wept with relief.

"That's the end." She pulled his head away. "You owe me another answer."

For a second, she thought he might not obey her, for he gave her nipple one last teasing nip. Then lifting to her a gaze feverishly bright, he licked his lips like the ravenous wolf that he was. "Ask me another question quick. I'm not even close to being finished with you, *ma belle ange*."

His words made a naughty excitement surge through her, swamping her senses, frightening her with its force. Perhaps she should end this. Each time he touched her, she lost more of her will to stop him. Even now she couldn't seem to take her hands out of his glossy, thick hair. She wanted to keep smoothing it, caressing it.

But there was one more answer she needed. At least one more. Curse him, she'd get her answers if it killed her. "Why did Lord Ravenswood tell you that I'd reported you to the magistrate?"

With a low curse, he glanced away, but he didn't hesitate to answer, speaking in a frenzy as if to be done with it. "Because he and I are friends. I knew him when I was in the navy. He wanted to warn me about your possible interference."

It took her a moment to absorb that astonishing answer. "Does he know that you're a fence?" she exclaimed in outrage.

His gaze shot back to her, fiery and seductive. "That's a new question, angel."

Good Lord, it was. And she couldn't honestly say he hadn't answered the previous one fairly.

But the devilish intent in his face sparked her alarm. How would she ever make it through the next song? With a show of rebellion, she thrust her breasts up at him. "Do your worst," she said mutinously, hoping to rouse his conscience.

It didn't. Instead, it seemed to rouse something else entirely, for with a reckless and unrepentant smile, he slid her skirts up her thighs.

The rustle of satin sounded a warning knell, and she grabbed his hand in a panic. "Now see here, I thought you wanted to keep tasting my . . . my . . ."

"We never specified what I could taste or touch. You said whatever I wanted."

"I thought—"

"I know what you thought. But lovely as your breasts are, my angel, I have a more intimate spot I wish to explore." Keeping his heated gaze locked on her face and his hand on her thigh, he listened for the next dance to begin.

Once it did, a triumphant grin crossed his lips. He shook off her hand, then slid his fingers up beneath her cambric petticoat. While she watched with a mixture of outrage and impatience, he delved inside the slit in her drawers to touch the curls between her legs.

Her most private place, mind you! How brazen of him! She didn't know whether to be appalled or thrilled at his daring. She did know that her heart beat louder than the orchestra's music in her ears, that his touch provoked her to dream and want and ache.

He knew it, too, judging from his dark smile. "*This* is what I want to caress." He found a particularly sensitive piece of flesh and thumbed it lightly, making her jerk upright. "I don't think you'll have any cause for complaint when I'm done."

Oh . . . good . . . Lord. He was as deft as a thief with a picklock, opening the clasp to her pleasure with one flick of his finger. Only he didn't stop there . . . he went on and on and on, working the flesh until she writhed and moaned beneath his hand, wanting more, needing his touches, craving the excitement that he doled out too sparingly.

"Does that please you, *cherie*?" he rasped. "Do you want more?"

"Yes . . . bother it all, yes."

Pure satisfaction filled his face as he stroked her more firmly, satisfying her cravings only to raise them higher with the next stroke. Her fingers still lay in his hair, and she flexed them with every caress, wondering if she might die if he stopped.

"Heavens," she murmured, "that's . . . oh, Morgan . . . yes, like that . . ."

"God, you're so warm, so wet for me. My sweet, wanton angel . . ."

Her eyes had drifted closed, but she could hear his pleasure thrumming in his voice. And she felt it beneath her bottom, for her mews of satisfaction made the bulge in his breeches thicken, until she wondered if he might burst right out of them.

"*Bon Dieu*, but you feel good, inside and out," he said hoarsely.

Inside?

That's when she realized that his finger had dipped inside her. Her eyes sprang open. "Morgan!" she cried, grabbing for his wrist. "You can't . . . that's not . . ."

"Shhh, angel, I won't hurt you, I promise. It's just my finger. To please you. Like this." He thrust deeply inside her, wringing a startled cry from her lips.

Then he bent to kiss her hungrily, taking her mouth with violent stabs of his tongue, like the plundering beast that he was. In some hazy, distant part of her brain, she wondered if this wasn't against the rules—a kiss and a caress at the same time. Yet she couldn't bring herself to protest.

Nor did she protest when he trailed his open mouth down her neck to her breasts and began sucking her again, teasing and tormenting her on every front. His hot breath made her skin hum and her heart flutter wildly. Between her legs, she felt tight and eager and needy. "More . . ." she whispered, arching into his hand. "Oh, Morgan . . ."

"Have I answered enough questions for you?" he growled against her breast.

"Yes. No. I-I don't know . . ." Her mind was completely blank. For the life of her, she couldn't remember what the questions had been all about.

"Either ask them while I touch you or don't ask at all. Just don't make me stop."

"I . . . can't . . . think . . ."

"Good. Neither can I. Oh, *cherie*, you feel like heaven." With one swift tug, he bared her other breast, but any feeble protest vanished in the hot, swirling pleasure of his mouth and his hands on her. God forgive her, but she couldn't stop him, didn't want to stop him. Only Morgan seemed to rouse that Doggett blood of hers, and now that it was kicking up again, she'd lost any will to fight it.

Especially while his finger . . . no, two fingers now . . . drove urgently inside her, exciting her, making her yearn for . . . oh, she didn't know what. But all the restless energy he'd provoked in her since she'd met him seemed to bunch into one pulsing need centered beneath his thrusting fingers. It built and built until suddenly it arced inside her, making her cry out and clutch him tightly to her breast.

For a moment, she glimpsed a heaven that only he seemed able to give her. Then as the vivid pleasure subsided to a dull throbbing, his fingers stilled inside her.

She fell limply against his shoulder, still gasping. "Oh . . . good Lord . . . Morgan, what did you do to me?"

He tore his mouth from her breast to press tender kisses up the arch of her throat. "Gave you pleasure, that's all."

"Why?"

"Because I wanted to. You were wrong before, you know."

"A-About what?"

"I wasn't touching you only to distract you. It might have started out that way, but—" He dusted soft kisses to her

cheek, her ear, her jaw. "Do you know how long I've wanted
to do this, *ma belle ange*? How often I've imagined stripping
you down to nothing, laying you down on my bed, and then
tasting and fondling every sweet inch of you until you were
rapt and eager for me?"

He'd thought of her? Dreamed of her? The way she'd
dreamed of him?

Despite all her cautions, a little thrill coursed through her.
"I've imagined touching you, too," she admitted as she lifted
her hand to stroke his smoothly shaven cheek.

He drew back to stare at her, but there was no smugness in
his look, no cockiness now. "Have you really?"

Something about the disbelief in his face, the sheer yearning made her ache to reassure him. "Yes. Especially that day
in the street when you—" Her eyes trailed shyly down to his
chest. "When you weren't exactly . . . um . . . dressed properly." She ran her hands over his waistcoat. "And I could see
your chest showing through your shirt."

Swiftly he unbuttoned his waistcoat, then took her hands
and pressed them to his chest. She could feel his heart race
beneath the fine lawn.

He dragged in a breath. "I'd take every stitch of my
clothing off just for the pleasure of having your hands on
me, but I don't know if I'd ever get my cravat tied right
again." He smiled faintly. "Not with you watching me, making me insane."

She wished he'd stop saying such delicious things. They
roused her Doggett blood to even keener heights, tempting
her to be naughty. Like now, when she splayed her fingers
over his chest, eager for any chance to stroke his muscles,
even if it was through a shirt. "Do I really make you insane?"

"*Sacrebleu,* yes." He shifted her forward on his lap until she
was balanced on his knees, then grabbed her hand, flattening it
against the bulge in his breeches. "Don't ever accuse me again

of not desiring you. I can't sleep for desiring you, and when I finally do nod off it's to dreams of you touching me like this."

He rubbed her hand over him, and a hot, predatory look etched his features. "Oh, God, if only you'd be willing to—" He paused. "Tell me, angel, do you know how a man and woman make love?"

Her cheeks flamed. "Yes, of course."

How could she work in Spitalfields and not know? She'd heard the act described in the coarsest detail, seen it painted on the walls of the brothels where some of her children's mothers lived, and even happened upon people engaged in it.

But she'd never imagined she might actually want to do it.

"Then you know that as long as this"—he pressed the bulge into her palm—"is beneath your hand, I can't be putting it inside you, can I?"

She nodded slowly, wondering what he was leading up to.

"As long as it stays in your hand, you remain chaste."

"So I've been told." She'd gone way beyond blushing to outright mortification. She couldn't believe they were having this outrageous conversation.

Suddenly his hand left hers to fumble with his breeches buttons. "Don't be alarmed, Clara. All I want is for you to touch my bare flesh with your sweet fingers."

The fall of his breeches now gaped open. Grabbing her hand, he slid it inside and beneath his drawers, then closed it around his hot, iron-rigid length. "This is what I'd like you to caress, angel. Only for a bit. The way I caressed you."

For a moment, she was too stunned to react.

"Does that shock you?" he asked.

What a question. "Certainly not," she said dryly. "I touch men's privates all the time. Such behavior is quite the rage among women of my set."

He managed a smile. "Then touch me, too."

When she saw the intense longing in his face, she couldn't bring herself to deny him what he wanted. Besides, she was curious. "Very well, if you insist." Tentatively, she explored him.

He sucked in a harsh breath, his eyes drifting closed. "If you never let me near you again," he choked out, "thank you for giving me this."

"Why would I never let you near me again?"

He gave a wry chuckle. "Because you're stubborn. Because you hate me."

He sat there with his eyes closed and his breeches open, showing more vulnerability than she'd ever seen in a man, and her heart melted.

"I don't hate you. If I hated you, why would I do this . . . this scandalous thing?"

He opened his eyes. Though glazed with need, they showed every portion of his uncertainty. "You ought to hate me."

"I know. I've tried, but I just can't." She dropped her gaze, embarrassed. "I-I think I'm doing this wrong. Show me how to give you the same pleasure you gave me."

"You're not doing it wrong, but if you really want to please me . . ."

He showed her how to caress him, with long, tight pulls that made him groan every bit as much as she'd groaned when he stroked inside her. Arousing him gave her a heady sense of power. It was so forbidden, so very beyond what was acceptable for a woman of her station that it spiked her own excitement to new heights.

And piqued her curiosity. "Doesn't it hurt? I mean, to have me grab you like this?"

With a weak laugh, he leaned forward to nip at her ear. "It drives me absolutely mad. Which is why we must . . . stop soon. Before I embarrass myself."

"You? Embarrassed?" she teased. "Never!"

"You'd be surprised . . . oh, angel, that's too much . . . damn, you have to stop."

Delighted to have this little bit of feminine control, she whispered, "Are you sure?" as she gave him a long, firm tug.

"Yes," he growled, forcing her hand out of his breeches. For a moment, he sat there, breathing hard, as if trying to get his bearings. Then he cast her a regretful smile. "This isn't the place or the time, I'm afraid."

She arched an eyebrow. "I tried to tell you that before."

"Aren't you glad I didn't listen?"

He drew up her bodice, but then kissed her again, hot and deep.

They sat kissing a while longer, both loath to leave their private little sanctuary.

Then the ornate clock atop the mantle chimed, and she bolted upright. "Good Lord, look at the time! Aunt Verity will be frantic with worry, wondering where I am!" Sliding off his lap, she fumbled to restore her clothing.

He watched her with a hooded gaze as he stood to refasten his breeches buttons, then went to work on his waistcoat. "Clara, we should talk."

She cast him an uncertain glance. "Yes, we should. You didn't answer all my questions."

"I didn't mean about that."

"Oh." She dropped her head to concentrate on her clothing. Now that he wasn't holding her, she felt much more self-conscious. And not quite sure that she *wanted* to talk. She didn't want to spoil what had been a wonderful interlude. One that she shouldn't let happen again.

So instead she focused on something else. "I still want my questions answered about you and Ravenswood and the shop."

"None of that has anything to do with you, so stay out of it."

She lifted her gaze to his. "I can't. Something is going on, and I want to know what it is." When he only glowered at her, she swished her hips and smiled teasingly. "If you'll answer more questions later, I might even let you touch my bottom."

Frustrated desire and the tiniest bit of humor flickered in his face. "Don't tempt me. As it is, you'd best be grateful we're in a somewhat public place, *ma belle ange*. Otherwise, we wouldn't have stopped with touching and kissing."

There went that silly quivering in her belly again. "Rather sure of yourself, aren't you?"

"I recognize when a woman is ripe for seduction, yes."

When his gaze trailed knowingly over her wrinkled bodice and rumpled skirts, her mouth went dry. He was right, curse him. Deep in some naughty part of her, she'd wanted him to seduce her. She still did.

The realization stunned her. She hadn't known how badly she'd craved such intimacy with a man until she'd found it with the wrong one.

Or was he the wrong one? She began to wonder. How many unscrupulous scoundrels would have given her pleasure without taking their own? And restrained themselves from taking advantage when they had a woman perfectly willing to let them?

For that matter, how many fences would have given a lady's footman lessons in how to guard her? Or taken in a pickpocket, then not availed themselves of his talents? If Samuel was to be believed, that was exactly what Morgan had done.

She began to think that Samuel *could* be believed. Until now, she'd had no trouble considering Morgan's strange actions as maneuvers calculated to further his criminal aims. But not after tonight. Not after he'd shown such astonishingly unexpected consideration for her virtue. That was why she must have her answers.

She tore her gaze from his and headed for the door. "I must go. But after the ball, I'll expect a full accounting from you, even if I must camp outside your shop to get it."

"Don't go to the shop tonight, Clara. If you want to talk, come by tomorrow."

"Why?"

"For once in your life, do as I say without asking a million questions, all right?"

"Fine. I suppose it can wait until tomorrow." In a pig's eye. If he didn't want her there tonight, it was because he was hiding something, so she would definitely be there to find out what it was.

Unlocking the door, she slipped out into the hall, grateful beyond words that no one lingered there just now. As she headed back into the ballroom, she started to shake, a delayed reaction to the magnificent experience she'd just had in Morgan's arms.

He was driving her mad, layering enigma upon enigma until she swam in a pool of questions. Well, if he thought she'd keep swimming without answers, he was mad.

Her thoughts so absorbed her that she scarcely noticed where she was going when she emerged from the passageway. So in her haste to find her aunt, she nearly barreled into a gentleman.

"Whoa there, madam," said a rich, familiar voice as a man's hand shot out to steady her.

Her gaze rose to the man's face, and she started. "Morgan! But how did you—"

He laughed. "No, not Morgan. I'm his twin brother, Templemore."

Twin? Belatedly she realized that this man was dressed differently and his hair was shorter, more evenly cut.

"I-I didn't know Morgan had a twin," she stammered. "I didn't even know he had a brother."

Just then, a young woman approached. "Lady Clara! It's so good to see you."

Embarrassed and confused, Clara fumbled for a name. "Yes, it's good to see you, too."

"You probably don't remember me," the woman said, laughing. "I was Lady Juliet, now Lady Templemore." She tucked her hand in the bend of the gentleman's proffered arm. "This is my husband."

Lord Templemore? Oh, heavens, now she remembered who they were.

Two things registered at once. One, Morgan had been hiding more than she'd suspected. And two, he was the brother of a baron.

Her pool of questions instantly deepened into a sea.

Chapter 13

With Step so majestic the *Snail* did advance,
And promis'd the Gazers a Minuet to dance.
The Butterfly's Ball, and the
Grasshopper's Feast, *William Roscoe*

Morgan waited in the library a few minutes after Clara
left, trying to calm the raging erection in his skintight
breeches before he made a spectacle of himself in Merrington's ballroom.

But it was difficult when he kept playing over and over
how sweet it had felt to have Clara moan with pleasure in his
arms, accept his kisses eagerly, grow silky wet beneath his
fingers. And then to have her admit she wanted to touch him,
too! He'd thought he would explode when she put her hot little hand inside his breeches to stroke him, all shy curiosity
and womanly temptation.

He wiped sweat from his brow. *Bon Dieu*, if that was what
she could do to him when her surroundings kept her from ac-

tually bringing him to release, only think what she'd do to him at leisure in his bed. Which is where she'd end up if he wasn't careful.

And what a temptation. She wanted him, too. So why not let her have what they both wanted? Ah, to be able to touch her without restraint . . . to part those long, luscious legs and bury himself inside her soft, waiting flesh—

He swore as his cock stiffened again. At this rate he'd never get out of here. She was driving him mad. He had to stop thinking of her, that's all.

No, what he had to do was remind himself of the havoc she'd wreak on his plans if he followed his prick. She was already badgering him with endless questions. If he involved himself with her, there was no telling how far she'd go in her quest for the truth or what she'd do once she learned it.

Besides, he wasn't what she truly wanted. If they shared a bed, nothing could come of it except ruin for her. Unless he married her, of course, which he couldn't do. Even if he was ready to marry—and he wasn't—why would a marquess's daughter want to be stuck with a rascal like him? What possible advantage could she find in having a naval captain sail in and out of her life from time to time?

That sobering thought thoroughly dampened his ardor, and a few moments later, now depressed in both body and heart, he left the cozy library.

His business with Ravenswood was done, so he might as well leave the ball. He couldn't stand by and watch Clara dance with a series of eligible gentlemen, all of whom would make her better companions than he would.

But he hadn't counted on running into her right outside the passageway. Nor, worse yet, his brother and sister-in-law.

Panic surged in him as he hurried up in time to hear Juliet say, "So Lord Ravenswood tells us that Morgan has been helping you at your home for pickpockets."

"Helping me?" Clara said, clearly bewildered.

Morgan stepped up and took her arm, squeezing it to beg her indulgence. "Lady Clara doesn't like to think of it as 'helping.' She prides herself on not needing any help from a ne'er-do-well like me. But I hope I'm offering some small service by staying on the premises at night."

The gaze Clara leveled on him was coolly curious. He tried to ask for her silence with his eyes, but he feared that she would call him an out-and-out liar.

Instead, she smiled. "Oh, yes, you're offering all sorts of helpful services. I wonder what possessed you to do so?"

Weak with gratitude, he swept his fingers down to her hand, then lifted it for his kiss. "That should be obvious, my dear Lady Clara."

As color suffused Clara's face, he cast a sidelong glance to find his sister-in-law beaming. His brother, however, was looking past them to the passageway. Confound it, Sebastian probably had seen them both come out.

Very well. Morgan might as well maintain the illusion that he was courting Clara.

An illusion that Clara seemed less eager to maintain, for she slipped her hand quickly from his. "We both know that if not for Lord Ravenswood, you wouldn't be 'helping' me at the Home at all, Captain Pryce."

"Why is she calling you Captain Pryce?" Sebastian broke in.

Damn, damn, damn, damn, damn.

Clara's eyes narrowed. "I beg your pardon, Lord Templemore. Your brother led me to believe that he was a naval captain."

"He was," Juliet put in, clearly anxious to smooth away any misunderstandings. "He is. It's just that he hasn't used that name in some time. His real name is Blakely."

His family was unwittingly digging a hole for him that grew deeper by the moment. Morgan cast his brother a rueful smile. "I'm afraid that when Ravenswood introduced me to Lady Clara, he . . . er . . . neglected to use my proper name. He's so used to calling me Captain Pryce from the old days."

"Ah, yes, the old days," Sebastian said dryly. "When you spied for him and got yourself into trouble."

"Why, Captain Pryce—" Clara began, then caught herself. "I mean, Captain Blakely, you never told me about this fascinating previous life. I'm surprised you could settle for the dullness of my institution after being a spy. You must tell me all about your exploits. Here I was led to believe you were only a naval captain fallen on hard times—"

"What hard times?" Sebastian broke in, outraged. "Morgan, what the devil did Ravenswood tell Lady Clara anyway? What is he up to?"

"You can ask him yourself, dearest," Juliet interjected, "for here he comes now."

With a groan, Morgan turned to find Ravenswood fast approaching. To all outward appearances, the man was utterly unperturbed by the sight of the little group standing there, but Morgan knew him well enough to read alarm in his quickened pace.

It served the arse right for having this meeting take place at a public ball. Then again, neither of them had expected Clara to show up.

"What a nice surprise," Ravenswood boomed as he met them. "How delightful to see four of my favorite people conversing together."

Morgan shot him a dark glance. Ravenswood ignored it.

"Lady Clara tells me you've been spreading lies about my family," Sebastian snapped.

Ravenswood managed to look unconcerned. "Really?"

Morgan hastened to explain. "My brother is upset because you introduced me to her as Captain Pryce and implied I had no income of my own."

"I must apologize, Lady Clara," Ravenswood said smoothly. "I shouldn't have let you believe that my friend was strapped for funds, but I thought you'd be less willing to let him stay in your Home otherwise. I know how you hate to feel obligated. I figured a little white lie about how he needed a place to live would ease your mind about his presence. Since you're so kindhearted, I knew you couldn't resist helping him. And me."

His mute appeal was unmistakable. Morgan stood there marveling at Ravenswood's sheer audacity. And his quick thinking.

Clara didn't look quite so impressed. "Lord Ravenswood, you ought to be ashamed of yourself—"

"Indeed I should," Ravenswood broke in expertly. "I'd completely forgotten that this dance was ours, my lady." He held out his arm. "If you would do me the honor?"

She hesitated but apparently couldn't pass up the chance to interrogate his lordship. "Yes, I'd be delighted. Good of you to finally remember."

As soon as Ravenswood and Clara were gone, Morgan let out a breath and turned to Juliet and Sebastian. How much of that claptrap had they believed, anyway? Judging from Juliet's happy smile, she'd believed every word. But Sebastian looked a little less trusting. He knew Ravenswood too well.

"So you've got a tidy setup down there at Lady Clara's Home, have you?" Sebastian asked with obvious suspicion.

"What's wrong, *mon frère*?" Morgan said, going on the offensive. "Can't you believe that I would come to the rescue of a lady as worthy as Clara Stanbourne?"

"No one is questioning her worthiness," Juliet put in, her

little matchmaker's heart clearly thumping with glee. "Or your gallantry. You always have been gallant to ladies. But you're not fooling me—this is clearly more than mere gallantry."

"Clearly," Sebastian echoed, though his thoughts were obviously taking a different turn from his wife's.

"Now tell the truth, Morgan," Juliet went on. "Are you in love with her?"

"Yes, brother of mine," Sebastian repeated, eyes gleaming, "are you in love?"

Morgan groaned. But it was either be "in love" with Clara or tell his brother the truth. If he claimed the former, Juliet would badger him for details. If he did the latter, his brother would strangle him.

He pasted a smile to his face. "Looks like you've found me out, Juliet."

And it looked like it was going to be a damned long night.

Almost as soon as Clara and Lord Ravenswood left, she spotted her aunt and gave her a nod from across the room. Aunt Verity lit up immediately to see her niece being led to the floor by the very eligible Lord Ravenswood. After flashing Clara a blazing smile of approval, she returned to her conversation with the other ladies.

But Clara wasn't terribly surprised when Lord Ravenswood took a detour and bypassed the dance floor entirely. Or when he asked to speak to her in private and then ushered her out through the cut crystal doors onto the marble balcony.

It didn't matter to her where he answered her questions, as long as he answered them. Because somewhere during that bizarre conversation with the Templemores, she'd remembered who Morgan was. The fellow named Blakely who'd been aboard that pirate ship when Lord Winthrop's ship was attacked.

"You have a great deal of explaining to do, Lord Ravenswood," she said as soon as they were alone.

"I must thank you for your indulgence a few moments ago. My friend is in a sticky situation with his family, and you were gracious enough to save him from their wrath."

"I don't care about his cursed family. I want to know why your friend is really in Spitalfields. Why he's acting as a fence for stolen goods."

He feigned surprise. "Captain Blakely? A fence? Surely you jest. He told me he was staying at your Home to protect you."

"Nice try. But the Templemores already told me that *you* were supposedly the one to introduce Captain Blakely to me. You maintained the fiction, too. Which came as quite a surprise, since we both know you never introduced me to anyone. So find another lie."

His lordship strolled to the rail and leaned on it. "I was merely trying to help my friend by supporting his tale. I had no idea he was involved in anything illegal."

"Oh, stuff and nonsense!" She strode up to him. "I saw you and Captain Blakely conferring in Merrington's library just now."

She'd finally managed to startle him. His gaze shot to her in alarm. "You did?"

"Yes. And I know you told him that I reported him to the magistrate. Why would you do such a thing?"

A sudden warning gleamed in his eyes. "Lady Clara, you're dabbling in matters beyond your purview. I suggest you go on about your business at your little Home and leave matters of this sort to me and my office."

It was bad enough that Lord Winthrop referred to it as her "little Home," but to have this duplicitous scoundrel do it was too much.

"You and your office seem to be consorting with the enemy." Her eyes narrowed. "Perhaps I should speak to the Home Secretary about this. I'm sure he'd be interested to hear how you are covering up the activities of a known fence."

"Now see here—"

"If that's indeed what you're doing. I suppose a good spy could come in handy in Spitalfields, too."

He seemed to be restraining his temper, but only with great difficulty. "My lady," he said after a moment, "the difficulties of running your Home have clearly taxed your strength, or else you'd never be indulging in such wild fantasies about me and my friends. But in the interests of lightening your load so that you aren't tempted to . . . er . . . speak of these fantasies to unwitting strangers, I'm willing to offer you a donation. I'm sure you'd find a thousand pounds useful for your children."

Good Lord, now he was resorting to bribery. But this must be enormously important if he'd offer her so high a sum for her silence. The trouble was, what did he want her to keep silent about? An illegal web of such insidious breadth that it involved even the Home Office? Or an official endeavor?

And if it was the latter, why didn't he simply say so?

"I don't respond well to bribery, sir."

"Bribery? Who said anything about bribery?"

"Come now, Lord Ravenswood, I know a bribe when I hear one. But as it happens, I've just come into a rather large fortune, so I don't need your thousand pounds. If you want my silence, you'll have to offer me something I want more than money. Like the truth."

Though his eyes glittered dangerously, he twisted around to lean against the rail with apparent nonchalance. "Why do you ask *me* for the truth? Why not ask Captain Blakely, since it is his activities that alarm you?"

"I've already tried that. But as you probably already know, he refuses to answer."

"A pity. Because you won't get anything from me. I don't make a practice of revealing to civilians the particulars about matters that are none of their concern."

"Civilians? You mean this is an activity sanctioned by the Home Office?"

He scowled at her. "I mean to say it's none of your business. And before you threaten again to go to the Home Secretary, I should point out that any more of your interference could easily result in trouble for you. All I need do is speak to the magistrate about your precious institution. If Mr. Hornbuckle is told that some illegal activity is going on there, he will make your life hell, evidence or no. Especially if I ask him to."

"You wouldn't dare!"

"I'd dare a great deal to make you stop being an annoyance, I assure you. And if you'll tell me what I can offer you to accomplish that amazing feat—other than answers I will not give—I'll do my best to oblige you."

They stood a moment in hostile silence. Lord Ravenswood wasn't a man she'd ever felt easy with anyway, but at the moment, she could cheerfully wring his neck. How strange that she felt much more comfortable with a fence than with this well-placed lord of the realm.

If Morgan really was a fence.

Clearly Ravenswood wouldn't tell her. She'd be better off coaxing Morgan to do so. At least he wasn't a haughty official of the government. "All right, if you won't tell me what's going on, at least enlighten me about Captain Blakely himself."

He eyed her warily. "Why?"

"Because I might be persuaded to keep silent about his present activities if you can convince me that he is an honorable man."

He hesitated, then said, "All right. What do you want to know?"

"I remember hearing last year that he spent time aboard a pirate ship. Is that true?"

"Yes."

"That doesn't strike me as the act of an honorable man."

Ravenswood sighed. "He wasn't there by choice. When the pirates met up with him, he'd been marooned on an island for two years by a group of smugglers he'd been spying on. The Pirate Lord and his crew rescued him. He remained with them a few months before he could gain his freedom."

"And what exactly did he do to gain his freedom?" she said dryly.

Ravenswood shrugged. "Showed them how to make the best use of the island. Kept out of their way. Taught them a thing or two about sailing."

"No slicing people in half for their valuables?" she asked, only half joking.

He shot her a penetrating look. "Does Captain Blakely strike you as the sort of man to do such a thing?"

She shifted her gaze to the lantern-lit gardens. "No."

"Then perhaps you should trust your instincts."

"I do. And they're telling me that you and Morgan are up to something."

" 'Morgan'?"

Too late she realized she'd used his Christian name. "I-I meant to say 'Captain Blakely.' "

"No, you didn't. Take care, Lady Clara. Our mutual friend is not the sort of man to . . . well . . ."

"Don't worry, my lord. I know Morgan isn't an appropriate suitor for me, if that's what you're trying to say."

He regarded her speculatively. "Actually, I didn't think you'd gone so far as to think of him in that regard. Yet."

She blushed, cursing herself for having given so much away. "It was a joke, that's all. What *were* you trying to tell me?"

"That he's not like other men you've known."

A small smile touched her lips. "Which 'other men' do you mean? Those in Spitalfields? Or men like my father and Lord Winthrop and you?"

"Forgive me, I tend to forget that you don't lead quite the sheltered life of other ladies. I meant the latter, of course. Despite Morgan's family connections, he isn't quite as civilized as he can seem."

That was certainly an understatement. "I've figured that out for myself, thank you very much."

"Please don't mistake my meaning. I have enormous respect for him. But he doesn't play by the same rules as the rest of us."

"And you assume that I do? How odd."

He broke into a smile. "I see your point. I only meant to warn you in case your discovery of his true station has given you the wrong impression. Made you think more . . . how shall I put this . . . *fondly* of him."

"Don't worry about me. I can . . . how shall I put this . . . *handle* Captain Blakely."

He chuckled. "Funny, he said the same thing about you when he first met you. But I think he's revised his opinion since then."

She laughed. "I do believe he has."

They fell into a more companionable silence this time. At last he pushed away from the rail. "So have we reached an agreement, Lady Clara? You will mind your own business in this matter?"

No, she would not. But it didn't seem particularly wise to tell him that. "I'll do my best," she said blithely.

"For some reason, I don't find that reassuring," he muttered.

But he let her lead the conversation to his new groom, one of her former charges. By the time they returned to the ballroom, he had her laughing about his stable-master's adventures training the pickpocket to work with horses. She was still laughing when Morgan encountered them coming in.

He, however, was not laughing.

Chapter 14

With Carefulness watch
Each moment that flies,
To keep Peace at Home,
And ward off Surprize.
A Little pretty pocket-book, *John Newbery*

Morgan couldn't believe it—Clara and Ravenswood coming in together from the balcony so chummy, looking as if they'd been friends all their lives.

Which they probably had. The thought provoked an unfamiliar tightness in his gut. "You two seem to be enjoying yourselves. I thought you'd gone off to dance."

"We never made it there," Ravenswood said calmly.

"That became readily apparent when I went looking for you." Stepping up to Clara, Morgan laid his hand possessively in the small of her back. "I hope you won't mind if I carry her off for a dance myself."

Ravenswood looked suddenly amused. "I rather think that's up to Lady Clara, don't you?"

"Dance with me, Clara," Morgan said curtly.

To his vast annoyance, she laughed. "Is that a request or a command, Captain?"

"Whichever you prefer, *ma belle ange*."

Curiosity flickered in Ravenswood's eyes at the endearment, but he merely tipped his head toward Clara. "I can see when I'm not wanted. Thank you for the discussion, my lady. It was most . . . enlightening."

"Yes, it was, wasn't it?" She held her hand out to Ravenswood. He took it, but instead of pressing it as was usual, he lifted it to his lips to kiss it. Then with a smile at Morgan, he left.

A fierce urge to throttle his friend seized Morgan, and he didn't know how to handle it. *Bon Dieu*, what had come over him this evening? "So are you dancing with me or not, Clara?" he asked, hating how peevish he sounded, like a besotted idiot.

She faced him, eyes twinkling. "I do believe I shall, since Lord Ravenswood deprived me of the dance I apparently promised to him."

With a scowl, he led her to the floor for the waltz. "You seemed to be having a grand time with Ravenswood."

"I was. He's quite an interesting gentleman."

He gritted his teeth. He could easily see how a woman like Clara would find the viscount "interesting" . . . and titled and rich and very eligible. Everything that Morgan was not.

Taking her in his arms, he held her closer than was proper, feeling some primitive male urge to stake his claim on her, to remind her that she was *his*. Even though she wasn't, not in any real sense of the word. Even though she never could be.

Yet she didn't seem to mind his possessive hold. She danced easily with him, as light-footed and blithe as any winged angel. Her grace and self-assurance were that of a woman who knew her own mind, yet she yielded in his arms with all the sweetness she'd shown in the library. It was enough to make a man trip over his own feet.

And her scent . . . oh, God, the scent of jasmine in her hair made him want to howl at the moon, to carry her out into Merrington's gardens and ravish her like the devil he was. He settled for stroking her satin-covered back, holding her close, running his thumb along her ribs where he held her at the waist.

Still, he couldn't get Ravenswood out of his mind. "How is it that when you're badgering *me* for answers, you rage and accuse and torment, but with Lord Ravenswood you're the soul of amiability?"

Her startled gaze shot to him. "What makes you think I am?"

"The two of you were all smiles just now, as comfortable as two old friends."

"We've known each other for some time, you know. It's not as if we're strangers." An impish light crossed her face. "Not the way you and I are, in any case."

"What's that supposed to mean?"

"When were you planning to tell me that you're the Honorable Captain Morgan Blakely—brother to one baron, son to another, a notorious spy, and Lord knows what else?"

He didn't know why, but it bothered him that she was so interested in his family connections. "Does it make a difference to you who I really am?"

"It makes a difference that I didn't know. That you lied to me about your name and Geneva and the rest of it. That you won't even tell me *why* you lied to me."

The hint of hurt in her voice tore at him more effectively than the actual words. "I didn't lie. Not really. I truly did go by the name of Morgan Pryce when I served in the navy. Most naval officers still know me by that name."

"But why would you take a different name—"

"It's a long story, Clara, too much to go into now."

"Give me the short version," she said tersely. "Or is that something else you and Ravenswood feel that I cannot know?"

He sighed but could think of no reason not to tell her. "My brother and I were raised apart. Shortly after Sebastian and I were born, my mother left my father and took me with her to Geneva. She gave me her maiden name for a surname. She summoned my uncle Llewelyn when she was dying, and Uncle Lew came and fetched me. I was thirteen. Sebastian didn't know about me, and my uncle and the baron urged me to keep the secret to make matters less . . . complicated."

"Less complicated for whom?" she asked, so softly that he almost didn't hear her above the orchestra.

The sympathy in her face caught him by surprise. He squeezed her hand. "I didn't mind, *cherie.* I understood. The baron and my uncle were concerned about claims to the title. Although Mother did assure them that Sebastian was the eldest, they thought it best to keep us apart until he inherited. They put me in school, and when I was of age they used their influence to start me as a midshipman in the navy, where I was presented as the baron's ward. They took good care of me. I have nothing to reproach them for."

"Except denying you the company of your brother."

He glanced away. She read him so well it frightened him. "I have him now, and that's all that matters. After the baron died, I saw no reason to keep the secret, and I sought Sebastian out. When he knew the truth, he insisted that I take my place with the family and use my birth name. That's how I started out as Morgan Pryce and ended up Morgan Blakely."

His gaze swung back to her. "So you see, I really didn't lie. I just . . . left some things out."

She lifted an eyebrow. "Indeed you did. Like the fact that you used to be a spy. That you spent time with pirates. That—"

"Ravenswood told you about the pirates?"

"Only because I asked. But he wouldn't tell me much of anything else."

He tightened his hand on her waist. "Yet you were out there with him a long time."

A teasing grin played over her lips. "I suppose I was."

He didn't like this new coyness of hers. He hated it almost as much as the tightness in his gut that he was just beginning to recognize as jealousy.

Jealousy, for God's sake! He'd never felt such a thing in his life. "What did you talk about, the two of you, while you were out on the balcony?"

She tossed back her head. "That's between me and Lord Ravenswood, isn't it?"

"Then I'll just ask him myself," he bit out.

"What makes you think he'll tell you?"

"Because he has nothing to hide from me." When she averted her gaze, he pulled her closer. "Or does he? He didn't try to . . . kiss you or anything, did he?"

Her gaze shot back to him, full of amusement. "Why would you think that?"

"That's generally why men bring women out onto balconies at these affairs." When she remained stubbornly silent, he snapped, "Well? Did he?"

"Did he what?"

"Try to kiss you, confound it!"

All the mischief drained from her face, and she eyed him with deep solemnity. "Would you mind if he did?"

He thought about lying, but there seemed no point to that.

"The truth is, I would mind very much. Though I'm damned if I know why."

That seemed to please her. "If it makes you feel any better, Lord Ravenswood didn't attempt anything. Just because you try to kiss me whenever we're alone doesn't mean *everyone* does, you know."

"Then they're all either blind or fools or both."

He regretted his honesty instantly. Her tender, hopeful smile made him want to cut loose and run, abandon her right here on the floor. Before she wrapped her web of soft, womanly caring tight about him and he *couldn't* run.

Who was he fooling? She already had that web wrapped tight. All he could think of was getting her alone so he could kiss her again, so he could taste her and touch her. Madness, sheer madness.

Clara was experiencing her own sort of madness, thanks to Morgan's sweet words. They made her feel all hot and bothered, and this intimate waltz didn't help.

Until now, she'd never understood the outcry against the waltz when it first appeared in London. There had seemed nothing "shameful" or "outrageous" or "destructive to the moral fiber of decent people" to her.

But then she'd never waltzed with a man she cared for, a man who'd kissed her and caressed her in her most private places. That changed every movement into an erotic and sensual step toward seduction. The brush of his thigh against her skirts, the feel of his powerful hand guiding her at the waist, the intimate clasp of their hands . . . all of it, when combined with the breathless pace of the dance, made her weak in the knees.

And being weak in the knees was a decided impediment to dancing. As was the close way Morgan held her, as if afraid she might bolt.

Bolting was the last thing on her mind. She should use this opportunity to question him further, yet she'd lost the heart for it. When she was with Morgan, she forgot she had to be safe and responsible and moral. She forgot about everything but the possibilities he showed her, the freedom from her self-imposed prison that he offered.

Besides, it was too late for questions now. The waltz was ending, and Morgan was leading her off the floor. With a sudden panic, she saw her aunt squinting at them from a short distance away, as if trying to make out Clara's companion. Lord Winthrop stood at her aunt's side, and after a short conference with her, left her to elbow his way through the crowd toward Clara and Morgan.

Just what she did not need—another dance with Lord Boring. Hadn't she run him off for good? Heavens, what did it take to discourage the man?

Lord Winthrop reached them as they cleared the floor, but his attention was on Morgan, not her. "So it *is* you. I thought that it was. I doubted it was your devil of a brother—he would never hold a lady so improperly in public."

Too late Clara remembered that Morgan and Lord Winthrop had a rather unpleasant history together. She hastened to smooth things over. "Why, Lord Winthrop, I wondered where you'd gone off to. I was hoping you might fetch me some—"

"Lady Clara, I know you're unaware of this scoundrel's true character," Lord Winthrop broke in, full of pompous righteousness. His eyes shot daggers at Morgan. "But you should take care who your companions are. That's all I'm saying."

"Don't leave us in suspense," Morgan said lazily. "Go on, Winthrop. Enumerate for her ladyship all the details of my poor character." He paused, and when Lord Winthrop merely stared at him, tight-lipped, he added, "I forgot—you can't do that, can you? I seem to recall your signing a piece of paper . . . what was it . . . a stipulation of some kind? That in exchange for a sum of money far larger than what was taken from you, you'd keep quiet about certain affairs?"

So *that* was why Lord Winthrop had refused to speak of his attack by the pirates. He'd been paid off.

"Perhaps we should ask my brother," Morgan went on. "I'm sure he remembers."

"No doubt he does," Lord Winthrop said viciously, "since the money came out of *his* pocket. It could hardly come out of yours, could it?"

Clara sucked in a breath. Lord Winthrop trod dangerous ground now. She could feel the muscles of Morgan's forearm tense up beneath her hand, could almost smell his anger.

Yet when he spoke, he managed to sound cooler than the aristocratic Winthrop. "Only because he's the one who cares about public opinion, and I don't give a damn. So if you want to again be free to rail against me in society, by all means return my brother's money to him. Just don't be surprised if you succeed only in making yourself look foolish."

That didn't appear to sit well with the tightfisted Lord Winthrop. "I . . . er . . . wasn't trying to breach the terms of our contract, sir. I was merely pointing out to Lady Clara that a man of your history is by no means an appropriate dance partner for her."

"And you'd be a better one?" Morgan slid his own hand over to cover hers, stroking it casually as if to taunt the stuffy earl. "There must be a few ladies somewhere who'd prefer the sedate pace of a man your age, but I doubt Lady Clara is one of them."

Lord Winthrop looked as if his eyes might pop right out of his head. He was gathering a head of steam, and if she didn't do something, it would blow. So she gauged whom it was more important to placate and decided Morgan could take care of himself.

Releasing his arm, she moved to Lord Winthrop's side and said swiftly, "Didn't you ask me for this dance, my lord?"

He blinked at her. "I beg your pardon?"

"A dance. I believe I promised this dance to you."

"Why . . . why, yes. You did indeed, Lady Clara." Looking down his nose at Morgan, Lord Winthrop held out his arm to her with a triumphant smile. "And I am most happy to show you how a *gentleman* dances."

She cast Morgan an imploring look. "Thank you for the waltz, Captain Blakely. It was very enjoyable."

Fire sparked in Morgan's eyes, but he merely tipped his head with apparent nonchalance. "You're welcome, my lady. You know I'm always pleased to satisfy any whim of yours."

She turned hastily to Lord Winthrop. "The music is beginning. Shall we go?"

"If you wish, my dear." As Lord Winthrop led her away, she glanced back at Morgan. He watched them with a brooding expression that boded ill for Lord Winthrop. And perhaps her as well.

But she couldn't just stand by and watch them come to blows in a public place. That would do neither of them any good.

"How do you know that fellow?" Lord Winthrop asked, breaking into her thoughts.

"Captain Blakely and I were introduced for the first time this evening." Technically, it was true, for although she'd met Morgan Pryce, she didn't know Morgan Blakely at all. But she intended to remedy that.

Lord Boring eyed her shrewdly, as if he didn't quite believe her, though why he shouldn't was beyond her. "I caution you, my lady. He is not the sort of man with whom a lady of your standing should associate."

"Thank you for the advice, Lord Winthrop. I shall keep it in mind."

Just not in the way he meant. All these cautions against Morgan were having the perverse effect of rousing her interest in him all the more. Everyone seemed determined to paint him a black creature, yet the more she knew of him, the more she saw an entirely different Morgan. It intrigued her enormously.

"I've been thinking about what you asked of me earlier," Lord Winthrop said, as if he'd read her thoughts. "I do believe I shall come help you at your little Home after all. Your aunt seems to think you could use a man's influence with your urchins. Teach them how to respect their elders."

Stifling a groan, she silently cursed her aunt. Just what she needed—the self-important Lord Winthrop trying to take her boys in hand. Although if anything were to run him off, a day or two at the Home surely would. "Thank you, my lord. Feel free to come whenever you wish. I'm there every day." She'd wager half her new fortune that he never showed up.

The music started then. To Clara's vast relief, it was a lively reel that precluded speech. But it also made it difficult to scan the ballroom, which she did in every turn, looking for Morgan.

He'd vanished, curse him. After the dance was over and she'd excused herself to Lord Winthrop, she discovered that Morgan wasn't the only one who'd disappeared. Lord Ravenswood was nowhere to be found. And even Morgan's family seemed to have left.

When half an hour passed and she found none of them, she was forced to accept the truth. Morgan had escaped her without answering the rest of her questions.

Fine, let him evade her if he wanted. Because if she couldn't get answers here and now, she would get them, one way or the other. Even if she had to corner the wolf in his den.

* * *

Clara shivered and drew her serviceable cloak more closely about her as she hurried down Petticoat Lane to Morgan's shop. This was probably not such a good idea, coming here alone near midnight. But after she'd returned home from the ball, she hadn't been able to find Samuel anywhere, and she dared not have any of the other servants accompany her while she went snooping on such a notorious man.

It was bad enough that she'd roused suspicions at the Home an hour ago when she'd arrived and announced that she was spending the night. It wasn't something she did often. And when she did, it was usually because she'd been summoned there to deal with a sick or runaway child. It was rarely for no reason at all.

Nonetheless, one advantage to being in charge was that she could make seemingly arbitrary decisions without much comment. With any luck, the servants at the Home would merely assume that she was checking up on them.

She'd had a bit more trouble sneaking out to come down here to Morgan's shop, but she knew the Home better than almost anyone. And she had copies of all the keys.

What choice did she have, anyway? Having one of the stalwart male servants from the Home accompany her would have meant questions and protests. Two people would also be less quiet than one, so Morgan would have had fair warning of her approach. She certainly didn't want that. The success of her plan depended on surprising him in the midst of his secretive activities.

So she'd had to sneak out alone. Thankfully, the streets were fairly deserted. It was too early for residents to be leaving the taverns and gin shops, and too late for any respectable merchants to be heading home.

Besides, the Home was just a cry away—if she screamed, someone there would surely run to her rescue. And Morgan and Johnny were undoubtedly both inside the shop, and they would help her, too.

Just thinking of how Morgan had vanished after their dance made her scowl. Why, he hadn't so much as said good night! That only proved he'd been rushing down here to do something devious.

It was most vexing how he and Lord Ravenswood seemed determined to be mysterious. She'd had quite enough of their coy evasions and blatant attempts to either pay or frighten her into silence. She would learn the truth on her own, since they'd left her no alternative. If Morgan wasn't at the shop, she'd press Johnny into telling her what he knew. But somebody would give her answers if it took her all night to get them.

Still, when she approached the shop to find it completely dark, an uneasy shiver crept down her spine. She'd expected lights and activity, not this utter stillness. She peered through the dirty windows but could see nothing, not even the faint glow of a burning lamp in the back. She knocked but no one answered, and a quick check of the door showed it was locked.

How very strange. Could their dastardly activity involve something off the premises? Just to be sure, she slipped around to the alley and tried the alley door. It was locked, too, and nobody answered when she knocked. Her blood began to pound. If Morgan wasn't here, Johnny at least should be. Unless Morgan and Samuel both had lied about Johnny's lack of involvement in criminal activities.

No, she couldn't bear to think that. But where would he be otherwise? Could he simply be sleeping so deeply that he didn't hear her?

She rapped more sharply on the door but succeeded only in making it rattle. No other sound emerged from inside. She held very still, listening hard to make sure.

That was the only reason she heard the creak of a boot behind her. Whirling around, she was struck dumb by the sight of a man clothed entirely in black, looming large at the entrance to the alley. Or at least she thought it was a man. She couldn't see his face, for it was hidden deep within the hood of a black cloak that swirled around him with the faintest breeze.

With a heart-chilling jolt, she realized who he must be. Only one man in Spitalfields was known to prowl the night in such garb.

"What are *you* doing here?" growled a voice that seemed vaguely familiar.

She didn't dare tell him she was here to question Morgan about his activities. "I . . . I could ask you the same thing," she hedged, hoping evasion might help her escape the fearsome form.

He drew nearer. Now that she could see him better, she realized that although he was taller than her he was only slightly built. But that didn't stop her from shrinking instinctively against the wall as he approached.

He halted momentarily, as if surprised by her fear, then advanced again until he stood a few feet away. She glimpsed his chin, but the hood hid the rest of his face.

"You know who I am, don't you?" he snapped.

She nodded, though it was hard to believe that *this* was the Specter. His accent was coarse, and he didn't seem big enough, yet she'd always heard he had a gentlemanly quality and was massively built. So much for pickpocket rumors.

"My business ain't with you," he said in that guttural voice that couldn't possibly be natural. "Where's the cap'n?"

"I don't know."

"You're here to meet him, ain't you?"

"No! I mean, I . . . er . . . wanted to see . . . that is—"

His hand disappeared inside the cloak, and suddenly a

pistol appeared in the man's hand. Her heart thudded frantically in her chest. If he wanted to frighten her, he was certainly going about it the right way.

"Tell me where your friend is," he demanded, "and I might let you go."

"He's not my friend!"

"That ain't what I asked!" he cried, almost peevishly. Then he lowered his voice. "Tell me where that bloody Cap'n Pryce is, or you forfeit your life."

"If I knew, I'd tell you, I swear. I came here hoping to speak to him, but he doesn't answer when I knock."

A low curse erupted from beneath the hood. He steadied the pistol, aiming it straight at her. Well, not quite straight at her. He seemed oddly unsure of himself for a man who'd undoubtedly used a pistol many times. The pistol wavered in the air.

"Now you listen to me," he rasped. "I want you to give your friend a message."

"Whatever you ask." A message was good. A message was *very* good. She couldn't pass on a message if she were dead. "Wh-what's the message?"

"I don't want him keeping that boy around anymore, you hear?"

She blinked. "What boy?"

"That boy of yours! You know, the Perkins boy!"

"Why not?" she blurted out, surprised that the Specter should even know about Johnny, much less care what happened to him.

"Because that boy's sister is friendly with a police officer, that's why! And I don't want the magistrate hearing all the ins and outs of my business from a loose-tongued lad, you ken?"

"Yes, I 'ken'," she snapped. "But Captain Pryce can't very well just throw the boy out."

"He'll do whatever I say. He'll send him back to that Home of yours or to his sister. That's what should be done with that boy anyway. He don't belong here."

Remembering how Johnny had insisted on remaining at Morgan's, she flinched. "What if the boy won't leave? What then?" Surely the Specter wouldn't kill a child for so frivolous a reason as a loose connection between Lucy and the police. Would he?

"He'll leave. He ain't gonna cross *me*, is he?" The man loomed up close, brandishing the pistol rather recklessly before her. "Your friend Pryce won't neither."

"I wouldn't be so sure." Somehow she couldn't see Morgan bowing easily to the dictates of anybody, even his cohort in crime. And if Morgan wouldn't do as the Specter said . . . "He's very attached to the boy. H-he might not do what you want."

The Specter waved the pistol in the general vicinity of her chest. "You tell him he'd better! Or I'll make him regret it!" He cocked the pistol and added in a menacing growl, "And if you don't persuade him, I'll make *you* regret it, too!"

A new voice sounded from the top of the alley. "Damn it, Samuel, I told you two not to come back tonight—"

"Morgan!" she cried. "Run!"

Cursing, the Specter whirled to face Morgan, and the pistol went off. Clara watched in stricken silence as Morgan staggered back against the opposite wall.

"Godamercy, I've kilt him!" cried the Specter. "What have I done?" Then he dropped the pistol and fled the alley at a dead run.

Clara darted forward just in time to see Morgan slide down the wall. "Morgan!" she screamed as she raced over to him. "Oh my word, Morgan!" Her heart ground to a halt as she dropped to her knees beside him. "Speak to me. Tell me where you're hurt."

"Clara?" he rasped. "Is that you?"

"Yes, yes, I'm here." Frantically, she searched his slumped body, trying to find where he'd been hit. *Please don't let him die, God*, she prayed. "I'm right here with you, my darling. What can I do? How can I help?"

He lifted his face to hers, and the moonlight shone fully on eyes that looked surprisingly lucid for a dying man. "You can start running, *cherie*. Because when I get my hands on you, you won't be able to sit down for a week."

Chapter 15

> . . . the clock struck nine, yet no Beast appeared.
> Beauty then feared she had been the cause of his
> death; she ran crying and wringing her hands all
> about the palace, like one in despair . . .
> *"Beauty and the Beast" from*
> The Young Misses Magazine,
> *Jeanne-Marie Prince de Beaumont*

Morgan could tell from the way she blinked that he'd surprised Clara. But then the reckless woman seemed to think he was dying. He should let her go on thinking it after the fool thing she'd done by coming here.

He'd lost ten lifetimes when he'd realized that it was *her* the Specter had been confronting, *her* who'd nearly gotten shot before Morgan had scared the arse off. He still reeled from his terror.

And the searing pain in his thigh. Grabbing her by the shoulders, he used her to heft himself to a stand.

She rose and slid her arm swiftly around his waist. "What do you think you're doing? You're hurt!"

"You're damned right I'm hurt!" He steadied himself on his feet, relieved to find that standing wasn't much of a problem. "And why the devil are you here? Don't you ever listen, for God's sake?"

"Never mind all that now. You shouldn't stand until I fetch a doctor."

"I don't want a confounded doctor!" He could hear voices in the street now, people calling out about the pistol shot, questioning where it had come from. And the last thing Clara needed was to be found here with him at night. Draping his arm about her shoulders, he ordered, "Get me inside the shop before anybody sees us, all right?"

"I-It's your leg, isn't it?" she said when he leaned on her. "He shot your leg?"

"Either that or wild dogs ravaged me while my back was turned. Of course it's my leg!"

She sniffed. "You don't have to be surly about it." She helped him limp toward the door. "It's not as if *I* were the one to shoot you, for pity's sake."

"You're going to wish you'd shot me by the time this night is over," he grumbled. "I swear I'll take you over my knee—"

"Oh, hush, and give me the keys to the shop. Even if I'd let you take me over your knee, which I wouldn't, you're in no condition to do it."

"I wouldn't bet on that if I were you." But he handed her the keys anyway. She unlocked the door, then helped him across the threshold.

He shut the door behind them quickly and locked it, relieved that they'd escaped the alley before anybody had seen them. Releasing her shoulder, he limped forward.

She hastened to his side. "Wait, let me help you."

"I'm fine. I just need to sit down." He suspected the wound wasn't very serious or he wouldn't be able to walk, but it hurt like the devil, and he figured he should examine it.

The shop was black as coal dust, but Morgan was used to moving about it in the dark. Clara wasn't. She nearly walked into the stairway banister before he jerked her back.

"Should I call Johnny to come down with a lamp?" she asked.

"He's not here. I sent him off with Samuel for the night."

"Why?"

"Why do you think? For the same reason I didn't want *you* here!"

"You were expecting the Specter, weren't you?" she accused as he grabbed her arm and led her through the shop to the back.

"That isn't the point. I told you to stay away tonight, so you should have listened. Why didn't you listen?"

"I might have, if you'd actually explained things instead of barking out orders."

"I thought you had more sense than to come here alone at night."

When she answered, contrition filled her voice. "Looking back, I'll concede it wasn't a very bright idea. But I knew you were up to something. And I was right, wasn't I?" She was so intent on accusing him that she nearly stumbled over his bed.

"Whoa, angel, hold up there before you break your shin. Then we'll have two injuries to deal with."

Sighing heavily, he dropped onto the bed, then reached for the lantern he always kept beside it. He lit it, and instantly a warm light filled the room. As he reached behind him to hang the lantern on a hook, he heard her gasp and glanced back to find her staring at his leg in abject horror.

"Heavens, Morgan, there's so much blood."

Damned if she wasn't right. Blood stained the entire left

leg of his breeches. But that didn't daunt him. He'd seen too many wounds to be much surprised that this one was bleeding. "I doubt it's as bad as it looks." He examined the side of his thigh carefully. "No holes and only this tear here . . . the bullet must have just grazed me."

"But the blood—"

"Sometimes the mildest wounds bleed the most. It burns like hell, but flesh wounds often do."

"But you must see a doctor."

He glanced up at her. "And who's going to fetch me one? You? And have it be known that you were with me when I was shot?"

"I don't care about that."

The hell of it was, she probably didn't. "But *I* do. Besides, I can handle this myself. I've done it before." When she started to protest, he added, "If I need a doctor, I'll send Johnny for one when he returns in the morning. But I don't think I will. All it needs is a dressing—"

"Oh, you can be so infuriating!" Removing her cloak and tossing it over his dresser, she took off her gloves as she turned and scanned the room. "People die of 'mild' wounds all the time, you know." She looked frantic, her gaze darting this way and that. "Where the devil am I to find water in here? And bandages and—"

"Calm down, Clara, it's all right." Her concern for him both touched and amused him. He gestured behind her. "The washstand is over there. And there's clean linen underneath— you can use that."

Turning on her heel, she headed with a purposeful stride toward where he pointed.

"You have dressed a wound before, haven't you?" he asked.

"Once or twice at the Home, when a child was hurt and we couldn't wait for the doctor." As she knelt to search the washstand, she shot him a panicky look. "But never one so serious."

"I keep telling you—it's not that bad. I can do it myself if I have to. I've done it before."

"I shan't make you dress your own wound, for pity's sake." But her face was the color of chalk as she jerked out towels and tossed them onto her shoulder. "I'm the one who got you into this, and I'll be the one to take care of you."

He eyed her skeptically. "If you insist. But you look like you're about to faint."

"I am not the fainting sort, I assure you. I can handle this."

"Nobody said you couldn't, *ma belle ange*." He bit back a smile. Having Clara fuss over him went a long way toward diminishing the pain in his thigh.

She went on as if he hadn't spoken. "I've seen plenty of horrific sights in Spitalfields, you know—men shot in cold blood, a woman battered by her lover, some gin-loving matron emaciated from lack of real nourishment. This is no different."

She was babbling now, but he let her talk. If his experiences in battle had taught him anything, it was that people reacted differently in times of crisis. Some of them grew morbidly quiet. Others, like Clara, talked to keep their minds off the difficulties at hand.

While she poured water in the basin, he removed his boots, then rose and stripped off his skintight breeches and stockings. The cloth was already starting to stick, and he cursed as he pulled it free of the wound. Removing his coat and waistcoat to keep them from being further soiled by blood, he tossed them aside. Then he hitched up his shirt and sat down to examine his leg.

A sudden clatter of metal against wood made him jerk his head up. Clara stood there mute, having dropped the basin of water she'd apparently been carrying to him.

He raised an eyebrow. "Something wrong, *cherie*?"

"You're not wearing any . . . um . . . breeches."

The blush rising in her cheeks made him chuckle . . . until he saw her staring at his bared legs in clear fascination. Despite all that had happened, he felt a stirring in his drawers. With a curse, he leaned forward, hoping his shirt would cover his annoying reaction. "I figured the breeches would get in the way of your dressing the wound."

"Oh, of course. Yes. Certainly." Kneeling to pick up the basin, she poured more water in it and brought it to the bed. She wouldn't meet his eyes. "Forgive me, I'm not used to seeing grown men . . . well—"

"Half-naked. No, I don't imagine you are."

When she set the basin on the floor and knelt down, all flushed and angelic, he stifled a groan. The one time he'd imagined her kneeling at his feet she'd been performing an entirely different service for him. Unfortunately, his cock remembered the fantasy only too well.

Quickly, he turned his attention to his wound. "Looks like it's just superficial." He almost wished it weren't. Then he'd be focusing on his pain instead of his pesky arousal. "I expect it will heal all right."

"Thank God!" she said fervently as she soaked a towel in the basin.

When she began to wash away the blood, fire leaped up his thigh, and he swore under his breath.

Two spots of color stained her pretty cheeks. "I'm sorry," she whispered. "I'm so sorry. For everything. I didn't mean for this to happen."

"Remember that the next time you go snooping where you're not wanted."

She ignored his grumbling, apparently too intent on cleaning the wound to argue with him. "Have you any strong spirits here? Brandy? Whisky?"

"Good idea." He could certainly use some brandy. "Look

behind the towels in the washstand." As she rose and headed in that direction, he added in a teasing voice, "I thought it wasn't proper for ladies to drink strong spirits."

She arched one elegant eyebrow at him. "I somehow think watching a man get shot is an acceptable excuse for flouting the proprieties. Unless you have a problem with that?"

"Not me. Women should always flout the proprieties. Makes life more interesting."

"You *would* think that." She found the bottle and pulled it out. "It's strange, but I don't think the Specter meant to shoot you at all. I think it was accidental. After it happened, he said, 'Godamercy, I've kilt him!' as if he were surprised."

"I'll give him a surprise, all right," Morgan said grimly. "That arse will *not* get away with this. I'll tear him limb from limb for daring to assault you."

"Me? I'm sure he didn't mean to assault me at all. Even though he threatened me some, he—"

"What? He threatened you? I thought you'd just come upon him while he was waiting for me, and you'd accosted him."

She drew herself up, stony with offense. "I'm not an idiot, you know. I would never have accosted a stranger in your alley."

"You accosted me a week ago."

"That's different. It was broad daylight, and I wasn't alone. And you weren't draped in a black cloak." She came toward him with the bottle. "No, I was here knocking on the door when he came up and demanded to know where you were. When I couldn't tell him, he pulled out that pistol and started waving it around—"

"*Bon Dieu,* he could have killed you! I'll wring his damned neck, I will!"

He started up from the bed, but she pushed him back down. "It wasn't like that. Not exactly."

"Then tell me 'exactly' how it was." The realization that it could be *her* sitting here wounded staggered him, made the hair rise on the back of his neck. "Why did he threaten you? What did he want from you? What was he saying?"

She sat on the bed beside him and uncorked the bottle. "It was very odd. He seemed concerned about Johnny, of all things. He told me to give you a message about him."

When she poured brandy on the wound, he swore a foul oath, then snatched the bottle from her, temporarily distracted from their discussion. "What in the hell do you think you're doing? Trying to kill me, for God's sake?"

"Why do you think I wanted the brandy? To help stop the bleeding. Mrs. Carter swears that cleansing a wound with strong spirits will help it heal faster."

"Mrs. Carter is entitled to her opinion, but I'd rather not have it tried out on *my* leg."

She tipped up her chin. "She said her brother, the surgeon, used it in the navy."

"We didn't waste good brandy on a scratch like this in the navy, I promise you." Lifting the bottle to his lips, he drank several gulps, then set it down again. "*That's* what we used brandy for in the navy."

"Fine. Use it for whatever you wish. I'm done with it anyway." She stood and glanced around, hands on her hips. "Do you have anything I can use for bandaging?"

"Here, use my cravat," he said as he removed it.

When he handed it to her, she scowled at him. "This is silk. I'm not going to ruin silk by wrapping it around your wound. Besides, silk isn't absorbent enough. Don't you have any clean sheets and a scissors or a knife to cut them with?"

He reached behind him for the sheathed knife he sometimes wore inside his coat when his pistol was inconvenient. He'd had to leave it off for the ball, since evening clothes made it difficult to hide.

He handed it to her. "You can use my knife, but the only sheets are on this bed, and I'm not letting you tear them up."

"All right, I'll use my petticoat. It's made of cotton, perfect for bandaging." Taking up the knife, she marched off to the front, apparently to preserve her privacy.

"Wonderful," he called out behind her. "Wouldn't want to have my wound dressed in anything but the latest female fashion."

"Sorry," she called back from the front room, "that'll have to wait until the next time you're shot. This petticoat is out-of-date—I never dress in my finest for Spitalfields."

"I noticed. Just as I noticed that you changed into a black gown for your little escapade this evening. I assume you thought that would make it easier for you to snoop about without being detected."

There was a long silence from the front room. Then she said in a small voice, "Something like that."

He would have lectured her again, but the rustling of her skirts distracted him. He tried not to imagine her lifting them to cut strips from her petticoat. Tried not to imagine the filmy, calf-length chemise she'd be wearing underneath, the silky stockings clinging to her eloquent thighs and dimpled knees and . . .

Need roared through him with typhoon force, and he swore under his breath. He should have sent her to fetch a doctor after all. Anything would be better than this torture.

Especially when she returned to the room with strips of cloth in one hand and the ruined petticoat in the other. As she tossed the piece of clothing aside, he couldn't help staring at her skirts, which now clung to her legs, though the black bombazine was too impenetrable to allow him to see much.

Too bad he didn't have more wounds. Then she'd have to cut up her gown and her chemise to bandage all of them. Not to mention her drawers—to get her out of those, he'd shoot the damned pistol at his leg himself.

A tantalizing image of Clara naked rose in his fevered brain, and he squelched it ruthlessly. He had more important things to deal with right now than seducing Clara. "You said the Specter gave you a message for me. What was it?"

"That was the odd part. He said he wanted you to kick Johnny out. He was very adamant about it. He didn't like that Johnny's sister is friendly with a policeman."

Morgan turned that over in his mind. Why would the Specter care about that, especially if he really did have connections in all the police offices? It made no sense. None of this made sense.

His eyes narrowed. What if the man who'd attacked her hadn't really been the Specter? The man who'd fled the alley tonight hadn't been husky and broad-shouldered, like the man who'd fled last time. And there'd been no horse waiting in the street when Morgan approached—tonight's attacker had fled on foot.

"Something else I forgot about," she said as she came to his side. "He dropped the pistol after he shot you. I imagine it's still lying in the alley."

"Damn it, Clara, that's important! I'd better fetch it and bring it in here."

He started to rise, but she shoved him back onto the bed. "You're not going anywhere until I've bandaged you, Morgan."

"Bossy wench," he muttered.

"Besides, he's probably already returned for it himself by now," she said matter-of-factly as she sat down and propped his leg over her knee so she could bandage him.

She had a point. What fool left their weapon lying in an alley? But that reinforced his suspicion that her attacker hadn't been the Specter. And if it hadn't been, then the real Specter might even now be lurking about.

He watched impatiently as she folded a towel into a thick square, pressed it firmly against the wound, and then wrapped the petticoat strip around his thigh.

When she tied it off, he set the brandy bottle on the floor and took her hand. "Clara, I need you to give me a moment-by-moment account of what happened in the alley." She opened her mouth to speak, but he pressed two fingers to her mouth and added, "No, not yet. Not until I'm sure we're alone."

"What do you mean?"

"I'll explain in a moment." When he was sure the real Specter wasn't listening in.

He rose from the bed, and she cried, "Morgan, what do you think you're doing?"

"It's all right. I can walk."

"But you might injure your wound further!"

He smiled down at her. "I once fought a battle with a bullet embedded in my arm, *ma belle ange.* Trust me, this is nothing."

He limped through to the front room and checked the door to make sure it was still locked. Coming back into the room, he closed the door between the shop and his bedchamber. Then he climbed to the second floor to search the storage room, ignoring Clara's cry of protest. Other than Johnny's meager belongings and the few stored boxes, there was nothing upstairs, thank God.

When he came back down, she stood at the bottom, hands planted on her hips and eyes flashing. "I swear, if you make your wound bleed again, I'll . . . I'll make you dress it yourself!"

"What? And miss torturing me with brandy?" He reached her side and chucked her under the chin. "Relax, angel, I know what I can handle." He headed back to the bed. "Now tell me exactly what happened tonight. Start at the beginning. I want to know everything you saw, everything your assailant said. All right?"

She stood there with a mutinous look on her face until he sat down again and leaned back against the wall. Then she hurried over to check his bandage. Satisfied that no fresh blood seeped through, she sat down beside him and began to talk.

In a surprisingly calm voice, she recounted the incident, so fully describing it that he smiled. The woman ought to be a spy herself. She had a fine attention to detail, even down to describing a hint of clean-shaven chin that she'd glimpsed beneath the hood. But the more detail she related, the more convinced he became that she had *not* met up with the Specter. The ill-educated accent, the erratic behavior . . . none of it fit.

He stopped her from time to time to clarify something, and when she finished, he leaned forward, scowling. "When you say that the pistol shook," he asked, "what do you mean? The man was trembling? Perhaps even frightened?"

"At first. But later he was clearly just agitated, waving the thing wildly about and—"

"That wasn't the Specter," he said firmly.

"But he was wearing the cloak, and he acted like—"

"It wasn't him, I tell you. For one thing, he speaks excellent English. And though I've only had a glimpse of him, he's a hulking brute, very husky. Not the slightly built fellow you describe. Besides, no one with an ounce of knowledge about pistols would ever wave it around. It gives the person's intended victim too many chances to snatch it or knock it aside. The Specter's too clever to let himself be that vulnerable."

"He was angry."

"He doesn't get angry. Or not angry enough to make that

many big mistakes. Besides, he never uses a pistol; he prefers a knife." The Specter liked to threaten his lackeys by coming up behind them and holding a knife to their throats. And Ravenswood's last spy, Jenkins, had been found stabbed, not shot. "No, this sounds like somebody with little experience in weapons and even less sense."

"Somebody who wants Johnny gone."

"Yes, but who could that be?"

They both fell silent, thinking. Finally Clara said, "Lucy. Johnny's sister."

"What? But he told me she didn't care about him."

"She cares more than he gives her credit for. She's been trying to get him to leave, but he won't." Clara slanted him a dark glance. "He says he prefers living with *you*."

Morgan shrugged but felt absurdly pleased.

"And the person who assaulted me did say that he—or she—wanted to speak to you. The message was certainly designed to scare *you* off, not me."

"True, but a woman threaten somebody with a pistol? It doesn't seem likely."

"You haven't met Lucy," she said dryly.

He considered that. "There's another suspect we're ignoring—Lucy's Mr. Fitch."

"How do you know about Mr. Fitch?"

"Johnny told me. And he said the man doesn't approve of him or his brother."

"Well, that's true, but then why would he want Johnny gone from here?"

"Because it damages his reputation to have the brother of his lady friend consorting with a known criminal."

She nodded. "He did say as much to me at the police office." She sighed. "Well, I suppose we won't figure it out tonight. I'll talk to Lucy tomorrow and see how she reacts. We could always be wrong, you know. It could still be the Specter himself."

"It's not, of that I'm certain. If Johnny's presence here bothered the Specter, the boy would be dead by now."

She shuddered. "Wonderful. You've chosen a fine associate—a man who would kill children if it suited his needs."

His gaze shot to her. She now watched him with a darkly accusing expression that tore through his defenses.

"Clara, you don't underst—"

"I won't let you put me off this time, Morgan. After what happened, I deserve answers." She drew a shaky breath. "You expected him to come here tonight, didn't you? That's why you didn't want me here. That's why you were railing against him when you found me."

He hesitated, then sighed. "Yes. He said he would come for his answer."

"And I suppose you were all ready to promise your allegiance to him." Bitterness laced her words. "I don't understand it. I don't understand *you*. You obviously have dealings with him, given how well you seem to know him. But how can you work with a man like that? You're not his sort. You're a baron's son—"

"As if that matters," he growled. "You're like all the rest of those fools in society—thinking that all it takes to create a gentleman is to put a man in impeccable evening clothes and give him a titled father. But you don't know what I really am."

Her eyes were huge in her face, but she thrust her chin up stubbornly. "I know what you're not. You're not a murderer like him. And God help me, but I don't believe you're a fence, either. So why are you here?"

Dragging his hand through his hair, he glanced away. After he'd left Clara with Winthrop, he'd tracked Ravenswood down and demanded to know what the man had discussed with Clara. Ravenswood had been evasive, but he *had* given Morgan free rein to tell Clara what he felt was necessary.

How the hell did he know what was necessary? And did he dare reveal everything?

Then again, did he dare *not* reveal it? She could have been killed in her confounded quest for answers tonight. He would shoot himself in the other leg before he'd risk that happening again.

The trouble was, she wasn't a sailor who'd blindly follow orders without knowing why. And she was right—she deserved to know why. Why her life had been turned upside down. Why he was here so close to her Home, providing ample temptation for her children. Why Ravenswood refused to do anything about it.

With a sigh, he leaned back against the wall. "All right, damn you, all right. I suppose you do deserve answers."

Chapter 16

Thus youth without Thought,
Their Amours pursue,
Though an Age of Pain
Does often accrue.
A Little pretty pocket-book, *John Newbery*

Clara listened as Morgan related the whole story from start to finish. She didn't find his explanations particularly amazing—she'd already guessed he wasn't what he seemed.

Still, it was vastly reassuring to learn that he was a man she could be proud to know. Her attraction to him hadn't been unwarranted, and her instincts had been right, however much her mind had chided her for them. He was indeed a fine and honorable gentleman.

Perhaps *too* fine and honorable. He was risking his life, for heaven's sake! From what she'd heard, no one had ever crossed the Specter and lived.

Her heart leaped into her throat. Her attacker tonight might not have been the Specter, but his pistol had been just as terrifying, just as dangerous. She'd hated being cornered, hated the dread and helplessness that had rocked her. Even though it was over now, she started at every sound, her pulse still raced, and the sight of Morgan's poor bandaged leg closed a cold fist of fear around her heart.

Yet here Morgan sat, calmly relating how he intended to catch the real Specter, a far more deadly criminal. It was too much.

"Morgan, you can't do this," she said as he finished his tale.

He cast her a defensive look. "Do what?"

"This! Lay a trap for the Specter. You could be murdered! If anything goes wrong—"

His expression softened. "Nothing will go wrong, angel. Not as long as you keep silent about my real purpose in Spitalfields."

"Of course I'll keep silent. What else would I do?"

A faint smile touched his lips. "You could berate me for involving your pickpockets in this sticky affair. For deceiving you. For unwittingly tempting Johnny back into the life."

"I don't care about all that. Not when you're risking everything to catch a man who is such a danger to us all."

"You're not angry at me," he said incredulously.

"What? No! How could I be angry to learn that you're not a criminal after all? That I had it all wrong—that everything I feared about you, everything I thought Lord Ravenswood was trying to warn me about . . ."

Bother it all, she hadn't meant to mention that.

His eyes narrowed. "What exactly did Ravenswood tell you? He claimed he'd merely evaded your questions and tried to bribe you into keeping quiet."

"He did. That's true."

"But obviously he did more than that."

She flashed him a wan smile. "It was nothing very awful. Truly. He merely . . . well . . . warned me not to assume from your family connections that you were like other gentlemen. His exact words were, 'He isn't quite as civilized as he might seem.' "

Morgan stared at her bleakly. "He's right, you know." Snatching the brandy bottle from the floor, he lifted it to his lips and took a swig, then wiped his mouth on his sleeve as if to emphasize his point. "I can pretend when I choose, but at heart I'm not in the least civilized."

A rush of tenderness filled her to see him so unsure of himself. "Civilized or no, you're a *good* man, and that's more important."

He shook his head with a harsh laugh. "Yes, I'm a 'good' man. I'm so good that I daily tempt your pickpockets to return to the criminal life just by being here." He stared down at the bottle. "Though I think you've had your vengeance for that tonight."

"I didn't come for vengeance. I only came here to learn the truth."

"Well, it was a damned fool thing to do. What did you hope to accomplish?" His voice was silky soft, but his eyes blazed fire as he lifted them to her. "You could have waited until tomorrow to ask all your questions. When I think what could have happened if that man had proved to be the Specter—"

"All right, I admit I blundered in where I shouldn't have. But how was I to know you were meeting the Specter?" Agitated by his perfectly justified anger at her for nearly ruining all his careful plans, she rose from the bed to pace the room. "In my own defense, I must point out that if you'd told me the truth when I asked this evening, the entire fiasco might have been prevented. If you'd explained why you didn't want me here, you can be sure I would not have shown up."

His exasperated sigh told her that her barb hit home. "I'm not entirely convinced of that. I suppose I can see why you might ignore my order, but to come here prepared to spy on a notorious criminal . . . For God's sake, what were you thinking?"

Tired of being lectured like a child, she whirled to face him. "I was thinking that you and Ravenswood were up to something criminal. That a conspiracy of enormous proportions, involving you and the Home Office and the Specter, was afoot."

"But Clara—"

"I was thinking," she went on in high dudgeon, "that if I allowed this . . . this illegal scheme to go on without trying to prevent it, I'd be betraying all those people out there who trust their government to mete out justice, those who can't speak or act for themselves. Like my charges." Crossing her arms over her chest, she glared at him, daring him to lecture her any further.

It didn't work. He rose, looking amazingly menacing for a man wearing only drawers and a shirt and a bandage around his leg. As he stalked toward her, eyes gleaming like black diamonds in the lantern light, she caught her breath, then backed up a step.

"Suppose you'd been right," he growled, "and we were indeed 'up to something criminal.' Even if you'd found us all conspiring together, what could you have done? In your eagerness to save the world, you pranced down here without a weapon, without a companion or policeman to aid you . . . without any protection at all."

It suddenly dawned on her that he wasn't angry at her for interfering in his plans. He was angry because she'd put herself into danger. Why, the man was actually concerned for her!

That changed everything, deflating all her own anger. "I

didn't plan to come alone, you know. But I couldn't find Samuel, and I didn't want anyone else to learn I was visiting you—"

"Damn it, Clara, that wretch—Lucy or whoever it was—might have shot *you* instead of me." He grabbed her by the shoulders, his face wrought with frustration and fear. "He—she—might have killed you!"

She swallowed. "But he didn't, thanks to you."

"And that alarms me most. If I hadn't come along when I did . . ." A shudder rocked him, and his fingers tightened on her shoulders. "Do you know what it would have done to me to see you hurt? In that split second, when I realized it was you he had cornered, you he was waving a pistol at . . ." He shook his head, then went on in a voice hoarse with emotion, "God, Clara, I never want to feel such terror again."

"I hope you won't have to." Her heart thundered in her chest, and not from fear either. He cared for her—he truly did. Why else would he be so angry? "From now on—"

"From now on, you're staying clear of me, do you hear? For the duration of this investigation, you're not to come anywhere near me or this shop." Releasing her abruptly, he strode to where her cloak was draped over his dresser. "In fact, I want you to leave right now. If you'll wait while I dress, I'll walk you to the Home or fetch you a hack, whichever you prefer."

She blinked at him. Surely he wasn't kicking her out. Not now, when she was just beginning to discover what kind of man he was and how deep his feelings for her ran. And certainly not when his wound still needed attention.

"I'm not leaving you alone tonight," she protested. "You're still hurt. You shouldn't even be standing. What if the wound festers or you turn feverish? There's no one here for you to call, no one to help you."

"I'll be fine." He brought her cloak to her. "I've been wounded before, you know, and managed through it without anybody coddling me."

"I am not leaving," she repeated fiercely. "Don't you understand? If you felt terror at seeing me almost shot, what do you think I felt when I saw you really shot? And then to know that it was my fault, that you might die because of me . . ." She jerked away from him when he tried to put the cloak about her shoulders. "No, I'm not going anywhere until I'm convinced that you'll be all right. Now get back into that bed, and I'll see if I can't make you some tea. If you have a kettle, I can start a fire in the stove—"

"I don't want any damned tea!" he roared. When she flinched, he let out a frustrated sigh. "Clara, be reasonable. If I'm right about your assailant not being the Specter, then the Specter himself might still be on his way."

"And he might not be, too. The pistol shot might have alarmed him enough to make him reconsider approaching you tonight." She tipped up her chin. "For all you know, he was outside waiting for you the whole time and saw everything. Isn't that what you were worried about when you searched the premises a few moments ago?"

"Yes, but—"

"For all you know, he could be arriving now. Then while we're leaving, we'd both run into him. I'd love to see you talk your way out of that one." She squared her shoulders. "No, I may understand why you felt the need to be so secretive before, but now that I know what you're up to, I see no reason to leave. At least not until it's almost time for Johnny to return."

He gritted his teeth. "Sometimes your stubbornness goes beyond the pale. Even if you're right about the Specter, don't you care about your reputation? What will people think when they see you running out of here in the morning?"

"What will they say when they see me running out of here

now, well after midnight? I'd think that would be more suspicious. Especially if you accompany me. At least in the morning, I can leave at a decent hour and they'll assume they just never saw me come in. Or if they see me on the street, I can give them a plausible excuse—that I went out early to the bakery or something. Besides, you know quite well there are less people on the street in Spitalfields in the early morning than there are between midnight and dawn. I probably won't even be noticed if I wait until morning."

"But if you are—"

"Let me worry about that if it happens. And why do you care if I stay here? I promise I won't get in your way. I'll sleep upstairs where Johnny sleeps. You can have your meeting with the Specter, and no one will be the wiser. In the morning, after I'm convinced that you're still all right, I'll leave. It's as simple as that."

He stared at her a long moment. "As simple as that, eh? You think you've thought of everything."

"That's because I have."

"Oh no, you haven't." His burning glance gave her pause, reminding her of a wolf eyeing a plump chicken. "There's one little problem you've neglected to address, *ma belle ange*."

"And what's that?"

"I want you." His gaze skimmed her body with clear intent. "And if I have you under my roof all night—alone—I will have you."

Every sense in her body went on full alert. She knew that look of his only too well. It ought to frighten her, but it didn't. It excited her, yes. Thrilled her, most assuredly. But not a scintilla of her soul was frightened at the thought that he might "have" her.

Yet years of breeding and moral lectures made her protest. "What if I refuse to let you 'have' me, sir?"

He lifted one eyebrow. "If you'll recall, the last time you invaded my shop and refused to leave, I threatened to ravish you if you ever returned. You're here. You think you're staying. So it seems to me I have every reason to make good on my threat."

"Nonsense. You're wounded. You can't—"

"I'm wounded, not dead. And yes, I can." His voice grew husky. "I most certainly can, if you're involved."

He'd made such threats before. Was he merely bluffing her again? Or did he truly mean it this time?

And did she want him to mean it? She very much feared that she did. "When you threatened to ravish me before, you were only trying to scare me off. It worked then, so you're trying it again. But it won't work this time, because now I know too much about you. I know that you're a gentleman, and you'd never—"

"You don't know a damned thing about me." He advanced on her so swiftly that she had no time to escape. Backing her against the staircase banister, he trapped her between his two muscular arms and leaned in until they were eye to eye. "I am not a gentleman. I am not civilized. I am not any of those things you admire in Ravenswood and Winthrop and all the other gentlemen from your circle."

He certainly looked uncivilized—raw and hungry and rebellious. It sent an electric pulse of excitement through every part of her.

He went on fiercely. "I'm used to taking what I want when I want it. And I want you. I have wanted you from the day I saw you. If you think I'd have any compunction whatsoever about 'ravishing' you when I finally have you alone, you're out of your mind. So either leave right now or stay and warm my bed. Which is it to be?"

"You wouldn't take an unwilling woman to bed," she whispered.

A slow smile curved his lips. "You wouldn't *be* an unwilling woman, Clara. And we both know it."

They stared at each other a long moment, each assessing the other's true intent. She had to admit he was right. If he made the slightest attempt to seduce her, he would have her.

Yet was that what she wanted? He hadn't spoken of marriage—it was too "civilized" a thing for him to speak of. But after how he'd touched her earlier tonight, she couldn't conceive of marrying any other man. She certainly could never bear to share another man's bed.

So the way she saw it, she could either relinquish the hope of ever experiencing physical love with a man, or she could have a brief affair with Morgan that might end in nothing but ruination and heartache.

Then again, it might not. She'd wager every pound of her newfound fortune that he felt more for her than mere desire. Why else would he take such risks to shelter Johnny on her behalf? Or threaten death to the man who had accosted her tonight? Or teach Samuel how to protect her?

No, he cared for her beyond the physical. And that was enough hope for her. She'd gone a little insane tonight when she'd thought he was dying. It had changed everything, shown her how short life could be, how recklessly he lived, how little time they might have together. She didn't want to waste that time with a man who might be perfect for her re-forming aims and bad for her heart. She wanted to spend it with a man she cared for.

She wanted to spend it with Morgan. Any way she could get him.

"Well?" he demanded, as impatient in his desires as he was patient in his spying. "What's it to be? Will you flee to somewhere safe, somewhere you belong? Or will you stay and let me 'ravish' you? Because those are the only choices I'm giving you."

And there was only one choice she wanted.

She slid her arms about his neck and pressed her body

against his, delighting in his sharp intake of breath and the fullness she felt swelling against her thighs. "Ravish me, Morgan," she whispered. "Ravish me tonight."

Sheer fierce desire leaped in his eyes as he caught her head between his hands. "Taunt me at your peril, angel. I'm only a man. So before you tumble from heaven into my bed, be very sure it's what you want. Because once I've got you where I want you, nothing on earth or heaven will save you from me."

Her mouth went dry as anticipation blazed through her body. "Then it's a good thing I don't want to be saved, isn't it?" Stretching up on tiptoe, she placed a tender kiss on his unsmiling mouth.

It was like waving Red Riding Hood's basket right in the Wolf's face. His eyes glinted dangerously seconds before his mouth seized hers with a ravening fervor she'd only imagined she'd seen before. He kissed her deeply, greedily, sweeping the breath from her with the vastness of his need. He gave her no quarter, demanding a response from her that she was only too glad to give.

A fierce triumph possessed her when his arm manacled her about the waist and anchored her to him, belly to belly, breast to chest, soft loins to hot, hard groin, as if to stake his claim. He would make her his now. And oh, how she wanted to be his.

She slipped her hands up beneath his shirt and spread them over the warm contours of his chest. She wasn't at all surprised to find it sculpted and firm, the chest of a man who'd known physical labor in his time.

A choked groan erupted from him, and his mouth left hers to rain kisses over her cheeks and nose and eyelids. "So you want to be ravished, do you, Clara?" he rasped against her ear.

"Isn't that what I just said?"

"You tend to say what you don't mean to provoke and distract me. But you always manage to escape before I get what I want."

"You see how hard I'm trying to escape." Taking her hands out from underneath his shirt, she lifted them to unfasten his buttons, but he was too impatient for that.

With a growl of satisfaction, he ripped open the vee of his shirt, sending buttons flying, then tore it off over his head. "Ah, Clara, you don't know what you do to me," he whispered as she stroked the hair-roughened skin of his bared chest, marveling at its fine texture and wondering at the scars scattered here and there.

She glanced up to see him watching her with an avaricious wanting so intense that it unfurled her own want, bringing it fully into the open. She couldn't deny it and didn't want to. She was as wicked as he, aching with desire, eager to have him take her.

And worst of all, entirely unrepentant.

He reached behind her to unbutton her gown so recklessly that she wondered if she'd have any buttons left when he was done. Nervous at being undressed by a man, she fingered a thin scar across his breastbone, too near his heart. "How did this happen?"

"I don't know," he murmured, fully absorbed in getting her out of her gown. "Some sea battle or another, I expect."

That he could have been hurt so often he didn't remember the origins of his scars astonished her. No wonder he was "uncivilized." Who could remain civilized in the face of such savagery?

Her gown fell open, and he shoved it off her shoulders with impatience, then went to work on her corset ties. She kept exploring the many scars on his chest, finding a particularly deep one across his ribs. "And this one? Another sea battle?"

His face grew shuttered. "No. Geneva."

"But I thought you were only a child then—"

"Turn around," he commanded, ignoring her comment. "*Bon Dieu*, you women and your corsets. The man who invented the corset never tried to get one off a woman, I suspect." Nonetheless, when she did as Morgan bade, he made short work of removing hers. She tried not to think of why he knew his way so well around a corset.

But the realization made her peevish. "We wear them for you men, you know. You're the ones who want the perfect figure, the tiny waist and—"

"Don't lump me in with those society idiots," he broke in. Her corset dropped to the floor, and he swept his hands up to cup her breasts. "I'm just ungentlemanly enough to prefer a woman's real flesh, angel. I like the softness, the fullness of it. If I wanted to feel whalebone, I'd fondle a whale." He bent his head to nip her ear, his whiskers scraping the soft flesh beneath it. His hands kneaded and teased her breasts through the chemise, making them ache for his touch. "I much prefer to fondle you."

His breath wafted over her, fragrant with brandy, and his face smelled of bay rum. Over all of it drifted the musky scent of their desire. The longer he fondled her breasts, the more she swayed, drunk with the pleasure of having his hands on her. And when he slipped one hand down to rub between her legs with an uncanny ability to know where she wanted to be touched, she nearly cried out aloud.

Her own hands itched to fondle him, too, but it was difficult with her back to him. Feeling the hard bulge of him press against her derriere wasn't enough, so she caressed the only thing she could reach—his thighs. She stroked the rigid muscles, dragged her fingers up them eagerly. Until her left hand hit his bandage and he groaned.

"I'm sorry," she murmured, jerking her hand away.

He caught it in his. "No problem. Just move your hand higher past the bandage, *cherie*." He laid her hand on the bulge in his drawers, and when she closed her fingers around the thickness there, a shudder rocked him. "God, I've wanted you in my arms like this for so long . . . ever since I saw you in that alley with Johnny and knew I could never have you."

"You have me now, don't you?" she whispered, caressing him as best she could through the stockingette.

"Not quite." Pushing her hand away, he turned her around to face him. Hunger shone stark in his face as he reached up to unfasten the ties of her chemise. "Let me see you. Let me see what I've only been able to imagine all this time."

She dropped her gaze, a sudden shyness assailing her. "Aunt Verity says that a woman should never be naked with a man. Not even with her husband."

Did she imagine that his hands hesitated on the ties of her chemise at her mention of a husband? If so, it wasn't for long. Before she had time to protest further, he was drawing her chemise down her body.

"Much as I like your aunt," he murmured, "I don't think you should rely on her for lessons in how to behave when you take a lover."

A lover. She didn't know whether to be disappointed that "a lover" was all he meant to be to her. Or heartened that he would want her for more than one night.

"Besides," he went on, his voice husky, his hands roaming freely down her belly to her drawers, "no self-respecting ravisher would leave all this beauty covered." He unfastened her drawers and slid them over her hips. Only her stockings remained, but he left those on.

Still, she was mostly naked. With him. The thought sent a hot blush flaming her skin . . . and excitement trilling along her nerves. Nor did it help when he stepped back to look at her.

His gaze seemed to eat her up, to drag greedily over her as

if storing up her image for future spells of hunger. "No man—even a gentleman—could see you like this and not want to have you. And since I am by no means a gentleman . . ."

Stepping in to cover her mouth with his, he took greater license with her body than he had earlier at the ball. The fiery fondling of her breasts and thighs and belly, the intimate strokes between her legs . . . they all marked her as his as surely as if he'd slapped chains on her wrists. Because the thought of ever letting any other man touch her like this revolted her.

She even reveled in the swell of his hard flesh against her belly, the promise that it offered. It made her want to touch him everywhere—his broad chest, his wiry arms, his thick, well-wrought thighs. She delighted in the exquisite firmness of his muscles, the hairy skin like rough velvet beneath her questing fingers, the flat male nipples that tightened to knots when she thumbed them.

He groaned and tore his mouth from hers to whisper, "You're not at all what I expected, angel."

"How so?"

Eyes gleaming, he caught her hands, then held them out to the side and pushed them back until she felt the rough wood of the banister bars against her knuckles. "All this time I thought you were meddling in my affairs because of your high moral sense. But that's not the only reason, is it?"

"I don't know what you mean."

He closed her fingers around the bars with a knowing smile. "In your soul, you have a secret craving for wickedness. You enjoy the thrill of danger, don't you? It's like those children who tweak the nose of a sleeping beast, then run as fast as they can. You enjoy tweaking the nose of the beast to catch his attention."

She started to protest, then hesitated. Was he right? Was it only some combination of her Doggett blood and the influence of working in Spitalfields for so long that had attracted her to him?

Perhaps that was part of it. But not all, not by any means. "Yes, I do enjoy tweaking the nose of the big bad wolf," she whispered. "But yours is the only wolf's nose I've ever wanted to tweak. You're the only rogue whose attention I've ever wanted."

He stared at her a long moment, his expression giving nothing away, though she thought she glimpsed satisfaction in his eyes. "Then hold on to the bars, *ma belle ange*. Because you've certainly captured *this* big bad wolf's attention. And I won't rest until I've satisfied every craving for wickedness you've ever had."

Fear mingled with feverish expectation to course through every vein, every muscle, every nerve as she did his bidding. Her position thrust her breasts out boldly toward him, but any embarrassment faded when he began lavishing hot, openmouthed kisses over each one. He tongued the nipples erect, then sucked until they were tight, aching kernels. Both breasts received his attentions for what seemed like endless moments before he dropped to his knees and buried his face in her belly.

How strange to have him at her feet. To have him kiss circles around her navel as his hands reached behind to cup her buttocks and pull her into his kisses. Oh, Lord, what he could do with his mouth. His teeth grazed her skin, his tongue darted into her navel, and his lips tantalized her quivering flesh. He made her squirm and—shameful thought—want his mouth lower still.

Suddenly, he drew back to cast her a mysterious smile. When his hands forced her legs apart, her mouth went dry. Still clinging to the bars, she felt exposed . . . flagrant . . . embarrassingly wanton.

"Morgan?" she whispered uncertainly when he parted the

curls in the juncture between her legs and eyed the soft flesh there with lascivious intent. A warm gush of fluid right in the spot he was contemplating made her swivel her hips back instinctively to hide her shameful reaction.

But he caught her hips in his hands to stay them. "Be still, angel, and let me taste you." Then he put his mouth right on the source of her shame.

He gave her no chance to be mortified, for he began to caress her with his tongue in such an astonishing manner that she could do no more but sway there, intrigued.

Good Lord in heaven. How utterly wicked. How utterly delightful. His mouth devoured her, his tongue lapping at her as hungrily as a wolf at his last meal. She clutched at the bars as heat spiked through her, consumed her.

Then his tongue was inside her as his finger had been earlier, a devilish invader stroking where it should not, making her ache where she ought not. She writhed against his impudent mouth, wanting more, needing more.

Soon the same sensations that had overtaken her in Merrington's library were rushing her toward the conflagration, making her groan ... then utter a keening cry ... then scream out his name as the fire consumed her entirely.

As the flames licked at her, she shook uncontrollably. Somewhere in the midst of his attentions, she'd released the bars. Her hands now clasped his head to her thigh as her breath fell slowly to a normal pace.

"You are ... very good at this business of ravishment, aren't you?" she whispered. Twice in one night he'd shown her the stars without yet reaching his own fulfillment. "I fear I may disappoint you with my inexperience."

He rose to cup her head between his hands. "As if you could ever disappoint me." A rakish grin split his face. "Besides, the cure for inexperience is practice. And I look forward to hours of practice with you in the months to come."

As he tugged her away from the stairwell and headed for the bed, she pondered his words. Clearly, he didn't see this night as a single occurrence for them. But what did he see it as? The beginning of a short affair? Or something more? And did she really want to know?

He pressed her down onto the bed, halting only long enough to strip off his drawers before kneeling between her legs.

She gaped at his loins, unable to tear her eyes away from the thick, erect flesh jutting proudly from a nest of dusky hair. "That's a rather . . . um . . . sturdy-looking instrument," she said shakily.

He chuckled. "Sturdy enough to pleasure us both, I should hope."

Sturdy and *pleasure* were not words she would have used in the same sentence just now. *Sturdy* and *battering ram* seemed more apt. She began to question the wisdom of allowing that . . . that *thing* anywhere near her tender parts.

Sensing her hesitation, he leaned down to brace one hand beside her shoulder. The other reached between her legs to fondle her. "Do you like it when I put my finger inside you, Clara? You seemed to like it earlier."

His finger stroked inside her, and a blush rose to her cheeks, which was utterly absurd given that she lay naked beneath him and had just been pleasured by his mouth in the most intimate manner imaginable. "Yes, I . . . I like it."

"And two fingers?" he rasped as he delved a second finger inside. "Do you like that?"

Already the heat was building again between her legs, that astonishing heat he always roused. "Y-Yes," she murmured, wondering where this was leading. "Oh, yes."

"My 'instrument' isn't much bigger, *cherie*. But I promise

I can give you ten times the pleasure with it if you'll let me."

She felt the tip of his "instrument" graze her flesh, then felt him guide it between her slick nether lips. Panicking a little, she whispered, "Bigger isn't always better, Morgan."

He gave a strained laugh. "We'll see if you feel that way in a week or two." As he entered her, slowly, surely, inexorably, he bent to brush a kiss against her mouth. "I want to be inside you, Clara. Open and let me in."

"How?"

"Just relax, *ma belle ange*." His hand left the juncture between her legs to fondle her breast. "I know you can take all of me if you'll only relax."

So she relaxed. To her surprise, what he was doing wasn't so bad. Indeed, it grew less bad the farther he inched in. It was a bit uncomfortable, but the remarkable sensation of having him inside her compensated for that. The sheer intimacy of having him fused to her did funny things to her, made her crave more, made her open her thighs and arch up to meet him.

He groaned. "For a virgin, you have good instincts."

"I have a good teacher."

A weak smile tipped up his lips. "You won't think so in a minute, I fear. I've never 'ravished' a virgin before, but I know it hurts the first time."

She swallowed. "So I've been told."

The strain of easing into her showed in his taut lips and rigid jaw. "If I could take you without hurting you, angel, you know I would."

"I know." She stretched up to kiss his mouth.

He returned her kiss greedily, his tongue stabbing deeply with the urgency he couldn't show elsewhere. Then he halted his movements abruptly and tore his mouth from hers to whisper, "If you want me to stop now, say so. Because after this, your virtue will be irretrievable."

"It became irretrievable the first time you kissed me," she admitted. "And some things are worth any hurt."

A fierce satisfaction leaped in his face. "I'll *make* it worth the hurt," he vowed, then lunged deeply into her.

At her involuntary cry, more of surprise than of pain, his eyes darkened, and he caught her mouth in another long, aching kiss. He lay still inside her a moment, as if allowing her time to adjust to him. Then he began to move. To ravish her.

There was no other word for it. The powerful drive of his flesh within her, the hot probing of his tongue in her mouth . . . they were meant to overcome her, to conquer her, to make her so vividly aware of him that she couldn't do without him.

It was certainly working. Every thrust seemed to provoke the next until she was straining against him, writhing beneath him, craving the same sweet satisfaction as before, the release he always gave her.

He tore his mouth from hers to drag it over her cheek and her neck, his teeth grazing the skin, nipping her earlobe. "I could eat you up, angel . . . and still not be satisfied. God help me . . . you're in my blood."

As he was in hers. She met the savage beat of his every stroke . . . rose to them with the hunger of a she-wolf welcoming her mate. She kissed everything she could reach, tugged at his nipple with her teeth until he gasped. Now she was ravishing him, too. They were ravishing each other, each feeding on the other's frenzy, satisfying the other's need.

Wildness built to unbearable heights within her body. She clutched at his arms, struggling to pull him further into her.

"Give me everything, angel," he rasped, his breath hot against her cheek as he drove harder and faster and deeper. "I want all of you . . . all . . ."

"Take it . . ." she whispered. "It's yours."

With a ragged cry, he thundered into her one last time, and all at once her release hit her, a bright, piercing explosion that shook her body. Seconds later he spilled himself into her, moaning her name, his face rapt with his own release.

It was the sweetest moment of her life. And in that moment of aching clarity, when his body sank onto hers and his mouth sought her mouth in a soul-searing kiss, she realized one thing.

She'd fallen in love with the wolf.

Chapter 17

Ill do they listen to all sorts of tongues,
Since some enchant and lure like Syrens songs.
No wonder therefore 'tis as overpower'd,
So many of them has the Wolfe devour'd.
"Little Red Riding Hood," Charles Perrault,
English translation by Robert Samber,
Tales of Times Past with Morals

Sated and relaxed, Morgan lay beside Clara, one arm about her shoulder and her head resting on his chest. He'd never felt so content in his life. In the past, lovemaking had made him feel only more restless, more alone.

Not with Clara. To have her lying naked in his embrace, with her arm draped over his belly and one of her legs thrown over his, felt utterly natural, utterly right. Utterly pure.

She nuzzled his chest. "I do believe I like lovemaking, Captain Blakely."

He smiled. "My instrument proved sturdy enough after all, did it?"

"Mmmm. Nicely sturdy. A very useful instrument you have there."

"Always glad to oblige, my lady." As a sweet languor stole over him, he indulged his urge to hold her close a few moments longer. "I hope you were right about the Specter being scared off tonight. Because if he comes knocking any-time soon, I fear I'll be too weak to answer the door."

Her head shot up from his chest, her eyes filling with alarm. "Your wound isn't paining you again, is it?"

He laughed, warmed by her concern. "Not in the least, an-gel. Our lovemaking was what drained the strength out of me."

"Never!" A mischievous smile played over her well-kissed lips. "A big bad wolf like you? Who calls your wound a 'scratch'? I thought you were invincible."

He slanted her a glance. "Don't provoke me, you teasing wench. I can barely summon the energy to breathe, much less bandy words with you."

With a grin, she dropped her head onto his chest. "Well, at least now I know how to end all your lecturing."

Chuckling, he wrapped his arms about her and savored the feel of her in his arms, the intimacy he'd never known with anybody else.

She snuggled against him. "I must say I'm very glad they chose you for this particular spying job."

"So am I." To his astonishment, he realized it was true. Despite his dislike of Spitalfields, he'd enjoyed the challenge of trying to outwit the Specter, the satisfaction of helping Johnny, and most of all, the wonder of knowing Clara.

After a moment, she said, "Morgan?"

"Hmm?"

"Why *did* they choose you? Did you volunteer?"

"Not hardly," he said.

She propped her chin on his chest and stared up into his face. "But I thought you'd done this before."

He stiffened. "Ravenswood told you about that, too?"

"Not really, but your brother did mention the spying, and I got the impression—"

"Oh, the spying," he said, relaxing again. "Of course."

She eyed him solemnly. "What did you think I meant?"

Confound it all. He should have known this blessed sweetness couldn't last. Now he would have to tell her something of his past, if only to show her what she was getting herself into with him. And she would undoubtedly realize how foolish she'd been and thrust him away. So he mustn't let himself grow too accustomed to this sensation of belonging.

Yet when he tried to withdraw, she clutched him tightly. "Tell me, won't you?"

As he stared at her serious expression, he sighed. She had foolish notions about his gentlemanly character that he had to shatter before she learned the truth about him some other way. Like from Ravenswood, who seemed determined to warn her away from any personal involvement with Morgan.

"Actually, I thought you were referring to my thieving." He dragged in a breath, preparing himself for her reaction, then went on. "You asked why they chose me—well, it was largely because I used to be a pickpocket and a thief myself."

Disbelief clouded her features. "But how can that be? You were a baron's son. Even if you weren't raised in England, surely your mother didn't allow—"

"She didn't know I was a thief. And I didn't know I was a baron's son."

"What? When you said your mother took you, I assumed it was in a formal separation from your father."

He gave a harsh laugh. "Not quite. Mother stole me away, actually. She'd had enough of the baron's philandering, so when she gave birth to twins, she bribed the servants to hide it from the family and care for me until she left her childbed. Then she took me and her jewels and fled with her lover, her dancing master. Apparently she thought that since the baron had his heir he wouldn't look for her."

"And did he?"

"No. She'd judged him rightly. He had Sebastian—he didn't much care about anything else. He told the world, including my brother, that Mother had died in childbirth." He glanced away, throat tight. "I didn't know the baron, but by all accounts he was something of an arse."

"I should say so!"

He swung his gaze back to her, surprised by her fervency. "You certainly are an opinionated wench."

"No feeling man who loved his wife would let her simply walk out on him without searching for her, lover or no."

"Ah, but I wonder if English lords *are* feeling men. Their pride often seems stronger than any softer emotion. Though perhaps you're right. I sometimes doubt that the baron ever loved my mother." Neither Uncle Lew nor Sebastian seemed to know one way or the other. It would explain why Mother had never gone back to the baron.

Not that it mattered. The past couldn't be changed.

"Well?" she prodded. "You still haven't explained how that turned you into a pickpocket."

The fact that Clara took this all in stride astonished him. But then she always did astonish him. "Unfortunately, my mother picked the wrong year to run and the wrong place to run to. Not to mention the wrong man to run with. She fled with me in 1788, you see. Less than a year after our arrival in Geneva, the rabble in Paris stormed the Bastille."

Horror filled her face. "Good Lord, you were in Geneva during the revolution?"

He nodded. "And Geneva was affected far more than England. It even had its own Reign of Terror. Almost from the time we arrived, there was chaos in the city. As you might imagine, it wasn't the best place for an English dancing master, an adulterous English lady, and her newborn child to make a home."

"But why Geneva, of all places? Why not America or . . . or Spain or something?"

"I don't know all of my mother's reasoning, only what she told me when I grew older, but apparently that first lover of Mother's had friends in Geneva. Unfortunately, they were nobility, which didn't help the situation."

"First lover?"

He sighed. "Yes. About a year after we arrived in the city, the dancing master stole all the jewels she'd meant us to live on and then disappeared." He cast her a wry smile. "Mother was never very . . . wise in her choice of men, I'm afraid."

The clear pity in Clara's face was hard to stomach. He glanced away and went on more stiffly. "With no money, no friends she could claim, and a baby to support, Mother decided that the only way to survive was to take another lover. To be fair, there weren't many options for her. And we did live fairly well with the second man until he fell victim to the guillotine."

He ignored her sharp gasp, though he knew all of this must be hard to fathom. He'd lived with it, so it didn't strike him as odd. But he'd never told this to anybody before, probably because, aside from the mortification of having anyone know the sordid details of his childhood, he knew it sounded like something out of a novel.

The only other person who knew everything about the early history of his life in Geneva was his mother's brother, and that was only because Mother had told Uncle Lew in her last days of life. Ravenswood only knew about the thieving, and Sebastian knew nothing, which was the way Morgan wanted it.

"Anyway," Morgan continued, "that's how Mother supported us—by taking lovers. But it was a dicey existence at best. Her value as a pretty Englishwoman plummeted in Geneva once the Terror began."

"So you decided to supplement the family income by picking pockets," she said with quiet sympathy. "How young were you when you started?"

A vise tightened around his heart. He was tempted to stop the conversation here. He didn't even like thinking about those days, and it unnerved him that Clara could guess his motives so easily. Or that she might see him as one of her sad little urchins. Though he supposed that was indeed what he'd been.

Yet he answered her, compelled by some unnamable urge to tell it all. "I was six the first time. It wasn't planned. Mother was arguing with our current 'benefactor,' a very stingy man. I left to escape the shouting. I was hungry, so when I came upon a baker setting out baguettes I waited until his back was turned, took one, and ran. A pickpocket saw the whole thing and befriended me. He taught me how to filch things and sell them to a fence." He cast her a grim smile. "I even developed a specialty. I was what the boys around here would call a silk snatcher."

"You stole bonnets and hoods from people in the streets."

"Very good. You know your thieves' cant."

"After spending so many hours in the company of thieves, one can't help but pick up a little. But why bonnets?"

He stared down at her own bare head of tousled chestnut hair. "Mother liked them. For every ten or so I stole and sold to the fence, I'd keep one for her. It was foolish, I know. She could have used the money more, but—"

"It made the stealing all right."

"*Nothing* made the stealing all right," he said fiercely.

She soothed him with the stroke of a hand over his chest.

"No, of course not." Her fingers drifted idly down his waist. "In my experience there are two sorts of thieves—those who steal to survive and would prefer a real job if they could get it, and those who begin by stealing to survive but soon learn that it's an exciting way to make a living. The former are easier to reform. The latter . . . well, let's just say that not all my boys end up living useful, productive lives."

"So which sort was I?" he asked, the vise around his heart threatening to crush it entirely.

"The former, of course." She said it as if it should be obvious. "The latter have little shame for what they do. I mean, it was shame that kept you from telling your mother about the stealing, wasn't it?"

He blinked at her. "How do you know it wasn't a fear of how she'd punish me?"

"Because she doesn't sound like an uncaring mother."

That Clara could accept the necessity of his mother's whoring without also assuming it made her a bad mother awed him. He'd never met another person who saw the difference. "She was the best mother she could be under the circumstances."

She nodded. "And you were the best son you could be."

The vise snapped, and he could feel his blood rushing freely again. She understood about his mother. Not even his otherwise understanding uncle had understood that.

Words poured out of him, words he couldn't seem to stop. "I always gave Mother some excuse for where I got the money. I told her I got it plucking chickens for a poulterer or running errands for the painter next door or whatever I could think of."

He snorted. "As if such jobs were to be had. Jobs were scarce enough during those tumultuous times, even for natives of Geneva. But I was a fatherless boy whom everyone assumed was the 'English whore's' by-blow, so there were certainly none for me." He ruffled Clara's hair. "And no Home for the Reformation of Pickpockets, either."

"I wish there could have been one." Clara tightened her arm about his waist. "No child should have to suffer such responsibility alone."

The passionate outrage in her face on his behalf made a lump settle in his throat. "I wasn't entirely alone in my hell, you know. I did have my mother."

"Yes, but you couldn't talk to her about it, and that makes all the difference. You had to bear the weight of your guilt alone." She rubbed her cheek over his chest. "But were you never caught?"

"A few times. They didn't find the goods on me, however, so I always managed to convince the judge I wasn't guilty. But I spent the night in jail each time. I told my mother I stayed with friends. Since I often liked to be gone when one of her lovers was there, she accepted that explanation."

"Are you sure? Many mothers know when their children are lying, although they may not admit it."

"I think she chose to believe my lies. The alternative was facing the truth of how far we'd sunk, and she just couldn't. It would mean acknowledging how badly she'd blundered by trusting her first lover. I suppose that's why she didn't tell me about the baron until the very end."

Clara cast him a questioning glance. "Why do you call him the baron?"

Bitterness clogged his throat. "What should I call him— Father? He wasn't a father to me in any respect. Even after my uncle fetched me, the baron wanted naught to do with me. Uncle Lew was the one who administered my care from that moment on."

"I don't understand—your uncle sounds like a good man. So when things deteriorated in Geneva, why didn't your mother return to England? Surely her brother would have helped her even if your father would not."

"I've often wondered about that. There were the practical problems of escaping Geneva during the Terror and then afterward, with Napoleon taking control . . . I suppose it would have been difficult."

As Clara listened, she stroked him, wordlessly giving him her sympathy. And oddly enough, her coddling didn't make him as uncomfortable as he'd expected. In truth, it soothed him.

"But it was more complicated than that," he went on. "For her to come back, after having been pronounced dead, meant bringing shame upon her family. The truth would have come out, and they would have had to bear the scandal of her disgrace. At least in Geneva she was anonymous, and her shame didn't stretch to anyone else."

"Except you," Clara said softly.

"Yes, but in England it would have stretched to me, too. They probably would have taken me from her, and I don't think she could have borne that. I was all she had left." He shrugged. "And Mother always had high hopes about the men who entered her life. She was always convinced that her latest lover was a good man who would set us up for life, treat her well, and take me under his wing. She was a woman of endless hopes until—"

"Until what?"

No, he couldn't tell her about that. He just couldn't. "Until she realized she was dying." He dragged in a ragged breath, fighting down the pain. "Then she knew she had no choice but to provide for my future. So she wrote to my uncle, and he used his influence to gain passage into Geneva, since it was under Napoleon's rule by then. That's when we learned that Uncle Lew had never given up hope of finding his sister, though he'd had no success tracing her flight from England. Thank God he had a few days with her at the last."

"What did she die of?"

"Consumption." The lie came easily. He'd said it often enough—to Sebastian, to Ravenswood, to whoever asked about his mother. Only he and his uncle knew the truth.

Clara cast him a searching glance as if she sensed he was lying. But how could she? Nobody else ever had.

He shook off the eerie sensation. "You know the rest of it, for the most part. After I left Geneva, I was sent to a school in Ireland until I was old enough to be put in the navy." He smiled. "The navy proved perfect for me. All the discipline and all those pesky rules were just the thing to set straight the wild boy I'd become. I had an excellent captain who whipped me into shape—"

"Not literally, I hope. I know that there are harsh captains."

"Mine wasn't, thank God. He was a very good man. By the time we first saw battle, I was itching to fight, to prove myself to my uncle who'd saved me from a life in the streets of Geneva and to all the others who'd given me a chance. So I fought like the devil and distinguished myself."

"Until you ended up a captain yourself."

"Yes."

"And a spy in Spitalfields." She paused. "But you said you didn't volunteer, and I get the distinct impression that this isn't the sort of assignment you would have wanted."

"No."

"So why are you doing it?"

"Ravenswood has promised me a first-rater ship to command. It may be the only way for me to go back to sea." He didn't mention Ravenswood's offer of a position in the Home Office. She would never understand why he'd prefer going back to sea to that.

She turned her head to stare off across the room. "And are you . . . very eager to return to the sea?"

He couldn't mistake the hitch in her voice. She was certainly a Woman with Expectations. And what was he to tell her now that he'd ruined her? She had a right to her Expectations, after all. He might not be a gentleman, but he'd never been a cad.

"I'm eager to return to commanding a ship, that's all. It's been a few years now. The navy has been a bit perturbed with me, you see, because I . . . er . . . got into that sticky business with the pirates, and although I was cleared of blame—"

"Lord Ravenswood told me about that. And even if he hadn't, I knew a lot about it from Lord Winthrop."

"Don't believe a word Winthrop says." Morgan scowled. "I had naught to do with his being robbed. I was merely a sailor on the Pirate Lord's ship, earning my way back to England. I didn't receive a shilling of the prize money, yet Winthrop acts as if I masterminded the entire attack."

She surprised him by laughing, then running a caressing hand down his thigh. "Yes, well, Lord Winthrop is a rather unpleasant man."

"So I gather." He paused, then added in as light a tone as he could manage, "He has his eye on you, it appears."

With a teasing smile, she rubbed her foot along his calf. "Are you jealous of Lord Winthrop?"

He wished she would stop touching him so temptingly. It was rousing him where it shouldn't, and she probably didn't even realize it. "That arse? Certainly not."

"You ought to be. My aunt is determined to see a match made between me and Lord Winthrop. She thinks the earl would make me the perfect husband."

When she innocently laid her hand near his already burgeoning erection, he sucked in a breath. "And what do you think?"

"I think that if I married him, I would either die of tedium or brain him with a poker within the week. The last man on earth I shall ever marry is Lord Boring. He possesses none of the qualities I desire in a man."

"Oh?" he eked out as her hand inched in an unmistakable direction. "And what qualities might those be?"

"A quick brain. A good heart. A generous temper." She caught his now rampant erection in her hand. "And a very sturdy instrument."

She knew exactly what she was doing, the little witch! With a growl, he rolled her beneath him. Staring down into her laughing face, he rubbed his hard length against her soft nest of hair. "Don't tease me, angel, unless you're prepared to face the consequences."

She smiled impishly, then entwined her arms about his neck and pulled him down to her. "Don't tease *me*, sir, unless you're prepared to face the same."

He didn't even attempt to fight her. Not when her concern for him made him desire her again with a fierceness bordering on pain. He wanted to lose himself in her warmth, bury his past in her soothing smile, find peace in her embrace. He didn't know what god had sent him such an angel, but he was devil enough not to resist when heaven was handed to him.

Much later, when they'd finished a second soul-searing consummation and Clara lay asleep, he slid quietly from the bed and reached for his drawers. But before he could put them on, he spotted the blood smearing his thighs. It startled him. For a second, he thought his wound had started bleeding again.

Then he realized what it was. Clara's blood. Her virgin's blood.

Self-disgust roiled in his belly at the sight. Moving quietly so as not to disturb her peaceful sleep, he found a stray towel and washed the crimson stain from his loins.

He wished he could wash it from his conscience as well, but that was impossible. How could he have deflowered a woman he admired so much? He'd stolen from her what most people of her station prized, and without offering so much as a promise of marriage.

Such a promise must be given now, no matter what difficulties it presented. He'd often ignored his uncle's teachings about gentlemanly behavior, but one stricture he'd always abided by: no man worth his salt took advantage of a woman.

If he did—as Morgan in a moment of weakness had taken advantage of Clara's sensual nature—then he paid the consequences. Very well, Morgan would marry her. He refused to be like his mother's lovers, satisfying his own needs at the expense of a woman's reputation and future. Whatever it cost him, he would make it right.

And if she refused his suit? Morgan eyed her thoughtfully as he drew on his drawers. From what he'd heard, she'd never sought a husband.

But then she'd never bedded any man either. No, she was too sensible not to accept his suit. Women like her didn't take lovers, and if they did let themselves be seduced, they prayed that their seducers would marry them.

So Morgan would marry her, even if the thought scared him witless. Marriage to Clara . . . oh, God. She would try to make him into a replica of Ravenswood and his brother, a gentleman in truth instead of in name. She would meddle in his affairs, expect him to come to heel, want him to behave as his station demanded.

And care about him, fuss over him, cradle him in her welcoming arms.

That was worst of all. Because he craved that too damned much, and craving something was the surest way to lose it. It was safer not to yearn—he knew that in his head. Yet he still hadn't driven the yearning from his heart.

It was this cursed Spitalfields, where the yearning was amplified in every person around him. It hung in the air like fog, seeped into house and tavern. It drove boys to steal, women to sell their bodies, men to drink. And it drove him to desire things he'd given up on long ago. Love. Children. Happiness.

He had none of that at sea. He didn't want it or miss it there. Once buried in the routine of ship life, breathing air that smelled of naught but salt and fish, he could function like a cog in a wheel. Something always needed doing on a ship. Battles must be fought, ports explored, maneuvers attempted. He could forget for months at a time all the things he craved so badly.

All the things Clara made him crave again. That's why he must marry her and return to sea before she found out what he really was and turned from him in disgust. Before he was lulled into thinking his cravings might finally be satisfied.

Yes, he could handle that sort of distant marriage. She could live here and take care of her beloved Home, and he would see her between his sails to Africa and Gibraltar and wherever duty took him.

So why did that prospect seem suddenly so unappealing? Casting her a quick glance, he sighed and moved toward the front shop. He had to get some air. He needed to make plans that didn't involve holding her close every night for the rest of his life, and he couldn't do that with her lying there so sweetly sleeping, making his blood thunder in his chest and his throat draw tight with longing.

He started for the front room of the shop, then halted to grab his knife as an afterthought. Sliding it inside the waistband of his drawers at the small of his back, he left the back room and closed the door behind him. He felt his way to the side door and found the candle he usually kept there, the one he should have looked for when they'd first come in. Lighting it, he walked to the front and set it on the counter.

As he stood in the shadows near the window, he stared out at the nearly deserted street. A glance at the clock said it was 3 A.M. Soon he'd have to wake her. No matter what she said, he refused to have her leave his shop in broad daylight when anybody might see. If she covered her head and face, he could easily sneak her into a waiting hack tonight, and she could go home.

Home, away from him. And she'd have to stay away from him for as long as his investigation continued. Unfortunately, it might be months before this mess was settled, and that presented another problem. What if after tonight she found herself with child? What then?

The thought of Clara carrying his babe filled him with a yearning so intense it terrified him. *Bon Dieu*, but he should never have gone so far with her. He should have kept his damned prick in his breeches.

A knock at the side door broke into his thoughts. He tensed. It must be the Specter, which meant it was time to return to business. Checking to be sure the door to the back room was firmly closed, he strode to the side door and opened it.

The hooded figure who stood in the alley a few feet away bore little resemblance to the one Clara had described. For one thing, there was no hint of a face beneath the deep hood, not a single flash of the pale, clean-shaven chin Clara had spoken of.

Despite himself, Morgan felt a chill skitter along his skin. Of course the man had a face—he was no supernatural being. Yet it was strange how he could hide it so entirely beneath that hood of his. Morgan had the unsettling impression that if he jerked the hood back, there would be nothing underneath.

He shook off the ridiculous thought. Leaning against the doorway, he said, "You're here for your answer, I suppose."

"Come outside, Captain Pryce," the Specter rasped, his voice disguised as before. "We wouldn't want you to disturb your lady friend. And we certainly wouldn't want her to overhear our discussion."

Alarm knotted in his gut. The Specter knew Clara was here? Ah, but perhaps he thought his "lady friend" was merely a tart. "What lady friend do you mean?"

"Don't play dumb. Did you think I missed that ridiculous confrontation earlier? The impostor trying to frighten Lady Clara? Your springing to her rescue so gallantly?"

The arse knew it was Clara, damn him. She'd been right—the Specter *had* been watching all along.

Morgan walked out into the alley, ignoring the dirt beneath his bare feet, the brisk air stippling his skin with goose bumps. Closing the door behind him, he thanked God he'd thought to don his knife. It gave him a distinct advantage, since the Specter probably thought him unarmed. Otherwise the man would never venture close enough to risk Morgan's killing him. Not that Morgan was ready for that yet.

Morgan turned to his enemy and said noncommittally, "So I have a woman here. What of it?"

"Not just any woman. I must say I'm impressed. I expected you to be talented with the ladies, but this is talent beyond measure—to seduce the moral and lofty Lady Clara."

Morgan tensed, even though he knew that the door to the windowless back room had been closed the whole time and it was impossible that the Specter could have known what they'd done. "What makes you think Lady Clara would relinquish her virtue to a man like me?"

"I'm no fool. It's 3 A.M., you're wearing only drawers, and the lady has been here two hours at least. Can you blame me for drawing the obvious conclusion?"

Morgan scrambled to think of a response that wouldn't ruin Clara, his investigation, or both. "This particular lady had become a nuisance, so I silenced her the best way I know how, short of murdering her and drawing unwanted attention to myself." When he realized this might provide him with the chance to determine the Specter's connection to the police offices, he added, "Did you know the wench actually reported me to the magistrate?"

"I've heard of the trouble she's made for you. She hasn't exactly been discreet in her disapproval."

And the Specter's words hadn't exactly revealed anything, curse his hide. The man was too crafty for such a blatant ploy.

The Specter went on in a deceptively casual voice. "So you seduced her to gain her silence, did you?"

Morgan shrugged. "What else could I do? She was making too much trouble."

"Indeed. Though I'm surprised you could coax her into your bed. Considering that she wants to save the very pickpockets you'd like to recruit, I can't imagine how you convinced her to overcome her personal objections to your profession." The suspicion in the Specter's voice was unmistakable.

Morgan knew he treaded dangerous ground, but he saw no other way out. "I didn't even attempt to overcome her objections—as you say, she's too moral a lady to overlook my sins. Instead I persuaded her that her information about me and my sins was wrong."

"Oh? How did you manage that?"

"For one thing, I pointed out that I hadn't had Johnny pinch one item for me since he began his stay here."

"Yes, I know. I'd wondered about that."

Damn. The man had eyes everywhere. "Surely you didn't think I'd be that foolish. How did I know the boy wasn't

Lady Clara's spy, planted in my shop to catch me in the act so she could persuade the magistrate to have me arrested?"

"Good point. And very clever of you to think of it. Though if you didn't want him to steal for you, why did you take him in?"

The man sounded less suspicious now. Sensing he was gaining the advantage, Morgan pressed on. "Her ladyship's charges are her weakness, you know. I can afford to be kind to Johnny if it gains me her help in the end."

"Her help?"

"All those pickpockets, of course. She has an entire houseful of willing little thieves only waiting to be tapped. Just think of what I can accomplish with them under my charge. And the authorities wouldn't touch her, since they think her a moral sort, so I wouldn't even have to worry about their interference. A tidy setup indeed. I'm surprised you haven't attempted it yourself. Or at least worked to woo her children to your side."

"I've considered it. But I don't like to draw attention to my activities by public scraps with a well-known lady philanthropist, so I left well enough alone, thinking she would do the same. Which she has." He shrugged. "But then I didn't realize that seduction would work on Lady Clara, or I might have attempted more."

Though the idea of the Specter seeking to seduce Clara nauseated him, Morgan forced himself to continue the loathsome conversation. The villain would only let his guard down if he felt comfortable with Morgan. And if he thought Morgan was as vicious, sly, and unscrupulous as he.

"You know these moral sorts," Morgan said casually, "all prim and proper on the outside, but secretly burning for a man on the inside. Once I gained her interest, I was able to persuade her of whatever I liked. A lusting woman would rather believe a lie—no matter how far-fetched—than admit that her desires have overwhelmed her good sense. I only gave Lady Clara what she wanted by telling her what she needed to hear."

Morgan held his breath, praying that the Specter was cynical enough about women to believe the tale. When the Specter chuckled, Morgan nearly slumped in relief. He'd passed the test.

"You're more devious than even I gave you credit for, Captain Pryce. Though if she turns moral again—"

"She won't." Morgan tucked his thumbs inside his drawers suggestively. "I know how to keep a woman happy. But if she should have temporary moments of rationality, I can use blackmail to squelch them. After all, how long do you think her Home would last if a scandal about her criminal lover erupted?"

A low whistle escaped the Specter's lips. "God help the poor woman once you have her entirely under your thumb. You're certainly going about it the right way. To control a woman, one must tread carefully, lulling her natural fears, taking one's time in building her gilded cage around her until she doesn't even see the bars."

"Exactly," Morgan answered, though the Specter's callous assessment of womankind unsettled him. "And once I have the bars around her cage, I'll have her pickpockets out of theirs."

The Specter gave a brief bow. "Very good, Captain Pryce. You're clearly a man after my own heart." Then he stepped suddenly nearer. "The question is, are you a man after my business as well?"

Morgan chuckled. "Don't tell me I've got the great Specter worried."

"Not at all." A knife flashed suddenly in the Specter's hand. "*You're* the one who stepped into the alley unarmed."

Morgan drew his own blade before the man could even blink. "And you're the one underestimating me. I never go anywhere unarmed."

The Specter's sharp intake of breath showed that Morgan had taken him by surprise. Good.

"Is this your answer?" the Specter snapped. "Has your triumph with Lady Clara made you foolish enough to think you can take me on as well?"

"Not at all. But I don't like being threatened."

"Very well." The Specter's knife vanished into his vast cloak as quickly as it had appeared. "Then I shall not threaten you. Yet."

"And I shall not take you on. Yet." Morgan slid his own blade back inside his waistband. "Now that we understand each other, I have a proposition for you."

"I've already given you the terms of our agreement. Take them or leave them."

"Not so fast. You'll want to hear this. You see, I've asked around about you—"

"I know."

"—and I've learned that while you have adequate sources for your stolen bank notes on the Continent, you have to rely on the mails to get them out of England. You risk theft and exposure every time you send a packet through the mails. Not to mention that it probably costs you an average of a shilling out of every pound to mail them."

The Specter crossed his arms over his chest. "There are costs and risks in every endeavor."

"Yes, but I can eliminate both for you."

"How?"

"As you know, I have a connection with a very successful band of smugglers. I don't have to bother with mailing stolen notes—I simply use the notes to purchase the smuggled tobacco I sell in my shop for good coin. The smugglers pay for the tobacco in France with my notes, and they circulate there very successfully. Everyone is happy."

"Go on."

"Moving your notes in that manner as well would be no hardship for me."

"Yes, but why would you do me such a service?"

"I want the police off my back. You say you have connections there. Very well—you grease those palms and I'll grease the path of your notes out of the country."

Jack Seward, the notorious smuggler, owed Morgan a favor after the man's part in seeing Morgan marooned four years ago. Morgan had already spoken with Seward. For a promise that Jack could continue his brandy and tobacco smuggling unopposed, the man was more than willing to cooperate in setting the trap for a murderer.

"What about your other receiving?" the Specter asked. "I want a portion of your profits from that as well."

"All right. I'll give you twenty percent. Considering what I'm doing for you with the notes, that ought to be ample profit."

They bargained back and forth until they settled on twenty-eight percent. The Specter sighed. "You drive a hard bargain, Captain. I hope you'll make as formidable an ally as you have an enemy."

"I've never been your enemy, just your competitor."

"Same thing. Which is why I'll want some reassurances. First of all, I want the name of your smuggler, so I can make sure he's everything you say he is."

"You'll get his name when the three of us meet for the first exchange of bank notes, and not before. I won't have you trying to cut me out by making your own connection with him."

The Specter backed up a step. "You said nothing about a meeting. I generally deal with this sort of thing through lackeys."

Yes, that was why the man was so hard to catch. And why this was the most important part of the transaction. They had to catch him with the notes in his possession. It was the only way to have him dead to rights. "You're not the only one who wants reassurances, you know. My smuggler likes to know everyone he's dealing with—smuggling is a dangerous business, and it wouldn't do for him to find himself caught because some stranger turned him over to the excisemen. So he wants to speak to you in person at the first exchange, or there's no deal."

A long silence ensued, and Morgan had to bite his tongue to keep from adding other reasons why they needed a meeting. If he sounded too eager, the Specter would smell a rat.

But an easy outlet for the thousands of pounds the Specter would want to move would be hard for the man to pass up.

At last the Specter said tersely, "Very well, you shall have your meeting. But only if I set the time and place. And only if you give me your smuggler's name now."

Morgan hesitated, but Jack had already come to London and was staying somewhere no one would think to look for him. "All right. But I set the day, to give me enough time to reach my smuggler." And Morgan enough time to prepare his trap.

"Fair enough. What's his name?"

"Jack Seward."

The Specter nodded his approval. "I've heard of him. One of the largest smugglers of brandy and tobacco in Sussex."

"Soon to be the largest smuggler of bank notes in Sussex. As for the day of the meeting, is three days from now too soon?"

"No. I'll send you a message that morning with the time of the meeting. When the time comes, be waiting here with your friend, and I'll send a man to bring you to me. Understood?"

"Understood." That was the way the Specter always

worked, which meant he didn't suspect anything, thank God. Morgan backed toward the door. "Now if you don't mind, I'd like to return to building Lady Clara's gilded cage."

The Specter laughed. "Of course. Is she as passionate in bed as she is in defending her young charges?"

Morgan forcibly suppressed a shudder at the thought of discussing such intimacies with the Specter. "Let's just say I have no cause for complaint."

"Ah, a gentleman," the Specter said sarcastically. "All right, I'll leave you to it then. Look for my message in three days."

"Three days," Morgan repeated.

His blood racing, Morgan waited until the man left the alley, then let out a heavy breath. The bait was set. Now it was only left to him and Ravenswood to spring the trap.

Chapter 18

Time rolls like a Marble,
And awes ev'ry State;
Then improve each Moment,
Before 'tis too late.
A Little pretty pocket-book, *John Newbery*

Clara slipped into the back room and eased the inner door shut seconds before she heard Morgan close the outer door and move into the front of the shop. She hadn't missed much of the men's conversation—the moment Morgan had gone outside, she'd awakened. Hearing the murmur of voices in the alley, she couldn't resist listening in.

What she'd heard told her two things. One, Morgan was right about the difference between the person who'd attacked her tonight and the real Specter. The real villain was as terrifying a character as the impostor had been clumsy. She didn't envy Morgan having to match wits with *that* creature of the night.

Two, if anybody had the cunning to capture the creature, it was Morgan. Despite her annoyance with the tack he'd taken concerning her, she admired his quick thinking. He could spin a tale as easily and convincingly as any of her pickpockets.

But then she should expect that, since he'd once been just like them.

She shook her head. She still could hardly believe it. The man she'd recklessly fallen in love with had once been a pickpocket. And he still suffered for it, in his heart. She could tell. What's more, she knew, with an instinct she couldn't name, that he hadn't told her all of it. He hurt, and he hurt deeply. But he didn't trust her enough to tell her why or how.

A momentary fear shook her. Good Lord, what had she gotten herself into? She could hear him moving about in the front of the shop now, rummaging around for heaven knew what. Any moment he would return, and she didn't know how to face him. What could she say to the man she was only now discovering that she loved? Especially when love was probably the furthest thing from his mind?

Too soon, Morgan entered, then jerked to a halt when he saw her standing there in her chemise and drawers. "You're awake."

"So are you." That sounded stupid. But she had no idea how to proceed.

Apparently she wasn't alone, for he eyed her uncertainly. So she waited, wondering how much he would tell her of what the Specter had just said. That would be a measure of how much he trusted her.

Besides, she didn't want to admit she'd been eavesdropping. Again.

He tucked his thumbs in the waistband of his drawers. "I . . . um . . . that was the Specter."

She breathed a little easier. "Was it?"

His eyes narrowed. "You don't seem surprised."

"Why should I be? I told you he might come back."

"Actually, he never left. You were right about his seeing what happened earlier."

"Was I?"

Warily, he edged closer. "He knows you were here. He knows we were together."

"I see." She didn't want to say anything that might discourage him from telling her the rest. Scooping her corset off the floor, she slid her arms through the shoulder straps and turned around. "Here, help me with this, will you?"

That seemed to throw him off guard. "Where are you going?" he asked in an anxious voice, though he did as she asked.

The brush of his fingers against her skin as he laced her up made her ache for him all over again. "Now that the Specter is gone for the rest of the night, I see no point in staying. I think I'll return to the Home."

He rested his hands on her shoulders. "I thought you were staying because you were worried about my wound."

"If you're well enough to threaten the Specter in the alley, you're well enough to survive your 'scratch' until morning, I expect."

A groan erupted from him. "You heard what we said, didn't you?" His fingers dug into her shoulders. "Did you hear everything?"

She sighed. No point to hiding her eavesdropping now. "Yes, I heard everything."

He turned her around to face him, his eyes full of misery. "God, Clara, I didn't *mean* any of it! I was only playing a role to allay his suspicions so he didn't—"

"I know that," she protested before he could continue. "Really, Morgan, do you think I trust you so little?"

He frowned. "To be honest, angel, I never know what to

expect from you. You take me by surprise every moment."

"I'm not so foolish as to think you made love to me only to gain my compliance in some criminal scheme." That reminded her of everything else he'd said to the Specter, and her earlier annoyance reappeared. "Though I don't see why you had to make me out to be such a ninny."

He blinked at her. "What do you mean?"

Wriggling free of his hands, she mimicked his arrogant tone. " 'Once I have the bars around her cage, I'll have her pickpockets out of theirs.' " She crossed her arms over her chest. "As if I'd just throw away all my aims for my children because you bedded me. Good Lord, you made me sound like a pea-goose."

"Better you sound like a pea-goose than a threat," Morgan said grimly.

His blatant concern shook her to her toes, reminding her of all that was at stake. "I-I suppose you have a point."

Coming up to her, he drew her stiff body into his arms. "Listen, angel. Spying is a nasty, dangerous business. The last thing I wanted was for you to be hurt by it. I'm sorry I couldn't handle it any better, but he knew you'd been here, and he considers you the enemy. I had to present some reason for why I'd make love to the enemy."

"I realize that." She slid her hands about his waist and laid her head against his bare chest. "It's just . . . well, it's embarrassing to have that horrible man think me so easy to sway."

He held her in a tight embrace. "I was afraid he wouldn't even believe me. Nobody who'd ever met you could doubt your determination and strong will for one second."

"And all that stuff he said about how to 'control' women gave me the shivers."

"Me, too." He planted a tender kiss to the top of her head. "I would never try to cage you, Clara, even if it could be done."

"I know that." She mused a moment. "But the way he spoke made me wonder if he practices such a method on a woman of his own."

He hesitated, and when he spoke, there was a hint of surprise in his voice. "I hadn't really thought about it."

She drew back to look at him with eyebrows raised. "That's because you're not a woman. But suppose he has a wife or mistress in Spitalfields. If you can't reach him using your present methods, you might get to him through her."

"An intriguing thought, but without knowing who she is, it's not much help."

"Perhaps I could ask around. See if any of the women around here have spoken of a mysterious male friend—"

"No!" he thundered. "You won't do any such thing. Don't involve yourself in this more than you already have. It's too dangerous."

She found his protectiveness enormously endearing, though she dared not let him realize it, or he'd turn into a complete bear. "I'm only trying to help, you know."

"You're trying to get yourself killed is what you're doing, and trying to take ten years off my life in the process." He clutched her closely enough to squeeze the breath from her. "I swear, if the Specter hadn't already found out about you, I'd lock you up until the investigation is over. Now I can't, or it'll arouse his suspicions. But I can still keep an eye on you."

"What do you mean?"

"He thinks I'm trying to keep you under my thumb, so I'll do just that. I'll look in on you at the Home and escort you to your carriage at night. At least that won't surprise the Specter if he hears of it."

She pulled away to glare at him. "Yes, but what will everyone else think? The entire neighborhood knows I've been trying to close your shop. If I suddenly welcome you at the Home, they'll wonder why I now find you a fit companion. The children will be confused, and the servants will assume I've given my conscience over to darker forces. You can't let them think that, Morgan. It will ruin everything I've tried to build."

"It won't be for long, angel. A few weeks at most, now that the Specter has agreed to my terms."

"No." She crossed her arms over her chest. "We'll simply have to pretend we're still enemies until after he's captured."

"He'll wonder about that."

"Let him wonder." She sifted back through what she'd heard of their conversation. "Just tell him I realized my error and I retreated. But I'll keep quiet because of your threat to expose me. Yes, tell him that." She glowered at him. "After all, if anybody should come out of this looking like the fool, it ought to be you and not me. If you'd only told me what you were up to in the first place, I never would have meddled."

He snorted. "You're meddling now."

"That's different. I'm trying to salvage the situation."

Threading his fingers through his hair, he glanced away. "All right, I'll think about it. Your solution does seem more workable." His gaze swung back to her. "But if I get any impression whatsoever that you're in danger—"

"You can step in and save the day," she said dryly. "You'll do it anyway, whether I want you to or not."

He stared at her so long that she grew uncomfortable beneath his gaze. At last he said, "And what about when this is over? What are we to be to each other then?"

She went very still, trying not to hope too much. "What do you mean?"

"I may not be 'civilized,' but I do have some conscience. Marriage is the only way to fix what we did tonight."

She'd be overjoyed if not for the decidedly cautious

phrasing of his proposal. If it was a proposal. She ought to clarify before she leaped to any conclusions. "So you're saying you wish to marry me."

He muttered a curse under his breath. "I'm saying I mean to do the right thing by you. I refuse to leave you ruined. So yes, I intend to give you my name in marriage."

His name, but apparently not his heart. She tried to smile as she watched all her hopes dying. "But you've never spoken of marriage before. I got the distinct impression you weren't interested in it."

He glanced away, jaw taut. "I told you—I know what I owe a woman whose innocence I took. I'm not a complete barbarian."

"I never said you were," she choked out, though disappointment swelled in her throat, threatening to prevent all speech entirely. God forbid he should want to marry her for any reason other than to assuage his conscience. That was too much to hope for.

Wandering to where her gown stood, she picked it up and slid into it. "So what happened to your plans to return to the sea?"

He shrugged. "Nothing. When this is over, we'll marry, and we'll live together as man and wife until I take command of my ship."

Anger welled up in her. He wanted to assuage his conscience *and* keep his freedom, too. That was so like a man. "Once you're at sea, I shall see you how often, do you think? Once a month? Twice a year?"

"I'm a naval captain. I spend most of my time at sea." He paused, looking very uncomfortable. "I suppose you could always go with me. Plenty of captains carry their wives with them."

"I can tell from your enthusiasm that you can't wait to be one of them."

He had the good grace to look guilty. "It's just that I assumed you would prefer to stay here so you could oversee your Home."

"Of course." He wouldn't have proposed marriage otherwise, curse him.

She couldn't breathe through the crushing pain that weighted her chest. She didn't expect him to love her—not yet, anyway. Clearly, he was still unsure of his feelings. But if he had proposed a real marriage, she might have accepted, hoping that in time he'd feel comfortable enough to admit he cared for her.

But this! *This* was unconscionable. She'd finally found a man she loved, a man she wanted to marry, and his idea of marriage was worse than none at all.

Swallowing her agony, she dredged up some portion of pride within her battered soul. "It's very thoughtful of you to offer, but I'm not interested in that sort of marriage."

She'd expected him to look relieved, not stunned. "What the devil sort of marriage are you talking about?"

"A marriage of convenience to protect my reputation. I've waited this long to marry precisely because I didn't want to settle for such an alliance. And that isn't going to change because you're having a crisis of conscience."

"Clara, you misunderstand me. I want this to be a real marriage—not a . . . an 'alliance,' as you call it."

"Perhaps it would be real when you're in England, but the rest of the time—"

"Are you worried that I won't be faithful to you when I'm at sea? Is that what this is about? Because I would, you know."

"That's not it." How could the man be so blind?

He looked flustered. "Then tell me what it is, damn it! I thought you'd be pleased. It's not as if I propose marriage to a woman every day."

"That's painfully obvious. You do it very badly."

"What's that supposed to mean?"

She tipped up her chin. "It means that I deserve better than a marriage where my husband stashes me somewhere convenient while he continues to live his life precisely as before. Where I'm left to worry about his welfare and if I'll ever see him again, while he throws himself into danger at the drop of a hat—"

Choking back a sob, she put her back to him so he couldn't see her distress. "Please help me fasten my dress. I have to go."

But when he came up behind her, it was to slide his arms about her waist and hold her resisting body tightly to him. "I'm touched that you worry about me, angel," he nuzzled her hair aside to whisper, "but after a while you'll get used to having me gone and you won't worry anymore. You'll be too busy with your life at the Home to—"

"What kind of coldhearted witch do you think I am?" She wrenched free of his arms to face him. "How could you even say such a thing?"

"Sailors' wives, captains' wives, do it all the time. I'm told they get used to having their husbands away for such long periods."

"I doubt that. And those who do may feel they have no choice. But I have a choice, and it's not to have a husband who would rather be away from me than with me."

His eyes chilled to shards of black ice. "I didn't say that. This has nothing to do with how I feel about you—"

"Doesn't it?"

"No! This is my livelihood. You'd think you could accept it."

"If I thought that you truly loved commanding a ship and going to sea, I wouldn't quarrel with you, Morgan. But I've known a sailor or two. The ones who yearn for the sea speak of it often. Everything on land compares unfavorably to life aboard ship; they count the days until they can be back at the helm. You aren't like that. In all the time I've known you, you've never spoken of your longing to be at sea."

He clearly had no answer for that, because he came up and turned her around, then silently began to fasten her gown.

She went on in a low voice. "You're not running *to* the sea, Morgan. You're running *away* from me."

"I'm not running to or away from anything. This is just the way marriage is for women who marry sailors." He finished fastening her gown up, his breath beating hot and angry against her neck.

The instant she felt his hands leave her gown, she turned to face him. "Fine. Then I suppose I'm just not ready to be a sailor's wife. I have no desire to spend my life tied to a man who has little use for me while I sit yearning for what I can't have—a real husband at my side."

"My God, Clara, I . . ." He rubbed his hands wearily over his face. "You don't understand. I don't know how to be a real husband. I can't . . . give you what you want."

As she looked into his face, she realized he was telling the truth. Or what he thought was the truth. For whatever reason, he didn't believe he could be a real husband to her or that he was capable of a real marriage.

Perversely, that calmed all her anger. Because she believed he could. And a tiny, foolish part of her hoped that with time she could make him believe it, too. But not if she agreed to let him have this lesser version of a marriage now.

"If you can't give me what I want," she said softly, "then you can't give me anything."

His jaw tightened. "I can give you my name and protect you from a scandal."

"There won't be any scandal. With any luck, I can sneak back into the Home unnoticed, and no one will ever know what happened between us."

"And if you're carrying my child?"

The thought struck the breath from her. Morgan's child. *Their* child. A little boy with mischievous black eyes who dipped pigtails in inkwells. Or a chubby-cheeked girl laughing at danger as she fell into her father's open arms from a tree limb she'd climbed.

"That would change everything, of course," she said. "I have no desire to lay the stain of bastardy on any child of mine."

"Thank God you have *some* sense."

"Though that does raise an interesting question. If we were to marry for the sake of a child, I assume you would still not be around to raise him." She eyed him closely. "You were raised without a father. Tell me, is that what you want for your child? That he should grow up hardly knowing his father at all?"

Judging from his stricken expression, that was something he hadn't considered.

She left him to think on that while she went to the bed and drew on her stockings, tied her garters, and tugged on her boots. When she lifted her gaze again, he was watching her with unmistakable hunger . . . and a look she'd never seen in his face before, as if he were watching the ship to heaven pull away from the dock without him. His look told her instantly that he wasn't revealing *all* his reasons for his reluctance to stay in London with her. But until he did, there wasn't much she could do about it.

When she stood and swept her skirts down, he stiffened. "Clara, we're both tired, and it's late. We shouldn't make any major decisions just now. Promise me you'll take some time to think about this."

"I won't change my mind, Morgan." Not unless he changed his mind about the sort of marriage he wanted.

Without warning, he stepped close to grip her arms, then

held her still for a fervent kiss so fierce that she couldn't deny it to him. He kissed her long and deep, with a fiery passion meant to reduce her to ash. Which it did so effortlessly she could have cried.

When at last he drew back, his eyes shone overly bright, and his fingers dug into her shoulders as if to imprison her. "I could make it so you had no choice, *cherie*. I could keep you here in my bed until Johnny and Samuel arrive in the morning. Then you'd have to marry me at once to avoid the scandal."

She met his gaze with her own steady one. "Yes, you could do that. But what would the Specter think if you married the woman you're merely using? And you don't want to rouse his suspicions, do you?"

He stared at her a long moment, indecision flickering in his face. Then with a low curse, he released her.

Taking up her cloak, she settled it about her shoulders, then turned toward the door. She found no pleasure in her successful parry. She wished he would indeed keep her here, for that would show he cared more than he let on.

But he didn't. And she couldn't stay.

She'd nearly reached the closed door to the front of the shop when he said, "We're not finished, you and I. Not as far as I'm concerned."

A small smile touched her lips. At least he wasn't giving up too easily. Perhaps there was hope for them yet. "I won't be your mistress, Morgan, and I won't be your sometime wife. But if you decide you want more than that, you know where to find me."

Then she left.

Chapter 19

In Works of Labour or of Skill
I would be busy too.
For Satan finds some mischief still
For idle Hands to do.
"Against Idleness and Mischief," Isaac Watts,
Divine Songs attempted in Easy Language
for the Use of Children

Morgan watched her go with a sickening lurch in the pit of his stomach. He couldn't believe she was simply walking away like this—unprotected, ruined, teetering on the brink of possible scandal. Damned fool woman!

Slipping out the door after her, he padded barefooted up to the street to watch as his angel of the alley walked the short distance to the Home.

The cold glow of light on the horizon showed that dawn threatened to break any moment, yet she'd wisely chosen her time to escape. The street was entirely deserted. Not even a nightman stirred in the pre-dawn. When she disappeared inside the Home without apparently being noticed by anyone, he didn't know whether to be relieved or frustrated. He didn't want to have her at the cost of her reputation, but he didn't want to watch her walk away either.

Cursing under his breath, he reentered his shop. This hadn't turned out at all as he'd planned. She should have agreed to marry him. Then he could rest easy that he'd done right by her.

But Clara would never let him off easily. That would be too simple for her. It wasn't enough that he offered her his name. She demanded everything—hearth and home, children, his entire life at her disposal.

If only she knew what she asked. But how could she? She foolishly thought he was choosing between her and the sea. That would be no choice at all—he'd take her over the sea any day.

What he couldn't take was this place . . . and the fear that the longer he stayed here, the more likely that she'd see the real him one day and recoil in disgust.

As it was, he'd told her far more about himself tonight than he'd meant to. And the fact that she'd been sweet and understanding about it only made it worse. It increased his urge to confess everything, all his dark, nasty secrets. To show her the parts of him she would surely loathe.

It was this place, this despairing hole of London, that kept his past so near the surface. Perhaps away from here, he could be easy with her, and they could have a chance. Yes, perhaps if he took her to sea with him . . .

Bon Dieu, what was he thinking? She'd never leave her charges. Not for him or anyone.

But that didn't mean he would give her up. No, indeed. One way or the other, she *would* marry him. He'd wear her down somehow. It was for her own good.

Or so he told himself.

Exhausted in every muscle, he headed for his bed, then stopped short as he caught sight of the room. The place was a mess—the bloodstained sheet still on the bed, the other sheet tangled on the floor, the brandy bottle listing to one side on the floor with the contents spewing out. The whole place smelled of brandy and Clara's jasmine scent. Johnny and Samuel would be here soon, and they'd guess something had happened the minute they walked in if he left it this way, especially since Johnny had to come through here on his way upstairs.

He groaned. No rest for the wicked.

So he threw on his clothes and boots and set about putting the room to rights. He had to refill his pitcher at the tree in the street—the communal water pump—three times to wash the blood out of the sheet and scrub away the brandy. By the time he'd straightened the room, hung the damp bottom sheet from a rafter near the stove to dry, and remade the bed using only the top sheet, the sun had risen. He scarcely had time to stuff Clara's forgotten petticoat under the bed before the knock at the door signaled Johnny and Samuel's return.

When he answered the door, Samuel held up a pistol. "What the bloody hell happened last night? Found this in the alley, and Johnny claims it belongs to his sister. Their father left it when he was sent away. Johnny says she uses it for protection."

"That isn't all she uses it for," Morgan grumbled under his breath as he stood aside to let the two of them in. So Clara had been right again—Lucy had been the impostor.

Samuel and Johnny headed into the back room without paying him much notice. When he came up beside them, Samuel was scowling. "What's going on here? Lucy's gun lying out in the alley and now this?"

"What do you mean?" Morgan asked, worried he'd missed something.

Samuel glared at him. "You've had a woman in your bed. I can smell it. The whole room reeks of it."

It took him a second to realize what Samuel was implying. "You think that Lucy and I—" He let out a short laugh. "First she shoots me, and then you accuse me of lying with her. And I haven't even met the woman."

"Lucy shot you?" Samuel asked, his anger turning to bewilderment.

"You're bamming us!" Johnny lifted wide, shocked eyes to Morgan. "Aren't you?"

"Unfortunately, I'm serious." He smoothed his trouser leg over his thigh enough to show the bulge of the bandage beneath. "She came here last night all dressed up like the Specter, trying to scare me into kicking you out and sending you back to live with her."

Johnny's face lit up. "She did?" And then, as if aware he was being callous about Morgan's injury, he sobered. "She wouldn't do that. She wouldn't shoot you for that."

"The shooting was an accident, but I think we should make sure it doesn't happen again." He wanted Johnny out of here anyway, now that matters with the Specter had grown more serious. "You need to go live at your sister's, Johnny." He glanced beyond Johnny to Samuel. "Do you think you could see to it?"

Samuel nodded grimly. "And I'll see to it that she don't bother you no more, too."

"Now see here," Johnny protested, "I don't want to live with her!"

Morgan laid his hands on the boy's shoulders and stared down into the uncertain, frightened face. "You can come here during the day to work, and I'll pay you your wages. But I don't want you here at night."

When Johnny still looked crestfallen, Morgan changed tactics. "Your sister needs you, or she wouldn't have taken such extreme measures to get you back. You don't want your sister living all alone at the tavern, do you? Where men can get rough with her?"

It was clear the boy hadn't thought of that. "She can take care of herself," he replied, but he sounded doubtful.

"Perhaps she can. But it never hurts to have family around. So it's time for you to grow up and be a man, Johnny. It's time for you to take responsibility for your family. Which means living with your sister and looking out for her."

Johnny straightened his shoulders. "All right. I suppose I could do that."

"But no stealing," Morgan added.

Johnny shook his head. "No stealing."

At least he'd succeeded that much with the boy in the short time Johnny had been here.

"Come on then, Johnny," Samuel said, clapping one hand on the boy's shoulder. "Let's go upstairs and gather your things." He cast Morgan an apologetic look. "Sorry about what I said. About having a woman in here."

"It's all right," Morgan said, knowing that Samuel would change his tune if he ever learned Clara had been here. "Now go on, both of you. Before Lucy comes after me with a sword."

He felt oddly regretful as he watched Johnny head upstairs with Samuel. He'd grown attached to the boy. For that matter, he'd grown attached to Samuel. And God knows he was falling under Clara's spell so quickly he hardly knew how to break free.

When he left London, he'd not only be leaving her behind, but he'd be leaving them, too. The thought hadn't occurred to him before.

But he shook it off almost as soon as it came. He knew what he wanted, and it wasn't this place or these people. He couldn't live here, no matter how much Clara pleaded. He'd just have to make her understand that.

Clara was awakened midmorning by whispering outside the door of the small bedchamber she slept in when she was at the Home. Rubbing her bleary eyes, she sat up straight and cried, "Who is it?"

The door opened a crack, and Peg stuck her head in. "Begging your pardon, m'lady, but Miss Lucy's here to see you. And she won't leave."

"Let me talk to her," came Lucy's voice from beyond the door.

With a sigh, Clara slid from the bed and threw on her heavy wool wrapper. "I'm coming, Peg." Swiftly she crammed her tired feet into slippers and headed for the door, trying to clear the fog from her brain. Five hours was just not enough sleep for any sane person. And why was she so sore between her legs, for heaven's sake?

Lucy burst into the room before Clara could even reach the door. "I got to talk to you," she said, then shot Peg a glare. "Alone, if you please."

Clara nodded and Peg left, grumbling about girls who didn't know their place.

As soon as Peg left, Lucy burst into tears. "Oh, m'lady, I done an awful thing!"

Clara blinked, feeling an overwhelming need for coffee and a bath. And then it hit her. Why she'd spent the night at the Home. Why she was sore. And why Lucy might be standing here in a panic this morning.

She groaned. She wasn't up to this right now. "Lucy, this is not the time—"

"It was me last night. I admit it. It was me that stopped you in the alley."

Wonderful. Whoever said confession was good for the soul hadn't been forced to take one after half a night's sleep. "I figured as much," Clara mumbled as she headed for the basin to splash some cold water on her face.

"What?" Lucy said.

"Nothing. But why tell me this now?"

"Because they'll be coming for me soon. They'll find the pistol and know it's mine and . . ." She broke off with a wail. "And you got to tell them I didn't mean to kill Cap'n Pryce! You was there, and you got to tell them I didn't mean to do it!"

With a bewildered look, Clara faced her. "Kill him? What are you talking about?"

"You can't let them hang me for it! It was an accident, and I know—"

"It's all right," Clara broke in. "You didn't kill him."

Lucy lifted a face ravaged with tears. "What?"

"He's fine. You only nicked him a bit."

"But I saw him slide down that wall! I saw him! I saw the blood!"

"What blood?" Samuel asked as he burst into the room behind Lucy, then skidded to a halt when he saw Clara standing in her wrapper. He blushed a deep red. "Begging your pardon, m'lady, but they told me downstairs that Lucy was here and I been looking all over for her."

Clara bit back a smile. "It's all right, Samuel. Lucy and I were just discussing something. It doesn't concern you, so you can—"

"Oh, Samuel!" Lucy cried and threw herself into Samuel's arms, putting the lie to Clara's claim. "I done an awful thing! You got to help me!"

"There, there," Samuel murmured soothingly as he cast Clara a quizzical look. "It'll be all right."

"I shot him, Samuel! I shot the captain with Papa's gun!"

"Captain Pryce is fine, as I told you," Clara broke in

firmly. She'd had about enough of these dramatics. "You needn't worry about it any more."

"Lady Clara's right," Samuel added as he stroked Lucy's hair. "The cap'n is perfectly fine. Just a bit sore in the leg. And I brought your gun back, see?" Samuel held it up.

"You did?" Lucy took it from him with one hand while she scrubbed tears away with the other. "And you're sure he's all right? He ain't gonna tell the police and have me hanged?"

"They don't hang you for shooting somebody," Samuel said dryly. "Just for killing them. Which you didn't do. And no, he ain't gonna do nothing to you." He smiled and rubbed a wayward tear from her cheek. "What's even better, he's sending your brother home to you. Johnny's coming home, so you have naught to worry about, do you hear?"

Lucy's face lit up, and she sniffled. "Truly?"

"Johnny's outside waiting for you, I swear. Captain Pryce told him he had to take care of his sister, so that's what he's gonna do."

"Did you hear that?" Lucy exclaimed, beaming at Clara. "And it's all your doing, too. You talked to him, didn't you? After I . . . I was so foolish and nearly kilt you both. You talked to the cap'n and made him send Johnny home."

Clara figured Morgan's actions had more to do with the escalating situation with the Specter, but she couldn't say that, so she just shrugged. Too late, she realized what Lucy's words must mean to Samuel, for his face had darkened and he was staring at her.

"What's Lucy talking about?" he asked, eyes narrowing. "Were you with Cap'n Pryce last night when he was shot?"

Before Clara could chime in, Lucy answered, "You leave her be, Samuel. She was spying on him when I went to talk to him . . . when I nearly kilt him. She looked after him, didn't you, Lady Clara?"

Clara could see in Samuel's eyes that he suspected exactly what she'd done in "looking after" Morgan. But how could he guess? She couldn't believe Morgan would have said anything.

"Lucy, go wait in the hall for me," Samuel said. "I got to talk to m'lady in private."

Lucy hesitated, glancing nervously from Clara to Samuel. Then she sighed and left the room.

Clara couldn't breathe. Heavens, it was already happening—the suspicions, the lies she'd have to tell. What had she been thinking last night when she'd recklessly thrown herself into Morgan's arms? This could mean disaster for her reputation, for the Home . . .

Well, she wouldn't let it come to that. She wouldn't. She hated lying to Samuel, but it couldn't be helped. The alternative was too awful to contemplate. Clara waited until the girl was gone and then said in her most imperious voice, "Yes, what is it?"

Samuel met her gaze stubbornly. "The cap'n had a woman spend the night with him last night. In his bedchamber."

Alarm churned in her belly. "He told you that?"

"Didn't have to. I could smell it."

Smell it? Good Lord, that was something she hadn't prepared for. "I can't see what the captain's having a woman in his room might have to do with me."

"Lucy says you were there at his shop."

"And if I was?"

"I'm not talking about some friendly visit, mind you." He swallowed, then added, "He had a woman in his bed."

"Samuel!" Clara cried, summoning all the shock she could convey. "You cannot possibly believe that *I* was the woman."

Crossing his arms over his chest, he glared at her. "Then what were you doing inside his shop? At night? Alone with him? And don't try to deny it. I could smell that scent you always wear."

Clara cast Samuel her Stanbourne Stare, reminding herself that he might seem like a friend at times, but he could still destroy her life with one wayward word. "Not that it's any of your affair, Samuel, but Captain Pryce was hurt, so yes, I went into his bedchamber long enough to dress his wound. That's all. Then I came back here and spent the night." God forgive her for such a blatant lie.

Thankfully, her words seemed to bring him up short. "But his shop smelled of . . ." He trailed off uncertainly as she glared at him. "I mean . . ."

She didn't have to pretend the blush that rose to her cheeks. "Even if Captain Pryce had been in any condition to engage in the sort of inappropriate . . . behavior that you imply, I would never, ever do such a thing."

Apparently, it had begun to dawn on him how outrageous was the accusation he was making. "Well, I didn't think so, but I wasn't . . . I mean . . ."

"Why, the man is a fence," she protested, tamping down on her guilt at lying so egregiously. "If you think that I would ever—"

"I wasn't thinking! That is . . ." He hung his head, suitably chastened. "Aw, m'lady, I didn't mean it how it sounded. I'm only worried about you is all." He shoved his hands in his pockets. "He's got his eye on you—anybody can see that. But I know you would never consort with his kind."

"Certainly not," Clara went on, satisfied that she'd convinced him not to believe the truth. But that wouldn't work more than once, and she didn't think she could stomach lying to him again. Which made it all the more imperative that she stay away from Morgan until this matter of the Specter was finished. "Have you any more appalling accusations to make, Samuel?"

Flushing crimson, he shook his head, and she felt another

spurt of guilt. Still, it was frightening how perceptive Samuel was.

"Good," she said, determined to put the matter behind them. "Now I have a concern of my own regarding that pistol of Lucy's."

"Don't you worry none," he said, clearly relieved to abandon the subject himself. "I ain't letting Lucy shoot nobody else."

"She shouldn't carry such a weapon when she doesn't know how to use it."

"I agree, m'lady. I'll take care of it, I will. I'll take care of it right now." Turning on his heel, he walked out into the hall.

Clara followed, curious to see how he would handle the agitated girl. Lucy had wandered down to the foyer, where she was peering out the front window, obviously looking for Johnny.

"Lucy," Samuel announced as he and Clara approached, "I'm going to teach you how to shoot."

"What?" Clara said as Lucy whirled to face them. That was not what she'd had in mind.

Samuel cast Clara an apologetic glance. "It's better for her to have protection in these parts. But if I teach her how to use it all proper-like, then she can't hurt nobody."

"But Samuel—"

"Yes!" Lucy exclaimed. "Teach me how, Samuel. I asked Mr. Fitch to do it, but he wouldn't. He says girls have no business carrying pistols."

"He might be right about that," Clara mumbled, thinking of how wildly Lucy had brandished the pistol last night.

"I'm gonna teach you, and that's that," Samuel said stoutly. "I don't care what your Mr. Fitch thinks."

A troubled expression crossed Lucy's face. "Mr. Fitch

will already be sore that I'm taking Johnny back. He's not going to like *that* one bit."

"Lucy," Clara said softly, "don't you think you'd be better off with a man who'd accept your brothers?"

"Not if I can't support them," she said woefully. "Rodney's got that big house of his, and they wouldn't be no trouble if he could just get to like them—"

"Let 'Rodney' keep his big house," Samuel put in fiercely. Stepping up beside Lucy, he laid his arm on the back of her shoulder. "I can look after you and the boys if you'd only let me."

Lucy glanced uncertainly from Samuel to Clara. What the girl's heart wanted was clear, but her mind still worked against her. "You got no place to keep us, Sam."

"I'll find a place. Lady Clara will help us, won't you, m'lady?"

He cast her a look of such desperate appeal that her heart ached for him. "Yes, I'll help you. And perhaps I can find a job for you that would allow you to support a wife—"

"A wife!" Lucy exclaimed, ducking her head shyly. "Oh, no, m'lady, Sam ain't thinking of marrying me."

"Ain't I?" Samuel retorted. When Lucy lifted her face to his in surprise, he added, "I'm old enough to marry—nigh on to twenty years old. And . . . and I want to take care of you and the boys, honest I do." Tears filled her eyes, and he brushed one away with his thumb. "Aw, Lucy, I been in love with you since forever, practically since the first day I realized I was a man. You just forget that Fitch and marry *me*. The rest will take care of itself."

Lucy still hadn't said anything, was just staring at him dumbstruck. So Samuel took matters into his own hands, pulled her close, and kissed her.

Clara turned away, wanting to give them privacy and hide

her own tears of joy for Lucy. And if she were honest, her tears of envy, too. She would give anything to have Morgan want her as much as Samuel clearly wanted Lucy. Watching them kiss so sweetly was almost more than she could bear this morning.

She had no time to dwell on it, however, for the front door swung suddenly open, and her aunt's cheerful voice echoed over the threshold.

"This, Lord Winthrop, is the Home," Aunt Verity announced. Then as Clara groaned and turned toward the door, a little squeak sounded from her aunt. "Good lack-a-daisy, what is going on here?"

Good lack-a-daisy indeed. Lord Winthrop had apparently made good on his threat to volunteer his services at the Home. His eyes were agog as he took in first the kissing couple and then Clara standing motionless, still draped in her nightgown and wrapper and nothing else.

"What sort of heathen place is this?" he boomed. "There's a boy lolling about out front looking suspicious . . . people in here behaving like animals . . . why, this man has a pistol sticking out of his pocket . . . and I say, Lady Clara, where are your clothes?"

Clara sighed. Five hours of sleep would definitely not be enough to see her through *this* day.

Chapter 20

A Mushroom their Table, and on it was laid
A Water-dock Leaf, which a Table-cloth made.
The Butterfly's Ball, and the
Grasshopper's Feast, *William Roscoe*

Three days. Morgan couldn't believe he and Clara had been apart three days. It felt like three months. Three years. It felt like an eternity.

Bon Dieu, what had the wench done to him? She consumed his waking thoughts and bedeviled his dreams. The craving for her ate at him like a sickness, for which she was the only cure.

So he saw her the only way he could. Every morning, he made sure to be busy in front of the shop when her coach came by to bring her to the Home. Every evening, he watched from the same place as Samuel handed her back into the coach to go home. He'd even contrived once or twice to be heading to the tavern in the evening so he could pass her on the street, perversely wanting to test her determination to stay away from him.

She never gave him so much as a glance.

Today, she would give him more than that, he vowed as he strode up the street to her Home. He had come on a mission, and all her stubbornness wouldn't stop him.

Because tonight he was meeting the Specter. The man had already sent a message to say that Morgan should await his instructions at the shop at 8 P.M. Less than twelve hours from now, Morgan would be embarking on the most dangerous encounter of his life, and before it happened he wanted time with her. He deserved it, by God. He'd lived by her rules for three days. Now she could give him a few hours.

He'd nearly reached the Home when he noticed two children sitting in the shadow of the stone stairs, curled up together and giggling. Then they spotted him, and the giggling stopped. The boy grew sullen, and the girl went pale. Morgan tipped his hat to them, but as he started to climb the stairs, the boy sprang to his feet and leaped up onto the stairs in front of Morgan, blocking his path.

The boy jerked his shoulder toward the door. "You going in there?"

"I'd like to. If you'll get out of my way."

"All right. But if you please, sir, would you keep it quiet that you saw me and Mary out here?"

Morgan glanced over to where the girl eyed him curiously over the steps. "Why?"

Mary piped up. "If Lady Clara knows we're out here, she'll make me and David go back in. Then we'll have to put up with Winter."

"Winter?" Morgan gazed up at the clear spring sky, wondering what the hell she meant.

"It's *Lord* Winter, silly," David corrected the girl. "Not just 'Winter.' Odsfish, Mary, don't you know nothing?"

Lord Winter? Could they mean Winthrop? It had to be. And the idea of that pompous idiot spending time in Clara's Home didn't sit well with Morgan.

"What's Lord 'Winter' doing here?" he asked.

David tucked his thumbs in his trouser pockets. "He's been coming here for three days. Says he wants to help, but I think he just wants to keep an eye on Lady Clara, 'cause when she ain't around, he acts like he don't really like being here."

"I see. And what's he doing now?"

"He's supposed to be reading to us while Lady Clara works in her office."

"But he's awful at reading." Mary rolled her dark eyes expressively. "He won't read us stories at all. He reads these . . . what d'you call 'em, David?"

"Homilies." As David made a sour face, a shock of fine brown hair fell into his hazel eyes. "It's worse than the Bible Mrs. Carter reads afore bedtime. At least there's stories in the Bible. But this is just 'don't do this' and 'don't do that' is all."

"And he makes us memorize them, too," Mary said petulantly. She flashed Morgan a hopeful look. "Do you read stories?"

Morgan hid his smile. "Not today. I've only come to speak to Lady Clara briefly."

"Don't s'pose you could take that Lord Winter with you when you leave, could you?" David asked.

"I'm sure Lady Clara would rather that he stay."

Mary shook her head, her pigtails flopping. "I don't think so. The first day he came here, he made a big row, and Lady Clara's been sore at him ever since. I can tell when she's sore, too—she gets that look on her face, like somebody stuck a pin in her bottom. Whenever that Lord Winter comes in, she walks around like she's got a pin in her bottom. Only I wish somebody would stick a pin in Lord Winter's bottom instead."

Morgan wanted fervently to oblige her, but he had to

avoid Lord "Winter." The man would call him Blakely and ruin Morgan's carefully crafted image of himself as a fence. But damn, if he didn't tire of this double life. He'd be glad when it was all over.

"So what have you come to talk to Lady Clara about?" David asked.

"I hope you're here to cheer her up," Mary put in. " 'Cause when Lady Clara is sad, it ain't the same around here."

"Has she been sad?" Morgan's gut tightened painfully. He didn't like thinking she hadn't missed him, yet perversely he didn't like knowing she might be unhappy. *Sacrebleu*, the woman was turning him inside out.

"She's all right." David shot Mary a cautioning glance. "Why do you want to know about Lady Clara anyway? You're the cap'n, ain't you? Johnny's friend?"

"Yes."

"Then you ain't got no business being here. Lady Clara will skin your hide, she will, if she sees you talking to us. Being as how you're a fence and all."

"You may be right. Nonetheless, I need to speak to her privately about an important matter. So I'll make you a bargain. I'll keep quiet about you and your friend skulking about out here—"

"We ain't skulking!" Mary protested.

"—if you'll tell me how to get in to see Lady Clara without any of the servants or the other children seeing me. Do you think you could manage that?"

As David looked thoughtful, Mary mumbled, "We wasn't skulking, that's all I'm saying. It ain't skulking if a body's just sitting there leaving folks be . . ."

Paying her no mind, David nodded. "We can go round by the back stairs. It goes right up to the hall by Lady Clara's office. Won't nobody see you if I keep a lookout for Peg and Mrs. Carter."

"Lead on then. There's a guinea in it for you if you can manage it."

"A guinea!" Mary exclaimed, all her protests forgotten. "Can I help?"

Morgan hesitated, then said, "I'll give you a guinea of your own if you'll do something else for me. But it's not something you'll like, I'm afraid." He eyed her as if somehow finding fault, then shook his head. "No, I don't think you'll do it. Since you dislike Lord 'Winter' so much."

She planted her little hands on bony hips and thrust out her lower lip. "I can do anything you want for a guinea."

"Can you keep Lord 'Winter' busy until I've finished my business with Lady Clara? I don't want him bothering us while I'm talking to her."

Mary frowned. "You mean, I have to go back in there and listen to the old codger?"

"Yes. And if he tries to seek out Lady Clara, you have to coax him into staying put." He started to climb back down the stairs. "Oh, never mind, I knew you couldn't—"

"I'll do it!" She held out her hand. "But I want my guinea now."

He suppressed a smile. "Fair enough."

When he handed her the guinea, she bit it, then flashed him a toothy smile. Squaring her shoulders, she marched up the stairs with all the regal bearing of a miniature Clara. At the top, she paused to strike a dramatically languid pose. "If I die of boredom, Captain, pray give me a good burial."

As she sauntered inside, Morgan couldn't restrain a laugh. But David merely snorted and grabbed his arm. "This way, Cap'n, if you want to see Lady Clara."

Another guinea poorer and scarcely a minute later, Morgan found himself inside the building. He was in a hallway, facing the imposing door to what David had told him was

Clara's office. The hall was deserted, thank God, because all the children were downstairs.

He hesitated only a second before easing the door open to slip inside. And there she was—his obsession, sitting at an ancient oak desk etched with scratches and stained with ink. Sunlight from a back window streaked across the room to dab at her muslin-draped arms and shoulders, gilding them in morning gold. Her head was bent as she concentrated on the ledger lying open before her. She was so absorbed she didn't even notice anyone had entered.

But Morgan noticed everything—how ringlets of her pretty chestnut hair fringed her drawn brow, how the tip of her pink tongue darted out to lick her lips as she worked a sum, how her mere presence in the room made it brighter, bigger, sweeter.

When he moved further inside and closed the door behind him, however, her head shot up and the spell was broken.

"Morgan!" Pleasure briefly flashed in her face before agitation replaced it. "What are you doing here? I told you we mustn't be seen together!"

"It's all right. I sneaked in."

She jumped up, suddenly as skittish as a cat, her gaze darting to the door, her hands fluttering to smooth and straighten her skirts. It pleased him that he could unnerve her as easily as she unnerved him.

"You have to leave," she protested. "Lord Winthrop is here, and if he sees you, it will be disaster."

"Don't worry, it's taken care of." He rounded her desk. "What's he doing here anyway?"

"Oh, it's ridiculous." Her sweet mouth drew up into a pout. "He's got this foolish idea in his head that he should volunteer here. I asked him at the ball to come work with the boys, but I never thought he'd do it. I was trying to put him off for good." She sighed. "No such luck. I told you—my aunt is set on marrying me off to him, and now he seems to be falling in with her plans."

Morgan scowled and caught her about the waist before she could back away. "Well, that's out, because you're marrying me."

"Morgan—"

He cut off her words with a kiss, taking solace in her easy response, in the way she melted beneath his touch. He tasted lemons as he buried his tongue in the welcoming warmth of her luscious mouth over and over, wishing he could do more than kiss her.

Suddenly, she tore away from him, her eyes wide and her breath coming quickly. "We mustn't do this. Not here."

"I know," he said regretfully as he allowed her to slip from his arms. "That's why I'm taking you away for the day."

"What? You can't!"

"I can. My sister-in-law has invited you and your aunt to join her and my brother and me for an excursion into the countryside. A picnic, as it were. She has even convinced Ravenswood to come along to accompany your aunt."

"But . . . but . . ." she sputtered.

"Remember, Juliet thinks we work here together. She told me to convince you to come with us for the day. And if I can't manage it, she plans on coming down here to fetch you herself." He cast her a taunting smile. "So you see, angel, you have no choice. If you don't come out with us, she'll show up here with my brother and ruin my entire scheme to capture the Specter. Just think of how the denizens of Spitalfields would react to see my twin descend from the Templemore coach, accompanied by footmen in full livery. You wouldn't want to be responsible for that disaster, would you?"

"No, but . . . but couldn't you talk Lady Juliet out of her plans? You should have told her you couldn't do it or we were busy or . . . or . . ."

"Why would I do that? It was my idea." When her confusion turned to anger, he added softly, "I wanted to be with you, angel, and I knew you'd never come out alone with me, so I engaged Juliet's help. Now that the wheels are set in motion, you have to come."

Her eyes narrowed. "This is blackmail, Morgan, and you know it."

Reaching out, he caught her hand and lifted it for his kiss. "I do what I must to get what I want. And I want a day with you, *ma belle ange*. One day is all I ask." He swept his other arm wide to take in the room and beyond. "Away from this, away from Spitalfields. Can't you spare me even one day?"

She bit her lower lip, clearly undecided, though her eyes were fixed on the single window showing a perfect blue sky outside. He fancied that she tightened her grip on his hand as she stared out at the beautiful morning. "What shall I do about Lord Winthrop?"

He tugged her into his arms. "I can think of any number of suitable things—drowning, hanging, drawing and quartering—"

"Don't be absurd," she retorted with a weak laugh. "And I thought you said you weren't jealous of him."

He bent his head to nuzzle her hair and got a noseful of her sweet jasmine scent. Longing tightened a band around his chest. "I'm jealous of everyone who has your attention—the children in the Home, your aunt, Samuel . . . all of them. Because you give them everything while you begrudge me even a few hours . . ."

"And you begrudge me a lifetime," she whispered into his cravat.

He winced. Damn her for always cutting right to the point. "I'll begrudge you nothing today. Will you come spend the day with me?" He swept his hands along the curves of her waist, wishing they had time for more. "Please?"

"I-I can't very well just walk out the door with you."

"No. I'll leave the way I came. Wait a few minutes, and call for your coach, then go fetch your aunt and join us at the Templemore town house."

"Are you sure you want me to bring Aunt Verity? She knows you as Captain Pryce, and she's sure to say something to your family."

"Confound it all, I forgot about that." He cupped her cheek. "No, that would muck things up considerably. Is there any way you could leave her at home? You could tell Juliet that she's sick or something."

"I'll do that. It would hardly help for us to go to all this trouble to hide your true identity only to have my aunt blathering it everywhere."

His breath caught. "Does that mean you'll come?"

She cast him an arch glance. "You're giving me no choice, are you?"

"None."

"Then I suppose I *have* to, don't I?"

"Absolutely." The intensity of his relief that she'd said yes astonished him. "Sebastian and Juliet are taking us to an abandoned pleasure garden just outside London. He purchased it from a friend and hasn't yet decided what to do with it. But it has ponds and waterfalls and a little arbor. I think you'll like it."

A smile broke over her face. "I'll admit I could use a break from the Home." She gestured to the desk. "And I'd much prefer a day in the country to doing the books."

"Good." He took a slip of paper from his pocket. "When you leave here, send your coachman to this address. We'll be there waiting." He tipped up her chin with one finger. "And if you haven't come within the hour, I swear Juliet will drive down here and—"

"I know, I know. She'll ruin your entire scheme to capture the Specter, and it'll be all my fault."

He chuckled. "You're a fast learner, angel. But in case you get that little mind of yours working after I leave and think to change your plans—" Dragging her into his arms, he kissed her again, slowly, leisurely, taking his time to rouse her, letting his hands roam over the soft contours of her slender frame.

When he drew back, he was hard as iron and wishing he didn't have to share her with his family today. "God, how I've missed you," he whispered against her pinkening cheek.

"Me, too."

They stood there a moment until a rattling of pebbles against the window made him jerk back. That was the signal he'd agreed upon with young David to indicate that Lord Winthrop and the children had come out into the hall downstairs. "I have to go," he told her, pausing only to brush another kiss across her lips. "But I'll see you in an hour, angel."

Then he let himself out the way he'd come.

Clara could hardly contain her excitement as the Templemore carriage trundled out of the city. Her head told her to resent Morgan's manipulation, but her heart thrilled to it. That he had missed her would have been enough, but for him to have gone to all this trouble . . . It gave her hope.

So did the way his family had welcomed her, as if they expected an announcement of marriage any day.

Take care, she cautioned herself. But it was no use. She was too happy sitting across from Morgan in this delightful carriage, too pleased to be leaving the grimy streets of London behind on such a gorgeous day, if only for a few hours.

"Are you sure Lord Templemore is all right up there?" she asked Lady Juliet.

Lady Juliet, pretty and prim, smiled fondly at Clara. "Believe me, he's having the time of his life. Sebastian enjoys the outdoors almost as much as I do."

They'd planned to take two carriages until Clara had arrived without her aunt. When they'd realized that by fitting in only one extra person they could leave one carriage behind, Lord Templemore had chosen to ride with the coachman, and the other four of them had crowded into the lushly appointed but cramped family carriage.

She didn't mind the squeeze, not with Morgan across from her, his legs intimately interlaced with hers and his gaze hot upon her. In the hour since they'd left, she must have blushed half a dozen times at the way he looked at her, though she tried to suppress it whenever she caught Lord Ravenswood watching them both.

If Lady Juliet noticed the blushes, she was much too polite and well-bred to indicate it. "Do tell me," the young woman said, half-turning toward Clara, "how does our Morgan get on at the Home? Do you feel that the place is safer now that he spends his nights there?"

Clara swallowed. She hated lying to this perfectly nice woman, yet for some reason Morgan seemed determined not to tell his family what he was doing in Spitalfields. "Oh, yes, things are much better at night now that he's around," Clara murmured evasively. "I don't know what I shall do once he's gone."

Lady Juliet patted her arm. "Then we'll simply have to convince him to stay in London past the end of the wager, shan't we?"

"The wager?"

With a groan, Morgan cast his sister-in-law a long-suffering glance. "Really, Juliet, must we talk about that today? It's so pleasant out and—"

"Don't tell me he hasn't told you about his wager," Lady Juliet exclaimed. "Why, Morgan, that's too awful of you!"

"Yes, Morgan," Lord Ravenswood chimed in with a smirk. "You should have told her."

"Well, *somebody* should tell me," Clara put in. "My curiosity is thoroughly roused now."

As Morgan sighed, Lady Juliet explained. "About eight months ago, Morgan claimed that I wouldn't be able to tell him and Sebastian apart if they were both presented to me dressed exactly alike. I told him he was wrong, and we laid a little wager upon it."

Clara shot Morgan a teasing glance. "Really, Captain Blakely, how could you even take such a wager? A wife not be able to tell her husband from her husband's brother? It's ludicrous."

Morgan raised one brow. "I thought the identical twin thing would present an obstacle."

Clara and Lady Juliet exchanged one of those men-are-so-stupid glances. Deciding that she liked Lady Juliet already, Clara smiled impishly at Morgan. "I could distinguish you from your brother, I assure you."

"Could you really?" His eyes darkened to smoldering coals. "Even though I'm not yet your husband?"

The word *yet* hung in the air, and her mouth went dry. She really wished he wouldn't say things like that. It made Lady Juliet look speculative and Lord Ravenswood frown. "That's got . . . nothing to do with it. Anybody with good observational skills could tell the two of you apart."

"I don't know—I have trouble with it myself," Lord Ravenswood said dryly.

Morgan smiled his wolfish smile, clearly pleased at her claim.

Juliet clapped her hands. "Oh, we should do the wager again! We can use the same terms. Then Morgan shall be forced to spend yet another year staying out of trouble."

Morgan's smile vanished at once. "Don't even think it. I don't trust you two. And I learned my lesson the last time."

But Clara was more interested in Juliet's comment than

all Morgan's grousing. "What do you mean—he'd have to spend another year staying out of trouble?"

As Morgan glanced away, jaw tightening, Juliet said, "That was the agreement. When he lost the wager, he agreed not to leave England for a year and not to put himself into any danger."

A slow smile spread over Clara's lips. So *that* was why he was lying to his family about his activities in Spitalfields. Why, the little cheater!

When she glanced over to see that Lord Ravenswood had suddenly taken a great interest in straightening his gloves, her eyes narrowed. She knew exactly who'd put Morgan up to cheating on his wager, too. Both of them were scoundrels and sneaks, and they deserved to be put in their place.

"Tell me," Clara remarked, "is Morgan so eager to put himself into danger that you can only keep him from it by a wager?"

"Oh, yes," Lady Juliet answered, "Morgan is always throwing himself into the thick of things. Only last year he was nearly killed capturing a highwayman at Lord Ravenswood's request. And before that, there were the pirates and the smugglers. Why, Sebastian used to worry about Morgan's safety endlessly. Until the wager, that is."

"I see," Clara said. "Then I feel just awful, Lady Juliet."

Morgan's head shot up, and he glared a warning at Clara, but Lady Juliet merely asked, "How so?"

Clara smiled blithely at Morgan. "I'm sure it's been terribly difficult for Captain Blakely to stay in Spitalfields under such circumstances. What with the fences and the rough men causing trouble, he's probably wanted to break his wager a thousand times." She flashed Lord Ravenswood a mischievous grin. "And you, his friend—how could you ask him for such a favor? Forcing him into a situation where trouble dogged him at every turn, yet he's not allowed to act—"

"I figured he could handle it," his lordship retorted. "Morgan has always known what's most important in life."

"You mean his duty to his family?" she asked with an arch smile.

"And his country."

"Yes, but in this case his duty to his family conflicts with his duty to country."

"Then it's a good thing Morgan always makes the right choice, isn't it?" Lord Ravenswood said, eyes glittering.

Her gaze locked with his, and it was on the tip of her tongue to tell him exactly what she thought of his machinations. Especially when she knew how they'd affected Morgan.

Then Morgan said, "Ah, look, we're here." As if to give credence to his claim, the carriage jolted to a halt. "So that's enough talk of Spitalfields. I want to eat."

Lady Juliet laughed. "You always want to eat. I swear, Morgan, you have a stomach the size of a cavern."

Morgan opened the door and climbed out. "Don't tell Lady Clara, or she'll know where all the Home's food has been disappearing."

Lord Templemore appeared to help Lady Juliet down, and Morgan stepped forward to provide Clara with the same service. But he didn't release her hand right away. He merely used it to tug her close and whisper, "I'll get you for that later, you teasing wench."

"As long as you don't put yourself into danger in the process," she whispered back, "I don't think it's a problem."

With a searching glance, he took her arm. "What my family doesn't know can't hurt them. I only want to protect them."

"You have a funny way of doing that."

His jaw tightened, but he said nothing more as they joined the others.

The next two hours passed more enjoyably than Clara

had expected. The pleasure garden had long ago ceased to be viable—the formal walks were overgrown, the stone fountain of Cupid riding a swan had been overtaken by lichens, thus giving the young God of Love a green beard, and the elegant bridges crossing the nearby Fleet River had not been kept up.

But the place held a ruinous charm that made strolling about it in the company of friends a soothing experience. Especially when Morgan accompanied her as closely as any courtier of old, holding her hand when nobody was looking, even stealing a kiss once behind a cherry tree in full bloom.

His unfailing attentions gave her second thoughts about her decision not to marry him. Was she being unfair to expect him to give up his chosen profession? Throughout the afternoon, she heard a great deal about his years in the navy, enough to show her he did have some stake in that life. If he'd wanted to captain a ship again so badly that he would break his wager to his family and risk his life in Spitalfields, then who was she to expect him to give it up?

Especially when his only alternative was a gentleman's life, existing on the undoubtedly comfortable allowance his brother gave him. Though his family clearly wanted that for him, Morgan wouldn't be content to live like that for long. He needed activity. Like her, he needed to feel useful. He had ambition, and the navy seemed the only avenue open to him.

He'd probably been too proud to admit it, but what options were left for a second son? Depending on his brother's largesse or living on her income would chafe at him. No matter how little or how much he liked the sea, he probably saw it as his only chance for advancement.

Yet could she bear the life of a naval officer's wife? How could she stand seeing him only from time to time? Yearning for him while he threw himself into danger at every turn? How long would it be before she hated his absences, resented raising their children alone, tired of worrying about him constantly?

Then again, whenever he kissed her . . .

No, she must think this through rationally. She would regret any decision made solely on the basis of one night spent in his bed, no matter how glorious and thrilling that night had been.

"Juliet," Morgan called out to his sister-in-law as they all strolled away from the river. "Don't you think you've made me suffer long enough without sustenance? Are we ever going to eat?"

Lady Juliet laughed. "As a matter of fact, the servants are setting up our meal now, over there at the top of the hill. And there's plenty enough even for you, I expect."

"Thank God," Morgan stated, tucking Clara's hand more firmly in his elbow. "Come on, angel. Dinner is finally served."

Dinner consisted of an astonishing array of viands, breads, and cheeses, all neatly spread upon blankets beneath the open sky. Wine and punch had been provided, as well as fruit and cold tarts. Clara hadn't realized how hungry she was until she saw it all there.

She wasn't the only one. The outdoor air had heightened their appetites, so they fell upon the food like ravenous hounds, sparing little energy for conversation.

But once the first edge of hunger had been blunted, Lady Juliet grew chatty again. From her seat beside her husband, she stretched out one dainty foot to poke Morgan in the knee. "You see what you'll be missing if you sail away from us? I dare say you don't eat this well aboard ship."

Morgan laughed. "Why do you think I eat so much while I'm *not* aboard ship? I'm storing it up for the future."

The tart Clara was eating suddenly tasted dry as dust. The mere thought of Morgan sailing away killed her appetite.

As if noticing Clara's response, Lady Juliet turned to Lord Ravenswood, who was stretched out on the blanket with his eyes closed. "Can't you do anything about this, sir? Must you always send him off to sea and away from his family?"

Lord Ravenswood cracked open one eye. "Don't look at me. I've already offered him a lucrative position in the Home Office. It's his for the taking whenever he wants it. Thus far he's refused it. So I've done all I can to keep him here."

Clara sucked in a breath, then cast Morgan a questioning look. Surely this could not be true. He would have said something, he would have told her . . .

But she could tell it was true by the way he stared down into his wineglass, not meeting her eyes.

So it wasn't that he had no choice. It wasn't that his pride would not allow him to live off her or his family. Oh, no. He would simply rather be anywhere than here with her.

Her meal rose in her gorge, and blood rushed to her head. She had to get away from him, from all of them, before she betrayed herself. Rising unsteadily to her feet, she forced a wan smile to her lips. "If you'll excuse me, I have to find . . . is there a necessary on the grounds?"

Lady Juliet nodded and pointed down the hill. "Through the woods leading to the river. By that arbor we saw earlier."

"Thank you," she choked out, then charged off down the hill and into the trees.

Chapter 21

How blind is that Man,
Who scorns the Advice
Of Friends, who intend
To make him more wise.
A Little pretty pocket-book, *John Newbery*

Morgan knew in an instant what had made Clara so upset. He leaped to his feet and started after her. "I'll go help her find the arbor."

"Is something wrong?" Juliet called out.

He shook his head. "Just give me a few minutes alone with her, all right?" He wished Ravenswood had kept his damned mouth shut. Morgan would never forget the hurt that had spread over Clara's face the moment Ravenswood spoke.

Morgan felt his brother watching him, probably sensing in his unerring way that Morgan was upset, but he ignored his twin to hurry off after her.

"Clara!" he called out when he caught sight of her ahead,

but that only made her break into a run. Cursing under his breath, he ran after her. He lost sight of her for a moment, but kept heading for the place Juliet had spoken of. He reached it just in time to see Clara dart through a curtain of honeysuckle and into the arbor. No doubt she thought to hide from him, assuming that he'd look for her in the necessary instead.

But she didn't need the necessary—she was trying to escape him, and he wouldn't let her. He'd worked too hard today to tear down her defenses only to watch her erect them against him once more.

Ducking beneath the honeysuckle, he found himself plunged instantly into a semidarkness barely penetrated by the late afternoon sun. Long ago this arbor had probably held only enough vines to trail prettily over its flimsy trellis structure, but time had thickened the honeysuckle until it choked out nearly all the light, creating a cave of fragrant flowers.

But not so dark a cave that he couldn't see her. She sat hunched over on a stone bench beneath the overarching framework. Her face was turned away from him, and her shoulders moved convulsively.

She was crying, damn it. He'd made her cry.

"Clara—" he began.

"Go away," she choked out, twisting her upper body away from him. "I . . . just need a moment alone, Morgan."

He stepped nearer, feeling helpless in the wake of her obvious distress. "It's not what you think."

"You don't know what I think."

"I turned Ravenswood's offer down long ago. But even if I hadn't, I could never accept it. It would mean . . ." He groped for words that would make her understand.

"Staying here," she finished for him. "It would mean staying here with me. Which of course you don't wish to do."

"No! I mean, I want to be with you but . . . confound it all, it has nothing to do with us." Taking a seat beside her on the bench, he laid his hand on her shoulder. When she shrugged it off, the bottom dropped out of his stomach. "I'm just not suitable for the sort of position he's offering."

She lifted her head to stare off across the arbor. "I told myself that you were too proud to take your brother's money or mine. That you felt you had no choice but to go back to sea. I thought . . ." Her breath caught. "I thought you . . . truly meant it when you said you wanted to marry me—"

"*Bon Dieu*, I did!" He caught her by the shoulders, trying to make her look at him.

But she jerked free of his grasp and rose to step away. "No, you didn't, or you wouldn't throw aside the obvious solution to our problem. You wouldn't wish to flee me the first chance you get."

"It's not you I'm fleeing." He rose, too. "You don't understand, angel. It's not you."

"Don't try to tell me again that you miss the sea, because—"

"I can't live in this damned place!" he burst out.

She went still. Then she faced him, confusion spreading over her soft features. "What do you mean?"

"I can't live in London."

"But you already do."

"Yes, because I have to. But I hate it, do you hear?" He strode up to her, fists clenched. "I hate all of it! I hate the poverty and the dirt and the crime. I hate the thick air. I hate . . . My God, I hate so much of it."

"That's only because you're in Spitalfields now. But you won't have to see all that if you work for Lord Ravenswood."

"No one can live in London and insulate themselves entirely from the rest of it. You know that as well as I do." He whirled around and strode to the opening of the arbor, staring through the tangled curtain of honeysuckle into the woods beyond. "And it doesn't matter where I live or work, it will always remind me of—"

"Geneva?"

He shook his head. "Not Geneva, but what I was when I lived there. What I became." Idly he fingered a honeysuckle blossom. "When I'm at sea, I'm a different person, Clara. I'm in command. I'm the captain—respected, honorable. I'm all the things that my uncle and my father and even my brother want for me. But when I'm here—"

"You're still that man!" Coming up behind him, she slid her arms about his waist. "Where you are has nothing to do with it. I've seen how you behave with Johnny and Samuel and me. You're no less a good man here than you are aboard ship. I *know* what you are—here or anywhere."

He twisted to face her, thrusting her away. "You don't know, damn it! You don't know anything!"

"I know that you stole to make sure your mother could eat. If I thought that made you a bad person, what kind of re-former of pickpockets would I be? No, I won't believe ill of you, no matter what you say—"

"Did you know that I killed a man?" When her face clouded over, he added, "Not in the heat of battle, not in duty to my country. I killed a man out of sheer hatred. And the truth is—if I were given the chance to do it again, I would."

There, he'd said it. And judging from her shocked expression, she thought exactly what he'd expected her to think of his revelation.

She stepped back, her face ashen. "W-Was it . . . someone you were stealing from?"

"No, not that. Even in my most desperate hour, I would never have killed for property."

"Then why?"

"For revenge. Why else?"

She seemed calmer now. Gliding to the bench, she sat down and gazed at him with an expectant look. "Tell me what happened."

Bile rose in his throat at the very thought. "It's too ugly a story."

"I don't care. I want to know."

With a curse, he shoved his hands into his pockets. He'd always known he would tell her some day. He couldn't seem to resist this compulsion to force her to witness all his secrets. And for each secret that didn't sway her, he wanted to reveal more. Because he needed to make her face what he really was, force her to acknowledge it. Then he'd know for sure if there could ever be something between them more than a "sometime marriage," as she called it.

Yet he hesitated a moment longer, gathering his energy to tell a tale he'd kept hidden for so long.

"Morgan?" she whispered.

He sighed. "I lied when I told you my mother died of consumption."

Clara said nothing, merely waiting.

"That's what I told Sebastian. That's what I told everyone. Except my uncle. Mother told him the truth."

When he fell silent, Clara prodded, "And what *was* the truth?"

"First I have to tell you about my mother's last lover, Jean-Paul. He was the worst of them, yet I think she loved him. He knew how to tell her exactly what she wanted to hear . . . all about the plans he had for them, the places they would go once he had money again. Only he never had any money, and when he did chance to get some, he spent it all on cheap wine." It all sounded so sordid, so . . . Spitalfields.

He forced himself to go on. "One day he found out about my stealing. I don't know how—perhaps he saw me. But he confronted me while Mother was out buying beef for our dinner. He said he wanted a portion of everything I stole or he'd tell my mother what I was up to."

"He sounds like a lovely person," she said sarcastically. "So did you agree?"

"No. I knew he'd spend it on wine and we'd have nothing left. I told him if he laid a finger on anything of mine, I'd cut it off." He cast her a faint smile. "At thirteen, I was feeling my oats. I thought I could do anything."

"Boys at thirteen often do," she said, concern shining in her eyes.

He turned away, unable to see her willingness to excuse all his faults. "Jean-Paul wasn't so sanguine about it, as you might imagine. And he was drunk as usual, which only made everything worse. We got into a major row, and my mother came in during the middle of it. He told her about the stealing." He dragged in a heavy breath, remembering. "Only he made it sound like I was keeping the money to myself so I could run away from her. I lost my temper. I launched myself at him, and we started to fight."

The night came back to him vividly, despite the brilliant day outside the arbor. He remembered his mother shouting for them to stop. He remembered the blows raining down on him, and the extraordinary energy that kept him fighting a man nearly twice his size.

And then the flash of steel. "I was holding my own and he couldn't get me off of him, so he drew out a knife and thrust it into my side. That pretty much . . . ended the fight. I lay on the floor bleeding, too weak to stand. I remember trying to plug the wound with my fingers."

She gave a sharp intake of breath. "That's how you got the scar in your side? From the knife?"

Her sympathetic voice jerked him out of the past, and he nodded. "Mother screamed at Jean-Paul that he'd killed me, and she started pummeling him." His throat felt tight, raw.

"He really didn't like *that*." A shuddering breath escaped him. "So he beat her. Until she couldn't stand. Until her eyes were swollen shut and—"

The words caught in his throat, and he felt rather than saw Clara hurry to his side. She tried to put her arms around him, but he shrugged her off. "The landlady heard the noise and came upstairs. She threw Jean-Paul out, got me to the hospital, got Mother to the hospital. They patched me up pretty well, but with Mother . . ."

He could still see his mother lying still and pale in that hospital bed. "She held on for several weeks, but I think he'd injured her . . . inside. Or perhaps her heart broke after taking so much abuse over the years. I don't know." He dragged in a harsh breath. "But that's when she told me about the baron, had me send letters to him and my uncle. Fortunately, Uncle Lew came to Geneva at once, because she died two days after he arrived."

"Oh, Morgan," Clara said in a watery voice that threatened tears.

"That's not all." He made himself look at her, forced himself to continue. "It took several weeks for the letters to reach England and for my uncle to come. In that time, Jean-Paul found a new woman to push around. But I still saw him every day in the streets, in the market. He even had the audacity to ask about my mother. I wanted to tear his tongue out."

"That's understandable," she said softly.

"The worst of it was," he went on, ignoring the pity in her face, "I knew he'd never be punished by the local police. Who would care about the beating of an English whore and the knifing of her pickpocket by-blow? They'd say we deserved it. So I turned to the military authorities for my justice, and to get it from them I knew I'd have to make sure he was found guilty of something more serious than assaulting Mother and me."

"Like what?"

He ran a shaky hand through his hair. "Spying. I set out to frame Jean-Paul. I forged letters in his handwriting, I paid all my little thieving friends to be witnesses, and then I told the authorities that Jean-Paul was a spy for the English."

"What?" she said, clearly shocked.

"Geneva was in turmoil then. France had annexed it, but there were still rumblings left from the revolution, and nobody trusted anybody. I made sure I was very convincing." A biting laugh escaped him. "And do you know what? It worked. A few letters and some lying witnesses, and Jean-Paul was found guilty of treason within days."

"So you had your revenge," she whispered.

His voice grew fierce. "No. I had my revenge when they took him to the guillotine. That was the punishment for treason. And I knew it when I set out to frame him." He grabbed her by the arms. "I watched his execution myself. And do you know what I felt when they struck his head off, Clara? I felt glad—*glad*, I tell you."

The truth of it sickened him even now. He dug his fingers into her arms. "So don't say you know what kind of man I am. *That's* what kind of man I am. The kind who'd take any devious means possible for his revenge, who would lie and cheat and frame someone for spying. The kind who wouldn't feel one ounce of remorse when it was done."

He started to thrust her away, but she caught his head between her hands. "You feel no remorse? Then why are you so afraid to live in London, to stay in a place so like the one you grew up in?"

"I'm not afraid of anything!" he protested. "I just . . . can't . . ."

"You *are* afraid. You're afraid that this is the sum of what you are. That an angry, wounded thirteen-year-old boy seeking a rightful vengeance for his mother's death is all you'll ever be. That somehow London will drag you down into the hole again, and you'll never be able to crawl out."

"*Sacrebleu*, Clara, what are you doing to me?" he whispered. Why did she have to see so damned much? Why did she have to understand him so well, yet not understand?

"But you are not that boy, Morgan, no matter what you fear. You could never be him again. You've risen above it."

"Have I? Is that why I can be a fence so convincingly that even you were fooled?"

"That was your duty, and I understand duty. We do things for duty that we might not choose to do. Don't be ashamed of being good at what you do. I wish there were more Morgan Blakelys fighting for the soul of Spitalfields."

"I'm not fighting for anybody's soul, damn it! I'm fighting to escape this place—"

She shook her head. "That's not true. You know perfectly well that Lord Ravenswood would have done his best to see that you had a ship. Even I can tell that he respects and admires you. No, you did this because it was the right thing."

"Like I framed a man for spying because it was the right thing?" he growled.

"You behaved the only way you felt you could under the circumstances—"

"So you think lying and cheating to gain revenge is acceptable. Is that what you would tell your boys?"

"No, of course not. But then my boys have other recourses, and you didn't." She cupped his cheeks with all the tenderness of a lover. "If you'd watched your mother beaten and then *not* tried to stop the man from doing it again to someone else, I would think you unnatural."

"I didn't do it for that reason—"

"Didn't you? You saw him with another woman. You saw he felt no remorse. You knew he was a slave to liquor and would do it again. So you stopped him. Perhaps it wasn't the right way to go about it, but it was the only way a foreign boy in Geneva knew how."

Tears sprang to his eyes, and he squelched them ruthlessly. Oh, God, she made him want to hope. That wasn't fair of her, damn it.

Thrusting her away, he went to sit on the bench, sure that if he stood near her a moment longer he'd turn into a blubbering idiot. "You keep trying to fit me into this . . . noble image you have of me, but it's not what I really am inside." He buried his face in his hands. "You don't know—"

"What you think you are inside doesn't matter, Morgan." She hastened over to sit beside him. "In the end, it's what a man does, how he acts, that shows his character. And I've never seen you act anything but nobly."

He lifted his face to hers, astonished at how fiercely she defended him, even after knowing the darkest secrets of his soul. "How can you be so sure of my character when I'm not even sure of it myself?"

"I can't help it," she said, her voice trembling. She dropped her eyes to the bench, turmoil showing in her sweet features. "I love you. And loving someone means believing in them."

She loved him? Despite knowing what he was? A fierce joy seized him before he could prevent it. He caught her by the chin and forced her to look at him, but her clear blue eyes held no hint of deception. "God help you if you don't mean that, *ma belle ange.*"

"Of course I mean it, you big idiot." She cast him a watery smile. "Why do you think the thought of watching you sail away without me torments me so?"

In that moment, he knew he could never leave her behind. "Then come with me," he whispered. "Sail with me. Be the captain's wife."

"That's not what you want—"

"I do." He slid his hand along her jaw, caressing, stroking. "I want you with me, Clara. If these three days have shown me anything, it's that I can't bear to be without you."

Her eyes looked troubled. "But what about my children? They need me—"

"*I* need you," he countered. "I know it's selfish, I know it's unfair, but I need you as much as they do." He dared not call it love, for if he let himself love her and she still refused him, he didn't know if he could survive it. Instead he bent his head forward to kiss her, seeking some sign that she needed him as much as he did her.

Her mouth was soft and eager, but he could feel a distance in her that made him want to howl with frustration. He would not let it remain.

He broke free of her mouth to urge, "Come away with me, that's all I ask. Marry me and sail with me. Your aunt could run the Home. Or somebody else . . . I don't know who. Let somebody else save the world for a change." Hauling her onto his lap, he tightened his arms about her. "Save me instead . . ."

Then he gave her no chance to refuse. He sealed his mouth to hers, determined to remind her of the bond between them, the bond he wanted to strengthen by marriage. He didn't know how to convince her except with this—holding her, touching her, rousing the inevitable fire that leaped between them. If he could show her that she needed him, at least for this . . .

He slid one hand under her gown and between her thighs while he slipped the other inside her bodice to fondle the warm satin of her breast.

She tore her mouth free, eyes wide with shock. "Morgan, we shouldn't—"

"I need you, angel." He kissed a path along her cheek to her trembling throat. "And I need to know that you need me, too. You say you love me, but you love those children of yours more."

"That's not true." Her breath was ragged, her pulse beating madly beneath his mouth. "It's just that they have no one, while you—"

"I have no one if I don't have you." He thumbed her nipple until she gasped and arched into his hand. "Show me that you love me as much as you do them, Clara. Show me you need me."

The urge to lose himself in her warm, giving flesh became so overwhelming he thought he'd shatter if she refused. But she didn't refuse. She caught his head in her hands and stared at him a long moment, as if looking for something in his eyes.

Then with a tortured sigh, she pulled his head closer, bringing his lips to meet hers. When her legs parted for the stroke of his fingers, he could have crowed. She *was* his, no matter what she said. She belonged to him, and he'd make sure she always did.

With a savage need bordering on madness, he kissed and caressed her, exulting at her eager response. He slid his fingers inside her drawers to tangle in her curls, seeking the center of her pleasure, needing to prove he had some power over her, that he wasn't the only one consumed by this ever-present hunger, that she wanted him, too.

And when he found her wet and warm for him, he fondled the hot, silky flesh until she moaned and writhed beneath his hand, clutching his head close. He dragged the edge of her bodice down with his teeth and closed his mouth over her nipple, pleasuring her at both fronts until he thought he'd explode with his need for her.

Especially when she brought her hand down to stroke the length of his erection through his trousers. He moaned and pressed himself into her hand.

"Take me inside you, angel," he rasped when he could bear no more. "I want to be inside you . . ."

She drew her head back. Her face was flushed, tendrils of hair clinging to her damp brow. "Here?"

"Yes, here. Make love to me, *cherie* . . . here . . . now . . ." He drew his hand from between her legs to unbutton her drawers, then worked them down over her hips and down to her ankles. "Stand up for a second."

Though she blushed and glanced furtively to the entrance of their scented bower, she did as he asked. Swiftly, he unbuttoned his trousers and drawers and dragged them down past his knees. Then he drew her back to him.

"What if someone comes?" she whispered as he lifted her skirts, then urged her legs apart and pulled her down to straddle his lap.

"I hope they do. Then you'll be compromised, and you'll have to marry me, no matter what." He tugged her further up his lap. "Kneel on the bench," he ordered, and she did, grabbing onto his shoulders with both hands.

The tip of his swollen cock grazed her curls, and his mouth went dry. "Now take me inside you, angel. Before I go crazy."

And as if she'd been born to make love to him, she impaled herself on him, sliding slowly down to surround him with her heat. Her skirts whispered about his thighs, an angel's white wings brushing his bare skin.

"Do you like that?" she whispered so coyly that his gaze shot to her. Though her cheeks shone scarlet, a teasing smile played over her lips. She wriggled experimentally atop him, and he thought he'd erupt right there. "Do you?"

He clamped his hands on her waist. "If it gets any better than this, angel . . . they'll have to lock me away. . . . I'll be a raving lunatic."

With an uncanny instinct, she rose up on her knees and

came down on him, wrenching a hoarse cry from his throat. "That's what I should do with you, Morgan. Lock you away, so you can't ever leave me."

"Will you share my bed every night?" he whispered against her breast, then lavished open-mouthed kisses over the sleek, taut skin, seeking out the nipple, tugging at it with his teeth as she began to rock up and down on him.

"Every night . . . every day . . . and I'll tie you to the bed if you refuse . . ."

"Then lock me away," he answered, rising to meet her. "I can't think of anything I'd like more . . . than being tied to a bed with you."

Her fingers gripped his shoulders painfully. "Except sailing off to have adventures."

He heard the ache in her voice, felt the pain that laced all their pleasure. "I want to have them with you," he countered.

"You want to run away." She tossed back her head, her movements wild as she came down on him over and over, tightening on his erection until she had him gasping.

"With you," he vowed. "Only with you."

"Curse you, Morgan . . . you want my soul."

"Yes!" He clutched her fiercely against him. "I want your soul." With the thrust of his hips, he urged her to quicken her motions, and she did. "I want your body." He laid his head on her chest, reveling in the beat of her heart that matched the frantic beat of his own. "I want your heart." He buried himself inside her giving warmth over and over until he thought she would devour him. "I want it all."

"But what do I get in return?"

"Everything. Whatever it takes to keep you."

Then he felt the explosion coming, pulsing up through him. He strained against her with a cry as he spilled his seed into her sweet satin heat. Clasping him tight to her, she convulsed around him, wringing the last bit of his release from him as he chanted her name over and over, the mantra to his salvation.

Time stood briefly still, fragrant with honeysuckle and the tangy scents of their joining. But it could not last. Slowly she sank onto his lap, limp and drained, her cheeks wet with tears as she laid her head against his shoulder.

The sight of them sparked his alarm. "What's wrong?" He bent his head to kiss her brow and brush the tears from her cheeks with his thumb.

"Oh, Morgan, I want to marry you," she said through her sniffles. "Truly I do. And if I thought that the only way we could be together is if I sailed with you, then I would do it. I love you that much." She lifted her face to his. "But until you face and accept who you are, I'll never be enough for you. I'll always be just one more panacea."

"What do you mean?" he said hoarsely, hardly able to believe that she was saying this after yielding to him so sweetly.

She caressed his cheek. "You throw yourself into danger to keep from thinking about the past. But that won't work forever. Until you accept the bad parts of yourself with the good, you'll always be fighting what you are. And the more you fight, the more you'll resent anybody who reminds you of what you once were. Like me, with my children."

She dragged in a harsh breath. "That's the real reason you won't marry me and stay here, isn't it? Because every time you see my boys, you remember what you were, and it angers you. But what you were made you who you are, and I love all of it."

"Just not enough to give up your Home for me," he growled.

"Enough to know that giving it up won't satisfy you. Nothing will satisfy you until you're at peace with who you are." Her eyes looked lost, regretful. "So no, I won't abandon my children just because you're too afraid to face the bad as well as the good in you. And I won't run away with you and watch you grow to hate me because I see you for what you are, what you want to hide from yourself."

Anger exploded in him. The fact that she might be right only heightened his fury. Lifting her off his lap, he set her on the bench, then stood to jerk up his drawers and trousers. "That's just your excuse for attempting to make me do what you want, to make me stay here in a city that I loathe—"

"It's not the city that you loathe," she whispered as she pulled up her own drawers and fastened them. "It's what the city reminds you about yourself."

He whirled on her, clinging to the anger that kept the awful pain at bay. "Believe what you like. But the fact remains that you don't want me unless I meet your terms. Well, I have terms of my own. Unless you can meet them, you can find some other fellow to dance to your tune, because I don't intend to imprison myself in this confounded city, no matter what you say."

Turning his back on her, he strode willfully toward the opening to the arbor.

"Morgan?"

He paused to snap, "What?"

"Even a ship can become a prison if all you see around you are bars."

He didn't give her a response, just shoved his way through the hanging honeysuckle and out into the air.

But her words clamored to be acknowledged as he made his way back to the others through the overgrown woods. Because although he might deny it to her, he'd known for a long time that the bars were closing in around him. And if he didn't do something about it soon, he might never break free.

Chapter 22

From hence we may learn
That, by one thoughtless Trip
Strange accidents happen
'Twixt the Cup and the Lip.
A Little pretty pocket-book, John Newbery

Much later that day, long after night had fallen and he'd left a subdued Clara behind with his family at the Templemore town house, Morgan paced his shop with a growing sense of unease. Bad enough that he couldn't keep his mind on what he was supposed to be doing. Now *this* had to happen.

"Something's wrong," he told Jack Seward as he glanced at his watch. It was nearly nine o'clock, and the Specter had promised to send word to the shop at eight about where they should meet. No one had come. And he and Jack had been waiting here in the front room for over an hour.

"P'raps he's just late." Jack threaded his fingers through

his pepper-and-salt hair. "Might have been harder for him to set up his place than he expected."

"I doubt that. This is a man who plans every detail of his encounters. He's not late. Something spooked him."

"I'm afraid you're right," Ravenswood commented from the door.

Morgan whirled around. "Damn it, Ravenswood, if he's not spooked, you'll certainly do the trick." Though Ravenswood had dressed appropriately to keep his vigil with his men in hidden positions along the street, he could still be recognized.

The man seemed unconcerned about that, however. "We have a bit of a problem."

Morgan exchanged glances with Jack. "What do you mean?"

"Remember the fellow I told you about at Merrington's ball? Hornbuckle's officer, Mr. Fitch?"

"What of him?"

Ravenswood tugged nervously at his cravat. "If you'll recall, you *did* instruct me to tell Hornbuckle it was all right to have the man investigate you. And I *did* warn you that he was diligent."

"Oh, no, you don't mean—" Morgan began.

"Unfortunately, yes. Shortly after my men and I took our positions, he showed up to keep an eye on the shop. When I realized he was settled in for a while, I asked him to leave, but I suspect it was too late by then. The Specter probably saw him hanging about and didn't want to risk being seen by a police officer. I dare say our quarry is long gone."

"Sacrebleu!" Morgan exploded. All this for nothing!

He'd wanted to be done with this tonight. He was tired of playing this game, tired of lurking about at the shop. He was tired of being half a block from Clara when he couldn't have her. And now that he knew for certain she wouldn't marry him, he was even more eager to put some distance between them.

"What do you want to do?" Ravenswood asked.

"We don't have much choice. We'll have to try again later." Morgan shot Seward a glance. "I'm sorry, Jack, but you'll have to stay in town a few more days, until I can set everything up again. Fortunately, having a police officer sniffing at my heels will at least convince the Specter that I am what I say I am. But I'll have to wait for the villain to approach me before I can set up another meeting—"

"It's all right," Seward responded. "I don't mind staying in London, not as long as your friend here is paying for it." He grinned. "There's a good deal more tarts here than there is in Hastings, I can tell you that."

Morgan took out a guinea and flipped one to Seward. "Then go find yourself one. Somebody might as well get something out of this night."

"Thanks, mate!" With a wink and a nod, Seward shoved the guinea in his pocket and left.

After he was gone, Ravenswood leaned back against the counter. "Do you want me to tell Hornbuckle to call Fitch off?"

"I don't know. Let me see if he becomes a nuisance."

"Has he been hanging around here much since the ball?"

"Not that I've noticed. But if he's any good, I wouldn't have noticed, would I?"

Ravenswood shoved away from the counter. "I'll be off then. Unless you think that your sister-in-law's invitation to the Templemore house for supper still stands."

Juliet, apparently unwilling to end their lovely day, had invited both Ravenswood and Clara to stay to supper. Clara had accepted even though Morgan and Ravenswood had cried off with some flimsy excuse about another engagement. Clara was probably there even now.

"I'm sure it does," Morgan grumbled. "For some reason

unfathomable to me, Juliet likes you. Either that or she's hoping to use you to convince me to stay in London."

Ravenswood smiled thinly. "Perhaps you should explain how little influence I have over you."

"You explained it quite well this afternoon." When Ravenswood's words had sent Clara running. And provoked her into the decision that still cut Morgan to the heart.

"If you don't mind my asking," Ravenswood said, "what happened between you and Lady Clara this afternoon? You both disappeared for nearly an hour, and when you reappeared, the two of you were obviously no longer on speaking terms."

"You're the one who told her I'm not 'civilized,' " he snapped, "so I'm sure you've already decided what happened. After all, nothing makes a lady angrier than an uncivilized man daring to approach her."

Ravenswood eyed him calmly. "I didn't mean that in the way you clearly think I did. I only meant to caution her not to lose her heart, because I know you have no interest in a lasting relationship with a woman."

"Then you'll be happy to know your cautions were successful," Morgan said bitterly. "She has protected her heart very well."

"Isn't that what you wanted?"

"I wanted—" He broke off with a curse, staring at the black window that reflected his own candlelit image. Ravenswood was the closest friend he'd ever had. He at least would understand Morgan's frustration, would agree that Clara asked too much of him. And right now, he needed a sympathetic ear. "I asked her to marry me. She refused."

"I see." Ravenswood stood silent a long moment. "Actually, that surprises me. From the way she speaks of you, the way she looks at you, I had thought she might welcome such a proposal."

"Perhaps she would—if I agreed to live here. But I won't, and she has no desire to sail with me. Nor any desire to sit around for months on end while I sail alone."

"Ah. Now *that* does not surprise me. And to be honest, how could you even think of taking her to sea?"

Morgan sighed. "I know, I know, her confounded Home is too precious for her to even consider leaving it behind."

"That's true, but I wasn't thinking of that." Ravenswood crossed his arms over his chest. "I was thinking of you with a wife aboard. It would be one thing if you'd be content to take the less hazardous assignments, but you know you won't. You'd be putting her into danger at every turn, which would certainly be a distraction to you."

Morgan hadn't considered those things. He'd been too focused on needing her beside him to think of the practical problems. "Captains bring their wives with them all the time—" he began.

"Not wives like Lady Clara. You've seen the average captain's wife—she has to subsume everything to her husband's existence. She has to live with few possessions and be cut off from her family for months on end, depend on him for any attention, give birth to children without the help of another woman. It's a hard life for both the wife *and* the husband. Why do you think so many captains retire from the navy when they marry?"

Ravenswood had a point, and suddenly Morgan felt ashamed of his anger at Clara. She was too clever a woman not to have thought through all the practical matters Ravenswood spoke of. She'd probably realized, even if he hadn't, that he was asking her to give up everything—her family, her life's work, her independence. And all for a man who could promise her only a warm bed.

If I thought that the only way we could be together is if I sailed with you, then I would do it. I love you that much.

Too consumed by anger at her stubbornness, he hadn't believed her. But now he had to wonder. Could she truly be willing to give up everything for him? And ask only in return that he do the same? That he demonstrate to her satisfaction that he wanted her for herself and not as simply one more distraction from his painful memories?

For some reason, it suddenly seemed very important to know. Because if she could give up so much for him, perhaps he could find a way to give her what she wanted.

It was either that or face life without her. And he wasn't sure if he could.

"Why don't we go see if Juliet has held supper for us?" Morgan told Ravenswood. "I'm famished."

But it wasn't food he wanted. And he wasn't going to wait until tomorrow and take the chance that what, *who*, he wanted might already have given up on him.

"Where do you think they were going tonight?" Lady Juliet asked Clara as they finished their dessert. "Morgan and Lord Ravenswood were very mysterious about their plans."

Clara frowned. No doubt Morgan had used the claim of a prior engagement to escape her and had talked his lordship into going along. But she could hardly tell Lady Juliet that. "I don't know. Captain Blakely never confides in me."

"That's what worries me," Lord Templemore broke in. "Whenever Morgan keeps mum, it generally means he's up to something. And Ravenswood is usually behind whatever it is."

Clara started to lie for Morgan, then stopped. Why should she? *He* was the one who wouldn't let his family know the real him, wouldn't tell them why he always threw himself into danger, why he chose to leave them. She refused to make excuses for him. If he wanted excuses made, then he could stay here and make them himself.

But no, he'd rather run away. From those who loved him. From his past. From everything that he hated about his life. Well, she would not run with him.

Tears filled her eyes, and she squelched them ruthlessly. Bother the man, she would not cry over him. Just because he'd suffered so much, because he claimed to need her . . .

You say you love me, but you love those children of yours more.

That wasn't true. It wasn't! Her reasons had nothing to do with the Home and the duty she felt to her children.

Let somebody else save the world for a change.

All right, so perhaps she did feel compelled to save the world, or at least the tiny part of it that included her pickpockets. But that was a good thing, wasn't it? Who was he to say that she should stop, just because he could not deal with living in London?

Save me instead.

That was the trouble—she wanted desperately to save him. Was she being unfair, trying to make him conform to her image of him when he struggled with such awful realities?

Her throat tightened, remembering his tale about his mother. Good Lord, how had he lived with that all these years and not gone mad? To watch your mother being beaten while you could do nothing . . .

She shuddered. Perhaps she did ask too much. Perhaps he would never be able to live here when it meant facing the memories every day. But if he couldn't, was she ready to give him up forever?

"M'lady?" came a voice from the doorway.

They looked up to see the stony-faced butler awaiting their attention.

"Yes, what is it?" Lady Juliet asked.

"There's a 'person' here to see Lady Clara." It was clear what he thought of said "person." "She claims to be a Miss

Perkins. She says it's urgent that she speak with her ladyship. I tried to send her away, but—"

"I'll see her." Clara rose from her chair. She cast her hosts an apologetic look, though she was relieved to escape the interest of Morgan's family. She should never have accepted their invitation to supper. "That's Lucy, the sister of two of my boys. I really should find out why she went to so much trouble to track me down."

"Of course," Lady Juliet said kindly. "Let us know if we can be of any assistance."

Trying not to let the sudden appearance of Lucy at the Templemore town house alarm her, Clara followed the butler out into the foyer. Lucy paced the marble floor, her young face lined with worry.

"Oh, thank God!" she exclaimed as she looked up to see Clara approach. "You have to help him, m'lady. You have to help Johnny."

Clara's heart sank. "What has he done now?"

"It ain't what he's done. Not really." Shooting the butler a nasty look, she drew Clara aside. "You remember what you told me about Rodney the other day? How I'd be better off with a man who'd accept my brothers?"

Clara nodded.

"I decided you were right, so this morning I told Rodney that I was marrying Samuel." She shook her head woefully. "He didn't take it well at all, and I . . . that is, I sort of ended up telling him some of what you told me." Lucy began to dab at her eyes. "It made him sore angry, you see, but then he calmed down and I thought everything was all right. Until tonight when he—" She broke off with a little sob.

"Yes?"

"He arrested Johnny!"

"What?" Clara exploded. "He can't do that! I'll just march right down to the gaol and demand the boy's release!"

"Johnny ain't at the gaol yet, thank God. But when Rodney came to the tavern to take the boy away a short while ago, he said he was carrying Johnny back to his house, and I was to meet him there after I fetched you."

"Me? But why?"

"He says he wants to talk to you, seeing as how you're the one who parted me and him. He says he'll let Johnny go if you'll just come talk to him."

"What does he hope to accomplish by talking to me?"

"I dunno." A worried frown crossed her brow. "P'raps he thinks you can talk me out of leaving him, since you was the one who advised me to do it in the first place." When Clara looked upset, Lucy added hastily, "Not that I mind. You were right. But Rodney don't see it that way. Anyway, I told him I'd see if you would come."

Good Lord, what a mess. Clara supposed this was what she deserved for all her meddling. Morgan was right—she did try to save the world, and sometimes it came back to punish her.

"If you don't want to go," Lucy went on, "I'll understand. It ain't your fault that I got meself caught up with the wrong man. It's just that Johnny—"

"Of course I'll come. I shan't allow Mr. Fitch to use the boy so sorely. I'll come at once."

Lucy's relief was evident. "Oh, thank you, m'lady! I've got the hack waiting just outside."

"Good." Clara had sent her carriage home as soon as she'd arrived this morning, because the Templemores had said they would take care of seeing that she got home later. "Wait here while I make my apologies to my hosts. I'll only be a moment."

Returning to the dining room, she explained as briefly as possible why she was being called away.

"Is there nothing we can do to help?" Lady Juliet asked.

"I don't think so. I'm sure Mr. Fitch is a reasonable man and will accept the situation once it's put to him rationally." Or at least she hoped he would. She didn't relish engaging in an argument with a brokenhearted police officer.

Moments later, she and Lucy were on their way to the man's house in the hack.

"What does Samuel say about all this?" Clara asked.

Lucy frowned. "That's the oddest thing. I can't find him. Tonight when I went to Stanbourne Hall looking for you, I figured he'd be there, but he weren't. They told me where to find you, but they said he weren't with you. Nobody knew where he was. Though they did say p'raps you'd know where he'd gone."

Clara shook her head. "I haven't seen him since he left me at the Home this morning. Perhaps he's making plans for your wedding."

Lucy ducked her head with a shy smile. "I s'pose. He did tell me he was looking for a little place we could rent that would be big enough for the four of us to live in."

"You love him, don't you?"

Lucy nodded. "Even the thought of Rodney's big house and all his nice things that I'm giving up don't change what I feel. I would never have taken up with Rodney if I'd thought that Samuel—"

She broke off to shoot Clara a pained look. "When we was younger, I had a soft spot for Sam. Until he began stealing. So when Johnny fell into picking pockets too, I dared not let Sam into my heart. Even after Sam got himself reformed, I was afraid he might go back to it and take the boys with him. But then I saw how hard he worked for you, and Johnny told me all the things he was doing." She blushed. "And since that night in the tavern, he's been so sweet. . . . Anyway, Samuel says he's going to keep doing right, and I believe him."

Clara patted her hand. "I believe him, too. He's a good man at heart, you know."

"Aye, m'lady, I do know."

They sat in companionable silence until they reached Mr. Fitch's house in Grave Lane, only a few streets over from Petticoat Lane. Despite how Lucy had described it, Clara was surprised to find it so impressive. It wasn't expensive-looking as much as refined. It rather surprised her that Mr. Fitch had such good taste. Though it might explain why Lucy had been dazzled by his attentions.

As soon as the hackney came to a halt, Mr. Fitch himself opened the door, looking troubled and distracted. He told the hackney to wait, then led them back to a parlor, where Johnny sat cross-legged on the floor before the fire, being guarded by a burly footman.

Mr. Fitch dismissed the servant, then closed the door to the parlor. "It's good of you to come, Lady Clara," he said in that same obsequious manner he'd used at the police office.

Clara cast him a searching glance. "I saw no choice in the matter. You've taken one of my charges into your care, and from what I understand you have no reason for it. So I demand that you release Johnny at once. He has nothing to do with any problem between you and Lucy."

"That's true." Striding up to Johnny, he grabbed the boy by the arm and made him stand. "You go on home with your sister now, boy. I want to talk to Lady Clara alone."

Clara gaped at him. That had been easier than she expected.

Looking alarmed by this swift turn of events, Lucy glanced from Clara to Mr. Fitch. "I'd rather stay here with the two of you, Rodney."

"There's no reason," Mr. Fitch responded. "The hackney is waiting, so go on. I'll see that her ladyship gets home safe. I want to talk to her private-like, and you need to get your brother off to bed."

And out of Mr. Fitch's power. Though the thought of being alone with the police officer made Clara a bit nervous, she preferred that to Johnny's staying here where the man might grow angry and change his mind about arresting him.

"It's all right, Lucy," Clara put in. "I don't mind speaking to Mr. Fitch. Take Johnny back to the tavern, and I'll come along presently."

Johnny looked as if he might protest the scheme himself, but when Clara cast him the Stanbourne stare, he relented and left with his sister.

As soon as they were gone, Mr. Fitch gestured to a chair. "Have a seat, m'lady. I got a favor to ask of you."

She sat gingerly on the edge of the chair. "If this is about Lucy, you should know that I had no say in her decision to marry Samuel."

His lips thinned. "She won't be marrying the little runt anyway. I offered him a tidy sum to leave the city, and he took it."

Clara stared at him in surprise. That didn't sound like Samuel, to abandon Lucy for money. "I don't believe it."

Mr. Fitch shrugged. "The man ain't stupid, y'know. He can see she's a fickle wench. First she lets me court her and then she turns to him—he saw what was what, took the money, and ran." His eyes narrowed on her. "But never mind all that. It ain't Lucy I wanted to talk to you about."

That certainly roused her curiosity. "Oh?"

"You might remember that you asked Mr. Hornbuckle to put me to investigating that Captain Pryce."

Oh, dear, this couldn't be good. "Yes, I remember."

"He decided as how you were right, so I been watching the man."

Only with difficulty did she stifle a groan. "Glad to hear it. And what have you discovered about the villain?"

He cast her a sly look. "Come now, m'lady, we both know he ain't no villain."

Could he really know the truth? Oh, of course he did. Mr.

Fitch was a police officer. Lord Ravenswood had probably informed the police of Morgan's true purpose. Indeed, that would explain why Mr. Fitch and Mr. Hornbuckle had been so reluctant to pursue Morgan's "criminal" activities.

But if that were the case, why had Mr. Hornbuckle told Mr. Fitch to investigate? Perhaps it would be safer to pretend ignorance in this matter. "I can't imagine what you mean."

"Don't play me for a fool, m'lady. I spoke to that chap Ravenswood from the Home Office this evening. It was clear that he and the captain were up to something. I dare say you know it as well."

So *that* was where Morgan and Ravenswood had gone— to an assignation of some sort with Mr. Fitch, and probably with the magistrate, too.

But Mr. Fitch spoke as if he himself weren't involved in the attempt to capture the Specter and perhaps didn't even know the details. Since she had no idea how much she could say about it, she'd best continue playing dumb. "If they are up to something, I don't know what it is. Surely you don't think they'd tell a woman."

"Why not? If they're working to catch that Specter villain, which is what I expect they're doing, they might think you could help."

"Don't be absurd. How could I possibly help?"

"I was hoping you could tell me, or at least reveal how far they've got with it."

That gave her pause. "Why do you care?"

He shrugged. "A capture of the Specter is a big affair. My office ought to be part of it. There's a hefty reward for the villain, y'know." He looked put out. "Seems to me they oughtn't run the investigation without sharing the profits with those of us who make our living in this part of town."

That made sense. But she wished that Morgan were here to deal with this. She knew nothing of the politics of police investigations. Would Mr. Fitch normally be entitled to the reward? Had Ravenswood slighted him by not involving him?

All she knew was she couldn't help him. She rose quickly. "Truly, Mr. Fitch, you'll have to speak to Lord Ravenswood about this matter. I'm not involved with such endeavors." Smoothing down her skirts, she started toward the door. "If you'll excuse me, I have to go. I promised Lucy—"

"Tell me about his lordship's association with the cap'n."

She halted short of the door to look at him. "I can't tell you what I don't know anything about."

"You needn't pretend with me, y'see." His knowing smile shot a tendril of unease curling down her spine. "I know that you and the cap'n have—shall we say—an *intimate* friendship."

Alarm sprang in her belly. He couldn't possibly know about her and Morgan. He had to be guessing. "I don't know what you mean."

"Of course you do. You're lovers, the cap'n and you. That's the only possible reason you spent the night with him in his shop."

How could he know about that? "You're mad if you think—"

"I was watching the cap'n, remember? Like Mr. Hornbuckle told me to. I saw you go in late at night, and I saw you go out in the wee hours of the morn."

Feeling her reputation slip away from her with his every comment, she frantically tried to salvage the situation. "If you did, then you saw Lucy shoot the captain. Yes, I did stay there, but only to help him with his wound."

He snorted. "You helped him seduce you, that's what."

"I can't imagine why you would think that," she protested, reminding herself that it was his word against hers. "I'll wager you didn't even wait the whole night, or you would have seen the Specter there—"

She broke off as his eyes narrowed. Oh, dear, she'd said too much. She wasn't supposed to have known the Specter was there. And if Mr. Fitch *had* seen the Specter and was so eager to get the reward, he should have arrested the man right there. It wasn't as if he wouldn't have known who the black-cloaked figure was. Everybody knew.

Yet he hadn't attempted to arrest either Morgan or the Specter. Not to mention that he seemed awfully sure of Morgan's relationship to her, and the only person who knew about that for a certainty was . . .

Pasting a smile to her lips, she backed toward the door. "Anyway, it hardly matters. I know nothing about the investigation, as I told you. If you want to hear the details, you should speak to Captain Pryce or his lordship. Now I really must go, so if you'll excuse me—"

"That's impossible, my lady," Mr. Fitch said, his voice altering subtly to one that was deeper, more refined, more menacing. As her heart sank, she saw him draw a pistol from his coat and aim it at her. "I'm afraid I can no longer allow you to leave."

Chapter 23

The giant declared he'd devour
For breakfast who dared to come near;
And leizurely did Blunderbore
Walk heavily into the snare.
*"The History of Jack the Giant-Killer,"
edition by J. G. Rusher, Anonymous*

"What do you mean, Clara's not here?" Morgan demanded of his brother's butler.

The butler cast him his usual lofty look. "Lady Clara left a short while ago in a hackney carriage, accompanied by a young lady named Perkins."

Morgan could only gape at him. "Lucy? Lucy was *here*?"

Sebastian and Juliet, apparently having heard him and Ravenswood in the foyer, came out to greet them.

"What's this about Clara leaving with Lucy in a hack?" Morgan demanded.

Juliet shrugged. "Miss Perkins came to request Lady

Clara's help. As I recall, it concerned a police officer named Fitch. He'd arrested one of the boys from the Home."

"Fitch has certainly been busy tonight," Ravenswood commented. "Don't you find that curious?"

"Indeed I do," Morgan said, as the hair rose on the back of his neck.

"I believe the young lady had refused the man's suit," Juliet added helpfully. "And apparently he retaliated by arresting her brother. Or something like that."

Though the explanation was perfectly plausible, it disturbed Morgan. He turned to Ravenswood. "How much do you know about Rodney Fitch?"

"Only what I told you. He acts like a Dogberry, but he's quite competent as a—"

"Dogberry!" Juliet exclaimed. "I *knew* I'd heard the name Fitch before."

Morgan cast her a cursory glance. "What are you talking about? How would you know anything about a police officer in Spitalfields?"

"No, no, this man wasn't a police officer. He was an actor with a traveling troupe that came to Stratford when I was . . . oh, twelve, I suppose." Juliet's family lived in Stratford-upon-Avon and were great enthusiasts of the theater, particularly Shakespeare. "Come to think of it, that Mr. Fitch's Christian name was Rodney, too. And he acted the best Dogberry I have ever seen. That's why I remember him so well. He had us all rolling with laughter."

Morgan felt the blood drain from him. "Describe this actor, Juliet."

She frowned, then did as he asked. Morgan heard Ravenswood's sharp intake of breath, and apprehension knotted in his gut. He turned to Ravenswood. "Does it sound like him?"

"Afraid so."

"He's been playing a role all along," Morgan said, feeling the blood congeal in his veins. "He's been playing Dogberry. Because who would suspect a bumbling Dogberry to be the most notorious criminal in Spitalfields?"

"It would certainly explain why Fitch was at the shop tonight." A frown creased Ravenswood's brow. "He wasn't there to investigate you. Or at least not on behalf of the authorities. He was there to sniff out a trap."

"And when he saw you, he realized what we were about, so he left." Morgan's alarm grew. "The Specter did say he had connections in the police offices—I just never imagined they were so close."

"This might also explain Fitch's success at catching criminals. Whenever the Specter wanted to remove a competitor or eliminate someone who'd betrayed him, he knew right where to go and how to catch them. I suppose if Jonathan Wild could do it a hundred years ago, the Specter certainly could." Ravenswood shook his head. "Still, an actor become a ruthless criminal? It seems unbelievable."

"Not to me. Perhaps he tired of never having money, and saw another way to use his talents. I always did think the Specter had a strange knack for manipulating his voice. And there's his uncanny ability to escape capture—he probably disguised himself every time. As an actor, it would have been easy. He probably used padding beneath the cloak to make himself look husky, for example."

"But how did he manage that effect you described—of having no face beneath that cloak of his—"

"Face paint," Morgan said grimly. "Black face paint. At night with the cloak, he'd look nearly invisible." His heart thundered in his chest. "But what in God's name would he want with Clara?"

"A way to lure you?" Ravenswood answered, paling.

"I don't think so. If he wanted me, he would have caught

me in a dark alley later this evening and slit my throat." He turned to Juliet. "Did Lucy say where she'd been? How had the girl known to come here?"

The butler answered. "She told me, sir, that she'd come from Lady Clara's home. They'd sent her over."

"Good. So Fitch doesn't know that we know he has Clara. Not yet anyway. Besides which, I don't think he's made the connection between Morgan Blakely and Morgan Pryce, so even if he'd known that Lucy would end up here, he wouldn't know what that meant. That will work in our favor." He glanced to the butler. "Did the women happen to say where they were going from here?"

"No, sir, I'm sorry. They left in a hack, so I didn't hear where they were headed."

"Probably not the jail," Ravenswood put in. "The arrest of the boy was undoubtedly just a ruse, and Fitch would want privacy, anyway."

Morgan's hands grew clammy with fear. "Yes, but privacy for what?"

Sebastian stepped forward. "Do you mind telling me what the devil is going on?"

"I don't have time to explain," Morgan snapped.

Sebastian glared at Ravenswood. "He's been working for you again, hasn't he? Despite the wager, despite what he promised—"

"Morgan is my best man," Ravenswood retorted, looking distinctly unrepentant. "I was certainly not going to stop making use of him simply because you two came up with that silly wager."

"Morgan!" Juliet cried. "How could you?"

"I'm sorry, Juliet," Morgan bit out. "I don't have time for lectures right now. Lady Clara is in danger."

That changed everything. Juliet paled and grabbed hold of her husband's arm.

Sebastian squared his shoulders. "Tell me what to do. I want to help."

Morgan hesitated, but this was no time to refuse a perfectly good offer. "She's with Fitch, but we don't know where. My guess would be his house, but I'm really not sure." He gazed at his brother's worried features. "If you want to help, why don't you go to Stanbourne Hall and see if the servants know where Lucy came from or where she was headed? And see if you can find a footman named Samuel. He'll know where Fitch might go, and he's sweet on Lucy besides. Once you find out what you can, head for Lady Clara's institution in Spitalfields." He rattled off the address. "We'll all meet there."

He turned to Ravenswood. "You go to Hornbuckle's and find out where Fitch lives, then meet us at the Home. I'll go to Tufton's Tavern. Since Lucy lives there, they may know Fitch's address. Or perhaps she'll have told them where she was going."

"Surely he wouldn't be fool enough to hurt her, now that he knows you're working for the authorities."

"I don't know. The man has always been unpredictable." Morgan felt a wave of futility overwhelm him. Suddenly he was thirteen again and watching helplessly as a man beat his mother.

He shook off the memory. He might have failed to protect his mother, but he would not fail in this. He couldn't. Otherwise, life would simply not be worth living. "He won't be expecting us to look for him," Morgan said evenly. "That's one thing in our favor. So let's take advantage of it."

And pray that Clara was clever enough to survive on her own until they could get to her.

Mr. Fitch gestured with the muzzle of his pistol to indicate that Clara should move away from the door. His motions were far more assured and controlled than Lucy's had been that night in the alley, and Clara found that distinctly disturbing.

"You've proven a more clever woman than I realized," he said in that cool, refined voice so different from his earlier one. "Apparently clever enough to gain the captain's confidence. I didn't expect him to tell you that he'd met up with the Specter in the alley. It's a pity he did, because now I can't let you leave."

"I-I don't see why not. What has it to do with you and me?"

"Don't play the fool with me!" he ground out. "You've figured out who I am, and I can't allow you to tell anybody else."

She *had* figured it out, hadn't she? The Specter was here in the flesh, even if he wasn't hefty the way Morgan had described. And he might prefer to use a knife when he played the ghost, but clearly when playing himself, he used the more practical pistol.

If she weren't careful, she'd receive all the benefits of such practicality. "I truly have no idea—"

"Captain Pryce told you, didn't he? He told you everything that night, all about why I was there." He scowled. "I should have known better than to believe what he said about you and him. That tale alone should have shown me the trap was closing on me. You would never have let him bed you unless you knew he wasn't really a criminal. Because you're far too moral—and too intelligent—to be manipulated by a real fence."

He let out an oath. "But I wanted to believe him, because if a villain like him could have a woman like you, then it meant I had a chance with Lucy—" He broke off, jerking his head toward the chair she'd left only moments before. "Take a seat, Lady Clara. It's time you and I had a long and truthful chat about your friend Morgan Pryce."

She edged toward the chair, her eyes never leaving the muzzle of his pistol. "Yes, let's talk about him. You were right—we're lovers. And if you shoot me, he'll come after you."

Fitch laughed. "How can he when he doesn't even know who I really am?" His eyes grew cold. "Or does he?"

"He might. He's a very clever man. Besides, even if he doesn't, Lucy will tell him that she left me here with you—"

"Lucy will say nothing." A muscle flicked in his jaw as he stepped nearer. "Not if she wants to keep her precious brothers out of jail. I'll simply tell her that you were fine when you left me. Everyone knows it's dangerous for a woman to wander London alone unaccompanied, so when you end up dead in the river no one will be entirely surprised, given your reckless behavior."

She swallowed, her eyes fixed on the ugly muzzle. She was going to die, and nobody would ever know what had really happened. Panic swelled in her chest, but she fought it off. She had to keep calm. She had to keep him talking until she could figure a way out of this.

"Morgan and I were to meet at his shop tonight," she said, "so he'll know something is wrong when I don't show up."

"Don't lie to me—you do it badly. He didn't set up any assignation with you. I know that, because he set one up with the Specter." A frown darkened his face. "Him and Ravenswood. The minute I saw that devil from the Home Office sniffing about, I knew something was wrong. But I never expected them to be so clever. Not after that Jenkins fellow—" He glared at her. "Never mind all that. It's just as well that you realized who I am. Now we can stop playing games and get straight to the point. Tell me how much they know, how much they've figured out."

"Why should I when you're planning to kill me anyway?" she whispered.

"Ah, but there's more than one way to die, isn't there? If you tell me what you know, I'll make sure your death is quick and painless. If not, it's going to be a very long night for you."

He sidled around behind the chair and pressed the muzzle to her temple, then ran it slowly down her cheek. "Didn't your lover tell you? I'm known for my ruthlessness. I'll happily take my time about killing you, if I must."

He ran the muzzle of the gun around her ear in a grotesque parody of a caress, and she shivered.

He gave a low, evil chuckle. "Did you know that the human body can endure a great deal of pain before it shuts down? One shot can shatter your knee, yet you can live quite a long time suffering the agony of it. Not to mention how long you will suffer if I choose to shoot you in the belly—"

"Torturing me won't do you any good. I don't know anything."

"Oh, I'm sure you do. A strutting cock like Pryce would never resist boasting of how he planned to rid Spitalfields of the Specter."

"He didn't tell me anything, I swear!" she protested.

"We'll see if you still say that after I put a bullet through your leg," he rasped, and she heard the unmistakable sound of a pistol being cocked.

Then a new voice sounded from the doorway. "She's telling the truth, Fitch. She doesn't know anything, so you might as well let her go. Because we both know it's me you really want."

Chapter 24

Jack donn'd his invisible coat,
Sharp sword and swift shoes for the fray;
He rescued the knight and the fair,
And great mighty giant did slay.
"The History of Jack the Giant-Killer,"
edition by J. G. Rusher, Anonymous

Morgan hadn't known true terror until he stepped into Fitch's parlor to see the woman he loved being menaced by the devil himself. Only by sheer will did he keep his own pistol steady on Fitch. Because the rest of him shook violently at the fear that one misstep would make Fitch fire.

Clara smiled weakly when she saw him. "It's about time you got here."

Her face had never looked so pale, her eyes so wide and frightened, but the mutinous set to her shoulders told him he could at least count on her not to fall apart.

"I would have come sooner if you'd left word where you

were going," he retorted. And he would have waited in the hall until Fitch had moved the gun away from her if he hadn't heard it being cocked and known he had no choice but to step in.

"If I'd realized Mr. Fitch was such a dangerous man—" she began.

"Silence, both of you!" Fitch's face contorted with rage as he shoved the muzzle against her temple. "You stay back, Pryce, or I swear she's dead."

The terror seeped into Morgan's bones. "Let's not do anything hasty now," he said, though he kept his pistol leveled at Fitch's head. "If you don't add murder to your crimes, you might yet escape death."

"Hopkins!" Fitch called out. "Get in here, damn you!"

Morgan inched further into the room. "If it's the footman you're calling, there's no point. I knocked him unconscious when he tried to block my entry into your house."

"A pox on you!" Fitch growled. "I thought you and Ravenswood would stay at the shop a while longer. And how did you know to come here, anyway?"

"Lucy told me." Thank God the girl had been climbing out of a hack at the tavern with Johnny when Morgan had arrived there. "I don't think she likes you much anymore."

Surprisingly, Fitch winced before setting his mouth in a grim line. "She'll come round. When I show her what I can buy her with my hidden fortune, she'll do whatever I tell her. We'll flee England together."

"You're mad if you think I'll let you leave this house." Morgan edged further into the room, his blood pounding in his veins. "Even now Lord Ravenswood is on his way here with dozens of men to take you."

"You're bluffing!" Fitch cried.

Morgan certainly hoped he wasn't. He hadn't waited for Ravenswood or his brother—he'd sent Lucy to the Home to guide them here once they showed up. But judging from Lucy's outrage at the very idea that Fitch might hurt Clara, Morgan figured he could trust Lucy to do her part.

"You know me well enough to know I wouldn't come unprepared," Morgan said. "So you might as well put down the gun. Once the rest of them arrive, it's all over for you."

"I'm not waiting around for your friends, Pryce." Keeping the pistol aimed on Clara, Fitch hauled her to a stand with his free hand. "And Lady Clara is coming with me to make sure none of you follow." He dragged her back with him toward the other door to the parlor. "Don't try to come after me or she's dead."

Morgan forced himself to focus, not to let the fear overtake him. The thought of losing her . . .

No, he wouldn't. "I'm not letting you take her out of here." Morgan advanced further into the room. "So you can just forget it."

"You can't stop me," Fitch retorted as he forced Clara back toward the door.

Suddenly, a figure appeared behind Fitch in the doorway. Morgan struggled not to show his surprise to Fitch, but what the devil was Samuel doing here? Lucy had said he'd gone missing.

Behind Fitch, Samuel put a finger to his mouth and displayed the knife he held in his other hand, as if asking for direction. With a quick shake of his head, Morgan warned the man to hold off. Fitch's pistol was too close to Clara's head, and there was too much chance it could go off if Samuel attacked.

So Morgan had to convince Fitch to move the confounded thing. "Listen, Fitch," Morgan said as he lowered the muzzle of his own gun slowly toward the floor. "There's no reason to take Clara. I'm the one who ruined your plans. Take me instead."

Clara frowned, but she seemed to understand what he was attempting to do. "Lucy will never flee with you if you kill me," she told Fitch. "She's much too tenderhearted to love a killer."

"She'll do as she's told," Fitch bit out, but the pistol wavered at Clara's temple.

Morgan picked up on Clara's cue. "But why risk her anger? She won't care if you kill *me*. She doesn't even *like* me." Stepping over to a nearby table, he set his pistol on it. "See? I'm putting this down. You know you don't want to hurt Clara. I'm a son-of-a-bitch, but she's an angel, and those children depend on her. She's an innocent, like your sweet little Lucy. She doesn't deserve to die."

Fitch released his grip on Clara. "You're right . . . you should be the one . . ."

As Fitch's gun veered toward him, Morgan cried, "Now, Samuel!"

But Clara, who couldn't have known Samuel was behind her, had already grabbed for Fitch's pistol hand and was forcing it toward the floor. As Morgan lunged for his own pistol, Fitch's went off.

Morgan's heart leaped into his throat. "Clara!" he cried as he snatched up his pistol and vaulted across the room.

But Clara was fine, standing frozen over the man who now lay writhing on the floor, clutching his leg.

"Blast you, Pryce," Fitch choked out as Samuel hovered close, knife at the ready, "why didn't you just kill me? You want to torture me, is that it?"

"The shot came from your gun, not mine," Morgan said, rage making his voice tight. "You of all people should know the hazards of waving a loaded pistol in Lady Clara's face." He stepped up to Fitch, then pressed the muzzle of his own pistol to the man's head. "But if it's killing you want, I'm more than happy to oblige."

Fitch went still. Then he gazed unflinchingly up at Morgan. "Go on, and make it quick. My years of playing to the crowd are long past, and I won't give the rabble the satisfaction of seeing me hang."

The temptation to pull the trigger surged through Morgan—heady, powerful, and all the more seductive because he feared it was the only way to see justice done. Despite what Fitch thought, the man might not hang if he went to trial. No one could prove that the Specter had killed Jenkins or anybody else, and being a fence—even a master fence—wasn't a capital crime. So Fitch could end up with only fourteen years' transportation.

After almost killing Clara . . .

The blood rage filled Morgan's vision, and he tightened his finger on the trigger.

Then he felt Clara's gentle hand on his arm. "You're not like him, Morgan. Don't make yourself like him."

"He was going to kill you," Morgan rasped, the memory of his fear for her still seared into his senses.

"Yes, and the law will punish him for that, so you don't have to. You're not thirteen anymore. You can trust the law to take care of this. You don't have to endure blood on your hands in order to find justice."

Samuel made some inarticulate sound, and Morgan glanced over to see the young man watching, waiting to take his cue from Morgan. Samuel's knife was still at the ready, and Morgan could tell he itched to use it. However Morgan acted now would shape the man's life for years to come.

"You're better than this," Clara said softly. "I know you are."

Morgan looked at her, at her face shining with faith that he would do the right thing. A pure faith in him.

For the first time, he realized she was right. He *was* better than this. He was not and never could be a man like the Specter. Not even in Spitalfields.

As the blood lust died abruptly in him, he lowered his pistol.

"Kill me," Fitch growled, clutching his bleeding leg to his chest at Morgan's feet. "You know you want to do it."

"Yes," Morgan admitted. "But not badly enough to lose what remains of my soul. So get up. Ravenswood and his men are waiting."

Clara sat with Samuel on a settee out of the way of the commotion. Morgan had ordered them to stay put while he dealt with Fitch, and she'd been only too happy to oblige. For one thing, she still shook from the terror of watching Fitch raise his pistol toward Morgan. For another, she didn't want to interfere with the men who now swarmed over the house, searching for stolen goods and other evidence of the Specter's activities.

While some of Lord Ravenswood's men carried Rodney Fitch off, Morgan and his lordship questioned Fitch's still groggy footman. Then Lord Templemore arrived, and more chaos ensued as he demanded explanations and Lord Ravenswood had to provide them.

"Who's that fellow who looks just like the cap'n?" Samuel asked beside her, gaping at Lord Templemore.

"That's the Baron Templemore," Clara explained. "He's Morgan's twin brother."

Samuel gave a low whistle. "Does that mean Cap'n Pryce is—"

"Yes. And his real name is Blakely. He's been working for that other gentleman there, trying to capture the Specter."

"You knew?"

"I found out. The night I went to his shop, and he got shot."

"Ohhh," Samuel said, as if that explained everything. "I did wonder how you could take up with a fence. Didn't seem like you."

Eager to change the subject, Clara said, "How did you come to be here tonight?"

"Not by choice, I can tell you that." Samuel jerked his head toward Fitch's footman. "That fellow the cap'n is talking to grabbed me as I was heading toward the tavern to see Lucy this evening. He knocked me on the head and carried me back here. When I came to, I was tied up in the basement, and he was telling me how his master was gonna deal with me later personally after he got back from some meeting."

"Fitch claimed he had paid you to leave London. I suppose he had a more permanent removal in mind."

"S'pose he did." Samuel shuddered. "When the footman left me alone down there in the dark, I had time to get my blade out. Y'see, Cap'n Pryce had taught me how to hide it so nobody could find it. That henchman of Fitch's wasn't too smart, anyway, so he never took it off me. It took me all this time to work the blade free and cut myself loose, but soon as I did, I came upstairs to see what was going on."

"And did your part in saving my life and Morgan's." She patted his hand. "You paid us a good service tonight, and I'll make sure you're amply rewarded for it."

"Didn't do it for no reward," he said with a shy smile. "I did it for you, m'lady. You brought my Lucy back to me, and I can never thank you enough for that." He looked up and then broke into a grin. "And speaking of Lucy . . ."

"Samuel!" shrieked a female voice from the doorway as Samuel rose.

Lucy vaulted into the room and straight for her sweetheart. "Are you all right? They said you fought with Mr. Fitch!" She ran her hands everywhere, checking for wounds. "I swear, if he hurt you—"

"Naw, he didn't hurt me, love." He caught her in his arms. "And I didn't really get the chance to fight—"

"They're saying you're a hero," Lucy went on, ignoring

his protests. She kissed him soundly on the lips. "And you are—you're *my* hero."

"Aw, Lucy," he said, blushing a deep rose, "I only did what a man ought for the woman he loves."

Nonetheless, he was clearly basking in her worshipful words as the two of them drew off a ways to reassure each other that they were whole and safe.

Watching the two sweethearts bill and coo only solidified the decision Clara had made somewhere between leaving the town house and now. She glanced over to where Morgan conferred with Lord Ravenswood and Lord Templemore, and love surged through her like some life-giving potion.

How had she ever thought she could let him sail away without her? She couldn't, no matter what it meant. Indeed, she'd be hard-pressed to let him out of her sight again.

As if he felt her gaze on him, he glanced toward her and a smile leaped to his lips. Murmuring a few words to his companions, he left them to come sit beside her.

"We're almost done here, angel." He laced his fingers through hers. "Then I'll take you home."

"I don't want to go home," she said fervently. "I want to be with you."

His smile broadened. "That could be arranged."

"And not just for tonight," she went on, determined to say it all before she could change her mind. "I want to sail with you. I could never bear being too far away from you to pick up the pieces when you get yourself into trouble."

His eyes warmed. "I'm not getting myself into any more trouble, angel."

"You say that now, but I know you. The minute you see a wrong committed, you'll throw yourself into setting it right. Next thing I know, some villain will be hurting an innocent and you'll be rushing into danger to save them and—"

He kissed her hard, thoroughly, his mouth blotting out

every thought in her head. When he drew back, he was grinning. "I'm not getting into any more trouble, angel, because I'm not going to sea. I'm staying right here in London with you."

She stared at him, hardly daring to believe him. "Y-You are?"

"I hope that meets with your approval, because it's too late to change it. I just accepted Ravenswood's offer of a position in the Home Office. And in case you're worried, he assures me it has nothing to do with pirates or smugglers or fences or—"

With a squeal of delight, she threw her arms about his neck. "You're staying! You're really staying in London with me!"

He laughed as he hugged her to him. "Yes, *ma belle ange*, I'm staying in London. With the woman I love."

She drew back, startled. "You love me?"

"Of course I do. Do you think I'd give up my exciting life at sea for just anyone, *cherie*?"

His words made her heart sink. "Oh, Morgan, I don't want you to do anything you don't truly want to do, and you did say you couldn't bear to live in London."

"That was before you forced me to see myself the way you see me—not as a rogue masquerading as a gentleman, but as a man. One who makes mistakes like any other. And who can learn to live with them now that he has an understanding woman at his side."

Hope swelled in her, too irrepressible to resist. "Are you sure? Because if you truly need all the excitement you find at sea—"

"The only thing I need, angel," he murmured, lifting his hand to cup her cheek, "is you. And if I take you away from the work and people you love, I know I'll lose a very special part of you—the part that wants to save the world, the part that cries for children with no hope, the part that braves any danger for the sake of those you love. You're right—if we go to sea together, it would only be a matter of time before you grow to resent me, and I grow to resent your knowledge of who I really am."

With a smile, he caressed her cheek. "But I'm not afraid of who I really am anymore. Besides, you belong here, and I belong with you. So as long as you keep looking at me with love in your eyes, I intend to stay where we both belong. Even if it's in London."

Under the steady sincerity of his gaze, her fears melted away. This was not the same Morgan who'd balked at facing his past. This Morgan knew exactly what he wanted, and by some miracle what he wanted was her.

"All right," she said softly. "Stay here with me."

A wicked light entered his eyes. "But I do have a few terms you'll have to meet."

She eyed him warily. "Like what?"

"I'll want to take you away from your precious Home for a wedding trip."

Relief coursed through her. "I believe I can manage that."

"And you must swear never to go anywhere near a loaded pistol again."

She laughed. "What? And miss the fun you've been having all these years?"

"Very amusing, Clara, but there will be no negotiation on this one." He cocked one eyebrow up. "Every time a gun goes off near you, I lose half a lifetime, and if you think I'm going to—"

"All right, all right, you win. I swear never to go near a loaded pistol again."

"That's better." His voice dropped to a husky murmur. "And that leaves only one more condition, the most important one of all."

The way he was looking at her now made her blood quicken. "What's that?"

"You must promise never to stop loving me. Because I don't think I could stand it if you did."

Drawing his head down to hers, she murmured, "As long as you promise the same thing, my darling, that is one promise I can definitely keep."

Epilogue

He married Beauty, and lived with her many years,
and their happiness—as it was founded on virtue—
was complete.
"Beauty and the Beast"
from The Young Misses Magazine,
Jeanne-Marie Prince de Beaumont

Clara couldn't have asked for a more perfect day for the dedication of the Home's new site. Nothing but summer sunshine greeted them this morning, the fragrance of honeysuckle permeated the grounds, and thrushes provided the musical backdrop. Why, the children would be ecstatic when they arrived.

Taking a moment from overseeing the servants who were setting out refreshments on long tables, Clara surveyed her new domain. In under three years, the volunteers had transformed the abandoned pleasure garden into an idyllic place for children.

And it was largely thanks to Morgan and his family. Uncle Cecil's bequest, ample as it was, could never have built all this. But with Sebastian's donating the land to the cause and Morgan's convincing so many of his naval officer friends to help with the building and design, the overall cost of establishing a new site for the Home outside of Spitalfields had been much lower than expected.

It had certainly helped that donations to the Home had improved, thanks to her new notoriety. Ladies clamored to help the marquess's daughter who'd played a part in capturing a dangerous criminal. The Specter's trial had been the talk of London for months, and now even Spitalfields felt safer, though she was still glad to have her charges away from there.

Juliet strolled up, smiling broadly as she tugged two of her three children along. "I told the girls that Uncle Morgan would take us on a tour of the house before the guests arrive, but now I can't find him anywhere."

"He went to help Samuel open all the windows." With Mrs. Carter planning to retire to the country, Samuel and Lucy would be taking over the day-to-day operation of the new facility. "We didn't expect it to be so warm and fine today, but now that it is, Morgan says the fresh air will add to the house's attractions. Who knows, we might even weasel a donation out of Lord Winthrop?"

Juliet laughed. "I doubt that. If his lordship even shows up, it will be a miracle. He's still peeved that you married the man he sees as the devil incarnate."

Fortunately, Lord Winthrop was the only one who disliked Clara's husband. Who could not like the dashing naval captain who'd proven himself a hero? Not to mention that Morgan had done very well for himself in the Home Office. He'd impressed them all with his coolheaded, practical approach to matters concerning the policing of London. Robert

Peel, the new Home Secretary, even spoke of making Morgan head of the commission to discuss a metropolitan police force.

And with every accomplishment of Morgan's, his family grew only more ecstatic. Sebastian beamed with pride whenever his brother was mentioned, and Juliet had long ago forgiven Morgan for breaking his wager.

Especially, as she was so fond of saying, when it had brought her such an amiable sister-in-law.

"And where's my little niece this morning?" Juliet asked. "Surely you didn't leave her with the nursemaid."

Clara laughed. "Morgan would never have forgiven me. I can't seem to convince him that a nine-month-old baby has little appreciation for the finer points of architecture. He insists that she be part of everything. Although at the moment, Lydia is with her great-aunt Verity and her great-uncle Lew. In fact, here they come now."

Aunt Verity came up from the woods cradling Lydia in her arms and casting brilliant smiles upon her, just as Cinderella's fairy godmother had cast spells upon her own charge. Beside them gamboled Fiddle, Faddle, and Foodle, though Empress had taken the other side, next to the man who accompanied them—Morgan's uncle Lew.

"Don't they make a charming couple?" Juliet whispered. "Uncle Llewelyn has been a widower for so long I'd despaired of his ever marrying again, but I think your aunt might just be able to tempt him."

Given the worshipful way Empress dogged Uncle Lew's heels, as well as the man's continuing indulgence of all Aunt Verity's peculiarities, Clara was inclined to agree with Juliet. Certainly Aunt Verity deserved to finally find a companion in life.

Aunt Verity halted in front of them. "We'd like to take little Lydia down to see the swans at the pond, but Llewelyn—

I-I mean, Mr. Pryce—thought we should ask you first. He was afraid you might worry about having the baby so near the water."

"It's fine with me," Clara said, "long as you're not planning on dangling her over the edge or anything."

"No, indeed!" Oblivious to Clara's dry tone, Aunt Verity clutched the baby to her chest in abject horror. "We will keep her quite a safe distance away from the water, I assure you. Won't we, lassies?"

A chorus of barks signaled the dogs' agreement, and Morgan's uncle Lew chuckled.

"We'll go with you," Juliet said. "I know the girls would love to see the swans. Will you come, too, Clara?"

"Not yet. The carriages will be arriving any minute with the children, and I want to make sure we're ready, because once they storm the place . . ."

She didn't have to finish the sentence. They all laughed.

As soon as they were gone, she headed through the woods toward the house. Morgan met her halfway there, looking a bit disheveled from all his labors. Catching sight of her disapproving glance, he smoothed his hair down with a grin. "Come to check on me, angel?" He captured her with one arm about her waist, looking so endearingly repentant for mussing his clothes that she couldn't help smiling.

She straightened his cravat. "No, I just wanted to make sure everything is ready."

"I took care of it. And I assure you that anything I missed was caught by Lucy or Samuel or Johnny. I think even Tim had a part in readying the place."

She cast an anxious glance through the woods toward the house. "I should make one last check—"

"I've got a better idea," Morgan whispered, eyes twinkling.

And before she knew what he was about, he was tugging her off the path toward the arbor.

"Morgan!" she protested weakly as he dragged her beneath the honeysuckle curtain and into the cavelike interior. "You cannot possibly think to—"

His hot, needy kiss cut off all protest. When he drew back, he was grinning. "You were saying, my love?"

"The children will be here any moment, you randy devil," she warned, though desire pooled in her belly. "The guests won't be far behind. What will they think if they discover us in the arbor doing . . . well . . . you know?"

He laughed heartily. "Considering that you asked me to ravish you the first time we were alone together, you can sometimes be surprisingly modest."

"You think so, do you?" she said, eyebrows raising. "Very well, I'll make you a bargain. If you can restrain your manly urges for the entire day, I'll give you what you want tonight." She pressed her fingers to his lips. "A chance to taste me." Then she took his hand and flattened it against her breast. "To caress me." Stretching up on tiptoe, she nipped his earlobe and whispered, "Whatever you want."

His breath quickened against her cheek. "I want to ravish you."

"Fine," she retorted, then pushed him away. "But not until tonight."

He sighed. "All right, you win. But I'm holding you to the bargain, angel. And I want to do it here. After all the guests are gone, and the children are settled in for the night. Let Juliet take Lydia for the night. Or even your aunt."

She sucked in a breath. It had been months since they'd been completely alone together, without having to stay alert for the baby's cries in the nursery that adjoined their bedchamber. And Lydia was newly weaned, after all.

Besides, just remembering the last time they'd made love in the arbor did naughty things to her insides. And to do it secretively in the dark, on the grounds of the Home . . .

The idea was positively thrilling. "Very well, it's a bargain."

"Now we have to seal it with a kiss," he said, eyes gleaming as he reached for her.

"Oh no, you don't." She darted out of the arbor before he could stop her. "You must keep your part and behave. And you won't do that if you kiss me again."

He strode after her, a resigned look on his face. "You know me too well, wife of mine."

As they emerged from the woods, she heard what she first thought was thunder. She nearly panicked before she realized it was actually the sound of a great many carriages approaching.

"The children are here!" She grabbed Morgan by the arm to urge him forward. "I want to see their expressions when they first glimpse this place."

They reached the carriages just in time to watch as fifty-one children poured out. Their freshly scrubbed faces lit up with delight, sending a fierce satisfaction through her.

Morgan moved up behind her. "They seem to like it, my love."

"They do, don't they?"

Then she spied David sidling up close to Sebastian, who didn't even notice the boy eyeing his pockets with a calculated gleam.

Morgan groaned, having apparently seen the same thing. "Please tell me you offered the children a bribe to keep them from robbing our guests blind."

"I promised them a week's unlimited supply of sweets . . . as long as not a single one of them picked a pocket today."

Mary came up to David, and they exchanged a few heated words. Fortunately, the girl won the argument and succeeded in tugging David off to join the other children.

Morgan laughed. "I see that Mary at least doesn't intend to lose her sweets. You've got this bargaining business down pat, angel. You always know how to dangle just the right temptation to get what you want."

"I do my best."

He bent his head to whisper, "And speaking of temptation, are you sure I can't tempt you back into the arbor? I don't know if I can wait until tonight to seduce you."

She chuckled. "Ah, but the waiting will make the seduction so much sweeter, don't you think?"

Sliding his arms about her waist, he drew her back against his chest. "It's not the waiting that makes it sweeter, *ma belle ange.* It's the loving. It makes everything sweeter."

And as they stood there together watching the children swarm over the grounds with happy cries, she decided he was exactly right.

Author's Note

Contrary to popular opinion, there were indeed police in London other than the Bow Street Runners before Sir Robert Peel established the Metropolitan Police in 1829. In 1792, an Act of Parliament established seven police offices around the city in addition to the Bow Street office, each headed by three paid magistrates and staffed by six or so police officers, who reported to the Home Office. At that time, the magistrates served not only as judges but also as supervisors of the investigations, as does Hornbuckle. The office at Lambeth Street is most famous for catching Ikey Solomons, a notorious Regency-era fence. I loosely based the Specter on Ikey (who wasn't violent, but who did a thriving trade in stolen bank notes), and Jonathan Wild, an earlier thief-taker who played both sides of the law.